Giada De Laurentiis's
Recipe for Adventure
Rio de Janeiro!

written with Brandi Dougherty
illustrated by Francesca Gambatesa

Grosset & Dunlap
An Imprint of Penguin Group (USA) LLC

For Francesco Sedita, my editor and friend, who inspires me to explore outside my comfort zone, to never stop traveling, and to keep learning about new places and things I have never seen!

Para Francesco Sedita, editor e amigo que me inspira a explorar o mundo fora da minha zona de conforto, a nunca parar de viajar e a continuar descobrindo novos lugares.

GROSSET & DUNLAP

Published by the Penguin Group

Penguin Group (USA) LLC, 375 Hudson Street, New York, New York 10014, USA

USA | Canada | UK | Ireland | Australia | New Zealand | India | South Africa | China

penguin.com

A Penguin Random House Company

Text copyright © 2015 by GDL Foods, Inc. Illustrations copyright © 2015 by Francesca Gambatesa. All rights reserved. Published by Grosset & Dunlap, a division of Penguin Young Readers Group, 345 Hudson Street, New York, New York 10014. GROSSET & DUNLAP is a trademark of Penguin Group (USA) LLC. Printed in the USA.

Library of Congress Cataloging-in-Publication Data is available.

ISBN 978-0-448-48204-0 (pbk)   10 9 8 7 6 5 4 3 2 1

ISBN 978-0-448-48205-7 (hc)   10 9 8 7 6 5 4 3 2 1

Chapter 1

An alien ship whizzed past Alfie's head. He ducked just in time and turned around to shoot glowing globs of slime at it. "Yes!" he cheered as the aliens sunk under the weight of the slime and sailed toward Planet Zob far below. Now Alfie could focus on his mission to save the stranded battleship *Kotar*—just as long as no other aliens came along. Surely, he'd make it to the next level of *Alien Slime Universe* before dinnertime.

"Alfredo Bertolizzi!" Alfie's mom said. *Uh-oh*, Alfie thought. When his mom used his full name, he knew he was in trouble. "*Cosa stai facendo?*" she said in Italian. "What are you doing?"

"Playing *Alien Slime Universe*," Alfie said.

Mom set down the basket of laundry she was holding. "Why aren't you practicing your drums?" she asked.

"I will," Alfie said, his eyes still glued to the TV screen. According to his friend Jackson, when you beat this level, the aliens floated out of their ships and did a hilarious song and dance. He just had to see that!

"What about your drum solo in the spring concert?" Mom asked as she folded a T-shirt. "You need to practice!"

Alfie glanced out the window at the flakes of snow falling lazily onto the white-dusted lawn. "It's only February. I have plenty of time."

Alfie had recently learned to play the drums and had been chosen to do a solo performance at the spring band concert next month. It was just that practicing could be so ... boring sometimes—especially compared to Level 5 of *Alien Slime Universe*!

"Well, having a solo in the concert is a very big deal

and should not be taken lightly. Not to mention, you probably also have homework to do," Mom continued. "So I think it's about time to turn off the video game."

"Aw, Mom," Alfie said. "Just ten more minutes, okay?"

Alfie's big sister, Emilia, and their great-aunt Donatella appeared in the doorway of the family room. "Ten more minutes of what?" Emilia asked.

"Blasting aliens," Alfie said.

"Aren't you supposed to be practicing for your drum solo?" Emilia asked.

Alfie frowned. Emilia was only one year older than he was, but sometimes she acted like she was his mother.

"I don't feel like practicing," Alfie said. But he turned off his video game anyway. There was no way he was going to get any more game time in now.

"Everything takes practice, *mio amore*," Zia Donatella said, adjusting the brightly colored stone necklace she always wore. "Even cooking!"

Alfie nodded. Zia was an amazing cook. Ever since

she'd come to stay with Alfie and his family, she had made some pretty awesome food for them—and everything was always prepared from scratch. But having a fantastic cook in the house wasn't the only perk. Sometimes Zia's food was magic! Alfie and Emilia had been magically transported to Naples, Paris, Hong Kong, and New Orleans—all thanks to her special recipes. They were always ready for the next surprising adventure.

"Well, you should at least start practicing singing

'Happy Birthday' to me!" Emilia said with a big smile. "Don't forget, my party is this weekend." Emilia was turning thirteen, and Alfie knew she could hardly wait—especially because it would mean she could say she was two years older than Alfie instead of one, even if it was only for a few months.

"How could I forget?" Alfie asked. "It's all you've talked about since Christmas!"

"I can't believe my *bambina*, my baby girl, is going to be a teenager!" Mom said, shaking her head.

Alfie rolled his eyes.

"How are the party plans coming, you two?" Mom asked Emilia and Zia.

"Great!" Emilia said. "It's going to be perfect. All my friends are coming, and Zia's helping me plan the food. We're making homemade *Napoli*-style pizzas, baked pita chips and red-pepper dip, and spicy popcorn!"

"That sounds wonderful!" Mom said. Alfie had to agree.

"Oh, and we're making Doberge cake for dessert!" Emilia added.

"Doberge cake?" Alfie asked. "Isn't that what we had in New—" Alfie stopped himself midsentence when he saw the looks on Emilia's and Zia's faces. He was about to say "New Orleans," but Mom and Dad didn't know about any of their adventures. It was Zia, Emilia, and Alfie's secret. Doberge cake was a special chocolate layer cake that the amazing cook Delphine had made for them on their last night in New Orleans.

"Where did you have Doberge cake?" Mom asked. "That's so unusual."

"It was . . . uh . . . at Becky's birthday party," Emilia jumped in. "Her mom is from the South."

"I thought Becky's mom was from Maine," Mom said, looking confused. "We talked about going up to their cabin for a family trip some summer."

"Oh, um, I guess it was her aunt then." Emilia shrugged.

"Okay . . . ," replied Mom. "Well, your party menu

sounds *delizioso*! Just give me your grocery list and I'll pick up everything."

"Thanks, Mom," Emilia said.

"Of course. After all, it's not every day we have a teenager in the house!"

"Oh, brother," Alfie said.

Zia laughed and ruffled Alfie's hair. "Come on. If you're not going to practice your drums right now, you can help me start dinner. I'm making chicken Milanese."

Alfie hopped up from his beanbag chair and turned off the TV. "Chicken Milanese? Does that mean it's from Milan?" he asked, exchanging a glance with Emilia. He was eager to know if tonight's dish might take them somewhere.

"It's from the market. Now *andiamo*! Let's go!" Zia said, trying to be serious, but Alfie could detect a smile at the corner of her mouth.

"Okay, fine," Alfie sighed. It looked like tonight would just be dinner at home as usual. And that meant he'd have to practice his drums when he was done.

Chapter 2

"People, people!" Mr. Erikson stood in front of the band room and tapped his baton against the podium. "Drummers, your timing in the intro is throwing everyone off. You're coming in one beat late. You have to get that opening sequence just right. Let's start again from the top."

Alfie slumped in his chair. *How was it not the end of the period yet?*

"That means you, too, Mr. Bertolizzi," Mr. Erikson said, giving Alfie a look.

Alfie straightened his music stand and positioned his drumsticks over his snare drum. He waited for Mr. Erikson to count out the beat, and then they started the song over again for the fourth time.

Finally, after two more tries, the band made it through to the end of the song. Then they repeated it again before the bell rang. Alfie thought his solo went pretty well that last time.

"Okay, everybody. Good work today!" Mr. Erikson called over all the chatter and commotion as students packed up their instruments. "Don't forget to practice, practice, practice. The spring concert will be here before we know it!"

Alfie slid his drumsticks into his backpack as his sheet music fluttered off the music stand and onto the floor. He knelt down to collect the loose pages into his band folder. Mr. Erikson walked over and handed Alfie one of the sheets that had sailed the farthest.

"You know, Alfie," Mr. Erikson started, "I think your solo could use some more work. I'm happy to help you with it if you want to practice a little extra after school."

Alfie crammed his music folder into his backpack

and zipped it up. "Thanks, Mr. Erikson, but I can't really stay after. I . . . I have to get home to help my great-aunt Donatella." Alfie swallowed hard. He knew his family would happily let him stay after school to practice with Mr. Erikson. He just didn't want Mr. Erikson to know that.

"Well, I can always find someone else to do the solo, Alfie, if you're not up for it," Mr. Erikson said. "I know it's a lot of pressure, so that's fine if you don't want to do it."

"No, I want to do the solo. And I'll work on it more at home. I promise," Alfie said, turning toward the door.

"All righty then." Alfie's teacher smiled. "See you Friday."

"Bye, Mr. Erikson!" Alfie called back. He bounded up the steps and through the band-room door. Charlie was waiting for him just outside, in the hall.

"Yo, Alfie!" he said.

"Hey, Charlie," Alfie replied halfheartedly. Charlie was *kind of* Alfie's friend, but he could also be kind of loud and annoying.

"So you're having trouble with the solo, huh?" Charlie asked, nudging Alfie's arm.

"No!" Alfie said, walking quickly down the hall. He knew his voice sounded defensive.

Charlie hurried to catch up. "Oh, well, I just asked because I've been practicing it, too." Charlie waved his drumsticks in front of Alfie's face.

"You have?" Alfie's eyes were wide. Why was Charlie practicing *his* solo?

"Yeah, you know, just in case you don't feel like doing it, or can't do it, or whatever," Charlie said.

"I can do it," Alfie said. "I'm *going* to do it."

Charlie put his drumsticks in his back pocket and held up his hand. "Okay, cool. It just sounded like maybe Mr. Erikson was going to look for a replacement, that's all."

Alfie could feel his ears getting hot. Why was everybody bugging him so much about this drum solo? When he and Emilia were in New Orleans, he played with a real, live jazz band in a real jazz club on a real stage! And he was good at it! All the La Salle kids in the band had told him so. This was just some silly little school concert. It was nothing compared to that!

Alfie stood in front of the door to his math class and faced Charlie. "Mr. Erikson is not replacing me," he said. "I'm doing the solo and that's that." He turned into the classroom without waiting for Charlie's reply.

Chapter 3

After school, Alfie sat in front of his drum set in the garage. He stared at the sheet music and sighed. He just couldn't bring himself to play that song again. Before long, he heard pots clanging in the kitchen and Zia and Emilia talking. His stomach growled. He decided to take a break and see what they were making for dinner. Besides, it was getting cold, and the little space heater he set up next to his drums wasn't helping much. Alfie turned off the heater and went inside.

Emilia was at the sink washing vegetables. Zia wove her salt-and-pepper hair into a loose braid and looked at Alfie. "I didn't even know you were out there. I didn't hear you playing."

Alfie plopped down at the kitchen island and rested his chin in his hand. "I know," he mumbled.

"What's the problem, *ragazzo*?" Zia asked.

Alfie shrugged. "I guess . . . I guess I just want to be naturally good at playing the drums. I don't want to practice."

Zia laughed as she rolled up the sleeves of her yellow silk blouse.

"What's so funny?" Alfie was annoyed. He felt like no one was taking him seriously!

"I'm not laughing at you, Alfie," Zia said. "I'm laughing because I remember feeling the same way about cooking."

"But you *are* naturally good at cooking, Zia," Emilia said, reading Alfie's mind.

"It may seem that way now, but it took me years to be able to cook the way I do."

"Really?" Alfie was surprised.

"Sure," Zia continued. "I've always loved cooking and some parts of it have come easy for me, but I still had many teachers and I needed to practice a lot. You can't expect to get good at anything without practice."

"I had to practice a ton for ballet," Emilia added. "There's no way I could have remembered all the positions, otherwise."

"And I would get frustrated with recipes that I

couldn't get right," said Zia. "Some dishes are very complicated to make. But imagine if I had given up? I wouldn't be able to make all the wonderful meals that bring our family together."

"And that take us to new places!" Alfie added.

Zia smiled. "So just stick with it, and you'll be amazed at the progress you make!"

"Okay." Alfie nodded. He guessed Zia and Emilia had a point. He stood up and went back out to the garage.

"Another award-winning meal, Zia!" Dad said after dinner that night. Zia and Emilia had made baked salmon and risotto with roasted vegetables. Alfie had to agree that it was pretty delicious.

"*Grazie*," Zia said. "I couldn't have done it without Emilia's help."

"I'm always happy to help you in the kitchen, Zia," Emilia said. "Much more fun than math homework."

"Well, I guess we better get going." Mom pushed back from the table. "We don't want to be late for the PTA meeting."

"That's right," Dad said. "If we're late, we get stuck in the back and we can't argue with Mrs. Phillips as much."

"Oh, Mauricio," Mom said.

Dad winked at Alfie and Emilia, and they laughed.

Mom went to get her coat and purse from the hall. When she returned she said, "Alfie and Emilia, you're on cleanup duty."

Alfie saluted. "Yes, ma'am."

"And then it's time for homework—even math, Emilia. And no *UFO Goo World* tonight, Alfie."

"It's *Alien Slime Universe*, Mom!"

Mom kissed Alfie on the top of the head. "Right."

"Be good!" Dad waved as they headed out to the car.

Alfie started clearing the table while Emilia put the dishes in the dishwasher. Then Alfie noticed an egg sitting on the counter.

"Are you going to make something, Zia?" he asked.

"I thought I'd make some cheese buns for the morning," she replied, pulling the blender out of the cupboard.

"Can we help?" Emilia asked.

"*Naturalmente*! Of course! Grab the milk from the fridge. Alfie, set the oven to four hundred degrees so it can preheat."

Alfie turned the dial on the oven, and Zia placed two mini-muffin tins on top of the stove.

"I learned to make these cheese buns in Brazil," Zia said as she sprayed cooking spray into the muffin tins. Not only was Zia an amazing cook, she was also a world traveler. Alfie and Emilia loved hearing stories about all the places Zia had been and the experiences she'd had.

"Wow, Brazil!" Alfie could picture the South American country on a map. He was obsessed with geography and maps—even more than video games. "That's the biggest country in South America—and one of the largest in the world!"

"That's right," Zia said. She measured out milk and vegetable oil and poured them into the blender.

"And although Brazil is surrounded by Spanish-speaking countries, they speak Portuguese because explorers from Portugal settled there a long time ago," Emilia added. Emilia's love of history almost rivaled Alfie's love of maps . . . almost!

"I'm impressed, you two!" Zia said. "Now, this recipe is called *pão de queijo* in Portuguese. And I ate these delicious rolls almost every morning when I was there."

"*Powng-deh-kay-joo,*" Alfie said, sounding out the words.

"Correct," Zia said. She handed the egg to Emilia. "Want to add this to the blender?"

Emilia cracked the egg on the side of the glass container and added it to the mixture.

"And Alfie, add a teaspoon of salt, will you?"

Alfie measured a teaspoon from the dish of salt that Zia kept next to the stove and sprinkled it on top of the other ingredients.

"How long were you in Brazil?" Emilia asked.

"I lived in Rio de Janeiro for a few months, some years ago," Zia replied. "It is a magical place."

"What's magical about it?" Alfie asked.

"There is music and dancing everywhere you go. Brazilian people are really passionate about those things. And the landscape of the city is so dramatic. Alfie, pass me the tapioca starch. We add that next."

"What's tapioca starch?" Alfie asked. "Is it like tapioca pudding?"

"Not quite. Tapioca starch is the ground root of the manioc, or cassava, plant. Brazilians use this plant in several signature dishes."

Alfie sat down on a stool at the kitchen island. "What else do you remember about Brazil?" he asked.

"There are big mountains that plunge straight into the deep blue ocean. And there's a huge statue high on one of those mountains that looks out over the entire city. It's iconic."

"I've seen that statue in pictures!" Emilia said. "What's it called again?"

"The mountain is Corcovado, and the statue is called Christ the Redeemer," Zia said. "The statue is over eighty years old, and it's absolutely huge. You can see it from almost anywhere in the city."

"Hey!" Emilia jumped in. "Wasn't it named one of the new Seven Wonders of the World, too?"

"That's right!" Zia said. "It's really quite something. Going to Rio is an experience for all of your senses. The colors, sights, sounds, and smells are truly enchanting. And if you're lucky enough to be there during Carnival, then it's like all of those things are even bigger!"

"It sounds kind of like New Orleans," Emilia said.

Zia smiled. "It is! Carnival in Rio is like a much bigger version of Mardi Gras in New Orleans."

"Whoa!" said Alfie. "That's hard to imagine." They had been in New Orleans during Jazz Fest, not during Mardi Gras, but even that festival was one fantastic party that the whole city enjoyed.

Zia laughed. "It's definitely something you have to experience to believe."

She poured the tapioca starch into the blender and Alfie peered inside. "What else do we add?"

"It's time for the best ingredient—the cheese."

"Yum!" Alfie said. Cheese was definitely one of his favorite ingredients in anything.

Zia went to the fridge and took out a large hunk of white cheese. "We need to crumble this *queso fresco* before we add it."

Alfie hopped off his stool. "I'll do it!"

Zia handed Alfie the cheese, and he used a fork to crumble the pieces into a measuring cup. When the cup was full, Zia poured it into the blender. *"Perfetto!"*

"What's next?" Emilia asked.

"Now we're ready to blend," Zia replied. She put the lid on the blender and flipped the switch to HIGH. She stopped blending partway through to scrape the ingredients down the sides of the container.

Once everything was blended, Zia moved over to the stove and poured the mixture into the muffin tins, filling them almost to the top. Then she slid the trays into the oven and set the timer.

Alfie and Emilia finished cleaning up the rest of the dinner dishes. After that, they sat at the kitchen table and started their homework. Soon, the smell of fresh bread filled the air.

When the timer went off, Zia peeked into the oven. "I think they're done."

"Can we try one, Zia?" Alfie asked. Even though they'd just finished dinner, the rolls smelled too good to wait until morning.

"Sure!" Zia said as she popped the buns out of the tins and onto a cooling tray. "They're always best when they're fresh from the oven."

Alfie and Emilia were impatient as they waited for the buns to cool. "They weren't hard to make at all!" Emilia said.

"Not like some of the other recipes I learned in Rio." Zia laughed. "Talk about needing practice—some of the foods I learned to make there took a long time to perfect. But it was definitely worth it. Traditional Brazilian food is full of flavors and textures and colors, much like the city of Rio itself."

Emilia touched one of the puffy, golden rolls with the tip of her finger. "I think they're cool enough, Zia."

Zia tested a roll and smiled. "I think you're right." She took three small plates from the cabinet and put a roll on each one. Alfie and Emilia each picked up their rolls and blew on them. Alfie eagerly pulled his roll apart and watched the steam rise in front of him. He could smell the rich, cheesy center of the bread. They took a bite at the same time. The bread was surprisingly dense and chewy, which he loved. The cheese added a perfect, extra-tangy flavor.

"What do you think?" Zia asked.

"It's so good!" Emilia said.

"And chewy," Alfie added. "It's like a really good breadstick, but the cheese inside makes it so much better."

Zia smiled and closed her eyes. "Just imagine waking up surrounded by lush green rain forests, golden beaches, and azure blue ocean with the smell of these buns baking in the oven."

Alfie closed his eyes, too, and he took another bite of his cheese bun. He could see it perfectly. All of a sudden, he felt that now-familiar drop way down in his stomach— like reaching the bottom dip of a roller coaster and heading back up for the next twist and turn. It was time for another adventure!

Chapter 4

When Alfie opened his eyes, he noticed two things right away. It was Hot with a capital *H*, and it was sticky—like standing in the steam room at the gym. But he was outside on a bustling city sidewalk. Thankfully, Emilia was beside him as usual, and she seemed just as shocked as he was. Alfie turned in a circle, trying to get his bearings.

"Do you think we're in Brazil?" Emilia asked.

Alfie could see huge rocky cliffs, vivid green plants, and bursts of colorful flowers all around them. Then he spotted the big statue high above the city with its arms outstretched as if to say, "Welcome!" Alfie pointed to the statue and Emilia turned to look. "Yep. We're in Rio!"

"Is it really February here?" Emilia asked, pulling her golden-brown hair into a ponytail. "It's so hot!"

"Well, we're below the equator now," Alfie said.

"So?" Emilia replied.

"The seasons are reversed from ours down here, so it's summer!" Alfie told his sister proudly.

Emilia nodded. "This has to be the hottest summer I've ever felt!"

Alfie definitely agreed. He was glad he was wearing just a T-shirt and not the heavy sweatshirt he'd worn to school that day!

"Who do you think we're going to meet?" Emilia said, glancing up and down the street.

"I don't know," Alfie replied as he took in their surroundings. There were crowds in every direction, but no one seemed to be looking their way.

They took a few steps along the sidewalk, unsure of which way to go. All around them, the city buzzed with excitement. People rushed in and out of shops. Car horns honked and people pedaled by on bicycles. Across a wide, busy avenue, Alfie could see big brightly colored beach umbrellas lined up along the water. People swam in the ocean, lounged on beach chairs, and played volleyball and soccer in the sand. It was hard to believe they'd been in cold, snowy weather back home just a few minutes before. Alfie could definitely get used to this. He hoped they'd get to swim in the ocean! It looked so inviting in the heat.

"Should we walk over to the beach?" Alfie asked.

"I guess we could . . . ," Emilia answered, but she sounded unsure.

"Or we could walk into one of these shops and just look around," Alfie suggested.

On their last few adventures, they'd met kids their age right away. It felt weird not to know what to expect this time.

"Let's walk around for a little bit," Emilia said. "If we see a kid our age, we could always ask for directions just to get them talking."

"Okay, that sounds good," Alfie said, though he didn't know what they'd ask for directions to ...

They set off down the sidewalk trying to take in all the sights, but Alfie felt a little uneasy. What were they going to do, exactly?

Chapter 5

Alfie and Emilia walked down the wide avenue that ran along the edge of the beach. A sign said AVENIDA ATLÂNTICA. On one side was a white sandy beach and a sea of people enjoying the sun and surf. And on the other side was a row of high-rise buildings that towered over them. It seemed so weird to have a beach right at the edge of a busy city like this. Any time Alfie and Emilia had ever been to a beach, it was always outside of a city.

As they walked, Alfie enjoyed watching the other people on the sidewalks. Everyone wore vibrant outfits in every color imaginable. And some people just wore skimpy bathing suits and sandals! It was pretty different

from all the dark-colored wool coats and thick sweaters people were wearing back home.

Just then, a band marched across the street in front of them. The music was festive and had a great beat. The band members wore sparkly top hats, sunglasses, and multicolored T-shirts. Some of them banged on drums

and shook tambourines, others tapped on cowbells, and many just danced along to the music, waving small paper flags or other glittery props on sticks. As they marched and danced up the street, people joined in all around them, dancing, laughing, and cheering. Zia was right—it was like New Orleans with the volume turned way up.

"I already love it here!" Emilia said, putting a little wiggle in her step. "It's so fun and colorful."

"Do you want to go over to the beach or wander up one of these streets?" Alfie asked, motioning as they approached a street that pushed between two high-rises and away from the water.

"Let's see what's up here," Emilia said. She twirled in a circle and skipped toward the corner. Alfie stepped next to her just as a blur of activity flew around the corner and crashed right into them.

Alfie grabbed Emilia's arm to prevent her from falling. He steadied himself with his hand on the side of the tall building next to them. All he could see were colors flying everywhere. It looked like an explosion of fluorescent flags. Then a tall, tanned boy with black hair, wearing board shorts and a tank top, appeared in the center of the colorful whirlwind. "I'm so sorry!" he said. He began trying to gather the colors, which were strewn all over the sidewalk. Alfie now realized that they were giant bolts of different kinds of fabric. "Are you all right?" the boy asked.

"We're fine!" Emilia said. She bent down to pick up a bolt of hot-pink silky material that had pooled around her feet.

"Okay, good," the boy said, still out of breath and bundling several bolts into his arms. "Well, then grab some fabric and follow me!" And with that he took off down the street, fabric soaring out behind him like kite tails.

Alfie and Emilia smiled at each other. Then they each picked up a bolt of fabric, and off they went.

"Here we go!" Alfie said.

Chapter 6

Alfie and Emilia struggled to keep up with the boy as he rushed down the sidewalk. The canary-yellow cotton material in Alfie's hands flapped in front of his face, momentarily blinding him. He wound the fabric around the bolt and tried to tuck it under his arm as he kept jogging along.

"I'm Miguel Costa," the boy called back over his shoulder.

"I'm Emilia Bertolizzi, and this is my brother, Alfie," Emilia responded loudly.

"Nice to meet you guys. You must be from America."

"How'd you know?" Alfie asked.

"Your accents!" Miguel said. "Welcome to my city!"

"Thanks!" Alfie said.

"How old are you guys?" Miguel asked. "I'm fifteen."

"I'm eleven, and Emilia's tw—" Alfie started to say.

"I'll be thirteen in two days!" Emilia chimed in. Alfie should have known she couldn't pass up a chance to say her almost-age.

"Well, happy birthday! You must be in Rio for Carnival?" Miguel asked.

Alfie and Emilia exchanged an eager glance. They were here in time for Carnival! Zia Donatella really did have such amazing timing. "Yep," Alfie said. "We're really excited."

They dodged a crowd of tourists standing outside a restaurant. "Are you guys staying in Copacabana? Or Ipanema, maybe?" Miguel asked.

"Um, yeah, we're staying in Ipanema," Emilia said quickly. "With our parents," she added.

Alfie wrinkled his brow at Emilia. What if Miguel asked to meet their parents? Emilia shrugged, reading Alfie's concern.

"Cool. The beaches are great, aren't they?" Miguel asked.

"They look great," Alfie said. "We just got here, so we haven't done much exploring yet. We're excited to check things out. And to try lots of Brazilian foods."

"Well, there's no shortage of excitement or delicious food here in Rio—especially during Carnival," Miguel said. "You'll have to make sure your parents take you to some good places."

"Our parents are here for work, so they're letting us explore a lot on our own," Emilia said. "We just have to check in with them every once in a while." She patted her shorts pocket as if it contained a cell phone. Alfie nodded. She was getting pretty good at this stuff!

"Well, then I can definitely show you guys some of my favorite Rio sights," Miguel offered. "You know, to say thank you for your help."

"Thanks!" Emilia said. "That would be great."

"I'm sure we'll be able to squeeze in a few things," said Miguel. "I don't have a ton of free time right now because I'm in charge of coordinating the children's parade for Carnival. It's the first parade that kicks off the entire Carnival festival on Friday night."

"Wow!" Alfie said. "That sounds really cool."

Miguel grinned. "It is. We're just putting the finishing touches on our routine, and we have a few more costumes to make. That's why I was rushing—I have to deliver the rest of this fabric to our costume designer. We have only a couple of days left to prepare, and everything needs to be perfect!"

"Well, we're happy we could help!" Emilia said.

Miguel stopped short on the sidewalk in front of them. "Actually, there might be another way you can help. Do either of you play any instruments or dance?"

"Sure!" Alfie said. "I play the drums."

"And I do ballet," Emilia added. "Well, it's been a couple years since I took classes, but I still remember a lot."

"Great!" Miguel said. "Samba's pretty different from ballet, but if you've got any sense of rhythm I bet you can pick it up."

"I definitely have rhythm!" Emilia said confidently. "But what's 'samba'?"

"What's samba?!" Miguel's eyes were wide. "It's only

the most important type of music and dance in Brazil. And it's at the heart of Carnival! Have you heard the bands playing on the streets and seen people dancing along?"

"Yes," Alfie and Emilia said together.

"That's samba!" Miguel held a bolt of fabric out in front of him like a dance partner and stepped forward with his right foot and then his left while swaying his hips back and forth.

"Fun!" Emilia said. "That looks way more exciting than ballet."

"Definitely!" Miguel laughed. "Well, I'd love it if you'd be in the children's parade. Part of our theme this year is to celebrate diversity and other cultures, so it would be great to add a couple American kids to our mix. What do you say? Do you want to help me kick off this year's Carnival?"

"Yes!" Alfie and Emilia cried. They could hardly contain themselves. This was going to be one of their best adventures yet.

Chapter 7

"Come on in," Miguel said, pushing open a big wooden door. "This old colonial building is our practice space." Alfie and Emilia entered a hallway and followed Miguel to a wide-open room with wood floors and high ceilings.

"This was the ballroom. They used to throw fancy parties here, and politicians and celebrities would mingle and dance," Miguel said.

"It's huge!" Alfie said, taking in the space. There were big arched windows on the far side of the room and a balcony at the other end overlooking the wooden dance floor. Spread out across the ballroom were at least ten small groups of kids. Most of the kids looked their age or a little older, like Miguel. Each cluster was busy working on something. There were several groups of dancers and musicians. And there were groups working on costumes and props. Everybody bustled around looking busy and super focused.

"The costume designer, Marta, is just over here," Miguel said as he motioned to the corner of the room. A round woman a bit older than their mother sat in front of a big sewing machine. She wore a bright pink blouse and her black hair was wound into a tight bun on her head. Mountains of fabric were piled all around her. She clenched two pins between her lips as the sewing machine whirred furiously through a piece of rich red fabric.

"Hi, Marta!" Miguel said. "I have the rest of the fabric for you."

"Oh, thank goodness!" Marta said. "I can finally finish all the bird costumes now."

"Marta, this is Emilia and Alfie. They're visiting from the States, and they're going to join our parade."

Alfie and Emilia waved as they set down the bolts of fabric next to Marta's sewing table. Alfie shook out his tired arms. It had been a long walk/jog to the parade practice space.

"Nice to meet you." Marta smiled, but she looked tired. "So I guess that means we need two more costumes, right?"

"I'm afraid so," Miguel said gently. "Do you think you can squeeze them in?"

"You know me." Marta laughed. "I can make it happen!"

"Yeah, you can! You're a miracle worker." Miguel patted Marta's shoulder. "Let's see, we need more butterfly dancers, so you can make a butterfly costume for Emilia. And Alfie will be one of our bird drummers."

Emilia gasped. "Oh, I love butterflies!"

"All right then," Marta said, holding up a measuring tape. "Let's get your measurements."

Alfie and Emilia stood with their arms out and their legs wide. Marta measured the length

of their arms and legs, across their backs, and around their waists. She scribbled notes in a small notebook as she went. Then she measured around their heads.

"Why are you measuring our heads?" Alfie asked.

"There's a headpiece that goes with each costume, too," Marta replied.

Wow, Alfie thought. *These costumes are serious!*

"All right," Marta said finally. "I think I have everything I need."

"Thank you!" Emilia replied.

Marta smiled. "Just wait until you see the finished product. You're going to look great!"

Emilia bounced on her toes. "I'm so excited!"

After Marta returned to the explosion of fabric around her sewing machine, Miguel led them across the ballroom floor to a stage area where a microphone waited on a stand. "Do you guys know much about Carnival?" Miguel asked.

Alfie and Emilia shook their heads. "Not really,"

Emilia said. "We know it's one big fun party."

"And that it's like Mardi Gras in New Orleans, but bigger. We've been to New Orleans," Alfie added.

"I've always wanted to check out Mardi Gras!" Miguel said. "Carnival is a lot like that, but grander and even more dramatic."

"How long has there been Carnival in Rio?" Emilia asked.

"It started hundreds of years ago. It's changed a lot, though. Now it's an amazing production of choreographed routines of music, dancing, and art. There's nothing else like it! People get to step out of their normal lives and pretend to be someone or something new. It's all about having fun and celebrating life to the fullest!"

"Sounds pretty awesome to me," Alfie said.

"During the opening ceremony of Carnival, the mayor of Rio gives the key to the city to a big, silly clown character called King Momo. King Momo oversees

Carnival and all the celebrations," Miguel explained. "Then the children's parade kicks off several days of parties, music, and dancing."

"Wow!" Emilia exclaimed. "I'm glad we're here for it!"

"But the best part is the parades of the samba schools that take place at the Sambadrome," said Miguel.

"What's that?" Alfie asked.

"The Sambadrome is like a permanent parade ground that was built with big stands on either side so that people can watch each samba school perform their parade routine."

"Are the samba schools where everyone learns to dance samba?" Emilia asked.

"You would think so, but not really," said Miguel. "The samba schools are like big community groups that come together to create a parade for Carnival. Everybody just kind of learns by watching each other. My mother is the Carnival designer for one of the top samba schools in the city," Miguel said proudly. "That's why being the organizer of this year's children's parade is such a big deal for me. If I'm able to make the children's parade a success, I hope that one day I can be the leader of a famous samba school for Carnival, just like my mother."

"That's amazing, Miguel," Emilia said. "Really!"

"Thanks. I'm pretty excited about it." Miguel motioned over a couple kids who looked about Alfie and Emilia's ages. "Nina and Lucas, meet Emilia and Alfie. They're visiting from the States, and they're going to be in our parade."

"Great!" Nina said, smiling at Emilia. "Are you a butterfly?"

"I am!" Emilia beamed. "Are there steps to learn? Can you teach me?"

"Yes, but the routine isn't too hard. I'll show you."

"Lucas, Alfie plays the drums, so he'll join your percussion group," Miguel told him.

"I'm kind of still learning to play," Alfie said, feeling self-conscious.

"That's cool," said Lucas. "You'll pick it up with some practice."

Miguel hopped up onto the stage. "I'm going to make a quick announcement about the rest of our rehearsal schedule and then we'll get started. You can join your groups."

"Great. Let's go!" Emilia said. She gave Alfie an enthusiastic smile as she hurried to join Nina and the other butterfly dancers.

Alfie tried to smile back as he followed Lucas over to the percussion group, but part of him was nervous about the whole parade thing. What if he couldn't get the hang of it?

Chapter 8

As soon as practice was over, Miguel thanked everybody
for their hard work and said they'd meet again tomorrow.
They had practiced for almost three hours, and Alfie was
exhausted. He couldn't believe they were supposed to
do it again the next day! Lucas and the percussion group
had shown him the routine and music, but Alfie hadn't
picked it up as quickly as he'd hoped. He was frustrated—
especially when he saw a crowd of dancers cheering
Emilia's great performance in her dance group. And she'd
never even done samba before!

Alfie and Emilia waved good-bye to Lucas and Nina.
Then as the remaining performers started to file out of

the ballroom, Miguel found Alfie and Emilia. "Great job, you two," he said. "Did you have fun?"

"Yes!" Emilia gushed. "Nina's a great teacher. I love samba!"

Miguel laughed. "I knew you would. What about you, Alfie?"

"It was good," Alfie said quietly. "I think I'm starting to get the hang of it."

"You will, don't worry," Miguel assured him. "We have a few more practices left!"

Alfie managed a weak smile. *Oh goody*, he thought.

"So, are you headed back to Ipanema?" Miguel asked. "Your parents must be wondering where you are."

Emilia shrugged. "I texted them earlier and they're stuck in meetings until late, so they were glad we had something to do."

"Well, I'm going home for a late lunch," Miguel said. "My house is close if you want to join me for something to eat."

"Really? That'd be great!" Emilia said.

"And the good news for you guys is that my dad is training to be a chef, so you're in for a treat!"

"How lucky for us!" Emilia exclaimed.

Miguel led the way as they wound through the narrow streets of Rio toward his house. "My neighborhood is called Botafogo, and it's in the South Zone of the city," Miguel explained, "just like the beaches you saw earlier today. It's easy to get to lots of other neighborhoods from here. And the Christ the Redeemer statue is right above us!" He pointed to the towering mountain not far in the distance. Alfie squinted his eyes against the sun to see the imposing figure above them. He hoped they'd get a chance to see it up close.

"Botafogo is a pretty residential neighborhood compared to the more touristy areas like Ipanema and Copacabana," Miguel continued. "Lots of cariocas live here."

"Cariocas?" Emilia asked.

"That's what we call people who are from Rio, or who live here," said Miguel.

They approached a large white apartment building with wrought-iron balconies. Alfie thought immediately of their time in New Orleans. Lots of old buildings in the French Quarter also had black iron balconies twisted into ornate shapes.

"We're on the second floor," Miguel said as he opened the front door of the building and bounded up the stairs. He used his key to open the apartment. As soon as Alfie and Emilia stepped inside, they were engulfed by the rich smells of cooking. Alfie's stomach instantly rumbled. All that practicing had made him hungry!

"Hi, Papa," Miguel said as they entered the kitchen and found Miguel's dad hard at work.

"How was practice?" he asked.

"Great! I think we're making really good progress. Papa, these are my new friends, Emilia and Alfie. They're visiting for Carnival, and they're going to be in the

children's parade. Alfie and Emilia, this is my dad. You can call him Señor Costa."

"Nice to meet you, Emilia and Alfie." Señor Costa smiled warmly.

"Nice to meet you, too," Emilia said.

"You're just in time for lunch," Señor Costa said.

"Thank you," said Alfie. "It smells amazing."

Miguel motioned to the round table with a bright red tablecloth draped over it. "Have a seat." Then he took four plates from the cupboard and brought them over to the

stove where Señor Costa was stirring a large clay pot. He spooned food onto the plates and Miguel set them on the table in front of Alfie and Emilia. On each plate was a rich stew that was a dark purplish-black color. There was also a serving of white rice, a heap of greens, and a side of something crispy and brown—it almost looked like bits of crisp rice cereal.

"This stew is called feijoada," Señor Costa said.

"*Fey-jwa-da,*" Alfie repeated.

Miguel nodded. "It's considered the national dish of Brazil. Brazilians love feijoada."

"It's a black-bean-and-meat stew," Señor Costa added. "This one is made with pork sausage, bacon, and beef."

Alfie took a bite of the stew. "Wow! That's really good." The black beans were rich and flavorful, and the meat was really tender and delicious. With the sausage, it reminded him a little bit of the jambalaya they'd had in New Orleans, but thicker and less spicy. It was like a really filling black-bean chili. "What is this crispy brown stuff?" he asked.

"It's called *farofa*," Señor Costa explained. "It's toasted manioc flour."

"We use it like a condiment," Miguel said. "You can sprinkle it on top of your food or serve it on the side."

"Are these collard greens?" Emilia asked.

Alfie thought he recognized the juicy sautéed greens they'd also had in New Orleans.

"Yes, they are!" Señor Costa said.

"This is all really delicious," said Emilia.

"I'm so glad you like it," Señor Costa replied. "Miguel may have told you that I'm training to be a chef, so I'm always happy to be able to cook for new people. Have you tried Brazilian food before?"

"No," said Alfie. "Well, actually, our aunt did make these cheese buns. *Pão* something . . ."

"*Pão de queijo*," Miguel and his dad said together.

"Those are another staple of Brazilian food," Señor Costa said. "But there are many, many more things to try. You'll have to come back for more food during your stay in Rio!"

"We'd love to!" Emilia said.

"Are you visiting Rio with your family?" Señor Costa asked.

"Yes, with our parents," Alfie told him. "They're here for

work, though, so they're going to be busy most of the time."

"You know what? You guys should just stay here!" Miguel said. "At least until after the children's parade."

Alfie and Emilia grinned at each other. "Are you sure?" Emilia asked. "That's awfully generous."

"That way I can show you around between rehearsals, and we won't have to worry about getting you back to your hotel or anything," Miguel said. "Right, Papa?"

"As long as Alfie and Emilia's parents are okay with it, it's okay with me."

"Want to call them and ask?" Alfie asked Emilia.

"Sure . . . ," Emilia said as she put her hand in her pocket, pretending to reach for a cell phone.

"There's better reception in the living room," Miguel said, motioning to the next room.

"Thanks!" Emilia stood up and walked out of the room. Alfie could hear her talking in a low voice. He almost laughed out loud thinking about her pretending to talk to their parents.

A minute later she came back into the kitchen. "We can stay! And our parents said thank you very much for your hospitality."

Miguel flashed a dazzling smile. "Great. It's settled then."

"Wonderful," Señor Costa said. "You will be perfect guinea pigs for my recipes during your stay!"

"I love being a guinea pig!" Alfie said, shoveling another heaping spoonful of stew into his mouth.

Everybody laughed.

At the end of the meal, Señor Costa served orange slices on a ceramic plate decorated with pink flowers. "The oranges help you digest the heavy meal."

Alfie bit into a section of orange. The citrus did taste really good and crisp after the heavy food. Alfie wasn't sure his stomach had ever felt so full—and *heavy* was a good word for it. Soon his eyelids were beginning to feel heavy, too.

"Are you tired?" Miguel asked with a smile.

Alfie thought about their busy day so far. "A little bit," he admitted. He looked at Emilia and decided she looked pretty sleepy as well.

"That's why we only have feijoada every once in a while. You always need a nap afterward!" Señor Costa said.

"Come on." Miguel stood up from the table. "I'll show you to the guest room where you can lie down for a little bit."

"Can we help you clean up first?" Emilia asked.

"No, no," Miguel's dad said, waving them out of the room. "You're our guests."

"Thank you for lunch," Alfie said lazily.

"Yes, thank you," Emilia added.

"You're very welcome. Have a good rest!"

Miguel led Alfie and Emilia down the hall to a small bedroom with two single beds. The beds were covered in bright pillows much like the colors of the fabrics they'd helped carry earlier that day.

"I'll wake you up in a little while," Miguel told them. "Then we can go see my mother's samba-school rehearsal."

Alfie sank onto the bed and nodded. He didn't think he'd really take a nap or anything—maybe he and Emilia would just talk about their experience so far. But when Miguel closed the door and Alfie let his head rest on the pillow, he was out like a light.

Chapter 9

When Alfie woke up, he looked out the window. The sky was beginning to get dark. Or maybe he'd slept all night and it was starting to get light. He had no idea what time it was. Then he spotted the digital clock on the nightstand between his and Emilia's beds. It was 7:45 p.m. Alfie reached over and turned on the lamp next to the clock. Emilia squinted awake from her bed.

"What time is it?" she asked.

"Almost eight," Alfie replied.

"How long were we asleep?"

"A few hours, I guess," Alfie said. "We had lunch pretty late."

Emilia nodded and rubbed her eyes. "I'm so glad Miguel asked us to stay."

Alfie smiled. "Me too."

"And Nina and Lucas seem really nice. I'm excited to practice for the parade with them again!"

Alfie nodded, though he didn't quite share Emilia's level of excitement.

"What do you think we should do about clothes this time?" Emilia asked. "I wonder if we could borrow from Lucas and Nina. But that might seem weird."

Alfie hadn't thought about this. He pictured tall Miguel. There was no way he could borrow from him—he'd swim in Miguel's clothes! He stood up and stretched. "I'm not sure what we should do," he said.

"Wait a minute," Emilia said, beaming. "I've got Grandma's birthday money!" She reached into her pocket and pulled out two twenty-dollar bills. "Her card came today, and I put the money she sent in my pocket!"

"Nice one, Emilia!" Alfie cheered. "Maybe Miguel can

change it to Brazilian money for us."

Emilia nodded.

There was a knock on the door, and Miguel poked his head in. "I thought I heard your voices. How'd you sleep?"

"Really well!" Alfie said.

"Excellent. Then let's go see how my mom's samba school is doing!"

When Alfie, Emilia, and Miguel stepped out onto the sidewalk, they hurried in the opposite direction from where they'd been earlier that day. Alfie stayed focused on Miguel as they weaved up the crowded cobblestone street.

"We have to hop on the bus to get to my mom's rehearsal space," Miguel said.

"We have some American money," Emilia said. "We just need to change it."

"Okay. We can do that tomorrow," Miguel replied. "I've got bus fare."

The bus was already crowded when it wheezed up to

the corner. Miguel got on first and paid their fares. Then he found one open seat and motioned for Emilia to sit down. Miguel stood over her and held the strap above the seat. Alfie wasn't tall enough to reach a strap, so he held the pole next to Emilia's seat. The bus lurched forward and they were on their way. Alfie looked out the window as the bus bumped through the busy streets. He could see restaurant and shop lights twinkling all around. They passed another couple of samba bands with crowds dancing in the streets. He sighed. He really hoped they'd get to do some exploring, too.

The crowd on the bus soon thinned, and Miguel pulled the cord to signal their stop. They exited the front of the bus and walked a couple of blocks to the rehearsal space. It was much bigger than the ballroom where Miguel's group practiced. It was like a big, open warehouse, and there were hundreds and hundreds of people inside!

Miguel scanned the sea of people and then finally said, "There she is! Come on."

They made their way over to Miguel's mother. Her face lit up when she saw him and she squeezed him into a tight hug, kissing him on both cheeks.

"This is Alfie and Emilia," Miguel told her. "They're going to be in my children's parade. This is my mother, Doña Costa."

"Nice to meet you." Alfie and Emilia smiled politely.

"Wonderful to meet you, too!" Doña Costa exclaimed. She had a dazzling smile just like Miguel's.

"Papa and I invited them to stay with us for a few days," Miguel added.

She looked confused. "Where is your family?"

"Our parents are here for work," Alfie said. "They're letting us explore as long as we check in with them a couple times a day."

"I thought I could show them around a bit between rehearsals," Miguel explained.

Doña Costa nodded. "Lovely!"

"How's rehearsal going?" Miguel asked. Alfie was

relieved he was changing the subject. He didn't want Miguel's mom to ask too many questions!

"Great! We're in really good shape," Doña Costa said. "We were just taking a break, but we're about to start up again. Why don't you grab a few chairs along the side and watch?"

Miguel nodded and motioned Alfie and Emilia over to the side of the room. Doña Costa used a microphone to call everybody to attention and explain which section of the parade they were going to rehearse. The percussion section led the start of the routine while the dancers got into place. Miguel paid close attention. He followed every move and every musical note. Alfie was surprised he was so attentive when it wasn't even his parade.

After watching intently for a while, Miguel spoke to Alfie and Emilia. "There are more than seventy samba schools that each represent a different neighborhood in Rio."

"That's a lot of neighborhoods!" Emilia said.

"Rio is a big city!" said Miguel. "So each samba school has its own flag colors and they choose a theme song, costumes, and floats for their Carnival parade."

"And your mom is the head of this samba school?" Emilia asked.

"That's right." Miguel smiled proudly. "She has been

the Carnival designer for *Borboleta* for seven years."

"Cool," Emilia said. "What does *borboleta* mean?"

"It means *butterfly* in Portuguese," Miguel explained. "*Borboleta* has been in the Special Group of elite samba schools for many years. It's a huge honor."

Emilia nodded and smiled. Alfie could tell she really enjoyed learning about Carnival.

Miguel stood up. "Well, let's head back home. My mom will be here for a while longer, but we don't need to wait for her. She practically lives at the rehearsal hall during Carnival season."

Miguel waved to his mother across the room. She blew kisses in his direction and waved at Alfie and Emilia before advising another large group of performers.

Alfie, Emilia, and Miguel took the bus back to Botafogo. The air was still surprisingly warm—it felt like most summer days back home and it was already nine o'clock at night. And Alfie expected the streets to be quieter now, but there were still plenty of people bustling around. "The streets are so busy," he remarked.

Miguel nodded. "Cariocas eat dinner pretty late. It's normal to sit down to eat at nine or ten o'clock."

"I can't imagine eating that late at home!" Emilia said.

"Yeah!" Alfie smiled. "I don't think my stomach would let me wait that long to eat dinner!"

"I'm guessing my dad made just a light dinner tonight," Miguel said. "After the feijoada this afternoon."

"I think I'm still full!" Emilia said, and they laughed.

When they arrived back at Miguel's apartment, Señor Costa was just putting out a salad, some fruit, and freshly baked bread. "Nothing fancy," he said. "Although I did make *brigadeiros* for dessert."

"This is definitely your lucky day," Miguel told Alfie and Emilia. "To have feijoada and *brigadeiros* on the same day!"

"What are those?" Emilia asked.

"They're a special chocolate dessert made from cocoa powder, butter, and condensed milk," Señor Costa answered. "The dessert was created in the 1940s and it was said that the first person to try it was a brigadier general in the army, so that's how it got its name."

"Now we usually eat *brigadeiros* at birthday parties and other special occasions," said Miguel.

"Or when we have special guests," Señor Costa added. "Go ahead, try one. I'm always a believer in eating dessert first."

Alfie grinned. He liked that idea. He wondered if he could convince his mom to let him start having dessert first! Alfie and Emilia each picked up one of the chocolate balls. They were heavy and looked like truffles rolled in chocolate sprinkles. Alfie bit into his *brigadeiro*, breaking the crust of sprinkles and sinking his teeth into a gooey center. The inside was the consistency of a soft caramel, but it was all chocolaty goodness.

"Yum!" Emilia said, taking the word right out of

Alfie's mouth. "It's sweet, but not too sweet. And I like the crunchy sprinkles."

Señor Costa nodded. "Traditional *brigadeiros* are always made with chocolate. But now people make them with all kinds of different flavors: pistachio, caramel, cherry, coconut—almost anything you could imagine!"

"I think I'd like to try every flavor!" said Alfie.

"I guess I better get busy then!" Señor Costa laughed.

Alfie ate the rest of his *brigadeiro*. It was only their first day in Rio, and they'd already had such amazing food. He couldn't wait to see what they'd try tomorrow. He just hoped there would be more exploring and less practicing on the menu.

Chapter 10

The next morning, Alfie and Emilia woke up early. Alfie could smell fresh bread baking again, and his stomach growled, despite all the food he'd eaten the day before.

Out in the kitchen, Miguel sat at the table sipping coffee and eating a bun. "Good morning!" he said.

"Morning!" Alfie said.

"My father made some *pão de queijo*. He had to head to the restaurant early, but he wanted to make sure we had something to eat for breakfast."

"That's very nice," Emilia said. "They smell just like the ones we made with Zia!"

Alfie thought it felt like ages ago that they'd been

helping Zia make cheese buns in their kitchen at home.

"Practice doesn't start until later this afternoon, so I thought we'd explore Rio a bit first," Miguel said. "Sound good?"

"Yefth!" Alfie cheered with his mouth full of cheese bun. This was what he'd been waiting for.

"Great." Miguel laughed. "First thing we need to do is get you two some sunscreen. You'll be redder than this tablecloth soon if we don't! Then I thought we'd go up to the top of Corcovado to see the Christ the Redeemer statue up close. And the view from there can't be beat."

"That sounds perfect," Emilia said. "Can we stop and get some new clothes on the way? That way we don't have to waste time going to our hotel."

"Excellent idea," said Miguel. "And you'll definitely need bathing suits if we're going to swim at the beach in Copacabana today."

Alfie grinned from ear to ear. "Let's go!" he said as he popped the rest of the cheese bun in his mouth. Emilia gave him a look like he was being rude, but he was too excited to care.

Outside, the day was already heating up. Alfie could feel the intense sun bouncing off the concrete sidewalks and the buildings as they walked. Miguel led the way to a bank to change their money and then to a small department store a few streets away. Alfie and Emilia bought sunscreen, beach hats, and bathing suits. Then Alfie picked out a T-shirt and Emilia chose a colorful cotton sundress. They also bought a cheap tote bag to put their stuff in. Once they paid for their things and slathered themselves with sunscreen, they were ready for their day of exploration.

"We'll go up to Corcovado first," Miguel told them. "It's less crowded with tourists in the morning, plus there's a better chance it will be clear at the top. It gets hazy in the afternoon, or sometimes it's even covered by the clouds—that's how high it is at the summit."

Alfie peered up at the towering mountain as they walked toward it. It was definitely high!

"How do we get to the top?" Emilia asked.

"You can actually hike to the top if you want to," Miguel said.

Emilia's face fell. "Are we doing that?"

"No!" Miguel laughed. "It's a pretty serious climb, and we don't have time for that today. There's a tram that takes you up the side of the mountain, if you don't hike. That's what we're taking."

"Good," Emilia said. Alfie could see her shoulders relax again.

They took the subway from Botafogo to the Cosme Velho station. Alfie was grateful for the air-conditioned subway ride. At the Cosme Velho station Miguel bought their tickets for the red electric train that ran up the side of Corcovado. Alfie strained to look up the mountain as they boarded. It was a steep climb, and he was excited!

As the train started climbing the rocky mountainside, Miguel told Alfie and Emilia a little bit more about the area and the statue.

"Corcovado is in Tijuca National Park," he said as he gestured to the dense green forest around them. "This is a rain forest, and it's the largest urban forest in the world."

"Whoa," Alfie said, taking in all the colors. The trees and plants were the brightest green he had ever seen. Red, yellow, and other brightly colored birds flew among some of the branches, and he could also hear animal noises that he couldn't identify. The rain forest was cool!

"Are there animals in this rain forest?" Emilia asked. *She must be hearing the strange noises, too,* Alfie thought.

"Sure," Miguel said. "There are tons of tropical birds, ocelots, and howler monkeys."

"Monkeys?" Alfie asked. Now he was really excited. "Will we see any?"

"We should be able to see some in the trees," Miguel answered. "They're pretty small, but keep your eyes peeled."

"Look at all the butterflies!" Emilia exclaimed. Alfie

could see tiny blue and yellow wings fluttering among the thick green plants.

The train continued its steep, steady climb, and the city started to spread out in front of them. Then some movement in a nearby tree caught Alfie's eye and he saw a flash of brown fur swinging between branches. "I think I saw a monkey!"

"Where?" Emilia pushed up against Alfie's side and he pointed to the trees where the monkey had been. It was long gone by now. It was so hard to believe they were still in the middle of a huge, busy city with all this wildlife around!

At the top of the mountain there was a chapel and a small souvenir shop. They took an escalator to reach the base of the statue, which towered high above them. Alfie drew in a long breath and held it. The view was like nothing he'd ever seen!

They walked below the base of the statue to the guardrail and looked out over the city.

Buildings spread out in every direction, but there was also so much rich greenery, dazzling blue water, and mountain scenery everywhere. And Miguel was right: There were even a few puffy clouds below where they stood!

Emilia looked up at the statue. "It's so tall!"

"It actually gets struck by lightning a lot," Miguel told her.

"Really?"

"Yeah. In fact, a strike not too long ago broke off one of the fingers on the right hand. They had to repair it."

"That's crazy!" Emilia said, still peering up at the huge stone figure.

"What's that round mountain out in the bay?" Alfie asked, pointing across the beach.

"That's called Sugarloaf," Miguel said. "You can also go to the top of that mountain to get a different view over the water."

"Cool," Alfie said. "But I think this view is probably better. It's so much higher!"

Miguel laughed. "Cariocas like to argue about which view they think is better."

Alfie, Emilia, and Miguel wandered around the base of the statue for a while and looked at the view in every direction. It was pretty spectacular. Soon, it started to get more crowded, and the air had grown much more hot and humid.

"Let's head down before there's a wait for the train," Miguel said. "I think it's about time to cool off at the beach, anyway."

Alfie nodded as he wiped the sweat from his forehead.

By the time they finally made it down to Copacabana, Alfie was more than ready for his first swim in Rio. And he was pretty hungry, too. Luckily, the gray-and-white swirling stone sidewalks were covered with cafés, kiosks, and vendors.

"The food carts remind me a little bit of Hong Kong," Emilia said to Alfie. Alfie nodded, remembering all the great street food they'd sampled there. He couldn't wait to try Brazilian street food, too!

"Let's go for a swim," Miguel said. "Then we can grab some snacks and hang out for a bit."

"Sweet!" Alfie said. They quickly found a public

restroom and changed into their bathing suits. They dropped their stuff in the sand and dashed straight into the sparkling blue water, ready for some relief from the heat. Alfie's feet sank into the warm white sand and he let the water wash over them. It was a little colder than he expected, but it still felt amazing. Soon, he was up to his waist, and Emilia wasn't far behind.

They swam in and out of waves, splashing and laughing. The sun shone strong on the water. Alfie could definitely get used to this, he thought. He wasn't missing snowy February back home at all.

Alfie floated on his back for a while and then remembered how hungry he was. He looked around for Emilia and Miguel. Emilia was heading out of the water and back onto the beach. Miguel bodysurfed a wave toward Alfie. "Hungry?" he asked as he swam close.

"Definitely!" Alfie said.

They stumbled out of the water and back onto the warm sand. Miguel ran over to a kiosk and rented a giant beach blanket and a red-and-white-striped umbrella. Emilia spread out the blanket while Miguel opened the umbrella above them to provide some shade.

"I'll go grab us some snacks so you guys can try a bunch of different things," Miguel said. He dashed across the beach.

"Alfie, look!" Emilia pointed to a group of kids who were playing soccer in the sand just down the beach.

Alfie watched closely. The players were really good. He thought about how fun it would be to play soccer on the beach! Back at home they had to play indoors until late spring.

Before long, Miguel returned with paper plates loaded with food. He set the plates on the blanket and pointed out each delicious-looking treat to Alfie and Emilia. "We have grilled shrimp, deep-fried salted cod balls, and *pastéis*, which are kind of like empanadas."

"I don't think I've had an empanada before," Emilia said.

"It's like a pastry, but it's filled with savory ingredients instead of sweet," Miguel explained. "*Pastéis* are similar to empanadas, but the dough is fried so they are crispier on the outside. These *pastéis* have cheese and chicken inside."

"Yum!" Alfie chimed in.

"Then I also got slices of mango and papaya and some fresh coconut water straight from the coconut." Miguel held out a large green coconut with the top hacked off and several skinny red straws sticking out. "I thought we might need something to balance out the *pastéis* and cod balls."

"It all looks delicious. Thanks, Miguel," Emilia said.

"Yeah, thanks," Alfie added, taking a bite of a salted cod ball. The whitefish inside was chewy and seasoned with a hint of salt.

"My dad makes really good salted cod," Miguel said.

"You have to soak it overnight to get just the right texture and flavor."

"Your dad's already such a great cook," Emilia said. "It doesn't seem like he's still training at all."

"Well, he's definitely had a ton of practice," Miguel said between bites of grilled shrimp.

"Alfie," Emilia started, "remember those fried fish sandwiches we had in Naples by the sea?"

"Oh yeah," Alfie said. "I wonder what kind of fish that was."

"Wow, it sounds like you have traveled quite a bit," Miguel commented. "Hong Kong, Naples, New Orleans."

"We've also been to Paris," Emilia added.

"I haven't been out of South America yet," Miguel said. "You guys definitely have me beat!"

Alfie smiled. They really had been to a lot of amazing places already, all thanks to Zia. And they'd tried so much fantastic food everywhere they went. Alfie felt lucky. He picked up the *pastéis* to sample yet another new food. The thick, fried crust was crispy on the outside and doughy on the inside. The melted cheese oozed out when he took a bite. The flavor of the cheese mixed perfectly with the slightly spicy shredded chicken.

Emilia took a drink of coconut water. "I've never had this before. It's so light and refreshing. I love it with the *pastéis*."

Alfie popped a grilled shrimp in his mouth and leaned back on his hands. He took in the scene of people frolicking in the water and laughing, playing, and eating on the beach. He could definitely see why Zia loved it here so much. He wasn't sure he ever wanted to leave!

Chapter 11

An afternoon rainstorm cut their beach time a little short, so Alfie, Emilia, and Miguel packed up their things and headed to the rehearsal hall early for the day's practice. Even though they weren't due to start for an hour, there were already lots of kids and adults there working on final preparations. Marta was busily sewing away in the corner, so Alfie and Emilia stopped by to check on their costumes.

"I'm almost finished!" Marta called over the whir of the sewing machine. "I will have yours ready to try on at tomorrow's final rehearsal."

"Ooh!" Emilia squealed. "I can't wait to see it!" Alfie

had a feeling she was super excited to try on the elaborate butterfly outfit.

Miguel motioned Alfie and Emilia over to a corner of the room near the stage. There was a flat-screen TV on the wall that Miguel had just turned on. "I thought I could show you a video with some of the highlights of last year's Special Group samba-school parades before we start rehearsal. That should help give you a better idea of this whole Carnival process."

Alfie and Emilia settled on a small couch facing the TV and Miguel perched on the arm, remote in hand. Soon, the first parade started with hundreds of performers lined up in different groups.

"Each samba school is broken up into 'wings,'" Miguel explained. "People in the same wing wear the same costume and have the same purpose in the parade. So, Alfie, you're part of the main percussion wing in our parade, and Emilia, you're part of the butterfly dancers' wing. In the big samba schools, each wing has its own president who is responsible for that wing's members."

"How many members are in a wing?" Emilia asked.

"Usually around one hundred. There are so many dancers and drummers that sometimes you need more than one wing to perform the same part in the parade. So then you have two wings that wear the same costumes and have the same role." Miguel pointed to one of the parade floats on the screen. It was a huge statue of a man that towered over the samba-school members. The man's arms and head moved as the float made its way down the Sambadrome parade route. "There are usually at least eight floats per samba-school parade. My mother's parade has nine this year!"

"Whoa!" Alfie's eyes grew wide. The floats were so big and intricate. And there were eight or more of them in each parade! "That must be so much work!" he said.

Miguel smiled. "Preparations for Carnival begin months and months in advance. Actually, almost as soon as Carnival is over, they start prepping for the next year!"

"That's crazy!" Emilia said.

"First the samba school chooses their theme for the year," Miguel continued. "Then they write a song for the parade. After that, the Carnival designer begins to design the costumes and the floats, and the crews start to work on making everything."

"What is *Borboleta*'s theme this year?" Emilia asked.

"Their theme is 'The Music of Nature.' It symbolizes

the importance of music and the natural world in our lives. That's why we have butterfly, bee, and bird costumes in our parade—and the children's parade uses the same theme of the larger samba-school parade."

"So how long has everybody been rehearsing?" Alfie asked.

"Rehearsals started in December for the main samba schools," Miguel answered.

"I had no idea it was such a big deal," Alfie said quietly. He was just now beginning to realize what a huge production each Carnival parade really was.

"The samba parades are very important to the people of Rio," Miguel said.

"And your mom's school is one of the top schools?" Emilia asked.

Miguel grinned. "That's right! *Borboleta* is one of the top twelve schools. They're the last parades to march."

Alfie watched the parade on the TV make its way past the crowd of spectators in the concrete bleachers on either side of the parade route. "How many people are in each school?"

"Thousands!" said Miguel. "My mother's school has over three thousand performers this year."

"Three thousand?" Alfie asked. "How does your mom keep track them all?"

"Well, it's not easy," Miguel agreed. "Each person has a specific role to play. Even though some performers have bigger roles, like the ones who ride on the floats and who lead the different wings, everybody is important in the samba school and every person's contribution to the parade is celebrated."

"It's all so beautiful," Emilia whispered as one parade ended and another began. "How do they ever decide who the winner is?"

Miguel laughed. "It's definitely not an easy decision. There are forty judges that score each school in ten different categories. Last year my mother's school placed tenth. So, she still qualified for the Special Group this year, but her school didn't perform in the Champion's Parade last year. Only the top six schools get to do that. The Champion's Parade happens the next week, after the main Carnival festivities are over."

Emilia shook her head. "It's an amazing production. I wish I could be a part of Carnival every year!"

"Now you know why the children's parade is so important to me," Miguel said.

Alfie nodded. He was definitely beginning to understand.

Chapter 12

The next morning Alfie and Emilia were up early again. Miguel had another place he wanted to show them before the final rehearsal that afternoon. Then tonight was the children's parade! Alfie couldn't believe it was already time.

They had a quick breakfast of fresh tropical fruit and leftover cheese buns. There were a couple of fruits that Alfie didn't even recognize, including some tiny bananas with rusty-red peels. The really sweet bananas were a creamy, almost pinkish, color inside and more delicious than any banana Alfie had ever had.

After breakfast, the trio headed out to the street.

Miguel whistled and hailed a cab. "We don't have much extra time today so we'll just take a cab through the Reboucas Tunnel."

"Where are we headed?" Alfie asked as the little taxi sped along.

"Somewhere I think you're really going to like," Miguel told him.

The area around the entrance to the tunnel was lush, green, and dotted with bright pink flowering trees. It looked like a big park.

"Is this the park we came to yesterday to go up to the statue?" Emilia asked.

"Yes!" Miguel said. "We're right on the edge of Tijuca National Park."

When they exited the other side of the tunnel, Alfie could see buildings with lots of graffiti near the elevated roadway. They made a left turn and sped down another busy street. Soon, a large round structure appeared up ahead. Miguel whispered something to the driver, and he

slowed to a stop in front of it. Miguel paid the driver and
they piled out.

"What is this place?" Alfie asked excitedly.

"This is our soccer stadium. It's called Maracanã
Stadium," said Miguel. "We've hosted the World Cup here
a couple times."

"Awesome!" Alfie said. "Seeing the World Cup here
would be so amazing."

"It was! Brazilians are bigger soccer fans than anyone
else in the whole world! Come on—we're taking a tour."

Alfie was pretty sure he didn't close his mouth
once during the entire tour. The stadium was just so

spectacular and huge. He had never been to a sports stadium that could hold so many fans. As they stood on the field looking up at the rows and rows of empty seats, he thought about all the famous soccer players who had played there. He could only imagine what it must sound like when it was filled with the screams of thousands of crazed Brazilian soccer fans. He definitely needed to come back to Rio for a soccer game as soon as possible.

At the end of the tour, they were walking to the main entrance when a man came out of the locker room with a big gym bag slung over his shoulder. Alfie's jaw dropped yet again. "Is that . . . ," he started to ask Miguel, but he couldn't get the words out.

"Yep!" Miguel beamed. "Excuse me, sir, would you mind

signing a quick autograph for my friend?"

"Who is that?" Emilia whispered to Alfie, who still hadn't closed his mouth.

"He's only the best Brazilian soccer player . . . scratch that—the best *soccer player*, period. On Earth," Alfie said.

"Oh," Emilia said, sounding not quite as impressed as Alfie thought she should.

"What's your name?" The player asked Alfie as he dug a piece of paper and a pen out of his gym bag.

"Um, uh . . . I . . . ," Alfie stuttered, unable to form a single word.

"His name is Alfie," Miguel said. "He's a big fan, as you can probably tell."

The player laughed. "Glad to hear it. Do you play soccer?"

Alfie nodded and then finally found his words. "Yes, sir. I do."

"Well, I hope you practice a lot," he said as he scribbled a few words on the paper. "That's the key to being a good player—that's why I'm here working even when no one else is. Practice makes perfect."

"And you are!" Alfie said as he took the autograph. "Perfect, I mean. Your game is flawless."

"Thanks." The player smiled. "But it wasn't always that way. It took a lot of hard work. Don't forget that." And with that he turned and headed toward the exit.

"Thank you!" Alfie called after him, still unable to believe he'd just met one of his idols.

That afternoon, Alfie was still flying high. He couldn't stop talking about the famous soccer player, or looking at his autograph. Emilia, on the other hand, would have been happy to talk about anything but soccer at that point. Before heading to their final rehearsal, they stopped back at the Costas' apartment to see if Miguel's dad was making lunch.

"Sorry, guys," Señor Costa said. "I'm just on my way to

the restaurant. I'm cooking for a private Carnival lunch party today. It's the first time I'll be the head chef. Wish me luck!"

"Good luck!" Alfie and Emilia said together.

"We know you'll do great," Emilia added.

"Thank you," Señor Costa said. "Oh, and don't worry, I'll be home in time to make a special dinner tonight after the parade."

"No problem, Papa," Miguel said. "I know just what we'll do instead. Good luck with your lunch!"

So, Alfie, Emilia, and Miguel took a detour down to the beach at Ipanema to sample some more food from street vendors. And that suited Alfie just fine. Miguel ordered *acarajé*, which were black-eyed pea fritters stuffed with shrimp, and fried cheese sticks called *queijo coalho*. Emilia had her eye on the cart selling frozen slushies made with açaí berries, so they bought one of those. They sat on a bench facing the water as they shared their food.

Miguel passed around the *acarajé*. It was kind of like

the falafel that Alfie and Emilia had tried at the Middle Eastern restaurant back home, but this was different, split open with the tender pieces of grilled shrimp and caramelized onion falling out the side.

"I love this slushie," Emilia said. "What did you say the berries were called again?"

"It's pronounced *a-sigh-ee*," Miguel said. "It's kind of like a blueberry, but bigger, and it grows in South America."

"Oh right!" Emilia said. "I've heard of that. But I've never heard of an açaí slushie before. It's so good!"

As the trio sat and enjoyed their afternoon snack, several samba bands and trucks carrying lots of revelers wandered past, either blasting music from stereos or creating their own music with instruments and singing. Everyone was definitely already celebrating the start of Carnival, even though it was still a few hours off.

"I bet they have Avenida Atlântica blocked off already, too," Miguel said. "They close that street to traffic every Sunday and for special celebrations so people can walk,

dance, bike, and skateboard without worrying about cars." Miguel stood up to throw away their empty plate. "Well, should we head to practice?"

"Yes!" Alfie cheered. With his soccer idol's words in his head, he was really looking forward to practice this time.

Chapter 13

As soon as they arrived at the rehearsal space, Alfie and Emilia jumped right into working with their groups. Alfie slung the strap for his snare drum around his neck and followed Lucas's lead as closely as he could. Luckily, he was used to the snare drum from band practice at school. It was the drum he used most for his solo. But the samba beat was very different from the music they were learning for the spring concert.

During a quick break, Alfie watched Emilia and Nina practice. They were at the front of their group and Emilia was even giving another dancer some tips! Alfie's shoulders slumped a little bit. It seemed like dancing came naturally to Emilia. She had picked up the routine in no time. Alfie was working so hard, but it still felt like he had a long way to go.

"Ready to go again?" Lucas asked.

"Sure," Alfie said quietly.

Lucas clapped him on the shoulder. "You're doing really well! This is a lot to learn so quickly."

Alfie picked up his drum and started again. He was determined to get it right.

Everybody worked hard all afternoon. Finally, it was time to put on their costumes. Emilia's and Nina's butterfly suits were magnificent. They wore black bodysuits and comfortable black shoes, but their wings were giant, multicolored masterpieces with small round mirrors sewn onto them. Emilia wore a fancy beaded headband with large butterfly antennae sprouting from the top and glittery face paint. Alfie could see her smile beaming for miles.

Alfie's, Lucas's, and Miguel's bird costumes were

just as colorful as Emilia's and Nina's, with a rainbow of feathers sewn onto the fabric. The wings were attached with stretchy armbands so that they expanded out to the sides but left their hands free for their drums. So when Alfie beat his drum, his wings flapped behind him. And his headpiece had a giant bird beak and an opening for his face. As they began to line up in the proper formation, Alfie started getting more and more nervous. What if his bird helmet shifted and he couldn't see? What if he tripped and fell, or forgot his part? Had he practiced enough? He should have paid more attention from the very first rehearsal...

But he didn't have time to worry about that now—the parade was starting! Alfie looked around at the sea of people gathered to celebrate the start of Carnival. Everybody was laughing, dancing, and cheering. Some people already wore costumes and carried props. It was like the biggest party he had ever seen!

Just then, Miguel signaled from the front of the

percussion group and pounded out the intro drumbeat.
The drummers shuffled forward and began their part.
Alfie stumbled through the first few notes before he
found his rhythm. Once he relaxed a little bit, he was able
to look around at the crowd more. He couldn't imagine
what the crowds must be like when the Special Group
samba schools performed!

The group made its way down the parade route. Alfie really got into the music as they went, and he found himself adding more rhythm to his steps as he walked. When they reached a tricky part in the song, Alfie fumbled the notes again, but he quickly recovered and finished strong. At the end of the route, the percussion group kept drumming, but turned to face the rest of the performers. Alfie was able to find Emilia and watch her dance her way toward him. She had a huge smile on her face and looked like an absolute natural. She moved effortlessly to the beat and tilted her butterfly wings so the mirrors flashed and blinked. It was amazing!

As the last dancers made their way to the end of the parade route and joined the rest of the performers waiting there, the crowd erupted into cheers. Alfie and Lucas found Emilia and Nina. They gave each other hugs and high fives. Then Lucas and Nina went off to see their families, and Alfie and Emilia found Miguel, who was standing at the edge of the stands with his parents. Doña

Costa was smooshing Miguel's cheeks with her hands and talking excitedly.

"Bravo!" she cried. "That was fantastic, Miguel. I'm so, so proud of you."

Alfie could see the relief and pride on Miguel's face.

"It was the perfect kickoff for this year's Carnival," Doña Costa continued. "And Alfie and Emilia, well done! You two looked great."

"Thank you!" Emilia said, slightly out of breath. "It was so much fun!"

Alfie nodded quietly. He couldn't stop thinking about the two parts he'd messed up. *I should have practiced harder from the start*, he said to himself. He thought about all the people he'd met since they'd arrived in Rio, who were working so hard at their dreams: Señor Costa and his chef training, Miguel and the Carnival parade, his favorite soccer player. Alfie thought about his drum solo during the spring concert. It felt different now. More important. And most of all, he wanted to make his parents proud like Miguel had done.

"Let's go home!" Señor Costa said. "We've got some celebrating to do!"

Emilia linked her arm in Alfie's as they walked. "You okay?" she asked.

"Yeah," Alfie said. "I just wish I'd practiced a little harder, that's all."

Emilia squeezed his arm. "I think you did pretty great. And it was fun, right?"

Alfie smiled. "It was fun. And you were amazing, Emilia! You could seriously be a dancer."

Emilia grinned from ear to ear. "I loved it! I wish we could do it again."

Back at the Costas' apartment, Señor Costa bustled around the kitchen preparing their celebratory meal. "I made *moqueca de camarão*," he said. "It's a shrimp stew with coconut-milk broth."

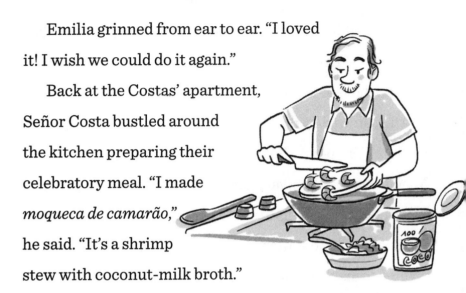

The steam wafting out of the pot made Alfie's stomach rumble. It felt like a lifetime ago that they were sitting at the beach eating fritters and slushies!

Miguel put five big bowls next to the stove and set the table while Doña Costa excitedly recapped the parade.

"Everybody knew their roles so well, and it was a wonderful performance," she gushed.

"Thank you, Mom," Miguel said. "That means so much to me."

"Here we go!" Señor Costa said as he set the first two

bowls of stew on the table in front of Alfie and Emilia. "Special guests first."

"Thank you, Señor Costa," Emilia said. "This smells so delicious."

"Yes, thank you," Alfie said as he peered in his bowl. The broth was a bright yellowish-orange color filled with huge pieces of shrimp and colorful chunks of red and green pepper and tomato. A sprig of cilantro on top was the finishing touch.

Señor Costa set the remaining bowls on the table, and Doña Costa lifted her wineglass in the air. Alfie, Emilia, and Miguel brought their glasses of fruit juice up to meet hers.

"To new friends and the most successful Carnival yet," Doña Costa said.

"Cheers!" Señor Costa cried.

"Cheers!" Alfie, Emilia, and Miguel added.

"Now, please eat!" said Señor Costa. "But save room for dessert."

Alfie glanced at the clock hanging next to the

refrigerator before taking his first bite. It was after nine thirty. And he'd hardly noticed how late it was this time— he was getting used to eating this late! Alfie lifted his spoon and the rich coconut broth coated his mouth with a sweet flavor. The shrimp were tender and juicy and made a nice contrast with the slightly crispy peppers and acidic tomato flavor. Before Zia had sent them on all their eating adventures, Alfie might have thought shrimp stew sounded gross. But now he was always willing to try new foods, and he was never disappointed!

"Another wonderful meal," Emilia said.

Alfie stared into his nearly empty bowl. "I could eat like this every day!"

Everybody laughed.

"And don't forget, there's dessert," Señor Costa said, getting up from the table.

Miguel's dad brought out a round yellow dessert. It looked a little bit like lemon Jell-O. He set five small plates on the table.

"Yum, you made *quindim*!" Miguel said. "Have you guys ever had flan?" he asked Alfie and Emilia.

They shook their heads. "I don't think so," Emilia said.

"Well, flan is a baked custard dessert, kind of like a firm pudding. And *quindim* is like a coconut flan."

It took just one bite of the *quindim,* and Alfie and Emilia were hooked. "I love the shredded coconut on the bottom," Emilia said, taking another big bite. "We should have Zia make this and the *brigadeiros*," she said to Alfie.

"Hey, wait a minute!" Miguel said. "Isn't it your birthday, Emilia?"

Emilia set down her spoon and smiled. "It is!" she said.

"Happy birthday!" Doña Costa cried. "How nice of your parents to share you with us on your special day!"

Emilia nodded. "We talked to them before the parade. We have a big celebration planned for when we get home. And we couldn't have asked for a better way to spend my birthday!"

"Great!" Doña Costa said. "Now I think we should find

a candle for this *quindim* so we can sing 'Happy Birthday' and you can make a wish!" She stood up from the table and searched a couple of kitchen drawers. "Here we go!"

Miguel's dad set the *quindim* in front of Emilia, and his mom added a candle. She lit the candle and they sang "Happy Birthday." Then Emilia closed her eyes and smiled before blowing it out and making her wish.

As Alfie and Emilia got ready for bed that night, they laughed about Emilia getting to celebrate her birthday twice.

"I wonder when we'll be going back home," Emilia said as she climbed into bed.

"I don't know," Alfie said. "Maybe we have more food to try first!"

"I really love it here," Emilia continued. "This is a place we have to come back to. We should convince Mom, Dad, and Zia to bring us back for Carnival next year!"

"Totally!" Alfie agreed.

"You know what else?" Emilia said. "I think I want to start a journal."

"A journal?"

"Yeah, to record all of these amazing adventures we've had. I don't want to forget a single thing—like how it felt to dance in that parade tonight!"

Alfie nodded. "That could be cool. We've definitely had some pretty fun adventures." He got in bed and turned off the bedside lamp. As he lay in the dark, he thought about their time in Rio so far. They were having a great time and he wasn't necessarily ready for it to end, but he couldn't help but wonder how much longer they'd be in Rio.

Chapter 14

Alfie woke up in the morning with a start. He'd been having a weird dream. He was down at the beach playing soccer in the sand and a woman in a butterfly costume kept running into the middle of the game, crying and shouting. But as Alfie wiped the sleep from his eyes, he realized he really did hear some sort of commotion. He looked over at Emilia and saw that she was awake and heard it, too.

"What's going on?" Alfie asked his sister.

Emilia sat up and shrugged. "I'm not sure. Maybe we should get dressed and go see."

When Alfie and Emilia appeared in the living room,

Doña Costa was pacing the rug while Miguel and Señor Costa sat on the couch, looking unsure of what to do.

"Good morning," Miguel said, getting up and coming over to them.

"Is everything okay?" Emilia asked quietly.

Miguel shook his head. "Three of my mother's top performers have dropped out of the parade. And it's tonight! There's no time to find replacements."

"What happened?" Alfie asked.

"Two of them caught some sort of stomach bug, and the other one broke his ankle dancing during a street party."

"Oh no!" Emilia said, covering her mouth. "How awful."

"My mother doesn't know what to do. They were all going to be on the first float of the procession."

"Can you bring any of your second-tier people up to the float?" Señor Costa asked gently.

"No!" Doña Costa cried, throwing her hands in the air. "They're too big. This float's spaces are very small, and

Luiza, Daniel, and Pedro were a perfect fit."

Doña Costa sank into a chair.

"Maybe we should go," Alfie said.

"Yeah," Emilia agreed. "We can get our things and head back to our parents' hotel."

Alfie and Emilia turned to leave the room when Miguel shouted, "Wait! I have an idea!"

Miguel rushed over to Doña Costa's chair. "Let me, Alfie, and Emilia do it."

"What?" she asked.

"Let us replace your performers. We're small—we can fit on the float."

"That's not a bad idea," Señor Costa said.

"But you'd have to learn our song. And the routine is

totally different," Doña Costa said. "You would have to practice all day. The parade is tonight!"

"I already know the song and the routine by heart—word for word and step for step," Miguel said confidently. And Alfie knew he was right. He'd seen how hard Miguel concentrated when they visited Doña Costa's rehearsal earlier that week.

"We can do it!" Alfie jumped in.

Emilia gave Alfie an uncertain look.

"I know we can do it," Alfie told her. "We just have to work hard today and give it everything we've got." Alfie wanted one more chance to prove how committed he was. "And besides, we need some way to thank you for making our stay in Rio so great!"

Miguel took his mom's hand. "You heard Alfie, Mom. We've got this!"

Doña Costa stood up. "All right! I trust you and I know you'll do a great job—especially after seeing you in the children's parade last night."

"We will," Alfie said. "I promise."

Doña Costa bustled around the room grabbing bags, folders, and props. "Let me get down to the rehearsal hall and start making arrangements. You kids eat a quick breakfast and meet me there. We've got a lot of work to do!"

Señor Costa hurried into the kitchen and served up bowls of yogurt blended with açaí and bananas and topped with granola. They ate quickly and Alfie led the way out of the apartment and to the rehearsal space. He couldn't wait to get to practice!

Alfie, Emilia, and Miguel practiced the entire afternoon. They barely took a single break except to have Daniel's, Pedro's, and Luiza's costumes fitted for them.

Emilia twirled in a circle, looking in the mirror at her dazzling butterfly outfit. It was even bolder and more elaborate than her costume for the children's parade, with extra swirls of color hand-painted onto the fabric. "I love it!" she cried.

Alfie's and Miguel's bird costumes were also more detailed. "Look at all these feathers!" Alfie marveled.

The other float performers rallied around their new teammates and showed them how they needed to stand, dance, drum, and move on the float. Once they had the routine down, they practiced keeping their footing on a moving platform since the float would be making its way down the parade route as they performed!

"The key is to not think too hard about the fact that you're moving," one performer told them as they wobbled on the platform. "Just keep your focus out in front of you and on your rhythm."

After that, they practiced their specific parts until they knew them by heart—Alfie's and Miguel's different percussion parts and Emilia's special butterfly dance.

Alfie listened to the *Borboleta* theme song over and

over, letting the heavy beat sink into his brain. For a while he just tapped his drumsticks against his leg, but soon he was ready to practice with his drum and add the steps to it as well. Miguel watched Alfie run through the song one final time. He clapped and cheered as Alfie performed without missing a beat.

"I think you're ready," Miguel told him. And Alfie had to agree.

Chapter 15

If Alfie felt nervous before the children's parade, it was nothing compared to how he felt now. He could hardly keep still as the costume designer put a few finishing touches on his costume to make it stand out even more. After all, the children's parade had been just for fun. But this—this was a fierce competition, and he didn't want to let down Miguel and his family.

"The parade lasts for over an hour," Miguel told Alfie and Emilia as they took their places on the float. "So just try to keep your energy up the entire time. We want the people at the end of the parade route to feel like they're getting as big of a show as the people at the beginning."

Alfie nodded, taking deep breaths to try to slow his heart. He was beginning to think that the rhythm of his heart was the same as *Borboleta*'s samba song! Alfie stole a quick glance at Emilia, who was on a small platform above where he stood. If she was nervous, he definitely couldn't tell. She smiled and spread her butterfly wings as wide as they would go. It was hard for Alfie to believe that back home Emilia could sometimes be shy. She was a lot more confident now, thanks to all their adventures.

The float they were on was amazing. Several drummers stood on platforms that looked like flowers. In the middle was a taller platform that looked like a beautiful tropical plant. And on that platform stood Emilia! Alfie knew she was excited—especially since she was also in charge of raining glitter down over the float as she danced.

"Okay," Miguel said. "It's time!"

Just then, an explosion of fireworks burst over their heads. Bright sparks in a million colors lit up the night sky and the lead drummers pounded out the beginning beat. The float started to move and they were on their way.

Alfie picked up the beat at the exact right moment and shuffled his feet in rhythm on the tiny platform of the float. He took one more deep breath and smiled. He knew he had worked hard that day. And now, with each new beat, he began to feel confident, too.

Alfie looked out at the masses of people lining the stands of the Sambadrome. People cheered and whistled, waved flags representing the different samba schools, and danced in place. He glanced at Miguel and watched his strong and steady drumming. Miguel nodded his head and smiled. Alfie smiled back and drummed even harder. He was proud to be part of such a big, important festival for the Costas and for Rio.

Alfie thought it would feel like the parade lasted a long time, but it didn't. It was over before he knew it. He was able to turn and watch Emilia dance a few times, and he could tell she was just as surprised when their float reached the end of the Sambadrome and turned off to the side. As soon as the float stopped, Miguel, Alfie, and Emilia jumped down and hugged each other. They jumped in an excited circle, knowing they'd given a great performance. Then they hopped back up onto the edge of the float and watched the rest of the *Borboleta* samba school make their way to the end. Everybody looked amazing. Their costumes dazzled, their music was strong, and their dance steps were perfect.

Before long, Señor and Doña Costa found them in the celebratory crowd.

"My baby!" Doña Costa cried. "You were magnificent!"

Miguel smiled from ear to ear. Alfie knew how much it meant to him to make his mother proud.

"You are going to make the best Carnival designer Rio de Janeiro has ever seen!" Doña Costa gushed. "And you two," she continued, looking at Alfie and Emilia with

tears in her eyes. "You did such a wonderful job. Emilia, you were like a dream up there. And Alfie, your beat and rhythm were perfect. I'm so proud of all three of you."

"Thank you!" Emilia said. "I think I was born to dance at Carnival!"

Everybody laughed and Doña Costa said, "I think you're right. You must come back and dance with my samba school again."

Miguel nudged Alfie with his elbow. "Nice job. I watched you a bunch and you were great!"

Alfie grinned. He hadn't messed up once, and it felt amazing. He'd had a great time in the parade, but all he could think about now was getting home to practice for his drum solo in the spring concert. He couldn't wait to make his parents as proud as Señor and Doña Costa were of Miguel.

Chapter 16

By the time they'd finished watching the rest of the samba-school parades, it was practically the middle of the night! It reminded Alfie of when they stayed up for the New Year's festivities in Hong Kong, but it was even later this time and he was struggling to keep his eyes open. Once it was finally time to announce the judges' decision, though, Alfie felt wide awake again—and ready to hear how *Borboleta* had performed.

The head judge began to announce how each samba school had placed. He started with twelfth place and made his way up the list. He announced tenth, and then ninth, and eighth. Alfie knew that Doña Costa's school had come in tenth last year, so he wasn't sure how many places they might move up this year. The list continued and Emilia clenched Alfie's arm as the judge read out seventh, sixth, and fifth place.

"And *Borboleta* is our fourth-place samba school this year!" the judge finally shouted. All of *Borboleta*'s fans and performers erupted into cheers and shouting. Alfie and Emilia danced in place while Miguel swung his mother into the air in a tight hug. Tears streamed down Doña Costa's face as she took the fourth-place spot on the stage next to the other Carnival designers.

The judge finished announcing the top three schools, and the stands exploded into a new round of celebration. Once things finally started to die down and Doña Costa worked her way through the sea of Carnival revelers and back over to her family, Miguel explained the announcement to Alfie and Emilia. "Now *Borboleta* gets to perform in the Champion's Parade next week!"

"I wish we could dance in that parade, too!" Emilia said.

"I wish you could, too, darling," Doña Costa replied. "I can't thank you and Alfie enough for coming to the rescue. You and Miguel saved our parade!"

"I'm just so happy we could help," Alfie said, feeling very proud.

"And now it's time to celebrate!" Señor Costa shouted. "What do you say, kids—do you have a little bit of energy left in you?"

Alfie still felt tired and part of him was pretty ready to go home at this point, but the announcement of Doña Costa's samba school making it to fourth place had definitely reenergized him. Not to mention that he'd just realized how hungry he was! "Let's go!" he said.

The family made their way to Señor Costa's restaurant. The entire dining room was decorated in *Borboleta*'s colors of green and white, and the samba school's theme song played out over the speakers. Señor Costa and the other chefs had prepared a smorgasbord of tasty Brazilian foods for the family and their friends. Alfie loaded up a plate with skewers of Brazilian-style grilled beef and chicken, crispy yucca fries, a couple of different salads, and an interesting snack called Romeo and Juliet. It was a hunk of sweet guava paste sandwiched between two slices of firm, mellow white cheese.

"It's like a little sweet-and-salty sandwich," Emilia said after taking a bite.

There was a passion fruit mousse for dessert, as well as several different flavors of *brigadeiros*. Emilia couldn't get enough of those, while Alfie couldn't get enough of the yucca fries.

Miguel found Alfie and Emilia in the crowd. "What do you think of the food?" he asked.

"Delicious!" Alfie said with his mouth full of grilled beef.

"I love this sauce," Emilia said, pointing to the green chunky sauce that accompanied the skewers.

"It's called *chimichurri* sauce," Miguel told her. "It's actually from Argentina, but we like it, too, especially on steak!"

"Argentina, huh?" Alfie said, looking at Emilia. "Maybe we should go there next!"

Emilia laughed. "We'll have to tell Zia."

"Is that your aunt?" Miguel asked.

"She's our great-aunt," said Alfie. "She's taken us to a lot of the places we've traveled."

"Well, you'll have to bring her back here next year for Carnival. And we'll have to meet your parents next time!"

"Next time, for sure," Emilia said, winking at Alfie.

"You'll probably be heading back to your parents' hotel now that Carnival is over," Miguel said.

"Yeah. They were just texting to ask when we'd be back," Emilia replied.

"Well, before you go, I just wanted to thank you again for all your help in the parades this week. You guys were really terrific."

"Thank *you*, Miguel," Alfie said. "Especially for showing us around Rio, and to your dad for feeding us such great food."

"And to your mom for trusting us in her parade!" Emilia added.

"Anytime. You're always welcome in our home, and you're honorary cariocas now, anyway," Miguel said. Then he held out his hand. "Here—I got you something as a thank-you gift." Miguel held two brightly colored ribbons. One was orange and one was yellow, and they both had black writing in Portuguese. Alfie had seen a beach kiosk selling these nylon ribbons down in Copacabana. "These are called Bahia Bands, or wishing bracelets," Miguel explained. "They're a tradition in Brazil. The orange one stands for courage and energy, and the yellow one stands for success and intelligence."

"Thanks, Miguel! That's so nice," Emilia said, picking up the orange one.

Alfie grabbed the yellow one. "Yeah, thanks!"

"So, you need to tie three knots into your bracelet and make three wishes," Miguel said. "Then you must wear your bracelet all the time until it falls off on its own. When it falls off, that's how you know your wishes have come true!"

"Cool!" Alfie said, tying his first knot.

"I better run," Miguel said. "My mother is waving at me from across the restaurant. I think she wants to introduce me to some of the Carnival organizers."

"You should definitely go!" Emilia said.

"I'll find you guys later," Miguel said before dashing to his mother's side.

Alfie and Emilia were quiet as they tied their knots and made their wishes. Then Alfie filled his plate with another helping of yucca fries.

Emilia gave him a wary look.

"What?" Alfie laughed. "They're like french fries, but better! Way better! In fact, I think I like them even more than the fries at Burger Heaven back home!"

Emilia's eyes were wide. "Really? I never thought I'd hear you say that!"

"Hey, remember that time we got Burger Heaven with Dad and took it to the park?" Alfie said, starting to laugh.

"And that duck kept trying to steal the fries right from your hand!"

Emilia scowled and crossed her arms. "I remember."

Alfie shook with laughter. "You were so scared! Of a silly duck!"

"It *was* scary! You would have been freaked out, too, if a bird had been trying to peck your hand off!"

Alfie made a duck face at Emilia and they both laughed. "Oh, give me one of those," she said, grabbing a yucca fry from Alfie's plate. "Mmmm, they are good."

"Told ya," Alfie said, popping another into his mouth.

"That was a really fun day in the park, though," Emilia said. "Even with the killer ducks."

Alfie and Emilia burst into a new round of laughter just as the air suddenly started to shift around them.

Chapter 17

Alfie squinted and waited for his eyes to adjust to the intense lights of their kitchen back home. It was much brighter than it had been in Señor Costa's restaurant. He also noticed how cool and crisp the air felt against his skin—even inside the heated kitchen—compared to the hot, humid air he'd grown used to in Rio.

Zia was just putting the cheese buns she'd made into a plastic container. Alfie's half-eaten bun still sat on his plate like he'd taken a bite just minutes before. Alfie looked at Emilia and she smiled, holding up her wrist. They were both still wearing their Brazilian wishing bracelets!

Emilia began to parade around the kitchen singing the *Borboleta* samba song. "You should have seen it, Zia!" she said. "The colors, the music, the costumes! It was glorious!"

"What was, *ragazza*?" Zia asked with a smile.

"Carnival!" Alfie cried. "It was one of our best trips yet. Rio was like no place I'd ever even imagined. And the food, Zia. Brazilian food is *so* good—especially the yucca fries!"

"Such dreamers you are!" Zia laughed.

Alfie spotted his drumsticks on the edge of the kitchen counter. He picked them up and followed behind Emilia in her kitchen samba parade. "I can't wait to practice my drum solo!"

Zia looked surprised. "Really?"

Alfie nodded. "Practice is important. And I want to make you, Mom, and Dad proud at the spring concert."

"You already make us proud," Zia said. "But I'm so happy to hear you say that! I know your solo is going to be *perfetto*! But for now, I think you two should practice some homework before your parents get home from their PTA meeting."

Emilia stopped parading and slumped into a chair, her tired eyes drooping with sleep. "I think I might just get up early to do my homework. I'm beat."

"Me too," Alfie said, feeling suddenly heavy.

"It must have been a big day at school today," Zia remarked. "You're both so tired."

"Zia!" Alfie and Emilia cried together.

Zia winked and strolled out of the kitchen. "Well, good night then, cariocas."

Chapter 18

It was Saturday afternoon. A light snow fell outside as the Bertolizzi family got ready for Emilia's thirteenth birthday party. Alfie was in the garage practicing his drum solo until Mom called him inside.

"Emilia's guests will be arriving soon," Mom said, peeking her head out the kitchen door into the garage.

"Okay," Alfie replied. "I'm just going to run through it one more time."

Mom smiled and nodded before going back inside.

In the three short days since Alfie and Emilia had returned from their Rio adventure, Alfie's solo had already improved noticeably. Mr. Erikson praised Alfie during band practice the previous day, saying that he had no doubt Alfie would be ready for the concert now. And even Charlie had stopped asking if Alfie needed a replacement. Alfie looked at the knots on his wishing bracelet and grinned. He knew he was going to blow everybody's socks off.

Alfie bounced into the kitchen to find Zia and Emilia arranging a tray of dark chocolate *brigadeiros*. Emilia had made the last-minute addition to her birthday menu because she'd liked them so much in Brazil.

"Where did you get this recipe again?" Dad asked, sneaking a *brigadeiro* from the tray. Emilia playfully slapped his hand away and added another one to the empty space. "Um..."

"I showed it to her," Zia said quickly. "It's a traditional Brazilian dessert to make on birthdays. I learned to make it when I was living there, so I thought it would be fun to include today since Emilia likes chocolate so much."

"That is definitely true!" Emilia smiled. Just then, the

doorbell rang and she ran to greet her first guest.

Alfie and Dad hovered near the food table as Emilia's friends arrived. Emilia's best friend, Felicia, came first with a giant package covered in turquoise paper and sparkly silver bows. Then Katelin and Becky skipped inside carrying matching gift bags. Soon the room was full of excited, laughing girls.

"How's the drum practice going, champ?" Dad asked, sneaking a piece of spicy popcorn from one of the mini movie-popcorn containers on the table.

"It's good!" Alfie replied, following his dad's lead and grabbing some popcorn before Emilia saw him. "I think I'll definitely be ready for the concert in a few weeks. I'm excited for you, Mom, and Zia to see it."

"We're excited, too. And I'm so proud of you for practicing extra hard the last couple of days. I know it's not easy, but it's worth it."

"Practice makes perfect!" Alfie said, echoing what his idol had told him at the soccer stadium.

"*Sì, sì!*" Dad said. "Wise words."

Everybody snacked on Zia's delicious treats while Emilia opened her presents. She mostly got clothes and jewelry from her friends, which Alfie thought was pretty boring. When it came time for Emilia to open his gift, though, Alfie felt his cheeks get warm.

Emilia tore open the paper and gasped. It was a pocket-size journal with a thick, cherry-red cover.

"To write about your adventures," Alfie said quietly.

Emilia jumped up and gave her brother a hug, making his cheeks even hotter. "Alfie, it's perfect!"

After all the presents were opened and the wrapping paper was swept aside, it was time for Emilia to blow out the candles on her Doberge cake.

Emilia sat in front of her cake with Zia on one side and Alfie on the other. She closed her eyes and made a wish. Then Alfie took out the candles while Zia sliced up the cake.

"*Buon compleanno*! Happy birthday!" Zia said. "What did you wish for?"

Emilia smiled as she touched her wishing bracelet. She looked at Alfie and said, "Another adventure."

A Note from Giada

I have traveled a lot in my life, but haven't yet made it to beautiful Brazil. It's at the very top of my list, especially because all my friends who have traveled to Brazil and visited Rio de Janeiro have raved about it! The people, the places, the food, the weather, the beaches! It all sounds so awesome. And as I worked on this book and learned so much more about this super-cool city, I realized . . . I can't get there soon enough! Rio is a big, bustling city, but there are beaches everywhere you look—it's an amazing combination. There is so much to see, from Sugarloaf to Corcovado to the marina—and so much to eat! The Brazilians have a way of combining savory and sweet into one meal that I just love. I never turn down the chance to try a Brazilian dish!

I can't wait to take a trip to this magical city one day very soon!

And now, a taste of
the next book in the series,
Recipe for Adventure:
Hawaii!

Chapter 1

Alfie and Emilia stood in the middle of the kitchen. Emilia had her hands on her hips and Alfie had his arms crossed over his chest. They scowled at each other. The overflowing trash can sat on the floor between them.

"It's your turn!" Emilia cried.

Alfie shook his head. "No, it's not!"

They stared each other down.

"Well, I'm not doing it," Emilia finally said.

"Neither am I," Alfie replied.

"Alfredo!" Emilia shouted, using Alfie's full name.

Dad appeared in the doorway. "*Quietare!*" he said in Italian. "Quiet down. What's all the shouting about?"

"It's Alfie's turn to take out the garbage and he won't do it," Emilia said.

"I did it last week!" Alfie cried.

"No, you didn't!" Emilia stomped her foot.

"Enough!" Dad held up his hands between them. "What's gotten into you two lately? You can't seem to get along for more than ten minutes at a time."

Alfie and Emilia were silent as they stared at the floor.

"Alfie, pick up the bag. Emilia, go open the garbage can in the garage. You can do it together," Dad said.

Alfie was about to protest again when he saw the serious look on Dad's face. He was not messing around. Alfie sighed, picked up the bag, and followed Emilia into the garage.

"I know it was your turn," Emilia whispered as she lifted the lid on the bin. "You're just being a *baby*."

Alfie rolled his eyes. Emilia could be such a know-it-all, especially now that she'd turned thirteen. She was only a year and a few months older than Alfie, but she liked to remind him of that fact every chance she got.

Alfie and Emilia stomped back through the kitchen and stood in the doorway to the family room. Dad had his back to them and was talking to their great-aunt Donatella.

"Maybe this is a bad weekend for us to go on our trip," Dad was saying. "Those two just can't seem to get along lately."

"Nonsense!" Zia Donatella replied, sweeping aside her long salt-and-pepper hair. "You and Arianna have waited ages to have a weekend away. You deserve it."

"We have been looking forward to it . . ." Dad said.

"We'll be fine here," Zia continued. "Don't you worry about a thing."

"All right, we'll stick to our plan." Dad picked up his briefcase. "Well, I'd better get to work. See you tonight."

"*Arrivederci!*" Zia called before turning to see Alfie and Emilia sulking in the doorway.

"Do you think we can all get along this weekend?" Zia

asked. Alfie and Emilia nodded. "Good. Now, anything you want to do while your parents are away?"

"I want to play video games and maybe watch a movie!" Alfie said. "And we're going to cook, right?"

"Of course!" Zia said. Zia was an incredible cook and ever since she'd come to stay with the Bertolizzi family she'd taught Alfie and Emilia some amazing recipes she'd learned from her travels around the world.

Emilia made her way over to the sofa and flopped down. "*I* have a history presentation I need to get started on," she said, giving Alfie a look like she was being more responsible than him.

"That should be fun." Zia perched on the arm of the sofa next to Emilia. Everybody knew that Emilia *loved* history. It was her favorite subject. Alfie, on the other hand, could never get enough of geography. His bedroom walls were plastered with maps of all kinds. And he was forever looking at maps online—everything from world maps to city maps—even climate maps!

"My presentation has to be on the history of a specific city or state," Emilia continued. "I just can't decide where to focus on!"

"Well, you've got plenty of options," Alfie replied, smiling at Zia. He thought about all the places they'd visited and experiences they'd had thanks to Zia's magical recipes.

"You could talk about any of the cities we've gone to," Alfie said.

"I know," Emilia replied. "I just can't decide if I should present somewhere we've already been or somewhere new we might go!"

Zia nodded. "That's a tough decision."

"Not to me!" Alfie said. "I'd definitely give a talk about somewhere we've been. That's much easier. You could talk about the Christ the Redeemer statue in Rio de Janeiro or the Eiffel Tower in Paris!"

Just then Mom walked down the stairs. "Who's going to the Eiffel Tower?" she asked.

Alfie looked at Zia, who busied herself picking lint off the arm of the sofa. Mom and Dad didn't know about any of Alfie and Emilia's adventures. It was their and Zia's little secret.

"Uh, no one," Emilia replied. "We were just talking about my history presentation."

"Oh, I just love Paris!" Mom gushed. "Eating fresh croissants every morning and going to all those sidewalk cafés..."

"And the markets!" Alfie chimed in before clamping his hand over his mouth. "I mean, you know...I remember how Zia was telling us about the markets..."

Mom nodded, but looked a little confused.

"Well," Zia said, straightening the brightly colored stone necklace she always wore. "Aren't you two going to be late for school?"

Mom glanced at the clock on the mantel. "Oh, goodness! It is late. Grab your stuff, kids. We've gotta go!"

"Bye, Zia!" Emilia said, giving her a quick hug.

"Bye!" Alfie gave Zia a grateful smile before slinging his backpack over his shoulder.

Zia winked. "Have a good day, *bambini*!"

MW00757238

THE
SHIP

THE
SHIP

ANTONIA
HONEYWELL

www.orbitbooks.net

Copyright © 2015 by Antonia Honeywell

Cover design by Lisa Marie Pompilio
Cover photographs © shutterstock
Cover copyright © 2017 by Hachette Book Group, Inc.
Author photo by Chris Honeywell

Orbit
Hachette Book Group
1290 Avenue of the Americas
New York, NY 10104
orbitbooks.net

Originally published in Great Britain by Weidenfeld & Nicolson, February 2015.

First Edition: April 2017

Orbit is an imprint of Hachette Book Group.
The Orbit name and logo are trademarks of Little, Brown Book Group Limited.

The publisher is not responsible for websites (or their content) that are not owned by the publisher.

The Hachette Speakers Bureau provides a wide range of authors for speaking events. To find out more, go to www.hachettespeakersbureau.com or call (866) 376-6591.

Library of Congress Cataloging-in-Publication Data
Names: Honeywell, Antonia, author.
Title: The ship / Antonia Honeywell.
Description: First edition. | New York : Orbit, 2017.
Identifiers: LCCN 2016050766| ISBN 9780316469852 (hardcover) |
    ISBN 9780316469845 (softcover) | ISBN 9780316469890 (ebook)
Subjects: LCSH: Regression (Civilization)—Fiction. | Teenage girls—Fiction.
    | Survival—Fiction. | BISAC: FICTION / Coming of Age. | FICTION / Literary. |
    GSAFD: Bildungsromans. | Dystopias.
Classification: LCC PR6108.O56 S55 2017 | DDC 823/.92—dc23 LC record
    available at https://lccn.loc.gov/2016050766

ISBNs: 978-0-316-46985-2 (hardcover) 978-0-316-46989-0 (ebook)

Printed in the United States of America

LSC-C

10 9 8 7 6 5 4 3 2 1

To James, who made it safe to open doors on dark places,
and to Oliver, Thea, Adam and Esme, who bring light.

THE
SHIP

ONE

A trip to the British Museum ❖ *the manifest*
is full ❖ *we leave*

Right up until the day we boarded, I wondered whether the ship was just a myth. There were so many myths in my life then. The display cases in the British Museum were full of them, and the street prophets crowding the pavements outside ranted new ones at my mother and me every time we walked past. From time to time, there was a government raid and, for a few days, the streets would be empty, except for the one prophet who always survived. He sat on the corner of Bedford Square and Gower Street, filthy in worn denim, holding up a board that said, "God has forgotten us." I don't know why the troops left him. Perhaps they agreed with him; in any case, he must have had a card. He was still there when we left, sailing past the car window as though he were the one on water. It was my sixteenth birthday.

I was born at the end of the world, although I did not know it at the time. While I fretted at my mother's breast, demanding more milk than she was able to give me, great cargo ships sailed out of countries far, far away, carrying people from lands that were sinking, or burning, or whose natural bounty had been exhausted. While I took my first stumbling steps, cities across the world that had once housed great industries crumbled into dust, and pleasure islands that had been raised from the oceans melted back into them as though they had never existed. And as I began to talk, the people in the surviving corners of civilisation fell silent, and plugged their ears and their hearts while the earth was plundered for its last scrapings of energy, of fertility. Of life.

I was seven when the collapse hit Britain. Banks crashed, the power failed, flood defences gave way, and my father paced the flat, strangely elated in the face of my mother's fear. I was right, he said, over and over again. Wasn't I right? Weren't we lucky that we owed nothing to anyone? That we relied on no one beyond our little trio? That we had stores, and bottled water? Oh, the government would regret not listening to him now. The government would be out on the streets with the rest of the population. Weren't we lucky, he wanted us to say, weren't we lucky that we had him? He ranted, and we bolted our doors; my mother tightened her arms around me, and for months we did not leave the flat.

Across the country, people lost their homes, the supermarkets emptied and the population stood, stunned and helpless, in the streets. My father watched the riots and the looting, the disasters and the forced evictions on every possible channel; he had the computer, his phone and his tablet and juggled them constantly, prowling about the flat and never seeming to sleep. The government resigned, and then came the tanks, and the troops with their terrible guns. My father vanished. Oxford Street burned for three weeks, and I watched the orange skies from the circle of my mother's arms, weeping for him. Hush, my mother whispered to me, hush. But I was only a child; I had not learned to be silent, and when he returned, tired and triumphant, I cried just as loudly and buried myself in him. But he was no longer the man who had walked away. The military government had listened; they had bought the Dove from him. He was a rich man now, and a powerful one, and he had more important things to do than cuddle me.

Within weeks of my father's return, the Nazareth Act came into force. I remember the queues, the identity checks, the biometric registrations, and surrounding it all, my father's jubilation at his success. Opponents called the Dove a violation of human rights, but as my father said, it worked. Your screen was registered, you were issued with an identity card, and from then on you were identified by your screen address, no matter where the social and financial earthquakes had left your land one. The satellites were still operational, so the authorities always knew where you were. What food there was could be distributed fairly. New laws could be communicated quickly and card-carrying citizens got the information they needed to survive. Food drops, medical assistance, re-registration requirements, work opportunities. New acts came in thick and fast: to the Exodus Act and the Optimum Resourcing Act were added the Land Allocation Act, the Prisoner Release Act, the Possession of Property Act— each heralded by a triumphant fanfare on the news bulletin, which was now the only source of information. The Dove was the ultimate firewall; anything it did not approve went onto the raven routes and over time, the raven routes became more and more dangerous. A screen open to raven routes burnt out in seconds; whether the virus that did so was a government initiative or a legacy from the days of unrestricted access, no one could say. And so, with cards and screens and the Dove, order was created from chaos. Regular biometric re-registration meant that stolen cards, and the cards of the dead, were only ever valid for a limited time. By the time I was ten, a valid card was the most valuable thing in the world, and my mother and I, duly registered, were able to go out for a walk.

"Where's your card?" my mother demanded the first time we went to unbolt the door. "Show me."

We'd practised so many times. I unzipped the inside of my pocket, felt through the hole, opened the card compartment of my belt and held it out to her. "Seven seconds," she said. "It's not fast enough."

"You do it then," I said, but my mother was holding her card up before I'd even started the timer.

"The troops will shoot me if you don't show your card," she said, "and it'll be stolen if it can be seen." And so I tried harder, but she wasn't satisfied, and took my card away to look after it herself. We went to Regent's Park, to look at the tents people had set up as temporary accommodation, although she wouldn't let me speak to anyone. We went to the new banks of the Thames, too, to see Big Ben and the London Eye peering mournfully out of the water, but even with the security of the troop patrols, London had become desolate and dangerous, and soon our outings became confined to the British Museum, just around the corner. We went there every day; it became my schoolroom, my playground, my almost home.

"Things will get better," my mother said, holding my hand, and I believed her. The bulletins said the same.

And yet—and yet. Time went by, and still people starved. Still they slept in floating death-traps, or in the campsites that had been created in London's parks, now surrounded by razor wire. I saw these things through the bubble of safety and relative plenty in which I lived; I saw them so often that I became immune. My father saw them too. I think he was a little bewildered that his great triumph, the Dove, had not saved the world, and so he set about saving his own world—my mother and I—another way. He always did like to be in control.

The paper ran out, so my mother tore labels from tins and taught me to write on the back of them; when there were no pencils left, we burned splinters of wood and made our letters with scratches of black. And after a year or two, a new word began to creep through the wall that divided my parents' room from mine, whispered at night in hopeful voices. *A ship. What about a ship?* I scraped the word laboriously with my burned sticks. Ship. Ship. I grew quieter as I grew older, and listened as hard as I could to my mother and father's intense, whispered conversations. I was spelling out the titles on the spines of my mother's old books when I first heard the word spoken out loud.

"A ship," he said to her. "Shall we do it?"

And my mother said, "But Lalage's future?" and my father said, "There's no future here. We'll make one for her," and from that time on he was barely ever home. It was years before I learned that Anna Karenina was the title of the novel and not the name of the author.

The ship. The word floated through my childhood, a thought with nothing to tether itself to. *There'll be paper on the ship*, my mother told me, when I complained about the labels. *There'll be rice on the ship*, my father said, when we ate the last of the rice in our stores. *The ship*, my father said when the public executions went from weekly to daily. When the marketeer riots spread from Oxford Street to Bloomsbury and the bodies stayed outside our flat for three days; when the screen crashed, or the rats got inside our building; when the water gave out, or a food drop failed, he always said, *Just you wait, Lalla. Wait until we sail.*

The only actual ships I'd ever seen were the stinking hulks that drifted up the bloated river every now and again, relics of the great evacuations, and I knew they weren't what my parents meant. Mostly they were empty; anyone left alive on them was shot as they swam to the bank, if they didn't drown first. The rusting carcasses lined the river from London to the sea, lowering into the water until they keeled over, complete with the homeless who'd taken refuge on them. My mother would go pale and clench her fists as we watched the bulletins on our screens. I hated seeing my mother so unhappy, but to me she seemed naive. After all, no one had forced those people to sleep on the Sinkers, any more than they were forced to live in London's public buildings. My parents and I lived in a proper flat, with food and clothes and locks on the door, and because we had these things, it seemed to me that they were available, and anyone who lived without them was making a choice. My father was very big on choice.

"Turn it off," my mother always said, but she never meant it. She would no more have missed a bulletin than she'd have let me go out into the streets alone.

Food became scarcer; on my twelfth birthday, for the first time since the Dove, there was no cake.

"There's no power spare for the oven," she told us.

"Why can't you just melt chocolate over the fire and stir in biscuits, like last year?" I asked, but my father told me to hush, and my birthday was ruined.

My mother got thinner, and when my father came home the two of them pored over papers and screens while I read and played approved screen games and tried to remember the things my mother had taught me during the day. Daytime London gradually emptied, drained by the curfews and the Land Allocation Act, and the terrible penalties of being discovered by the troops without a card. My father's appearances were gala days; the rest were about survival. Food drops. Hiding the car, which my father claimed we'd need one day. The fingerprinting and flashing lights of the biometric re-registrations, which became ever more frequent. And the ship, the ship, the ship, held out like a promised land between them, hung on words like equality, kindness, safety and plenty. "Wouldn't it be nice if the good people had a chance?" my mother would say, but in post-collapse London, my father and mother were the only people I knew, and in any case, she never seemed to expect an answer.

Who were the good people, anyway? The street people, or the prophets or petrolheads, who avoided me as instinctively as I did them? Were the strangers who came to the flat when my father was at home good people? I had no way of knowing; I didn't talk to them, and in any case they never came twice. You'll have friends on the ship, my parents told me. By the time I was fifteen, my parents were still all I knew, and their stories of the ship had become as fascinating and impossible as fairy tales. I didn't know that the people who came to the flat were being interviewed for berths, or that the hours my mother spent on the screen were spent exploring the forbidden raven routes, looking for stories of people who deserved to be saved. I didn't know that my father's frequent absences were spent tracking down supplies and vaccinations; I didn't know that he finally bought the ship itself from a Greek magnate who'd decided to tie himself to the land. I knew nothing. Except that I was lucky, and that was only because my parents kept telling me so. We walked to the British Museum almost every day, and the dwindling of the collections was the only marker of time I had.

The evening before my sixteenth birthday, I sat watching the news bulletin with my mother. At least, she watched the bulletin; I didn't bother. I couldn't understand how she could waste precious power when the bulletins were always the same. I never watched them; what I watched was my mother watching. She sat on the edge of the sofa, twitching and shifting as she sifted the presenter's words, her hand resting automatically over the pocket where she kept our identity cards, right up until the bulletin finished, as it always did, with the recording of the commander's original promise to the people. I could recite it word for word. "Keep your card. It is your life. This Emergency Government has but one task—to ensure fair distribution of limited resources. I, Marius, Commander of the Emergency Government, promise that no card-carrying, screen-registered, law-abiding man or woman in this country will go hungry, or homeless, or watch their children walk without shoes. But with that promise comes a warning. Do not let your registration lapse. Carry your card and keep it safe. My citizens are my priority. I cannot feed those who are not mine. And without your card, I cannot know that you are mine."

"Your card, Lalage," she said suddenly. She had handed it over to me just before the bulletin.

I felt in my pocket. "It's fine," I said. Her face tensed. "What?" I demanded. "I've got my card. It's here, all right?"

"No. It's not all right."

"Why not?"

"Because you'll be sixteen tomorrow. You'll be responsible for your own card. They will shoot you if you can't produce it. Not me. You. Your card, do you hear me, Lalage?"

"Happy birthday to me," I muttered. But I listened. I always listened to her, although I rarely let her know it, and on the day of my sixteenth birthday, as we walked to the museum, I was so conscious of the little plastic rectangle nestled inside the pocket my mother had made for it that I forgot to complain that my father was away for my birthday. I was an adult; the card in my pocket said so, and I looked around at the museum dwellers with judgemental eyes, asking myself how they could have been so careless as to lose their cards and end up homeless. While my mother spoke with them in undertones, and handed over the food we always brought, I wandered the display cases.

So many objects had disappeared over the years. The Mildenhall Treasure. The Portland Font. My favourite exhibit, a little gold chariot pulled by golden horses, had vanished just after my fourteenth birthday. Instead, the cases were filled with little cards—*Object removed for cleaning, Object removed during display rearrangement.* Lindow Man was still there, though, huddled, leathern, against whatever had killed him two thousand years before. I stared at him, and through the glass at the sleeping bags beyond, inside which living bodies huddled against what London had become. My mother made sure we kept up our registrations, and she took me to the British Museum and talked at me, and we read her old books and waited for my father, and scratched letters with burnt sticks, and that was my life. A closed circle shot through with irritations, soothed by the promise of a ship that never seemed to come any closer.

"If the ship is real," I asked my mother as we walked back to the flat, "why don't we just get on it?"

"It's not that simple." She tapped in our entry code and began to fit the separate keys into their various locks.

"Why not?" I asked. It was my job to keep watch while she did the door, but nothing ever happened. My mother liked things to be done properly, that was all. Even the milk, which came in cardboard bricks when it came at all, had to be poured into a jug before she'd let me or my father have any. When the outside door was safely bolted behind us, she began the long process of unlocking the front door of our flat. We went in, and the door clunked solidly behind us. As I began to fasten the bolts, she went to the pantry, took down one of the few tins on the shelf and stood staring at it. It didn't have a label. She held out the tin to me, smiling. "It's your birthday," she said. "You decide. What do you think? Shall we risk it?" I refused to look and went into the drawing room. We had always eaten roast chicken on my birthday, and I'd never forgotten it, even though the last one had been five years ago.

There was a bang at the door, then a pattern of knocks. Before it was finished, my mother and I were both there, our almost-quarrel forgotten, racing to see who could get the bolts and locks undone first. "It's my birthday," I protested, but she still got to him first, and clung to him, and left me to close the door and start on the bolts again.

"I've got something for you, birthday girl," my father said, leaning over my mother and kissing the top of my head. I wondered, wildly, whether he'd managed to find a chicken. But the box he produced as he grinned at my mother was smaller than the palm of his hand. "We haven't seen one of these for a very long time," he said, and I felt my mother trembling beside me, crowding in closely as he put the box into my shaking hands. I opened the box and her face fell. She began to cry and he moved away from me in consternation.

"I thought you had found a flower," she said. And he held her, and while she sobbed against him and he said sorry, sorry, sorry into her hair, I shook a pool of white fire onto the palm of my hand. I remembered him bringing home diamonds years ago, when the banks were teetering and there was still roast chicken, but I'd never even been allowed to hold them, and before long the diamonds had given way to rifles and grenades, piled up throughout the flat. My mother's face had become pale and lined, and my father went away, and then the rifles gave way to stacks and stacks of screens, pristine in their boxes. Then the Art Trials began, and my father was gone again. And so it went on, but now I had a diamond of my own. I stared at it, gleaming in my hand, and could not imagine how any flower could be more beautiful.

It was good to have him back on diamonds. I think my mother thought so too, because she looked at the diamond in my hand and said, "Another rivet in the ship," just as she had done all those years ago, and once again I imagined a boat studded with sparkling rainbows, like something from a dream.

"How was the trip?" she asked, drying her eyes and settling onto the sofa with her sewing.

"Fine. And I visited the holding centre. Roger told me that the people don't believe in Lalla because I never take her with me." He laughed, but my mother didn't even smile. He started to say more, then stopped and looked at me. "Kitten, is there any water? Could you fetch me some?"

I went to the kitchen. The boiled water in the stone jug was mine; my mother knew I hated the taste of the water sterilising tablets we were given at every re-registration. But it was hard to boil water when power was so scarce; my father and mother always used the tablets. I looked about for them, but the tone of my father's voice stopped me. "Anna, listen," he said quietly as soon as I was out of sight. "The troops are going to bomb St James's Park. They've put the razor wire round it, and moved out the people who've got cards. It's Regent's Park all over again. We need to leave."

Regent's Park. It had been one of the first places opened up for people who had nowhere to go. I was thirteen when the government bombed it. Hundreds, thousands of people eliminated in a series of explosions that had made the windows of the flat vibrate. "Be glad I didn't let you meet them," my mother had said, taking away my screen so I couldn't see anything more. "Then it would really hurt." My parents had shut themselves away for hours after that; I heard them through their bedroom door, talking about the ship, then and for weeks afterwards. The ship, the ship, the ship, but nothing happened. There had been more food available at the food drops after the bombing, and my mother said it was because things were turning a corner, as she'd always said they would. But it hadn't lasted, and now my birthday dinner was coming out of a single tin. I stood in the kitchen doorway, holding my diamond in my hand, and watched as my father knelt in front of my mother and took the sewing from her limp hands.

"You brought home a diamond," she said. "You haven't done that for ages. Surely that means things are getting better?"

"No. It means people have given up. I got that diamond for a tin of peaches."

"A tin of peaches?" she said. I opened my hand and noticed for the first time how hard the diamond was, how cold. My stomach rumbled, and I wondered what would be inside the tin my mother had lighted on.

"It was a kind of joke," my father said. "I was negotiating for the contents of a warehouse in Sussex. The guy said that diamonds were for those who believed in the future more than they cared about survival. I thought Lalla would like it, that's all."

"What did he take, if he didn't want diamonds?"

"Munitions. He traded one warehouse for the means to protect the other, and pistols for his family. There is nothing left, Anna. Nothing. We have to leave. You won't dissuade me this time."

My mother fastened her length of thread, shook out the material—it was a red velvet curtain that she was making into a skirt for me—and pointed the needle at my father.

"You created this situation," she said. She unspooled a length of thread and bit it off, looking up at him sharply.

"Me?" He stared at her. "Me? The Dove saved this country. Saved it."

It hadn't. You only had to look outside our window to see that. But my father no longer looked outside our window. His mind was made up, and his eyes were on places far beyond our London square. My mother picked a black button from her sewing box and said, "What about the people in the British Museum?"

"They're squatting," my father said quietly, sitting on the back of the sofa and stroking her hair. "It's all very cooperative, but how can they build an alternative society when there's nothing left to build it on? All the government can do—all it can do— is reduce the population in the hope of feeding what's left. Bit by bit. The museum dwellers are idiots, corralling themselves so they can be eliminated. It's time for us to leave." He frowned and jabbed at his screen. "It's been time for a long time."

She bent her head over the button, and when she spoke her voice was so quiet I could barely hear her. "I'm not ready, Michael. However dreadful the process is, soon the population will be manageable, and all this will improve. The ship will be the last thing we do."

"The last thing?" My father laughed, putting his screen down, swinging his legs over the back of the sofa and landing beside my mother with a bounce. "No, my darling, the ship is the start. Why do you cling to the end, when the beginning is waiting?"

"I want to grow things."

He stopped bouncing and turned away. "Still?" he said. "The Land Allocation Act's a failure. People are coming back from the countryside as fast as they left. And if they don't come back, it's because they're dead. I've seen it."

My mother put her sewing down. "What about the Lakes?" she said. "They didn't do industrial farming there. Or fracking. The soil might still be good."

"And you'd take that risk, even though we've never heard anything from any of the families who left? Remember the Freemans? The Kings? The Holloways? Think of the security we'd need just to get there. And the loneliness."

Freemans, Kings, Holloways—names from a time I could barely remember. A time of restaurants, a time when Regent's Park was a place to take a picnic, a time when people smiled at each other and sometimes stopped to talk. A time when there were still a few private cars in the street; when electricity was constant. Nothing but myths now, lost in time. But at sixteen, I knew about loneliness. I was lonely, so lonely that my stomach clenched with it at night.

"A life for Lalla," my father said. "Isn't that worth everything we have? A place to be a family, among friends, where we can learn and share without fear? A place for Lalla to grow in safety? Isn't that what we set out to create?"

"A place without money," my mother said softly, putting her arms around him. "No gold or guns. Just everyone working hard and sharing in the plenty we've provided."

"No homelessness," he replied, "and no hunger." He turned in the circle of her arms and stroked the hair back from her face. "Tell me when, Anna. Please tell me when."

"It was an insurance policy. Just that. Insurance. And now you're making it a life plan. I don't want to spend my life clinging to a lifeboat."

"How much worse do you want things to get?"

"If you loved me, you'd stop pushing."

"If you loved me, we'd have gone already."

"I love you, Michael. I just don't think you're right."

I stood in the doorway, forgetting I wasn't meant to be listening. I clenched my fist and felt the diamond cutting into my palm. "I want to go," I said. "If the ship is real, I want to go on it."

They looked at me in surprise. My father looked for his glass of water and realised that I wasn't holding one. My mother said, "You don't know what you're talking about," and took back her sewing, tucking her legs under her. "We're going to Mughal India tomorrow." But I had spoken out at last, and I couldn't stop now.

"I've seen Mughal India," I said. "I've seen Ancient Egypt and the Aztecs and Babylon and Abyssinia and Mesopotamia. I've seen them all day, every day, for years and years and years."

"But you've learned nothing," she said, standing up and marching past me into the tiny kitchen. I heard the drawer open and shut and the rattle of the utensils in it. I heard the tin opener puncturing the lid, and the ratcheting as she turned the handle. "Seriously, Lalage," she called over the rattle of the spoon as she scraped out the contents of the tin. "What have you actually learned from the British Museum? From me? From your father?" I drew breath, ready to tell her about hieroglyphics and lunar calendars, about crucifixes and fertility symbols and currency, about kings being buried with gold and sandwiches to see them safely to the underworld, but my father spoke before I could begin.

"I don't care what she's still got to learn," he called into the kitchen. "I want her safe. I want both of you safe."

"I want to go on the ship," I said again, and it was as though someone else had taken over my body, someone who carried their own card and owned a diamond and said what they thought.

"Lalla wants to go on the ship," my father said, and his eyes shone, and I felt the hairs on my arms prickle with electricity, because even though my mother had come back in the room, it was me he was looking at, my words that had brought that light to his eyes. I thought about the ship, and the promise of friends, and suddenly I needed to know, more than anything else in my limited, safe, grey world, that the ship was more than a theoretical hereafter for the hopeless, that it was not just one more of the many heavens I'd seen in the display cases at the British Museum.

My father stood up. "Lalla is sixteen now," he said. "Maybe that will persuade you better than I can." He held out a hand to me, and I stood beside him, his arm around my shoulder. My mother looked at us and, for a fraction of a second, her eyes widened. "It's over, Anna. You know it. That's why we bought the ship in the first place." He lifted his arm and I slipped out from under it, dismissed. He went to my mother, the two of them framed by the kitchen doorway, and stroked her cheek with the back of his hand. "Darling," he began.

I went to the window. It was quite dark now, and street people were gathering by the railings in the square opposite. One looked up at us, face stark white against his clothes. What did sixteen mean, when nothing ever changed? Behind me, my father and mother were kissing softly. Until recently, I'd just hidden behind the latest Dove-authorised game when they kissed, regardless of the power rationing. But now, I found myself staring, and wondering how it would feel to have my lips touched by someone else's like that, and whether it would ever happen to me.

"Come back into the room, kitten," my father said, and I did as I was told. I knelt down to see whether my mother had laid the fire. The wood came from a man my father knew. Everything we'd ever had came from a man my father knew.

"Of course we'll leave. When we have to," my mother said into the silence. "But, Michael, we need to stay for a little longer."

"What for? There's nothing left to see in the museums anyway. The stuff gets traded on all the time. What do you think the museum dwellers are living on?"

My mother's voice began to rise. "They need people like us. If we don't keep visiting the museum, then those people will be next on the government list."

"There are no more people like us." He gestured around the room, at the fire, the working screen, the spaghetti hoops in tomato sauce that my mother had emptied into three small bowls and put on the table in the corner. There were sausages hiding under the hoops, and I realised that my mother had known the contents of the tin all along and had saved it for my birthday. We went to the table. My mother didn't like sausages; I ate them for her, and for a few moments nothing was said at all. I waited for the miracle that sometimes happened on my birthday—not a cake, but chocolate or sweets; even a tin of peaches. But when my mother finally spoke, it was as though my birthday wasn't happening at all.

"You wouldn't want to leave the museum people if you'd actually talked to them," she said. "They're organising themselves, working together. If we desert them, it's over. We might as well kill them with our own hands."

"I talk to the people who matter. You, and Lalla, and our people in the holding centre."

"And people who give diamonds for tinned peaches."

"Yes," my father said flatly. "Face it, Anna. If we don't walk past the people who need us, we'll never save ourselves."

"I won't walk past them," my mother whispered. I took the

armchair, and thought about the people who had once lived in tents in Regent's Park, their bodies blown apart and scattered across the ruins of their makeshift homes. Who had gathered them up? And my own death. What would that look like? In a tent, by a bomb? *Lucky Lalla, lucky, lucky Lalla.* In the warmth of the fire, I lost myself in thoughts about people so valued that their dead bodies were buried with gold and jade, and of others so hungry that they would steal stories to feed themselves. Where did the difference lie? Which was I?

I sat up when my father said, "Tomorrow."

"Tomorrow?"

"We're ready. We've been planning this for years. What's it all been for if we don't go? It's time. I've warned you, Anna. For Lalla, if not for you."

My mother put another piece of wood on the fire. It was prettily shaped; it must have been part of a chair once. Or a table.

"Lalage," she said. "We named her Lalage." I waited for them to look at me, to bring me into focus, but they didn't. My mother sat staring into the flames; my father sat watching her.

"We had to find the right people," she said.

"We've found them. The manifest is full. Five hundred pages. Five hundred people. They're in the holding centre, waiting."

"But what if things get better?" she asked, turning to him. The light of the fire shone in her hair. "How can they get better if we leave?"

I could feel the press of people outside. Dark had long since fallen. There were firedrums lit on the street corners; I saw their burning orange on the white walls of the drawing room. I could feel the longing of the street people for what we had, pulling them towards us like gravity. I could feel the air, pressing change upon me, and a sensation in my belly that was new, gnawing at me like hunger, although we had only just eaten.

"I can't keep paying for the guards. For the holding centre. For all the food you and Lalla take to the museum dwellers. There's enough petrol to get us to the quay, but no more. Do you understand, Anna? I can't get any more."

"A little longer. Until the museum dwellers have a proper plan."

"What plan can they possibly have?" my father asked, but the words were barely out of his mouth when there was a scream from the street.

"Don't," my father said as my mother started up from the sofa.

My mother stood up. "Someone's hurt."

"Stay away from the window." He took her arm and pulled her back.

"I want to know what's going on out there."

"You know," my father said, tightening his grip. "You just won't see it. What do I have to do? What?"

"What?" I cried, suddenly panicked. "What is going on?" But they weren't looking at me. They were staring at each other, locked into a battle that was nothing to do with me.

"Didn't I see you and Lalla safely through the collapse? The establishment of military government? When have you ever been hungry, or in danger?"

"You're hurting me," she said through clenched teeth.

"Tell me we'll leave tomorrow. Tell me." He gripped her upper arms and held her against the wall. The screaming continued; more voices joined in, piercing and demented. "Tomorrow," he said. There were tears in his eyes; he was shaking. "I mean it. We've waited too long already. Say it. Say it."

She shook him off and ran to the window. I went to follow her, but he grabbed me and held me back, and I was too taken aback to protest.

The silence lasted for three heartbeats. Then the air was split by a sudden crack and the window fell away. The fire guttered in the wind and a sudden chill wrapped itself around me. My mother stood tall and beautiful, frozen in time, her eyes unnaturally wide and her lips parted in surprise. She folded in two and slumped backwards, and as she did so, the cord connecting me to the land snapped, fibre by fibre. There was blood, and as I ran to her, I knew that my sixteen years counted for nothing, and that nothing of this old life was relevant anymore.

"Close the curtains," my father said, and as I did so I saw a small black-clothed figure move away through the crowd and vanish into the dark.

"Look," I said, but my father was kneeling beside her body, kissing her cheeks, her hair, her lips, holding her hand in both of his as though he would never let her go, sobbing, "Anna, Anna," over and over again. I fetched a towel and pressed it to her abdomen, where blood seeped wet and dark, and he looked at me through his tears.

"I saw someone," I began, but he held a warning finger to his lips, and I stopped.

"Lalla," he said. "Help me to take her to the ship."

"The ship?"

He nodded, and even as I held on to my mother's hand, I felt my heart beating faster.

"Everything I have promised you is true, Lalla. Remember that."

Together, we laid my mother gently on the back seat of the last car in London. I remembered everything I had ever heard about the ship and sat with her head on my lap, whispering tales of doctors, of medicines, of healing. Every now and then, she tried to talk, but my father told her to save her strength. I watched her blood soaking the towel, but what I felt more than anything was the irrepressible beating of my own heart. It drowned out the engine starting, the protests of the street people as they moved out of the road, the cries of the children as we passed. It filled the silence of the empty streets beyond the city; it banished the fear of an ambush or a breakdown. On a smooth wide road in the middle of nowhere, two jeeps were waiting for us. "Our escort," my father said, and we drove on through the night flanked by guards and guns. It's beginning, I thought. My life is about to start.

TWO

The quay from above ❈ *my wounded mother*
❈ *the commander boards* ❈ *the fate of*
three women

The ship. The whispered word had done nothing to prepare me for the dizzying reality. It towered over us as we drove onto the concrete at the water's edge, solid and magnificent, a palace. A temple. It was as though my father had taken the British Museum, made it shine and put it on water. Ropes as thick as my father's arms tethered it to the quay.

"Doesn't it make you feel small, Lalla?" my father asked. But it didn't make me feel small. It made me feel that I could fly. I craned my head to marvel at the ship's whiteness, its grandeur, the rising sun reflecting on the windows and filling them with gold. I almost forgot my mother until she groaned in my father's arms.

"It's here," I breathed. "It's all true."

"Yes, little one," he said. "It's all true."

The escorting jeeps had disappeared. For a moment, the three of us were alone, the ship rising from the water before us. Then I saw the guards leading a procession of people towards us. As the people came closer, I realised that many of their faces were familiar. The man with the dark grey beard that had one white strand running through it; the woman whose eyes were like my mother's; another woman, old, old, with black eyes bright in her dark face. They had all come to the flat; I had watched them through windows, from behind doors, and now they were here. I remembered a boy with green eyes, who had smiled at me once. I looked for him, but when I saw him I pretended I hadn't, afraid he wouldn't smile at me again.

"Lalla," my father said as I stared, "run up ahead to the ball-room and open the doors." And it was their turn to stare at me as I ran across the quay. I was the first to touch the ship, and it was unyielding and real. My heart lifted as I unfastened the gangway gate. My red shoes set the gangway jangling as I ran up.

At the top, I stopped and turned around, breathing hard. I wanted to shout out to the sky up above and to my parents below. We were getting away. For years I had waited, dancing on the periphery of my parents' vision as they worked and prepared. Now my dress blazed orange against the white of the ship; I was a torch, a flame, I was forging the way. The gangway was held to the ship with a bolt on either side, each longer than my forearm. I put my hand on one, and imagined the moment when the bolts would be drawn back.

On the quay, the people parted to let my father through. Where he walked, they followed, like water swirling in the wake of a trailing hand. In my father's arms, my mother in her silk dress seemed to float like a flower. The ship. The beginning of every tomorrow there would ever be. The guards formed a corridor to the gangway; the people filled it. There would be a doctor among them, I was sure, and medicines and bandages. The deck rail was cold under my outstretched hand.

My father looked up and I remembered that he had told me to go straight to the ballroom. I had no idea where or what the ballroom was, but ahead of me I saw a pair of doors with golden handles and panels of decorated glass. I pushed them open and entered a vast hall, with blue velvet benches running the length of the walls and three chandeliers, sparkling with crystals, hanging from the ceiling. At the top of the room was a raised podium; on the podium stood a polished wooden desk; on the desk, fat and leather-bound, sat the manifest. This, then, was the ballroom, unreal in luxury and cleanliness. I stood and stared at the manifest. Those thick, dark covers held the details of every one of the people my parents had invited on board. If I read it through, there would be no such thing as a stranger, for as long as the ship sailed.

I saw my father through the window and ran to hold the door. He laid my mother on blue velvet and knelt beside her. Her palms were sticky, and her forehead shone with perspiration. Her skin was marble white. Only the movement of her eyes behind her closed lids and the blood seeping through the front of her dress said that she was still alive. I looked to my father for instructions, but he would not look at me, however hard I stared at him. He held my mother's hand to his forehead, his eyes tightly shut, while I watched the people coming in. "For Lalage," I heard him say under his breath, as though there was no one else in the room. He looked at the manifest, and then at me, and I was glad I had not touched it. He rose and I took his place beside her.

The people began to enter. First was a man with a grey face, lined and tired. As he came closer to my father, his shoulders straightened and he held his head higher, and I saw his blue eyes, eyes that belonged in a younger face. The rest of the people oozed behind him. They filed in and sat on the blue velvet benches, shuffling up, making room for each other, eyes meeting then looking away. Now, those people are Finn, Helen, Patience, Gabriel, Jamila. They are Luke, Emily, Tom. They have names, and stories that I know. But on that first day, they were images of hunger and sadness and loss, each as desperate as each other, and all I cared about was that one of them was surely a doctor.

From where I knelt, I could see the quay. The embarkation exposed its grey concrete in patches that grew bigger and bigger, until all that was left were the last few people stepping onto the gangway, the abandoned car and the two lines of guards. When we'd gone they'd tear the car apart for shelter, for food, for the dregs of petrol left in the tank. Beyond the car, the obsolete road unwound, hemmed in on either side by broken warehouses. Then my mother coughed and I forgot the guards. I forgot the ship and the people. I went and pulled at my father's jacket, as I had been doing ever since I was tiny. The six people he had been talking to left the ballroom at a run, and he turned to face me.

"Father," I said, "which one is the doctor?"

"Wait," he said.

"But Father…"

He looked at me then. "Lalla," he said, and his voice was low and urgent. "We've got to sail. The government troops will be coming. There is no doubt of that. And they will be armed."

"Then why aren't we sailing?"

"We have to start the engines. Register the people."

Register the people? My father's time and my mother's time were running at different speeds, and if I could not bring them together, my mother would die. This, then, was fear, and even as my heart pounded and my fingernails carved half moons on the palm of my hands, I thought how strange it was that I learned to feel fear the moment I was brought to safety.

"Roger!" My father beckoned to a man who had entered in a rush, looking anxiously about him, his floppy hair swinging lank across his face. In the flood of light from the huge windows, his skin looked translucent and crumpled. I wondered when he had last eaten, or slept. He thrust the parcel he was holding into the hands of a woman with red hair and ran to us.

"How is Anna?" he said at once. Then he saw her, and he closed his eyes as though he was in pain. My mother sighed, and then coughed again, rearing up as the bloodstains on the towel darkened and shone. The doctor grabbed a cushion from the bench—deep blue velvet, soft, new, untouched—and gave it to me. "Press this over the bleeding," he said. I started to try and remove the towel but he stopped me. "No," he said sharply, as though he'd expected better of me, "just hold it over what's already there." He put his hand to her forehead and snatched it away almost immediately. "She's burning up," the doctor said. "The wound must be infected."

"So quickly?" my father said, and I let go of the cushion; it fell to the floor just as the doctor was turning to my father, and his foot sent it spinning away.

The cushion came to rest in front of my father's desk, bloodstain uppermost. The manifest sat on the desk, fat and solid, and the three of us stared at it.

"Lalage," my mother whispered softly. "Michael?"

"I'm here," I said, squeezing her hand.

"Anna," my father said, kneeling. "Anna, I've sent the engineers straight down. The doctor's here. We'll be sailing soon. Try, Anna. Please try."

"Register them first," she breathed. Then her eyes opened wide, and no matter how many times I said, I'm here, I'm here, no matter how close to her I held my face, her eyes kept darting from side to side, seeing nothing. I kissed her forehead and was startled by its heat.

"The infirmary's ready, isn't it?" my father asked the man Roger. "It's all done?"

"It's been ready for a long time," the doctor said, and my father strode to the desk. The red-headed woman was standing next to it; she stepped aside, and my father opened the manifest. The cover thudded heavily; the pen sat fatly in his hand.

"Sign," he said, trembling. The doctor took the pen from my father's hand. He could not help lifting the pen to look at it first, and I thought the delay might kill her. Then he signed, and as he did so, my father leaned into him and whispered fiercely, "You save her, do you hear me? You save her."

The doctor paled, then lifted my mother in his arms. "I'll try, Michael. I'll do everything I can." A dark-haired woman opened the door for them, and I followed them.

"No," my father said. The word was a bullet. "Not you, Lalla. Let Roger do his job."

I stopped and turned, incredulous. Whenever our unit of three had been separated, it had been my father striding off alone, sometimes for weeks at a time, and my mother and I left together, counting the days until he came back. I did not know how to leave her to be with him. And whatever the doctor's job was, I was a part of it. The room had filled while I had been bent over my mother; wherever I looked, there was a face fixed on me. I had never been so close to so many people; I stepped backwards and tripped over someone's feet.

"We're going to register," my father said. I protested, but a voice above me spoke softly; I looked from the feet into the black eyes of an old woman.

"What would your mother do if she were with us?" she asked.

"But she's still with us," I said, looking around. Hundreds of eyes stared back at me, wide with sympathy, and I began to panic. "She's still with us," I repeated, as though repetition could somehow make it true.

"Come here, Lalla," my father said. I walked to the podium and sat down beside him; he placed his hand on my head with tears in his eyes, and I knew I had no choice.

No one picked up the cushion.

My father spoke into a small black stick. "Hello," he said, and his voice cracked a little and then suddenly came from every-where, as though a thousand of him had surrounded the ball-room and spoken together. He pulled back a little, startled, then leaned in again. "Can everyone hear me?" The people called back, and my father continued, "That's good. That works, then. So, welcome. We—we all—I mean, here we are, come to the ship at last. It's been a long wait but you've made it. You're free to breathe now. As you know, Anna's been hurt, but she's in good hands. In a few moments, we'll be off. But while the engineers are doing their work, shall we greet each other? I know you've been together in the holding centre for a long time, but let's meet each other once more, as the people of the ship."

All around the room, people smiled and held their hands out to each other. The people drew together before him, all rags and grime and hungry eyes, until I was utterly alone in the room.

I could not bear to look at them. The bloodstained cushion sat like a reproach; my mother was somewhere, bleeding, needing me. And I needed her. In this great crowd, I was still alone. I skulked behind my father, looking over their heads, desperate to avoid eye contact. Through the big picture windows I could see the guards on the quay gathered in dark blotches, waiting for us to unbolt the gangway so that they could wheel it away, release the ropes and send us on our way. They were hunched over; one of them, at least, was crying. Were they so sorry to see us go? Beyond the guards sat the little car. I went to the window and gazed at the car until I almost saw my mother's blood on its back seat. Along the road, the broken windows made dark gaps in the warehouse facades. And at the end of that road I saw a grey shape that had not been there before.

"Father," I said, moving closer to him, but the ballroom doors opened and six people walked in, nervous and proud.

"Our engineers," my father called through the microphone, and my plea was lost in cheers, and then in a wave of movement as people began to move towards the desk. My father called their names. The first—Diana Aabri, dark-eyed and serious—picked up the cushion and laid it gently on the podium where no one would step on it, and I felt a burst of gratitude that made me want to run to her. But there were other names, and Diana had moved away long before I had found the courage to approach her. One by one, they stepped onto the podium and signed the pages of the manifest, fascinated by the pen, the smooth ivory paper, the kindness of my father smiling upon them. One by one, they stepped off and gathered excitedly together, looking curiously and yet kindly at me as they did so, exchanging names, exchanging looks. Exchanging stories. And as they did so, I saw the anonymous mass resolve into dozens, hundreds of individuals, and wondered whether any one of them would help me.

"Father," I called again, my breath catching, but the buzz of the people drowned not only my voice, but another, fainter buzz that might have come from my father's microphone.

And then the new darkness at the end of the road spat out a globule of black. The globule moved with strength and purpose down the centre of the road, and as it grew bigger I realised it was a group, running in formation. In a few short seconds, they reached my father's guards and separated, and, for the second time since we boarded, fear rose in me. Those were uniforms. Not the makeshift clothes of the street in which everyone looked the same, or the worn fatigues my father had found for his guards, but clean, sharp, deliberate clothes, in unfaded black. I had seen them in the bulletins, batons lifted against marketeers. I had seen them at registrations and at food drops, patrolling the queues, removing those whose cards had become invalid, invalidating the cards of those who resisted. My card was always valid and I did not have to use the markets, but the black uniforms frightened me now. Government troops.

"Father," I said, more loudly this time, but the rhythmic jangling of heavy boots on the gangway silenced me. Beside me someone screamed; the whole room seemed to harden; people who had been smiling gently at each other stiffened and drew apart. The ballroom doors burst open and my father's chief guard strode in. The registration stopped.

"The troops are here, Mr Paul," the guard said, breathing hard. "Shall we shoot them?"

My father shook his head. "No, Greenlaw. Not as a first resort. And you should have left your gun with the others. You know the rules. No guns on the ship." But before Greenlaw could leave, the ballroom door was flung open by a man in true black. He had a craggy face, one which we had all seen on the bulletins. He, too, carried a gun. So did the two soldiers who stood behind him.

"Michael Paul," he said, and his voice needed no microphone.

"Commander Marius," my father said. His voice was pinched and light. "In person. We are honoured. And your armed guards. Delighted, I'm sure."

"We're here to arrest you."

"On what charge?"

"Stealing state property."

My father smiled with relief, and the room settled with him. Greenlaw went back to the quay, gripping his rifle. "The ship is mine," my father said. "It's registered to me, and it's been re-registered every time the regulations have changed. I've kept a hard trail." He took a sheaf of printouts from his case and offered it to the commander with a look of pity. "I'm sorry you've had a wasted journey. Did you run all the way?" My mother's voice floated over us. *Above board, Michael. Legal. Nothing that might shame us.*

I will be with you, I promised her silently.

"I'm not talking about the ship," Commander Marius said contemptuously.

My father leaned forward, his face alive with interest. "What, then? The provisions?"

"No. We can't trace those to government supplies."

My father raised his eyebrows as though he was acknowledging a compliment. "I didn't know that the state had any property left," he said. "Everything on board is mine, I assure you."

There was a gentle ripple of sound; I looked around me and realised that I had just heard strangers laughing. It felt light inside me; it was a feeling I liked, one I wanted to have again. My fear bubbled away; I thought this must be a game, something my father had arranged for everyone before we sailed away, and I laughed too, confident that I'd be with my mother shortly, and that she would be all right.

"Look," my father said, irritation shading his voice. "My wife and I have kept up with every single new law. There is no obscure amendment, no loophole, no adjustment you can surprise me with."

"The Exodus Act," the commander said triumphantly. My father's expression of amused tolerance did not change, but it set hard and the palms of my hands began to feel damp. "You've forgotten the Exodus Act."

"The Exodus Act?" my father repeated. Astonished eyes travelled from my father to the uniformed men and back again. My father spoke slowly. "The Exodus Act was twenty years ago. More. Under the previous government. The elected one," he added pointedly. The amusement had gone; now my father looked wary, alert, ready to produce whatever snippet of knowledge was required.

"But the principle still holds. No state assets can be exported from the state."

My father nodded. "Of course," he said. "But the ship is not a state asset. And how can I export when there's nowhere to export to?" He gave an exasperated sigh. "We're not your problem. We're just five hundred fewer people for you to feed. Please, Marius." He swallowed. "My wife is injured. I need to get to her."

The commander turned away from my father and indicated the ballroom. "Have these people all got valid identity cards?"

"Of course they have. They wouldn't have lasted long without them."

"Then they're state assets."

"State assets?"

"The Nazareth Act promised provision for all registered citizens. But it works both ways. You're stealing. From the state. And that's a death penalty." I heard a man whisper, "What isn't, these days?" but nobody replied. So many laws had just slipped in quietly, without fuss, like a stone held to the surface of the water before you let it fall in.

The commander stepped onto the podium and hefted a black armoured case onto my father's desk; the brass handles on the desk drawer rattled as it thudded down, and the red-headed woman flinched. He took out a screen; his bodyguards trained their guns on the crowd. A man in dirty checked trousers felt for his card, and he set off a ripple of similar movements along the benches. It was a market raid, except that no one was trying to escape. The very act of producing the cards seemed to galvanise my father.

"Look," he said. "Check our identities by all means. But you can't stop us from sailing."

"I can," the man said. "If nothing else, we're armed. You're not."

"They are," my father said, pointing at his guards on the quay.

"Fine," the commander said. "My men shoot your men, your men shoot mine, and then we'll carry on. Have you got a gun on you now?"

My father hesitated, then shook his head. *No guns on the ship,* I remember my mother saying to my father. *Let the guards keep them. God knows they'll have earned them.*

But...

Not on the ship, Michael. Do you know how many times I would have killed you if I'd had the chance? I don't want to have that chance. They smiled, the way they did when a serious point was wrapped in a joke and offered as a present, and the conversation ended in laughter and tinned peaches. But the truth is that my father did not want guns on the ship, either. When he went on his trips, he told me, he carried only his toothbrush and his wit. The episode in the flat, before my mother was shot, was as violent as I had ever seen him. He armed the guards because he had to, but words were what he liked. Words, arguments, debates. He liked to win. But for as long as I can remember, winning meant convincing you, drawing you into his vision so completely that you would defend it with your last breath.

Not your last breath, Mother, I whispered. *Not your last.*

"You should have a gun," the commander said. "Look." He gestured at the horizon. I looked in the direction he was pointing, past the quay and the car, down the road. The darkness I had noticed earlier had become a rolling cloud of smoke. My father left the desk and walked towards us. The commander lifted his gun, but my father pushed its barrel to the floor as he passed and the two men walked to the window together. In the silence I heard a noise that I thought was the whisper of conversation, but no one in the ballroom was talking. Then I realised that the noise was coming from outside the ship and that it was getting louder. The sound rose, at first like the rhythmic swish of the waves, then more insistent, harsher, like the noise the mighty ropes would make when they were let loose and sent crashing into the water. The black smoke in the distance was solidifying into a mass, like water made thick with detritus, oozing down the road we had travelled. The commander looked towards the approaching darkness. I saw fear in the way his hands would not stay still, in the way his head kept twitching as though he could not decide where his priorities lay. The people began to nudge each other, to exchange worried glances and to look, again and again, towards my father.

The commander turned to his bodyguards and said, "You'd better go down. Don't let them storm the ship. Yet." The bodyguards hesitated and the commander snapped, "He's not going to shoot me. He hasn't even got a gun," and the two men tramped down the gangway, guns raised, leaving my father and the commander facing each other.

"Are you going to shoot us?" my father asked.

"You're committing a crime."

"I'm saving the human race."

"No, Mr Paul. I am saving the human race."

"By killing off the surplus population?"

The commander shrugged, the crags in his face deepened and for the first time I saw a person behind the uniform. Here was a man; maybe he had a wife, a daughter. "This is not a democracy," he said. "This is government for survival. What else do you suggest?"

"It's over, you know," my father said gently. They leant on the sill; in another time, another place, they could have been friends contemplating a stroll on deck.

"I can't let you go," the commander said. "You've got food and medicine on board. Tools, equipment..."

"No more than we need," my father said hastily. "There's no law against holding the food you require for survival."

"Even so. Essential rations for five hundred—that's significant. We could create a few more citizens, get some people off the Sinkers... You've got all five hundred on board, I take it?"

"All except one."

"Your wife?"

"She's in the infirmary. She's going to be fine. No, a young man. He died last night."

"Then you're over-stocked. That's a criminal offence."

"I'll surrender his share. Just let us go."

The approaching mass became distinct; these were men and women, with voices raised in anger. Individual voices jutted from the cacophony—stop them, get them, take them, bring them down. Inside, the people of the ship, afraid and silent. On the quay, my father's guards and the government troops, armed and awaiting orders.

"You knew they'd come," the commander said.

"Of course." My father shrugged. "I had hoped to leave before they arrived, but they don't change anything."

The mob were surrounding the car now, and for a moment they were distracted, jumping on it, pulling at the door handles, kicking the doors, tearing at the seats. My father's guards and the government troops stood together, defending the gangway.

The commander looked directly at my father. "I have seen what hungry men will do for food," he said. "And if I were you, I would be afraid. I would be on my knees, begging me to let you raise the gangway and sail before they notice you standing here."

"Why?" my father said. "Why would I beg? You can shoot us all, one by one, and throw our bodies into the sea. You can de-register us and put us in tents and bomb us later. You can hold us up here until those desperate men and women swarm on board and destroy us all. Or you can let us go."

The commander looked from the mob on the quay to my father, from his black-clothed colleagues to the stricken faces in the ballroom. My heart was racing. We had to release the gangway and cast off the ropes. Part of me was waiting for my father to produce a weapon from some hidden store, for an army of his own to leap fully formed from the ballroom panelling and blast the commander and the mob and the quay into oblivion. But it didn't happen. Instead, the commander levelled his gun at my father and the horizon contracted so that the descending crowd and the road and the car and the quayside became one. *Fear makes men blind*, my mother said, and at that moment I understood what she meant. There was life, and there was death, and the fragile divide between them, held in the hands of a stranger. Metallic clangs echoed around the room, vying with the deeper, distant pulsing of engines ready for the off. I wondered how long it would take the crowd to break through the barrier of armed guards and storm the ship.

I needed my mother. My father's eyes kept straying to the internal door; he needed her too. He was restless, biting his lips and rubbing his thumb in the palm of his hand.

"I offered you a government post when you sold us the Dove," Commander Marius said. "You should have taken it. You'd have had food, security, privilege. But no. You wanted freedom. Look where your freedom's got you. I am arresting you, Michael Paul. If you resist, I shall have no alternative but to shoot you."

My father looked around at the people, his lips pale. "I…" he began, but his voice cracked and he said no more.

"We'll take you all off the ship and empty the hold. And if you're lucky, we'll shoot you quietly."

"Please…"

"And if you're not lucky," the commander continued, "then I'll tell my troops to stand aside and let the mob deal with you."

My father had failed. I saw the people being marched off the ship at gunpoint and sent away from the quay. I saw a chain of people in black uniforms passing boxes from one to another. I saw everything my father had worked to amass evaporating over the starving city. And in that one short moment, as my father crumpled on the window sill, his head in his hands, dwarfed by the commander's black case and the weapon at his side, I found myself growing angry. My mother would die. We would never sail; my father's vision would become dust, the ship would go back to being a myth and we too would starve, just to bring the commander a moment of glory on the bulletin.

And where I had felt fear and guilt, I now felt anger. I was angry with the commander, the troops, the government they worked for that my father had been too principled to join. I was angry at the stupidity of the generations before mine that had brought us to this place. And I was angry with the people—my father's chosen people—quietly shuffling into a queue before the commander's screen, cards in hand, as though this was just another registration. My father was shrunken and motionless. My anger spread through me, like a virus eating away the information on a screen. It destroyed all the questions, the doubt, the distance. It brought me on board. To untie the massive ropes that held the ship to the shore, to let the grinding engines leap into life—above all, to be gone and be with my mother, became my overriding mission.

"If he takes me, you execute him for stealing from the state?" I asked the commander. The crags in his face shifted as he raised his eyebrows and nodded. "What will happen to me? To all of us?"

"Nothing," he said. "You don't prosecute the bread for being stolen." He smiled sadly, and I remember thinking that, however sharp his uniform, his teeth would not last much longer. He addressed the people as a whole. "Leave now, and you will all retain your registration. My men will protect you, and you will be given food from the stocks we reclaim from the ship. For as long as you have your cards, you are citizens still."

A whisper of relief escaped the people. They were going to give in, I thought. They were going to walk down the gangway as quietly as they had walked up it. For a moment, I hated them all. For years, my parents had talked about them, planned for them, argued about them. Ignored me for them. And they were here, in this room. Not a bland mass, but individuals, each unique, all gathered in my father's name. The people. Men. Women. Even a scattering of children. My parents had chosen these people to be

my world. If I did nothing, I would never know them. Already I
knew that I couldn't go back. I had breathed salt air and spoken
to a stranger. I couldn't go back.

I undid the zip in my pocket and took my identity card from
its belt. I pulled open the door to the deck. The noise of the mob
on the quay hit me like a blow to the face. The commander followed me; the people followed him. Why aren't they more afraid?
I asked myself, looking at their empty faces. If they had been
marched back down the gangway and left to find a life, their
expressions would not have changed. *It was always too good to
be true*, they would say, just as my mother did every time a food
drop turned out to be no more than a rumour. But the ship was
not a rumour or a false promise. It was here, solid and white, the
giant engines throbbing under our feet, ready to take us away. I
climbed up onto the deck rail and braced myself against a verti-
cal bar. I held my card aloft. I didn't know what the ship was, but
I knew I wanted it. My blood coursed wildly through my veins;
I was alive; I was going to act. The latest biometric re-registration
had only been a couple of days ago; my card would be valid for a
week or two yet.

"Look," I shouted. My father joined the people on deck, staring at me until I met his eyes. His eyes grew bright, his shoulders
squared, and I loved him. On the quay, a woman in a pink dress
saw me and stopped still, pointing; the stillness rippled from her
until the mob and the troops and the guards were all staring up
at me, as silent as the people of the ship crowded onto the deck.

"This is my card," I called. "Without it, I am no one. Without
it, I have no state, no rights, no claims. Without it, I have no
screen access. I'll be a non-person, and no one will know when
I die."

"Don't," came a voice from the deck. "He'll shoot." I looked
towards the sound, and the eyes that met mine were green.

The commander raised his gun to his eye. Like mother, like

daughter, I thought, except that she had not known the shot was coming. I heard the click as he prepared to fire.

"Shoot me," I said, and as I let go of my card, he lowered his gun with incredulous eyes. My card turned over and over as it fell to the quay. It hit ropes that held the ship and rebounded into the water. I saw it floating, a speck of white on a grey-brown strip of sea.

The mob began to jostle at the water's edge. The woman in the pink dress lay down, stretching her hands to the water, but the water level was too low. A man held her ankles and she grabbed, but my card floated out of reach. Others joined in; a soldier bent down and used his gun to try and sweep the card towards him; yet others shouted advice.

"We must release the gangway," my father said quietly to the woman with red curly hair, who was standing beside him. "Now, while the people on the quay are distracted."

"What about the commander?" the woman said, moving to the bolts that held the gangway to the ship. She tried to draw them back, but they were heavy, and she looked about for help.

My father hesitated. "We've got a space, haven't we?"

I was too scared to ask what he meant. Now, I urged him silently. Now. The bodies on the streets had been ghastly; the government bombings had been horrific; the battles at the food points had been violent and bloody, but none of them had had anything to do with me. Now my card had gone, and with it any chance I had of survival in the old world. Like my mother, I had given myself wholly and completely to my father, or to death. We had to sail.

Then, as my father drew breath, the woman looked up from the gangway bolts.

"I've waited five years for this," she called out over the deck rail. "You can have mine, too." The crowd looked up, and she threw her card onto the quay. A group of people hurled themselves at it. My father watched, intent.

"And mine," shouted the man who had led the people on board. His card caught the sunlight as it fell into a mass of outstretched hands.

"And mine," called the green-eyed boy, climbing up onto the deck rail to join me. He swayed dangerously and I caught his arm, and for a moment we stood clasped together, high above everyone else, and I felt something glorious in the air around me, as though the ship really was studded with rainbows from the diamonds that had paid for it. And suddenly the air below us became full of white plastic rectangles with gold chips glinting, spinning and turning as they flew. The snarling mass separated into pairs of dancing arms. And the green-eyed boy and I climbed down and looked at each other, laughing, and for a moment we did not let each other go.

"I'm Tom. Tom Mandel," he said, but before I could answer, someone called out behind me.

"Be me," they said, and we separated to let others reach the deck rail, and my arms felt cold where he had let me go.

The commander looked down as the laughing crowd caught at the confetti of cards. My father, who had come to stand next to me, was laughing too, his body brimful of energy, his eyes alight. "Will you?" he asked the commander, pulling out his own identity card and holding it aloft. "We lost one of our number last night. You can have his place."

"It's suicide," the commander said quietly. "You'll never be able to come back."

"We don't want to. We know where we're going."

Commander Marius looked thoughtful. He looked from my father's card to his face, from the cards still raining onto the quay to his colleagues, as eager as the homeless to catch them. My mother's voice in my head said, *Michael, you can never know what depths people may have until the waters have a chance to settle.* What lay behind the commander's lined face, his yellowing eyes?

He took his card from a pocket and studied it, turning it over and over in his hands.

"Where are you going?" he asked at last.

"Join my people," my father said. "Find out."

"People?" the commander said wearily, putting his card away. "You know the Nazareth Act. No card, no presence. There aren't any people on this ship now." He put his gun into its holster. "The people are all down on the quay. I'll take my screen down to them while those cards are still valid. Then at least they'll be able to get to the next food drop."

My father held out his hand. "Why stay?" he asked.

"I have to do what I can. I don't have a choice."

"I'm giving you a choice, right now. Throw down your card."

"I don't think so," the commander said quietly. "I had a daughter once." He looked at me and took my father's hand without taking his eyes from my face. *I'm sorry*, I thought, although I did not know why, and before I could say anything he turned and walked along the deck and down the gangway. His ringing footsteps grew fainter. The gangway gate groaned, and as the commander stepped onto the quay, my father threw his own card. It paused in the air, a flash of gold, before the commander caught it. The people on the ship cheered. My father's guards ran to the ropes; others crowded around to help, making so much noise that no one heard my father's panicked shout. "Not yet," he screamed, running to the gangway bolts, but the ropes fell into the sea before the cheers had subsided. The engines kicked in with a deep roar, and the ship began to drift.

There was a screech of tortured metal. The gangway was still bolted to the ship.

"It'll slam into us," my father said desperately, struggling to slide the mechanism free. Others joined him. But the movement of the ship had tightened the bolts against their casings, and they would not give. As the ship moved slowly, inexorably out to sea, it dragged the gangplank across the quay. I shouted, but I was too late. Three women lay on the quay, still trying to reach the cards that had fallen into the water. They had no time to stand. The gangway swept them away with industrial efficiency; they barely had time to scream. The resistance of their bodies momentarily slackened the bolts; the bolts gave and the gangway fell into the sea with an incredible splash.

I watched the water crash white over the falling metal, and I watched as the waves subsided and the sea became smooth. The strip of brown water between the ship and the land became a river, a lake, a sea. But the three women did not come to the surface. Tiny figures lined the quay; I heard far-off cries. But we were gone. The gangway was in the sea, the ship was safe, and soon the land was nothing more than a panoramic postcard pinned to the sky.

My father returned to the desk and opened the manifest.

"Lalla," he said, inclining his head. He handed me the pen and I felt its unfamiliar weight between my fingers.

"But those women..." I said.

"Sign your name, then go to your mother," he answered, and I formed my name as quickly as I could, struggling with the strange sensation of the paper against the nib, my hands trembling with gratitude and relief. But at last there it was, Lalla Paul, thick, black, indelible. A pen with ink, a paper page. Irrevocable paper, that could not be reprogrammed, hacked, crashed, deleted. No matter what happened to the power supply, my name would stand there, for ever. I wondered whether this was why my mother had been so insistent on teaching me to write without using the screen. "Go, quickly," he said. "Up the first staircase, third door."

"Aren't you coming?" I asked.

He waved the pen at the queue of people before him, alight with hope and adoration. He shook his head. "I've got to register the people," he said. "Tell her..." he began, but his voice gave way and he stopped, breathing hard. "It's a metal door," he said at last.

Behind me, I heard my father calling out names, the shuffle of feet, the ordered method of things being done properly. Hope insinuated itself into the controlled space. I glanced over my shoulder as, one by one, the people signed the manifest. Three lives had been lost, but one hung in the balance, and that was the one I cared about most. I ran. I ran as fast as I could. To the infirmary. To my mother.

It never occurred to me to wonder how we would disembark, now that the gangway was gone.

THREE

A steel door ❖ _a doctor's joy_ ❖ _and now who is_
Lalla Paul?

I found the steel door and pushed it open, feeling the metal grow
warm under my hands. When I took them away, there were two
perfect hand shapes outlined in mist on the silver. They vanished before I had walked through. My mother lay still, her eyes
closed. The doctor was there too, adjusting the valve on a bag of
fluid hanging over my mother's bed.

"Miss Paul," he said, standing in the way of the bed. His eyes
did not meet mine. His hair was coarse and pale and fell over his
ears. He stepped aside as I approached the bed.

"Mother?" I said. "Mother?"

I reached out to stroke her face but the doctor caught my
hand. "Wash your hands before you touch her," he said gently,
"then rub them with the gel in the blue bottle. And put on a
gown."

I turned on the tap. "There's water," I said, surprised, watching it cascading into the silver bowl. I turned off the tap, then
turned it on again. "It's still there."

"There's electricity too," the doctor said. "All the time, apparently, although I don't quite see…" His voice trailed away. I
unfolded the gown slowly, and I began to feel that the change
in my life was not contained in the exchange of water for land,

but in the fact that the doctor could not meet my eyes, that his hands pulled restlessly at the elasticated cuffs of his own gown, that he had no words for me. He pushed his hair back and I saw that there were hairs growing from his ears, too. I didn't like it. The gel sat cold on my skin.

"We should wait for your father," he said, and his ear hair moved when he talked.

"He's registering the people," I said. "We've sailed now." The sound of the engines had grown fainter since the first great roar. "They're signing the manifest. My father sent me here. He said..."

"Yes?"

"He said the infirmary had a metal door," I faltered, watching the doctor take down a crisp sheet of startling whiteness from a stack on a shelf. "Can I...?" I nodded at my mother and he stepped aside. I kissed her and squeezed her cold hand and then I stared and stared, looking for the rise and fall of her chest until my eyes watered. Footsteps moved past the infirmary door in little groups. I heard voices and laughter. I heard doors opening and closing and the bubbling rush of taps being turned on and off. "Water!" I heard a distant voice shout, and a chorus of babbling voices took up the cry.

Water. How could there be water all the time, when time itself had stopped?

Then my mother heaved a sudden breath and an ooze of blood spread through the white cotton over her stomach.

"Mother?" I whispered. But she did not answer, and the doctor just watched, the white sheet folded over his arm.

In the cabins around us, the water continued to flow. Baths she had given me when I was a very little girl, when we still took water for granted, soap refusing to be caught as we chased it with slippery hands. Water cascading over her head as she washed her hair, turning it dark and shining. I forgot about the times I felt I had let her down, about never being quite clever enough, about feeling unimportant. I thought about rain making puddles on the pavement and the sudden anger with which she pulled me away when I asked why we couldn't drink from them as the street people did. I'd never thanked her for boiling my water. I'd just complained about having to drink it when it was hot. And so she had found a stone jug to cool the water in, and filled it, and poured cool water from it, just for me. She had to live, so that I could thank her.

I thought about the stone jug.

The blood spread but the very fact that it was there made me dizzy with hope.

The steel door opened and my father walked in.

"I'm sorry," the doctor said, hanging beside my father like a trailing thread, and my knees felt weak; I clung to her hand, although there was no answering pressure. My father approached the bed and the doctor did not stand in his way.

"Can she hear me?" my father asked.

I stepped back and leaned against the wall; I found myself sliding down it, the green gown rustling around me. I folded my arms over my knees and hid my face. I waited for my mother's voice to ask, *Lalage, what's wrong?* then felt the floor lurch as I realised that she was not going to ask.

"The bullet ripped through her bowel," the doctor said. "There isn't anything to be done except make her comfortable."

I looked up and saw that my father's face was grey.

"I'm sorry, Mr Paul," the doctor said again. "I'm so sorry. The blood loss, the infection. It was too much for her. It would have been too much for anyone."

My father closed his eyes. He clenched his hands into tight fists.

"It'll be peaceful," the doctor continued. "I'm making sure of that, at least." He gestured towards the bag of clear fluid dripping into my mother's arm.

I looked at my father, willing him to produce another miraculous ship, one in which my mother had not been shot. But he
kept his eyes closed and took a long time to draw breath. "Is
there anything you don't have?" he said at last. "Is there anything
you need that might make a difference? That might...save her?"

"No," the doctor said quickly. "I've got everything I want,
more of everything than I could possibly need. It's all here for
me. The morphine, the saline, the sterile needles and the drip..."

My father opened his eyes and colour returned slowly to his
face.

"I cleaned the wound with swabs and dressed it with surgical
muslin. Mr Paul, I had fresh water and antibiotics. If it had been
possible to save your wife, I could have done it with what was
here." The doctor finished, and my father stepped forwards and
held out his hand.

"Thank you," he said as the doctor took it.

"No," said the doctor, "it is you I thank. If I had had all
this..." He stopped, and my father put his free hand on the doctor's shoulder.

The sound of footsteps still surrounded us—pattering ones
underscoring chatter and effervescent giggles, heavier ones
accompanied by deeper voices—but this time they were going
the other way, back to the ballroom.

"What?" I demanded from the floor, pulling my hair away
from my face. "If you'd had all this, then what?"

Neither man replied. They stepped apart and silence flooded
between them.

"I told the people to gather in the ballroom after they'd found
their cabins," my father said. "I have to talk to them. If I'm not
there, they'll be uncertain. They'll look to each other, they'll
look back to what we've left behind. It could all...I need to be
there. She'd understand that. She told me to do it properly."

"But she's not dead," I said. They looked down at me. I

scrambled up with my back to the wall and faced the doctor. "You said she's not dead. She took a breath. And there's blood. The blood's still coming. Dead people don't bleed."

"It's only a matter of time," the doctor said quietly. My father stood bowed, his eyes on my mother, his senses alert to the sounds outside and the constant dark rumbling of the engines taking us onwards, onwards, we knew not where.

"Does she know we're here?" my father asked.

"The pain relief is very strong. It needs to be." The doctor paused. "I could go to the ballroom for you," he said. "They'll understand."

The footsteps on the walkway became quicker, skittering over the background bass of the engines and fading towards the ballroom. I took my mother's hand again. I felt the shallow quick fluttering of her pulse and watched the deep rise and fall of my father's breathing as he thought. I held my breath.

"No," he said. "It has to be me. They need to see me, to hear me. The ship was my plan. They put their trust in me. With all due respect, Roger..."

The doctor inclined his head in acknowledgement.

"Perhaps," my father said, moving towards the door and then coming back to the bed, "perhaps you could go to the ballroom and tell the people to wait." I breathed again and lifted my head. "Tell them that I...that Lalla and I...that we will be with them shortly. They'll wait. Of course they'll wait. They've waited so long already."

The doctor nodded. "Mr Paul," he said. "Michael. I want you to know—you need to know—that at no time in history could more have been done for her. And I thank you."

"You're happy," I said to the doctor as my father began to open the door for him. The doctor took a breath as if to deny it, then sighed. He leaned his forehead against the steel door and spoke to the floor.

"I've watched so many people die without being able to help. And to be able to help someone, to be able to do everything I can and then let what will be, be—that's life, Miss Paul. What's happiness, more than that?"

"And will you?" I said.

"Will I what?"

"Let what will be, be. You've stuffed her with drugs so she can't even hear me. She doesn't even know I'm here. She wouldn't want that. She wants to talk to me, even if it hurts her. She'd rather be in pain than be like this."

The doctor straightened up and turned to me. My father took a step backwards, as though he wanted a better view. "You think?" the doctor said. He pointed a finger at me. The slightest tremor at its tip betrayed the effort he was putting into controlling himself. "What do you know about pain, Miss Paul? What do you know?"

My father took my hand and held it tight. I felt the strong pulse in his thumb, the warmth and resilience of his flesh, and I stared into the doctor's face, which was as white as my mother's. "Life is pain, Miss Paul, and a pain-free death is a gift. You should thank your father. You should thank him on your knees for what he's given your mother. That's what you should be doing." He took a breath. "I'm sorry," he said, but this time he was talking to my father, not to me.

I pinched my lips together with my teeth and felt the blood being driven away. I hated him. I called down thunderbolts to strike him dead on the spot; I decided to find out where his cabin was and poison the water; I would track down the person he loved best in the world and shoot them through the bowels and see how strongly he held to his precious philosophy then. The door clanged shut behind him and the misty outline of his forehead faded with the noise. My father put his arm around me and we looked down at my mother.

"Don't be angry with Roger," he said. "He did all he could."

"But she's not dead."

"She's leaving us peacefully."

"I threw away my card," I said. "I stood on the deck rail and I threw it down to the people on the quay."

"I know."

"I did it for her," I said. "I did it so that we could sail quickly and I could come and be with her."

"No," my father said, tightening his arm around me. "You did it for me. For the ship. I knew you would make me proud, but I did not know how soon it would come. I owe you my life, Lalla. And so does everyone on board this ship. They are your people too, now. And so soon." He was excited; I could see his eyes dancing a little, even through the misery in his face.

"But I don't want them," I said, the image of my mother before me beginning to swim. "I want her." I blinked and she was back, pale on the infirmary bed. I took her hand and knelt down beside her. Her hand was cold; I rubbed it between my own, trying to communicate my warmth to her as I had done to the steel door. But her skin resisted me as wholly as the steel had absorbed me. I looked at my father, but his eyes were far away, seeing things I had never been a part of. He bent over my mother and kissed her forehead, but it was I who felt the warmth of his lips. "I want her too," he whispered.

We stayed like that for a moment, until he said, "Lalla. I have to go and talk to the people. Not for long. It won't be for long. I know exactly what I'm going to say." He patted his pocket and I heard the rustle of paper. "And then I'll be back. Right back."

I rested my head on the pillow beside hers and stared at him.

"It would be easier for me if you came with me," he said. "Will you, Lalla? Please."

"She's not dead," I said again, because that was the only thing I was sure of. I turned away from him and buried my face in my mother's pillow. I heard him sigh, then I heard the steel door open. I lifted my head and had to shield my eyes against the copper gold of the sun. My father hovered, silhouetted against the bright outside. He held out his hand to me; I shook my head and he was gone.

My father was always walking out of the room after an argument, leaving an important statement hanging in the air behind him. As soon as he'd gone, my mother's anger would melt and she would turn to me, eyes bright, ready to play or to walk or to teach. I thought she might sit up now, smile, ask me what I would like to do next. But this time there was no private wink, no secret smile to let me in on the joke. And my father was gone.

I settled my head on the pillow next to hers. The voices and running water had stopped; everyone was in the ballroom with my father. Through the silence, I felt the vibration deep in the heart of the ship. My heart learned to beat in time with the engine, and I was back in London, walking to the British Museum, my mother's steady steps undeterred by the emaciated faces, the blackened teeth, the smell of the end of the world. *What right do we have,* I heard her asking my father on our return, *what right do we have to a place to call home?*

It's for Lalla, he always said. *All of it. For Lalla.*

Yes, she said, *but has she ever eaten an apple?*

"Mother," I cried, and a cold gust of wind blew on me. My father had left the infirmary door standing open and I could see that the sun had set. I tried to stand and found that my legs had gone numb. My neck was stiff and I realised that I was cold and light-headed with hunger. We had not eaten since we left the flat. I shut the door. Where was my father? How long had he been gone?

"Mother," I said, and then again more loudly, "Mother." There was no response. I could not help myself; I pressed her stomach gently, and a fresh patch of blood glinted. Her blood was flowing, therefore she lived; only the doctor's magic bag of fluid was keeping her from me. "Mother," I said, "it's Lalla," as though that information alone would be enough to provoke a response.

I looked up at the plastic bag and the drip, drip, drip of the drugs that were keeping her still and quiet, keeping her away. The doctor was sedating her. Therefore, by stopping his drugs, I could wake her up. I could ask her what she wanted me to do. I reached up and turned the valve, and the dripping stopped.

I sat by the bed. For a few moments, nothing happened. Then her breathing became deeper and stronger. Her cheeks turned red. My heart outstripped the engines. I gripped her hand; I lined up my thousand questions.

Her eyes started open, pupils vast and unseeing.

"Mother," I began, but she did not answer me. Her face was turning purple. Her hands began to flail uselessly, reaching for help I could not give. Blood flowed faster, gathering in a pool and dripping from the bed to the floor. I stood over her, trying to give her wild eyes a glimpse of my face, to bring her back to me, but her mouth opened and she began to scream, an animal cry that carved out new lines in her face. She reared off the bed and curled into a ball, her head against her knees, as though pain was the only thing in the world. Then she fell back again, hard, her face drained grey and old. The bloody sheet fell to the floor, taking the sodden dressing with it. The wound beneath was swollen red and purple and black with white dots like dead maggots. I recoiled; I could not bring myself to go near enough to cover her again. Instead I screamed with her, and we filled the small room in ghastly unison, drowning the sounds of the ship. I stopped to draw breath, but she did not, and her scream became a thin wail that faded to nothing.

"Mother?" I was too scared to put my hands on her shoulders and shake her. My whole body was trembling as I waited for her chest to rise so that she could speak. "Mother?"

I heard pounding footsteps outside and the door burst open.

My father grabbed my shoulders and pulled me away from the bed; the doctor reached for the valve on the bag of fluid.

"What have you done, Lalla?" my father shouted. "What have you done?" The doctor stepped back, and the echoes of the screams and of my father's shouting rang from the walls as we stared at the thin, grey body on the bed and its terrible wound.

"She's gone," the doctor said.

"Gone?" my father repeated. They stared at each other. I tried to take a step towards the bed but my legs were not working. I fell, and neither man helped me up. The doctor took a clean white sheet and wafted it over my mother's body. It settled over the wound; he drew it gently over her face and I was glad, because the pain inscribed there made me feel so guilty I couldn't move. The light of the infirmary streamed out into the night; my father's shadow became a black path. The doctor looked at me, and his face was thin and sour. He did not like me, and I did not care. He passed before my father, through the open door and into the night, and if they exchanged words I did not hear what they were. But I saw my father's hand on the doctor's shoulder, and the way the doctor shook his head as he walked away.

My father turned towards me. I looked around; I saw the bed, the outline of the body beneath the sheet, the sink, the fluid in the plastic bag, dripping its contents once more. I did not dare turn it off again. My father and I stood alone.

"I just wanted to talk to her," I said.

He was silent. He stood staring at my mother. The bloody sheet lay on the floor between us. I wondered if the world without my mother was so different that he would raise a hand and hit me. I wondered whether I would feel anything if he did. But he did not hit me. He did not even look at me. Slowly, he slumped to the floor, folded on the threshold of the infirmary. Here, too, was pain, except that my father was not dying. Through the open door, the sky was black.

I listened for his breathing and saw that he was shivering. I looked at my own arms and realised they were covered in goose-bumps. Slowly, I crept towards him and sat beside him, so that our arms were touching. I thought he might push me away, but he lifted his arm and put it around me, and we stayed like that for a long time, staring at the shape on the bed that was my mother's body.

What would my mother do? I asked myself, over and over again, but my anchor was gone. My father shivered, and I remembered seeing blankets on the infirmary shelf; I think I had an idea of shielding ourselves against the inevitable dawn, when the sun would rise without her. The shelf was behind the door, and as I was standing there, reaching for the blankets, feeling the blood fighting its way back into my legs, the doctor came back. He did not see me, hidden as I was, and I said nothing. There was someone with him—the woman with red curly hair. The electric lights of the infirmary shone through it and made it look like fire. Together they knelt down beside my father; one on either side of him, they lifted him gently. He gave a start and looked around as though he could not remember where he was. Then he saw the bed and the sheet, and he rushed over and pulled back the sheet, and kissed the stricken face again and again. She was his wife, I thought, shrinking behind the door. She was his wife before she was my mother. And for the first time, I caught a glimpse of a world beyond myself. The woman and the doctor stood quietly by, and when he fell back, they caught him and led him away, supporting him on either side. I longed to call out, to go with them. But my mother was dead; I had made her death a painful one. And so I hid, unable to move, unable to cry out to the doctor who thought I'd killed her, or to the father who had, however briefly, forgotten me.

I sat on a chair beside my mother's body and felt under the sheet for her hand. I was so chilled that her hand did not feel cold in comparison. *I'm sorry*, I said, again and again. *I thought you'd want to know I was here.* Through the pain, I saw the face time would have given my mother, had she been allowed to grow old. I lay down beside her, undeterred by the blood, and stared through the door to the night sea beyond.

The doctor was right; I had never felt pain. I had never felt loss, or hunger, or genuine fear either. My parents protected me so well from what the world had become that I had no means to navigate it. They had surrounded me, made their plans to keep me safe, made sure that my only compass through life was my own experience of it. And it wasn't enough. How could it have been? A lifetime ago, the sun had set in front of the infirmary door. Soon, it would rise on the other side of the ship. Already the sky was imperceptibly lighter, like a screen that has just been turned off. And as the light grew clearer and brighter, I realised that my parents had been wrong. That, far from being the pivot around which the world turned, I was smaller than a mote of dust, less significant than a gnat.

FOUR

A new world ❧ *I choose to live* ❧ *the boy*
with the green eyes

I woke up in my father's arms, being borne into a new, colder
world.

"Hush, Lalla," my father said, "you're safe now."

I looked around. The sun hung high in the sky, bathing the
white painted metal walls and the lines of rivets in light. The textured surface of the steel walkway was set ringing by his London
shoes.

"Where is she?" I asked.

"She's in good hands," he said. We reached a door and he used
his elbow to open it, keeping his arms tightly round me. He set
me down on a bunk and stroked my hair. I ducked away from his
hand and looked around, sniffing for damp, expecting to see the
crumbling bricks and decaying plaster of our London walls. But
here was only polished wood and the smell of soap, and smooth
cotton pillowing under my hands. He kissed me and I missed
the scratching of the stubble on his chin.

"Darling," he said softly. "It's all right. Everything is all right.
My darling." He had never called me darling. Always kitten,
sweetheart, little one. *Darling* had been my mother.

My hands began to shake and I could not keep my voice
steady. "Did I kill her?" I asked.

"No, Lalla. Oh, no."

"I wanted her to know I was there. I just wanted to say good-bye. And she screamed." I began to sob. "I thought I could save her, and instead I—"

"Hush, darling, hush. All that pain—there are people here who will just smooth it away. When you see her again, she'll be beautiful, like she was before." *Before I killed her*, I thought, but I couldn't find the courage to say the words. "I've talked to the doctor, and to Emily. We're going to give her body to the sea, and as we sail, she'll be part of the seas that support us."

Except that she'll be dead.

I heard people walking the decks, learning the way around their new home, pulling their new-found safety about themselves. I overheard scraps of their conversations as they felt their way towards friendships, friendships that, only a few hours before, I had longed for. *I lost my home in the floods. My parents died in the first pandemic. My child was killed for the bread in her hands.* If there was any competition in their words, it was cancelled out by the undertow to every exchange: *What right do I have to be here? Why was I chosen? What did I do to deserve this haven? What did you?* And with every sentence that floated into my cabin, my father smiled slightly, and I saw my mother's death slipping away from him. The lines that appeared on his forehead when he cried for her were still there, but his mind was drawn to the people and the gratitude and awe they were pouring into the air outside.

"Where's the stone jug?" I asked suddenly.

"What?"

"The stone jug. Where is it?"

"What stone jug?"

"We had a stone jug. In London. Mother used to put the boiled water in it, so it could cool down."

He looked confused. "You don't have to boil the water on the ship. There's cool water flowing from the taps. We didn't bring a stone jug."

"But I want it."

"Why?"

Why? Why did I want something so redundant, so heavy, so futile? Because she had touched it. Because she had seen the need for it, and got hold of it, and used it to make my life happier, even as she scolded me. I closed my eyes and tried to hear her voice, to hear what she wanted me to do, what she wanted me to learn from the emptiness inside me, from the terrible thing I had done to her, but she was silent. I set my mind running through the galleries of the British Museum, searching for a stone jug, but although I ran from the jade axe to the Portland Font to the Mildenhall Treasure, all I could see were empty cases, and cards that marked where the treasures had once stood. *Object removed for rearrangement. Object removed for cleaning. Object removed for research purposes.* I could not find a stone jug, and from the far galleries, the sounds of hunger and loss hunted me until I was too afraid to stay silent.

"Come and have some breakfast," he said. But when I got to the door, I could not follow him. I could not step from my little cabin out into that bright white golden world of metal and rivets and endless sea. It seemed to me that if I were to take that step, I would become someone new, and I did not want to change. I wanted my mother, and my mother was dead.

"I can't," I said, and he put his arms around me.

"I have to," he said. "Please come, Lalla. I want us to be together. That's what all this was for."

I tried. I went to the door, and the air was so fresh it frightened me. I clutched at the doorframe, dizzy and heartsick. My mother would have led me out, holding my hand, or she'd have sat beside me and stroked my hair, and whatever she did would have been right, because she was doing it. Without her, I had nothing to lean on, and I flopped, empty and useless, back onto my bunk. I couldn't bring her back. Nothing I could do would bring her back, and so there was no point in doing anything. He held out his hands to pull me up, but I curled into a tighter ball. He put his hand on my head and I was grateful, although I didn't say so, because my head felt floaty; I thought I might fall if I stood up. I noticed red-headed Emily hovering in the doorway; my father saw her too.

"When did you last eat?" he asked me. "Emily, was Lalla given anything to eat yesterday?"

"I'm sorry," Emily said in consternation. "I didn't know—I didn't think—Oh, Michael, I'm so, so sorry. Our departure—the cards, and poor Anna, and...shall I fetch something?" Her voice went quiet and soft. "Michael, I'm sorry. I'll understand if you appoint someone else. Diana, perhaps. She seems very capable." Emily's voice shook; I lifted my head and dropped it again, bewildered by the abject misery on her face.

"It's all right," my father said. "We're learning. We're all learning."

Emily darted off, and my father said, "I have to go. They're waiting for me. But I'll be back, and Emily will bring you something to eat, and..." He put his hand on my arm and said, "Lalla. You're cold."

I wasn't cold. I was afraid. He was going to pull me out of the cabin, I knew, and force me into the terrible, unknowable world outside, without my mother to help me through it. How would I know where to go? What to do? How could I even put one foot in front of the other without her? She had walked alongside me for my entire life.

"It's going to be all right, Lalla." He was holding out a biscuit and a glass of water.

My hands felt too heavy to move; still, I picked up the biscuit, rested it on my bottom teeth and began to gnaw. But the crumbs were too dry inside my dry mouth. "Haven't we got anything else?" he asked the woman Emily, who was dancing about in the doorway holding a plate. "Something that might be easier for Lalla to eat? Some soup, maybe, or...?" His mind gave out. He had never planned our meals; that had been my mother's job. "Just something better," he snapped, and Emily flinched at the anger in his voice. I was glad, and then hated myself.

I put the biscuit down; I felt that to eat any more would be like Persephone eating pomegranate seeds, fixing me for ever in this world without my mother. And the thought of Persephone brought my mother's voice to life, and she was standing holding my hand in front of a little Greek bowl. "Which one is Persephone?" she'd asked, and I remember the way that I had looked and looked, searching for the big important figure at the centre of the story. But the Persephone moulded into the bowl was small, so small, holding her hands out to her mother as Hades drove away with her to the underworld. *Look*, my mother had said, *look*, but I couldn't see what she was trying to show me. I was overcome by the sudden conviction that all I had ever done was let my mother down, over and over again. I remembered the pain on her face, the terrible screams with which she had died. I hadn't told her I loved her. I couldn't even cry; instead I shrank, until I seemed to consist solely of a space in my chest made of compressed air that pushed outwards, against my ribs, squeezing my heart upwards to the base of my throat, where it beat painfully. I pulled my covers over my head. Everything was over. Everything.

"Go away," I wailed, my voice made dead by the blankets. "Go away."

"Lalla," he said, putting his hand where he thought my head was. "Lalla. Come on, darling. You can't stay in here for ever."

I heard Emily's soft, light voice suggesting I needed time, and my father asking her to go and tell the people he'd be there in a minute. Then something heavy landed just next to my feet, and for a wild, joyful moment it seemed that my mother had come to sit on my bed and tell me how stupid I was being, how selfish.

"Here," my father said, "look," and something in the tenderness of his voice made me reach out a hand, and he slipped something into it, something heavy and flat and smooth.

"It's a screen," I said, astonished.

"A screen," he said, "yes, but not the kind of screen you're used to. This is a screen for the ship. See? It's more like a portal. Let's call it a portal. We've had enough of screens." He opened it, and I wondered how he would access it without a card. But there were no demands for registration numbers, no requirement to scan a card and wait for the dove's wing to sweep the screen. There was not even a calendar or a clock. Just my father's smiling face. He tapped it.

"You see," he said, "there's the library, and there's the art collection—and here, Lalla, look." There, among the myriad of icons, was the British Museum. He tapped again. Every single gallery my mother and I had ever visited was listed. There was the Portland Font, its detail as clear on the display as it was in my memory. Lindow Man, just as I had left him behind the glass of his case. Even the little gold chariot with its gold horses was there. I called up object after object. "This was Anna's idea," he said, but I hardly heard him. "She said that the only thing to be said for technology was that we'd be able to bring every museum and art gallery in the world with us."

I took the screen—the portal—to my desk, and my father left, closing my door behind him very gently. I tapped and tapped, and in the darkness I felt that my mother had come, and that I had the chance to set things right. There, for example, was the Aztec mask. She had shown it to me so many times, but I always glowered and told her that human sacrifice was disgusting. Now, too late, the words I'd always known she wanted from me tumbled forth. *It's not bloodthirsty, Mother. They believed in human sacrifice, the honour of offering your own life for the continuation of the life force itself.* I found the jade axe. *It's ceremonial,* I said confidently, bathing in her smile. *It's to show people in the afterlife how respected the dead warrior was.* In the darkness of my cabin, we wandered the museum, together again. But this time, I made up for my sulking and silence, my resentment of the museum dwellers who took her away from me for hours at a time.

Someone knocked; I jammed a chair under the door handle. "Lalla," came my father's voice. "Lalla, let me in." But I didn't want him. I didn't want anyone except my mother, and she was in my cabin with me, and if I opened the door she would escape and fly into the golden sky and I would never find her again. I scrolled through the vases and statues and friezes until they began to swim; I could still see them when I closed my eyes, still hear my mother's voice. The banging at the door started again, but the door, and the person knocking on it, were both a long way away. I was looking at the Mildenhall Treasure—all the Roman silver had disappeared from the display cases long before we sailed, but I remembered the decoration, the size, the sheer beauty of it all, and I lost myself in wondering where it was now. I held the screen to my chest, put my head on the desk and tried to sleep, but I couldn't stay rooted. I floated, and when the voice outside the door came back and shouted that I would kill myself if I went on like this, it made perfect sense. To die would be to be with her always, to feel her hands, to walk with her, to drink cool water from the stone jug. I dragged my desk to the door, pushed it against the chair and took the screen under the covers of my bed, where I breathed and rebreathed the same warm air, resolved to stay shut up until I had used up all the oxygen and suffocated, or starved. I held my mother's hand, and together we carried tins of apple to the museum dwellers, only to drop them in the Great Court and see them bouncing up the staircase in defiance of the law of gravity, thumping and banging while people shouted. Bright spots danced across my vision regardless of whether my eyes were open or closed, and as the door moved and the desk scraped across the floor, the chair slipped and wedged against my bunk. Outside, my father swore and shouted, and I realised with delight that he would never get in unless I let him in.

I sank back on my pillow and my mother's hands weighed dry and warm against my cheek and sweetness spread over my tongue and I nestled under my quilt and searched for a word to describe the feeling, and then came to with a jerk and realised that I had been happy.

Before we sailed, we lived in England.

In England, my mother and father had lived and laughed and sheltered me.

Had my father loved her so little, that he could embrace this new life without her?

Fresh air came in through the partly opened door. My father was calling my name. I fought, but he was stronger, calling me on, on, into the ship and the world he had made.

"I'm fetching the engineers," he shouted. "We'll break this door down if we have to."

"Go away," I cried. "Go away," but the very act of speaking brought me back to myself, to my cabin, to the reality of my situation. "Go away," I said again, and as I heard his footsteps running away, I found myself reluctantly reborn, hungry and miserable, into the white order of his future.

I left my willingness to think behind, in the warm chaos where my mother had been killed. I moved towards the door like one already dead. I dislodged the desk and the chair and opened the door. The exhilaration was terrifying. I recoiled and stepped back, slamming the door shut, grateful to return to the warmth of spent, stale air that smelled of sweat and grief and the salt of tears. Of me and only of me. I regretted the familiar air I had allowed to escape and would never breathe again. But even as I sat on my bed, panting and shivering, I felt a tightly wound spring in my stomach suddenly come loose. I was desperately hungry. And my lungs, having snatched a breath of clean air, started complaining. I had stopped thinking, but I had not died, and my body started asserting itself. *Air*, said my lungs. *Food*, said my stomach, and I stood up, feeling dizzy. I opened the door once more, not out of disloyalty to my mother, but because I was not yet dead.

I almost tripped over a tray. Sandwiches. More biscuits, this time with raisins in them. A glass of clear water. As the fresh air brought warm blood to my cheeks, I realised that I had lived through a kind of death. I was alive. I would continue to live. But time and my mother were gone, and my life now would be defined, not by their absence, but by their absolute and irrevocable loss.

"Are you all right?" said a voice, a voice I recognised, a voice that belonged to a tall boy with green eyes who, once upon a time in London, had knocked upon my door. We had stood together on the deck rail, and he had taken my hand and we had smiled together. Tom, he had called himself, back in that different life, where my mother was still alive. He held a soft cloth; he was wiping the walls, but I had no energy to ask him why. My limbs were weak and I leaned on the deck rail for support. All around, the sea was grey and green and flat to the edges of the world.

"Where's my father?" I asked.

He looked at me. I remember thinking, *He is seeing me now for the first time*, and wishing that I had brushed my hair. We stood there, facing each other, and I felt a tiny shard of light cut through the dark emptiness inside me, as though I had lifted a corner of the blind in my cabin.

"I'm sorry about your mother," he said.

The air liquefied; the sun caught the green of his irises. I felt my heart beating again, and I stepped towards him. But he was not looking at me anymore, but past me, and I remembered that my mother was dead. I followed his gaze and saw my father approaching, with people running behind him.

"Lalla," he called. He waved the others away and said, "Tom. Go and tell everyone to wait in the ballroom." Then he put his arms around me and crushed me against the crisp cotton of his shirt, which smelled of soap. His body beneath the shirt was warm. I looked down and saw he had exchanged his London shoes for dark blue canvas ones with white rubber soles. "My darling," he said. Then faintness and nausea took over and I slumped against him. My father reached for the tray and gave me tiny sips of water, and although I strained for more, he would not let me control the glass. "Little by little," he said gently, "too much at once and you'll be sick."

Tom came back and between them, he and my father supported me to the ballroom, where the people swam in and out of my vision as my father settled me onto a bench. He's still called Tom, I thought, and my heart beat less reluctantly, for here was something that had not changed with my mother's death. As I grew accustomed to the light and the space, and the little sips of water spread through my exhausted body and brought the room into focus, I saw that the people were sitting upright, alert, excited. I looked on the floor for the bloodstained cushion, but it wasn't there anymore. This was a new, clean version of the ballroom and, I realised as he walked to the podium, a new, clean version of my father. His skin was glowing with certainty. He wore a white shirt, its collars and cuffs unmarked by any signs of wear or use. The people, too, were clean, their clothes bright. They've been updated, I thought, and for the first time in my life, I felt left behind and lost.

Then my father held out his arms to me from the podium. "My daughter," he called.

There was a heartbeat of silence. I looked down at my dress, saturated with the filth of the London air. My hair felt heavy, loaded with a build up of grease and grime. I wondered whether my father would tell me how I could wash it, and how it would feel to stand in the sparkling air of the sea and let it dry. And then the people began to cheer. They called my name, they shouted, they smiled and held out their arms to me as my father had done. They were cheering for me, and they would not stop.

"People," he said, and his voice was deeper than I remembered it, and more resonant. "Lalla has come. Lalla has chosen." Chosen? What choice had I made? I just hadn't been ready to die. But there was no chance for me to speak. "With Lalla beside me," he continued, "I can finally welcome you all. Here, together, we will create, not an existence, but a life. A life of like-minded people, joined together in love. A life, my friends, that may truly be called life. Remember work? Remember art, and music, and laughing over food in the company of friends? Remember conversation? Words exchanged, not in barter or pleas, but for nothing but the joy of sharing them with another human being?

"We have brought words, but left arguments behind. We have brought tools, but left weapons behind. We have brought love, but left betrayal behind.

"Together, Lalla and I give you safety. Not a temporary loan from a government that will take back as soon as it gives. An unconditional gift, given for nothing other than your happiness. We are a family now. People of the ship, we give you freedom."

The noise of the people was such that I thought the sea had crashed its way into the ballroom. I saw the man with the grey beard murmuring with his eyes closed. Michael, he said, as his tears flowed. He was not the only one crying. Michael, my captain. My father's name was taken up and whispered around the room. I read it on their lips, I heard the words *Michael* and *Captain* floating, bobbing up again and again above the soft wash of blended voices. They took my father from me and turned him into something new. Or something he had always been, that I had never seen before. He had grown and moved on, but I was simply me. Lalage. The babbling waters of a small stream, lost in an ocean of salt.

FIVE

The first meal ❧ pineapples ❧ I wash and change my clothes

From the ballroom we all moved to the dining room. There were no clocks on the walls or on our portals, but at the sound of the gong the people stood up and filed out. I was the only one unsure of where to go, and I simply followed my father. He led me to the seat beside him, at the head of the top table, and I thought, I am in my mother's place, and that is why he is not broken. He told me that lunch and dinner were served every day, and breakfast was set out on the buffet tables for everyone to help themselves. Emily, the woman with red curly hair, was in charge of the dining room; I would meet Gerhard the chef later. Freedom and plenty. I was lightheaded with hunger and dizzy with the sensations of colour and sound.

Plates were brought to us, filled with something that smelled savoury and maddening; I could smell garlic and salt and my mouth filled with saliva. It looked like chicken. I swallowed, and swallowed again, and I put my hand out for my fork. A quick hand prevented me from picking it up. A man with skin like a pickled walnut nodded towards my father. "Respect," the man said softly, his dark eyes shining. The chicken and garlic smell hung tantalisingly in the air. My father picked up his knife and fork; everyone in the dining hall did the same, and the moment was gone.

I ate, and the sensation of taste drove every other thought from my mind. I remember roast chicken, I thought, and I was eleven again, and my mother was holding out a plate of drumsticks and warning me that they were too hot to hold, and it was my birthday, and she was running to shut the window so that the smell of the chicken would not attract the street people to our home.

"Father," I said, because I wanted to see if he remembered it too, but the main course was over, and the kitchen team were bringing out rings of gold, set in squares of pliant cake and covered in sticky sweetness. A ripple of excitement spread across the room as the plates were placed on the tables.

"Pineapple," my father said, smiling at my amazement. "A tropical fruit, with sharp leaves and prickly skin. A symbol of hospitality."

"Which part of this is the pineapple?" I asked, prodding the cake with my fork.

"The round, yellow part on the top."

"You said it had leaves and prickly skin."

"Yes, but they weren't necessary. They were the parts we didn't need. The parts that prevented the pineapple from being truly itself, the best that it could be. They've been done away with already. The work has been done by those who came before us, and we are reaping the benefits now. This is a pineapple," he concluded, pointing at my plate.

"So a pineapple was not the same as an apple?" I said as he sat back down.

"No." He finished his cake and pushed his plate away.

"Was a pineapple an apple that grew on a pine tree?" I asked.

That's good thinking, Lalla, I heard my mother say, but my father was talking to someone else, and just said, "If you like."

The people began to get up and move around. I saw Tom hover at the doors and scan the room; my face burned and I stared at the table until he had gone.

"Where are the people going?" I asked.

"Some are going to the gallery or the cinema," my father said, coming back to me as the room emptied. "Some will be going for a walk on the deck, or to listen to music, or simply gathering together to talk. But most of them—" He paused, and I waited. He turned dark and stern, as he used to do when my mother disagreed with him. He sighed. "They're going to watch the bulletin in the ballroom. We usually have it before dinner, but today there was you." He smiled at me, as though he had just remembered how.

"The news bulletin? Like at home?"

He stroked my cheek. "The ship is our home now, darling," he said. "But yes, we have the news bulletin here as we did in London. We have everything we had in London, and a great deal more that we could never have had in London."

And suddenly, I had had enough. The food sat heavily in my stomach; the effort of digesting after not eating for so long made me sleepy. The noise of conversations and the constant movement of so many people had left me bewildered. I wanted our flat, and the little fire, and the dancing flames of the oil-drum fires in the street, and cooled water from the stone jug. I wanted my mother. *Have an apple*, she used to say when I asked for the impossible. Because there were no apples anymore where we had come from. I wondered whether the same would be true of where we were going. A pineapple was not the same thing as an apple.

He looked at me sadly. "Stop looking back, Lalla. She's gone. We'll have the funeral tomorrow, and then we move on. You've got everything here, darling. Everything she ever wanted for you. But you won't benefit from it until you let her go. Let her go, Lalla. Let her go." He wrapped his arms around me and pressed his new smooth face to mine; I felt damp on my cheeks, although I was not crying. "You have had the time to grieve," he said, wrapping himself around my shoulders far too tightly. "Be grateful for that." But I could not let her go. She was with me now; I had heard her voice. In life, her mind had always been on the next task, the next duty, the next thing that had to be done. In death, there was nothing to distract her. She was beside me, and I clung to her. My father let me go. I stumbled, and my dress caught on a corner of the table.

He stared at the dress as I unhooked it. "Do I remember that dress?" he asked.

"It was hers," I said. It had once been long and full with red and orange flowers all over it, so big that they were lost when my mother cut the dress down for me. Now, the dress was stiff with London dirt, with sweat and tears and loss and misery, flowers and flame puddled alike with grey. I held out the skirt to him, searching his face for a clue that he, too, was remembering her looking through her dresses for something to alter for me, the way she muttered *Impractical, impractical*, to the red silk, the golden gauze, the velvets she threw aside.

"She was making it the day you asked her to make the bags," I said. "Five hundred bags, for the five hundred people you were going to bring with us."

"I remember she didn't want to make the bags," he said. "I don't remember you being there."

That's because I stood so still, I thought. That's because I worried that if I moved, you'd remember I was there, and change the subject. "You said it would be symbolic," I told him. "A new start, the same opportunities for everyone."

"So it would have been. I could have got the material. I knew a man who had sailcloth. But it doesn't matter anymore."

He kept staring, and I wondered whether he, too, was remembering my mother draping the fabric round me, whether her voice was sounding in his head as clearly as it was in mine.

"We've got bags," she'd said through a mouthful of pins. "We don't need more bags."

"This is different."

"It always is. It always was. I thought we were trying to make sure that it won't always be."

"It would be nice if the bags matched. That's all I'm saying."

"Nice? Nice? Oh, for crying out loud. Have an apple, Michael." She looked up, and I saw dark circles under her eyes. She's tired, I remember thinking in surprise. She's really tired. "Shall we print them?" my mother had asked suddenly, falsely bright. "If we're going to use our precious resources to make bags we don't need for a plan that may never come off, we might as well have them printed. *I owe my life to Michael Paul.* That would be good. That's your vision, really, isn't it, Michael? A symmetrical line of grateful clean people, with matching bags."

"They will owe their lives to me."

"You've got to forget that, Michael. Life can only be given as a free gift. If our people come on board carrying bags that say, Michael Paul Saved My Life, we're sunk. They're sunk."

I had no way of knowing whether my father was thinking of that now. He only said, "You should go and change," and I watched him walk out of the dining room through an avenue of smiles.

I went to my clean and shining cabin and took off the dress. It had always seemed so easy—take a full, ornate dress and make it smaller and simpler. But now, as I buried my face in the fabric and tried to find her there, I saw the complexity of the task she had undertaken, the thousands of stitches all put in by her hands, the little darts and gathers that made the dress mine rather than hers. I realised then that I could never do what she had done. I could never ask the questions she asked, or tell the truth like she told it. She had resisted him, and through that resistance, she had disciplined his vision and given him strength. And that same resistance had given me my life. I had been born from it, nourished by it, educated by it. She had given me her life like she had once given me her clothes—carefully chosen, contrived from the best that was available, cut to fit. To fit me. Who was my father without her? Who was I? He was without boundaries now, and I half expected that the next time I saw the people, they would be sitting making five hundred matching bags from sailcloth, ready to be printed. *I owe my life to Michael Paul.*

I realised that the dress smelled foul and I was embarrassed that I'd worn it to dinner. I opened the cupboards. Clothes hung there, fresh and smooth. A pile of white squares sat on a shelf; I shook one out and saw that it was a nightdress. I could not hang my London dress amidst all that crisp purity. I showered, watching the grey water dancing lightly to the drain; I washed my hair, letting the soap run into my eyes and revelling in the pain of it.

Mother, I whispered quietly. *If this is what you wanted for me, I will do my best.* I scratched a mark on the wall beside me, slipped into my bunk and slept. When I woke up, the orange dress was gone.

SIX

The wind farms ❈ *the broken button*
❈ *I find my place of work*

On the morning of the funeral, as the sky in my porthole lightened, my father came and knocked at my cabin door. I let him in and climbed back into my bunk.

"Lalla," he said, perching on the corner of my desk. "How are you?"

"Fine."

"There are other clothes, you know." I looked down my cotton nightdress and felt exposed. I had never given a thought to what I was wearing in front of him before. This was a strange new world, in which I did not feel comfortable sitting with my father in my nightdress. "If you wanted to wear something new for the funeral," he said, "I can show you where the clothes are."

"Do you want me to wear black?" I asked.

"This isn't about what I want," he said. "Think about what would be fitting. Think of what would be the right thing by Anna."

"I don't think she would have wanted to die in the first place."

He frowned and his eyes darkened. "She chose what happened to her, Lalla. We all do."

I opened my mouth to speak, and my cabin went dark. A vast trunk of grey and rust was blocking my porthole. I got down from my bunk and looked out, so surprised that I forgot what I was going to say.

"What's that?" I asked.

"It's a wind turbine," my father said. "We're going through the wind farms." He got off the desk and stood beside me. "We were going to save the world with offshore wind farms." I stared at the peeling flakes of metal, the coastlines of rust, spread before my eyes as though my porthole were a magnifying glass.

"Look to the horizon," my father said, and as the ship sailed past the trunk, it moved aside to reveal a leafless forest stretching as far as I could see. On the horizon, I saw the motionless blades reaching uselessly to the sky, to the sea. I had only ever seen the wind farms on my screen before—now here they were, larger in life than I had ever imagined. It seemed a beautiful thing to me, to take the movement of the winds and turn it into power for humanity.

"Why don't they work?" I asked.

"They're disconnected," he said.

"But why? Why can't we connect them again, get the power going?"

"Look at them, Lalla. They're rusting away. Useless great hulks. Nothing lasts if it's not cared for. If no one could pay for the power, where was the money to come from to maintain the turbines? Or the oil derricks, for that matter? Who would create power only to give it away?"

I thought of the ship, of what it must have cost. "You could have done it," I said. "Instead of this."

"For Marius and his politicians to get fat on?" Anger flared in his eyes; I saw him control himself, and I did not dare to say more. Then he said, "Labour, and the fruits of labour. When those things were connected, the world turned. When the disconnect became absolute, it stopped. Politicians looking out for themselves. And all those street people in London, sitting around waiting for food drops. What were they doing, Lalla? Why weren't they working?"

"There wasn't any work."

"There's always work. Easier to sit around and complain than find it, though."

We passed another turbine and in the dark, I appealed to my mother, *Tell me what to think. Tell me what to ask.* It didn't seem to me that the street people had had an awful lot of choice.

"When we've passed the wind farms, we'll be on our way," my father said at last. "That's all the wind farms are now, a staging post on our journey."

"What's a staging post?"

"Somewhere they used to change horses. Before cars and trains and aeroplanes. So they could get where they were going more quickly." Horses. Aeroplanes. Words so impossibly exotic that they made little sense to me.

"Where are we going?" I asked.

My father smiled and went to the door. "You'll know when we get there," he said. "We all will." He looked at me and inclined his head. "We might not all arrive at the same time, that's all."

"But we're all on the same ship."

"Yes," he said. "Yes, we are. We are all on the same ship." He repeated my words as though they pleased him.

There was a gentle knock on my cabin door. My father called, "Come in," and the woman with red curly hair opened the door and looked in, smiling at me with pity in her eyes before turning to my father. Emily.

"We're ready for you," she said. He nodded and she withdrew, keeping her eyes fixed on him until the moment the door closed behind her.

He went to the door. "Shall we?" he said, holding out his hand.

"Why are you so angry with her?" I asked suddenly.

"With Emily?"

"No. With my mother."

"Angry?" He looked warily at me, and I remembered the way he had looked at Commander Marius when he mentioned the Exodus Act. As though he might have been found out.

"You said she chose what happened to her."

"She did."

The nightdress smelled of soap, not of London. "She didn't," I said. "She didn't, and neither did I."

I expected him to come over and put his arms around me as he had done before. I expected him to say that, although I had lost my mother, I would never, ever lose my father, and that he loved me, and that everything he had done in setting up the ship and this life was for me. That, at least, would be familiar, and by burying my face in his shoulder, I could maybe find a link back to her.

But he didn't. He just said, "Grow up, Lalla," and I felt as though a blanket had been ripped from me. "We could have left long before we did. Before the gangs began to gather. Before the Land Allocation Act, even. We didn't have to wait to see blood being spilt on the streets. We could have gathered you up years ago, Lalla, and brought you here."

"You could have forced her," I muttered sullenly.

"Anna would have kept finding excuses until London rotted and the people in the holding centre were all dead. I was terrified that something terrible would have to happen before she would agree to come away. That one of you would be hurt. I am only grateful that it was not you."

"Why did we have to come away at all?"

"Because of you." He smiled, and a terrible thought that had come into my mind popped like a bubble of soap. I was back at the centre of the universe, where I was comfortable because it was where I had always been.

"Me?" I asked. I felt warm again.

"You. I wanted you to have a chance to live with higher thoughts than where to find food. I wanted you to experience all the wonders of being human, without worrying that some starving, terrified soul was going to kill you. I wanted to give my daughter herself, so that she could find out who she is. When you were born, you gave me the strength and inspiration to reach for something higher, for everyone. And this is that place. Your mother will always be a part of you, so what need have I to weep when you are with me?"

At first I clung to him as I wept. I saw my mother walking down Great Russell Street, holding the hand of a little girl who looked a bit like me. Except that little girl was smiling, and I knew that I would never smile again. I wept for the water she had cooled for me in the stone jug, and for the dress she had died in, that would never be cut down for me. I wept because my days had been so empty, and because I had wasted so much time thinking that I was letting her down, when all she had wanted to do was to love me. My chest hurt; I could not bear that, if I stopped crying, it might stop hurting. And I wept in gratitude for my father's words, which had given me permission to cry.

"I've got something for you," my father said, putting a velvet jewellery box on the desk.

I stopped crying. Was I to be given another diamond? But I didn't want one. In death, I had drawn my mother closer. She had yearned for flowers, not for diamonds.

"Open it," he said.

I did so, and the world around me shifted.

One day, on the way back from the British Museum, I saw a couple standing on the corner of the street. I must have been ten or eleven, I suppose—after restaurants and shops, but before the museum dwellers became entrenched. I let my mother walk ahead and I watched, and I saw the man place his hands around her face and kiss the woman. It was a bitterly cold day, and he pulled his coat around the two of them so that they looked like only one person, and as he did so, a button fell from his coat and rolled to my feet. I wasn't allowed to talk to anyone, so I picked up the button, and when we got home, I put it into an empty jewellery box and gave it to my mother.

"That's a story, little one," she said. "We'll put it in our museum, shall we? With a label saying, *This button shows us that there was still love amongst twenty-first century man.*"

"It's just a broken button, Anna," my father said. "It's not worth anything. It's hardly a diamond."

"Diamonds are just diamonds," she said quietly, her skin shining soft in the pale daylight. "They're too hard. Nothing marks them. This button—look, those are the scratches where it rolled along the road. The pattern's worn away on one side. That must have been where the man used to push the button through the buttonhole. Think how long he must have been doing that for, to mark the button in this way. And think what it meant to him, to share his coat, maybe his only shelter, with someone else." She turned it over in her hand. "See?" she said, holding it out to both of us, although I was the only one who leaned forward. "The shank's worn so thin that it snapped." She turned to my father. "Don't you see, Michael? Don't you see that this button is more valuable than your diamonds?"

"What good's that button going to be when you get hungry?"

"So we're to eat diamonds, King Midas?" She pushed me towards him. "Go on, Michael, touch her and see if she turns to gold."

He held me, but I never did turn to gold. And yet, my father had taken the trouble to bring the button in its little box on board the ship. What could it mean, except that, in his own way, he loved me, just as my mother had in hers? Would he have to die, too, before I began to understand him? It was time to make of this life what I could.

The grey sea swelled around the ship. "It's you and me now, Lalla," my father said quietly. "Shall we go?" He gave me his arm, as though we were wearing the long, old-fashioned clothes I had seen on my screen and were about to dance.

And so the first funeral took place. My father hopped around, alternately exultant and subdued, disappearing after breakfast and coming back with artificial flowers, which he dumped in the ballroom before disappearing again and bringing a black dress from somewhere and giving it to me. Food was put out in the dining room and people snatched their lunch when they could, in between the dusting and the polishing and the dressing of tables. And at last, as the sun began to give up its gold to the sky and the wind farms disappeared behind us, we all came onto the lower deck. I wore the black dress, full-skirted and held at the waist by a thin belt with a gold buckle. All around me, people held handkerchiefs and looked sad. The children stood in a small group holding the flowers, and theirs were the only feet and hands that moved.

My father spoke over my mother's body. She wore the blue and green silk dress, cleaned and mended. She looked younger, as though at any moment she might open her eyes and jump off the board she was resting on and offer to play a game. My father was right; there was no trace of her suffering or her violent death upon her face, and I realised that this would make it easier for me to say goodbye. Someone had put her hair up. She looked as though she was going to a party in the time before the time before the ship.

"So lovely," someone whispered, and someone else said, "Such a terrible shame," and soft shimmery whispers moved around the gathering. Beside me, a woman wiped her eyes with a handkerchief. I saw her stare in wonder at the handkerchief, so clean and so new, and was not surprised that she found it more fascinating than death, which even I had seen every day until we sailed.

Then my father stood beside the body and faced us, and there was silence.

"We have come to let Anna go," he said. "We are here to say goodbye. We will commit her to the sea, which is our support now, and she will become part of it, bearing us up in death as she always did in life." I thought of the piece of paper he had patted in his pocket the night my mother died, upon which he had written his welcoming speech. He held no paper now. Where had he learned to speak like this? How much further from me was he going to travel?

"Love Lalla," he said to the people. A wind blew from the sea and I shivered. "Enfold her. Teach her the universality of goodness; show her your love for mankind, the love for which you were brought on board. Anna is dead. You lost her before you came to know her. But the very fact that you are here is testimony to Anna's vision, her love, her faith in you. You will find Anna in each other. Her death will draw you closer together, because during her life, she created this life for you. But Lalla— Lalla is just a child who has lost her mother. Can you bear that for her? Can you enfold Lalla in yourselves, as surely as the sea will enfold Anna and take her to itself?"

A child? Was I still a child? I felt that I had aged a hundred years since we boarded the ship. I imagined all the people coming towards me, holding out their arms, and I panicked and had to fight for my breath. A hand touched my arm but I pulled away. I did not need pity. I needed to be held. I needed to be held as my parents had held each other, as though each was only complete when the other was there. The people were alive, and my mother was dead, and I hoped they felt as guilty as I did. I stood and glared, my arm cold where the touch had been withdrawn, and the people shrank from me.

My father tilted the board on which my mother's body lay and she slipped into the sea with a small splash.

But the waters did not cover my mother's body. It floated without direction, without control, the blue green dress tracing its ebb and flow. As her dress took up the water, it clung across her body, outlining the wound on her stomach. The hair that had been arranged so carefully pulled loose with the water's weight and washed across her face in dark shadows. Each wave sloughed a layer of paint from her face, so that the peace and loveliness that had been created there melted away. She was no longer sleeping until we met again, the honoured guest of the sea; she was white and damaged and soiled and dead, and the pain I had forced on her was written all over her face.

I felt my father stiffen beside me. His fists were clenched. He did not move, but all around us, people began to look at each other. He continued to watch, his eyes fixed on the body as though he could draw the waters over it by the force of his gaze. I felt unease seeping into the atmosphere. People began to shift their weight from foot to foot; the children looked up ready to ask questions and were shushed; my father's lips thinned and his eyes became fixed and shone blue. He was Michael, their captain; food appeared on tables; stories were told, people gathered together, fresh water flowed, all at his command. And yet he could not push my mother's body beneath the waves.

And I understood that the next death would be different. At the next death, he would weight the body down with something, and the sea would rise to welcome the dead at my father's bidding. The next death would be perfect. But this time, my father stood white and unmoving, deaf to the rustle and shifting of the people around him. Slowly, they left the deck. Those with children went first, shoulders hunched apologetically over their fidgeting offspring still clutching their flowers. Others followed, throwing glances of concern at my father's granite back as they left.

He remained, staring at the body.

"He's grieving," I heard one departing mourner say to another, as the last of the people left the deck and the sun dipped slowly into the sea in front of us, glinting in the cabin portholes.

But my mother still refused to sink. Night came on, and her body became a stain on dark water. I grew cold, then colder. My arms and legs began to hurt; my fingers burned as I chafed them out of numbness. My father had not moved. I strained my eyes but the black water was unrelieved now. There was no moon, and I knew from the ancient calendars in the British Museum that this was because the earth was standing in the way of the light of the sun. The moon is still there, I told myself, even though I cannot see it.

Night time was new to me. In London, going out in the dark would have been akin to plunging a hand into boiling water or eating from the pavement. Although I had seen the night from our flat, there had always been some light out there—from the oil drums, from street fires, from screens. Here there was nothing. I could not even see whether my father was still there. I stepped carefully towards the sound of his breathing, feeling for the deck rail and gasping with the cold of it. Then I felt my father's hand, and I placed mine over it. He opened his coat and wrapped me inside it.

"Shall we jump?" he said quietly. "Now, before the sun rises. Before they come to start breakfast. Do you want to jump, Lalla? I'll come with you if you do."

To jump and to be with her. To jump, and join her in the sea.

"What about the ship?"

"It doesn't matter," he said, his arms tightly around me. "This was all for you. Only for you. Anna is gone. I can't change that. But if her death means there's nothing left for you, then I will jump, whether you do or not."

I burrowed into his chest. I imagined jumping, my body flying weightless through the air, my misery and loneliness left on the ship. Yes. Yes, I would jump, for the sake of that brief moment before the water hit. And when it did, the coldness of it, and the struggle for breath, and the fighting that would come before the peace would be worth it, because I would be with my mother.

The sun began to rise. I searched the horizon, but my mother was gone at last, taken by the receding darkness.

"What do you want me to do?" I said.

"Eat. Smile at me. Be happy."

I felt the deck beneath my feet. I saw how far it was down to the water; I saw the layers of cabins and rooms above us. I smelled the breakfast being prepared in the dining room; I felt my hunger and realised that my father was the reason it would be sated before I'd really realised it was there. And there was Tom, too. If I were to jump, I would never know him. What if I were to change my mind mid-air? My father stared out at the empty sea, waiting for my response.

"I don't want to jump," I said.

"But will you live? Really live?"

"I'll try."

"Promise me. Promise!"

I promised. In the half light, I slipped out of his coat and found my way to my cabin. No one took him from me this time; it was I who left. I took off the black dress and the belt with the gold buckle and pushed them into the laundry chute. I scratched another line upon my tally of the days. I put on clean clothes and made my way to breakfast. And I wondered whether these mechanical things could, actually, make a life. Whether, if I stopped thinking so much, I might find that my father was right, and that life without my mother was possible. After all, he was managing it. The rising sun warmed the air. People arrived in the dining room and smiled through me at each other, looking for the one person that was missing.

And then my father entered, red-eyed but touching every hand that reached out to him as he made his way to his seat. The woodwork glowed, the white paint on the deck outside gleamed through the windows, the plates and cutlery shone. My father stood at his place and raised his hand, and into the ensuing silence he called, "The sun has risen on a new day."

And so it had. From that day on, the new days just kept coming. The ship became a busy place, a bright place, a place where people smiled and talked and revelled in their safety and fullness. I watched the people as they went to meals, their cabins, the galleries. I explored my screen and found the library—hundreds, thousands of books. Books I had read with my mother, books I'd read on my own, but for the most part, books I'd never heard of. And for the first time since my mother's death, I felt a flicker of excitement. I was given work in the laundry; I had a role. I saw Tom talking with other people and vowed to find the courage to speak to him again. And I saw a life begin to take shape. What had seemed impossible only days before became normal, and any questions I'd had became less and less important, until they no longer mattered and vanished, like frost at sunrise.

The scratched markings by my bunk increased in number and the people began to coalesce in groups. New activities started—for example, a net was cast out from the lower deck and some people began to swim inside it. There was a little white boat on the lower deck too, a relic from the ship's former existence that my father had kept for its entertainment value. "A life boat, it was called," he said, faintly amused, as he watched the people lower it into the sea. It had a solar-powered motor and a small chamber below its tiny deck, where the children liked to hide. You could go all around the ship in it, although the novelty seemed to fade after the first couple of trips. Others got together and watched films, or went to Gerhard in the kitchen and learned to make cake. I couldn't walk from my cabin to the ballroom, or the kitchen, or anywhere without passing two or three people deep in conversation. Another group of people put the same book on their screens and then met in the dining room to talk about it. Emily with the red hair took them biscuits while they were talking, then she and her team set up for the next meal and collected the empty plate. I still spent hours in the British Museum on my screen, but my mother had fallen silent, as though she was waiting, watching to see what would happen next.

"You should join a group," Patience said when we were folding the ironed sheets. "Make friends." Patience was from Africa, and she was in charge of the laundry. When she smiled, her new white teeth flashed against the black skin of her face. My teeth had been passed by the dentist with an appreciative glance at my father, but many of the adults were in the process of having theirs repaired or, like Patience, replaced altogether.

"Aren't we friends?" I asked.

"I'm old. You are young. You cannot spend all your time working."

"I like working." And so I did—not so much for the lengths of fresh clean cotton sheeting, or the piles of laundered clothes ready to be delivered back to people's cabins, or even for the feeling of having something to contribute, but for my conversations with Patience. My father had always been hurried, determined, his every action dictated by a horizon that held something bigger and greater than whatever was happening in front of his eyes. Once he'd established that I wasn't going to jump into the sea, he was off again. My mother, too, had given everything to her part of the plan; I had simply been there, the reason for everything and the focus of nothing. But with Patience, on the ship, the horizon was a far off thing, a hazy line that meant and demanded nothing, and there was time.

"How did my parents find you?" I asked. "Were you still in Africa then?"

We had moved from sheets to clothes, and Patience's iron moved like a thing alive through the creases. "I was. In Mombasa, when the boats were leaving the burning lands with the last of the people."

"Why didn't you get on one?"

"If you thought your mother would return, would you have left your cabin? You chose to live. And to live, you must leave behind." She paused. "I was waiting for my daughter."

"Did she come?"

"Tola? No." Patience threw me the finished trousers, and began to work the iron's point into the gathers of a flowered skirt. "She took a different way. The way of the young. The young never believe there is an end. For them, there is always a tomorrow, and another, and another. But I remembered Africa before the earth baked dry for good, and I knew it was the end."

I checked the laundry mark on the trousers and began to fold them. "But you still waited for her?"

Patience added the finished skirt to the pile. I handed her a shirt and waited for her to speak.

She ironed the collar, the cuffs and the sleeves, then arranged the left front over her board. "Tola was angry," she said. "Her father put razor wire around our farm. He said it was for her, to keep safe the goats and chickens that fed us. She said he was a murderer, for the wire would kill anyone who tried to enter." I thought of the fences round Regent's Park, and their twisted barbs, that my father said could cut to the bone.

Patience rested the iron upright and lifted the shirt from the board. Her eyes rested on the wall beyond and above me, and her voice dropped so I had to lean forwards to hear her.

"One night," she said, "I looked out of the window. And in the moonlight, I saw the body of a young man, draped bleeding over the razor wire fence. I went out, but he was dead. So little blood, and so thin, I could lift him alone. I buried the body, glad to save my Tola this terrible sight. But Tola in the morning, she saw my cut arms. She said more people would come, and more, and were we to kill them all? Yes, said her father, if we must. And Tola left us. She was gone, and without her, her father moved around the farm like a forgotten spirit."

Patience's forearm caught on the iron. She flinched, and I ran to the sink and soaked a handkerchief in cold water. But when I took it to her, she waved it away, laughing quickly. "Michael warned us about looking back," she said, her voice suddenly light. "I look back, and see what happens? You are bad for me, Lalla. You and your questions. Join a group and bother some other person."

She rearranged the shirt and began smoothing the right front, then the back.

"But what happened?"

"It doesn't matter."

"Please, Patience. Tell me what happened in the end. Did Tola come back? Is that when my father found you?"

Patience's smile fell away and she worked on that shirt as though it was the only thing that existed in the world.

"Tola returned with fifty young people, all hungry, all wild. She told us we must feed them, with our goats, our cheese, our little bread. Her father fought them. But they were hungry, and they knew only to survive. They had clubs, and broken glass, and strength. Oh such strength."

"Did they kill him?"

"Tola killed him. She would not let her father be killed by a stranger."

"And then?"

Patience took the shirt and folded it carefully. "I gave Tola the keys to the farm. I walked three hundred miles to Mombasa, to the ships, and there I cared for the departing people. For their children, their elderly. I soothed their fears and promised good things in their new lives."

"But you chose not to go?"

"I had left all I had with Tola. And always, always, I hoped she might come."

"So you could punish her for killing her father?"

"So I could tell her she was forgiven. What else was she to do?"

"And my father? What about my father?"

"The people on the ships spoke of me. They wrote of me on their screens. Michael heard my story, and he sent a message to the authorities." She smiled. "In the office of the harbour master, I talked with Michael on the screen and I knew then that I would come if he asked me. And I wanted him to ask me. More than anything, I wanted that."

"But you said you were waiting for Tola."

"And so I am. She will come to me here, on the ship. In Mombasa, I had only a dream of Tola, and only a burning death to meet when the evacuation was done. On the ship, I know I will see her."

"But I don't understand. I don't understand why Tola ran away."

"You cannot understand what you yourself did not choose to do."

"Should I have run away?" I asked, perplexed. I saw Great Russell Street, unrolling diseased and dangerous before me, and the troops with their batons and their guns. "How could I have run away? Where would I have gone?"

"Forgive me, Lalla. You are a child still. Tola was a woman."

"How old was she?"

"Then? Thirteen. Now? Twenty-six. Maybe she is a mother herself, and her children will come with her."

"I'm sixteen."

Patience held up the iron with warning in her eyes. "Tola's was a different life. You had nothing to run from. But now— now, Lalla, you must become a woman too, and then maybe your mother will be holding Tola's hand when they come, and we will be women of the ship together."

The clothes were ironed, the piles made up. All there was now was the deliveries, and those were up to me.

"All right," I said. "I'll join a group."

SEVEN

A busy life ❀ *the last bulletin from land*
❀ *we destroy the mast*

I was busy. For the first time in my life, I was busy. There were my conversations with Patience, my trips to the cinema, the meals. I learned to swim and swam in the net most days. A little boy called Gabriel was often there at the same time; I played with him in the water while his mother, Helen, who taught the small children, looked on. I could call lots of people by their names. Above all, there was my work, and I walked with pride as I carried clean clothes and bedding to the cabins.

My busy life was plentiful, too. I cleaned my teeth, and when the bristles around the edges of the toothbrush began to bend outwards, a new toothbrush appeared in my bathroom. If the soap dispenser began to spit when I pressed the pump, the next day it would be back to laying a fat slug of scented gel in the palm of my hand whenever I wanted one. Meals were regular and varied, and the people of the ship gathered around tables to talk and to compare and to laugh. My sheets were smooth and soft, my mind occupied, my body nourished and exercised. Everything had its place, its allotted portion of the sun's journey over the ship and down the other side. There were even times when I looked up from the damp washing, or my screen, or Gabriel's little face, and realised that I had not been thinking about my mother. The sun shone, and although there were storms from time to time, they were nothing more than a reason to gather together in the ballroom and marvel at the sheer quantity of water that could fall from the sky.

My father watched me and I watched him watching. If he was there when I was in the net, I laughed just a little more loudly; if he came upon me talking to someone, I would nod more vigorously, agree more heartily, then pretend I had only just noticed him. And when he passed me carrying the clean laundry, I would hold myself just a little taller. *Are you happy?* he would ask me at dinner, and I would grin and say, *Yes, yes of course, of course,* and carry on talking with even more energy. He smiled, and I saw that he was pleased.

And Tom sat next to me at breakfast one day, and I found out that he liked toast with chocolate spread, but never drank coffee. He told me that coffee was for old guys, and I pulled my long hair over my chin so it looked like a beard, and he laughed, and the next day I saw him looking for me across the dining hall, and my breath came quicker and I sat next to him again. After the rain, the sun dried out the water on the deck and Tom and the deck team cleaned the tide marks away. Life can be like this, I remember thinking. Happiness is possible. Is this what my parents meant when they bought the ship? Is this what they wanted?

And I felt that it was, but for one thing.

The news bulletins.

My father made the bulletins available in the ballroom every other evening, just before dinner. And every other evening, the people came into dinner diminished and grey, walking as though time had turned backwards. On bulletin nights there were leftovers on people's plates and the goodnight meetings were subdued. I could see my father's frustration in the deep breaths he took before he spoke, in the emphasis he placed on the words "here" and "now" in his goodnight speeches. The bulletins brought heaviness into the air, and made people less ready to enjoy the films, the book group, even work. And yet they went, bulletin after bulletin, pulled there by a longing that was never satisfied.

I went to the bulletins because Tom went, but I spent more time looking at him and blushing wildly when he looked at me than I did watching the news. I sighed when the others sighed, but I quickly realised that the news never changed, any more than it had when we were still living in London. Riots, shortages, market raids, more Sinkers going down, the same stories over and over again, recited over film footage that never seemed to vary. As far as I could see, the bulletins depressed everyone and told us nothing, and I knew my father thought so too from the way he met my eyes across the ballroom.

And then, one night, when the scratches by my bunk numbered twenty-two and I had learned to fold a sheet without any help, the news was different.

"That's the British Museum!" I called out when the bulletin started. "We used to…" My father caught my eye and put his finger to his lips. The British Museum meant my mother, and as I stared at the screen, searching for her, my loss burst afresh through the sheet-folding and the Tom-following and the swimming and everything I had carefully built around myself since her funeral. I knew, sharply and absolutely, that the reason—the only reason—the people kept coming was to scour the footage for those they had left behind. My heart battered against my ribcage and I watched in silence. My mother was dead. I knew it, and yet I had trouble remembering to breathe.

"Today saw the commencement of the Heritage Restoration Act," the voiceover on the screen announced.

I don't have answers, Lalla. Only questions. That's how you learn. Mother.

"The Heritage Restoration Act restores citizens to the

enjoyment of public buildings. When government cleansing is completed, citizens will once more enjoy unencumbered access."

"What's happening?" a voice beside me asked, and I turned to see that Tom had come in late and was sitting beside me. But I was inside the museum with my mother, my head spinning. I could not speak for remembering, and I forgot to blush.

For a moment, it seemed that nothing was going to happen.

They wanted to show how valuable the man's life had been…

Then troops appeared on the roof of the museum. They stood for a moment, outlined against the sky, and then they abseiled down, like locusts swarming over the screen, slicing the building with dark ribbons. They stopped at the windows and produced great rolls of tape from nowhere. They ripped lengths of tape—the tearing sound was clear on the screen—and pressed them to the window frames.

"What are they doing?" I heard myself asking. *Watch, Lalla. Look at what you can see, then think about what you can't.* Yet more troops arrived in trucks bearing huge reels of yellow hose. They unrolled reel after reel into the Great Court, forming a yellow carpet through the main doors. Then they exited the museum and closed the doors. More abseiling troops sealed the doors, then released their cables and joined the others, positioned around the museum with their guns and rifles.

All around me, I saw hands stealing into hands, bodies moving closer together, faces illuminated by the screen, open-mouthed. Tom's hand lay next to mine; our little fingers were touching, and his skin was dry and hot. "I don't know," I heard myself saying. "I don't know what's happening."

For a few moments the only sound from the screen was the mechanical rhythm of the pumps starting up. The yellow hoses swelled, the carpet of hoses plumped into a mattress. The windows were dark and I briefly hoped that the faces I had seen there had existed only in my imagination.

Mother, what is the most valuable thing in the museum? I asked
her once.

Life, she said loudly. *Life*, and a woman looked out from under
a layer of cardboard, longing for ours.

Those staring faces appeared again now, marked not by hatred
but by despair. They pressed up against the windows, mouths
stretched into dark caverns. A woman held up a baby; another
dragged her away, then beat at the window with weakened
hands. Hundreds of them, thousands, hammering at the windows, kicking at the doors. Lifting their children to the glass,
hoping that someone, somewhere, might see them and care.
Desperate hands clawing at the inside of their giant sarcophagi.
There were no numbers. There were no names. The museum, the
announcer told us, was empty, and yet when she drew breath, we
heard distant screaming. The scrawled notice at the window—
Mums 4 Community—fell away.

I thought of everyone I had ever met. The men and women
who staffed the re-registration points. The people hiding in the
museum. The waitress who, back when there were still restaurants, had brought me a plate of food, unable to hide the jeal-
ousy and hunger in her eyes. A man whose coat was now missing
a button, and the woman who had sheltered with him. Commander Marius, who did not believe in suicide. I knew people
now; I knew what it meant to look forward to seeing someone, to
plan, to be glad that, when the sun rose, they would be there still.
And I knew that, although the museum would have been dirty
and crowded and full of fear, there would have been friendship
there too, and care. And that through the empty display cases,
a girl might have met a pair of eyes that made her heart beat
faster, and that even in the squalor and deprivation, a mother
would have lived and breathed for her child. Tom put his hand
on mine, and I took it, shaking.

They would all have died one day. But not like that.

Life, my mother said. *Life*.

The museum windows emptied, the last reaching hands sinking below the sills. The troops donned gas masks. They ripped away the sealing tape and stood with their guns as the main doors were opened. *Run*, I pleaded as seven hollow figures staggered through the doors, fragile and dazed. *Run*. But they collapsed before the troops had had time to aim their weapons. No one else came out, and soon, the troops entered in groups. They wrapped the first bodies in sheets and carried them out on stretchers. But after the first half an hour, the bodies were just slung into handcarts and wheeled into the backs of the waiting vans. Body after body. The British Museum emptied of its treasure. Reclaimed for the nation, the announcer said triumphantly. No identity cards, no casualties.

A woman with long dark hair began to cry first. "It could have been me," she said between sobs. I knew that my own dreams would be haunted by the thought of those people, whose eyes I had once felt burning into me as my mother explained what I was looking at.

Look carefully, darling. We can tell what these people thought about life by looking at how they treated their dead.

And what they think about death by the way that they treat their living.

The gong rang for dinner, but nobody moved.

"They've gassed the British Museum," Tom said, his voice a stunned monotone. Our hands were still woven together; bones and heat. "They ran pipes into it, and they've carried out hundreds of bodies."

"Thousands."

"There were faces at the windows..."

"They were trying to break out..."

"We have to go back," I said, and I felt my mother's arms around my shoulders, squeezing me tight as she did when I had given the right answer. I looked for my father, expecting to see his face stunned and overwhelmed, like those around him, but his face was fixed and stern. I spoke again, more loudly this time. "We have to go back," I said. Tom let go of my hand and I stood up. I waited for everyone else to jump up and join their voices to mine. It was our departure all over again, when throwing my card to the crowd on the quay had been the only thing to do.

"Turn the ship around," I told my father. "We need to be in London. We need to help. We've got to stop them before they gas the National Gallery too, and St Paul's, and . . ." Beside me, a pair of green eyes moved gently left to right as their owner shook his head and I shrank from him in disbelief. My hand was still warm where he had held it.

My father stood, and the people were silent. He looked around the ballroom. Savoury smells floated in from the dining room. The gong rang again. Still no one moved. Only the occasional lowering of a head here, eyes closed in pain there, said that these people were alive. I hated myself for thinking about food amidst such horror. But I could not stop the growling of my stomach, and wondered how long the horror was going to keep us all in the ballroom. We had witnessed a terrible thing. We knew what we had to do. We would eat, and we would go back.

My father looked at me.

"What good has it done you, to watch this?" he asked me.

"It's shown us what to do next," I said eagerly, watching for his approval and pride, certain that, somewhere, my mother was listening. "We must go, now. There are people sheltering in all the public buildings. Dr Spencer can treat them, and we can open our stores and give them food. And clothes." I thought of my orange dress and of the piles of clean clothes in my cabin. I did not need so many. "If they were stronger, they'd be able to do something. Resist the troops. I don't know." I searched the room for help. But no one would meet my eyes. My father remained unmoved.

"What good has it done you, to watch this?" he asked the ballroom as a whole.

The only sound was the clinking of plates in the dining room, and concerned voices wondering whether the gong had been heard.

"Are you surprised?" he asked, and his voice was deeper, his tone more certain than I had ever heard it. "Have we not seen it before, again and again? The consequences of criminal decisions squeezed downwards until the ones at the bottom pay the price?"

He looked around the ballroom. "I ask you again, what good has this bulletin done you?"

Helen stood up, her dark hair blending into the shadows. "Michael," she said, and I winced, because she was looking at him as though he was the only person in the world, and I still wanted him for myself.

"Yes, Helen?"

"While the bulletins are there, I must watch them. I might see Simon."

Across the ballroom, heads nodded in agreement and names were muttered. Tola. Paul. Grace. Nisha. Salvator. Mark. A gentle litany, murmured for the lost.

"Where's Gabriel?" my father asked Helen.

"I didn't bring him, Michael. He's still so young. He's helping Emily in the dining room, with the other children."

"In the dining room? Where your dinner is, even now, getting cold, while you weep here for something you cannot change?"

Helen looked at her feet.

"I did not bring you on board the ship for a ringside seat at the end of the world. I brought you that you might have life, and have it in abundance. We've left all that behind—the state murders, the mourning, the misery." Frustration broke through his voice. "I brought you here to be happy." He swallowed, and pulled himself up tall. "The past is over," he declared. "There is nothing now except what is here, on the ship, with us. We are the world. We are the entire universe. The old world is turning in on itself. We are no longer a part of it. In a few short weeks, they will have fallen apart. Will we fall with them?"

"I'm not watching another bulletin," someone said, and agreement spread through the room like a tide.

"No more bulletins!" came the cry. "No more news."

"No," I shouted over the cries of agreement. "We need to know what's happening." I thought of all the bulletins I'd ignored in London, back when I had been free to watch as many as I liked. Could I have changed things then? Is that what my mother had been waiting for?

"I don't want the bulletins," Helen said, turning on me. "While they're there, I'll watch them. Michael's right. We can't help those people."

"But we have to try," I cried, looking around the room, but it was too late. They had made up their minds.

"Lalla," my father said softly. "If we go back, we'll never reach our destination. Everything on this ship is necessary to get us there, and to support us when we arrive. Trust me." There was silence now.

"But people in London are going to be gassed. Or drowned. Or shot."

"So you want to return so that you can be gassed, or drowned, or shot? How is that going to help them? Or anyone?"

One of the engineers shouted out, "We're helping them by not being there." There was a murmur of agreement.

Then Tom stood up. He looked around and turned red, and then he coughed. For a moment I thought he was going to tell them all that I was right, and insist we should go back. I remembered standing on the deck rail with him as we threw our cards, and I clasped my hands together.

He said, "I think we should take the mast down."

"What?" I stood up too and looked around, waiting for the people to react. My father looked from Tom to me, from me to Tom, and said nothing.

"The thing is," Tom said, "if we don't want to see the bulletins, what's the point in having the mast?"

"So soon?" my father said. To anyone who didn't know him, his expression would have looked uncertain. But I knew that look. It was the look he used to give my mother and me when he had made up his mind about something and was waiting for us to catch up. And I knew, as surely as if it had already happened, that he would stand still and say nothing, and that the people would fall over themselves to do what he had wanted them to do all along.

"The bulletins rule my life," Patience said. "I wait all day for the next one, and when it comes, it is the same as the last, and the last, and the last. Tola will not come to me on a bulletin."

Tom turned to me. "If we could help those people, it would be different."

"But we can."

"No, we can't."

"They're already dead."

I couldn't keep track of who was speaking. Voices tripped over one another, and they were all saying the same thing. *Get rid of it. What good is it to us now? We don't want the mast where we're going.*

"Destroy the mast," they cried. "Destroy the connection."

And they did. My father sent the engineers off, and their dinners went cold as they untangled the wires that connected the mast to the ship. After our meat pie and vegetable bake we left our places to watch them drag it down to the small deck. Tom had not come to sit beside me, but I saw him cheering with the rest, standing with a group, clapping each other on the back. The engineers heaved the mast into the sea after my mother. It sank immediately, the water closing over it as though it had never existed.

I watched my father's face as the mast went down. His hand was on Tom's shoulder, and for the first time, I wondered how he had known to stock the ship with my mother's funeral flowers.

EIGHT

We remember our missing ❀ *the stores*
❀ *an apple*

When we came back from sinking the mast, everyone helped each other to pudding, hot from the kitchen. I put the first fork-ful into my mouth mechanically, but I was no longer hungry. I could see Tom, far away on the other side of the dining room, accepting the praise of his neighbours. He used his arms to mime the falling of the mast, and they laughed. The whole room pulsed with energy as though a great weight had been lifted from it. The woman to my right was talking energetically about what she was going to do with the extra time she would have spent watching the bulletin. The air was bright. But to me it felt brittle, as though the laughter was coming from people's throats rather than their hearts. Tom was talking away as though he had never held my hand, and I pushed my plate away.

"Is your meal not to your liking?" the man with the pickled walnut skin asked politely, but I didn't know how to answer him. He glanced at my father and back at my plate, then quickly swapped my full plate for his empty one and dispatched the crumble and custard efficiently into his own system.

"Are you hungry?" I asked, taken aback more by the appro-priation of my plate than by his appetite.

"No," he said quickly, "no, my dear. Not hungry. How could I be?" My father was standing now, waiting for everyone to notice and fall silent so that he could speak. "But Michael will not like to look out and see that his provision is not being enjoyed. Not tonight. Tonight of all nights. Tonight we have done a great thing."

"A great thing?" I queried, but at that moment my father drew breath, leaving my words ringing round the dining room like lost children.

"I am proud of you," my father said without preamble. "Your actions tonight have proved your worth. Had you not taken the decision you did, you would not be the people I thought you were. You would not be the people I brought onto the ship. Tonight, we say goodbye to the dead and the dying, and then we live. Live!"

I looked around the ballroom, expecting a cheer, but saw only thoughtful faces gazing at my father. He lifted his water glass.

"I offer myself as a father to your children, as a brother where a brother is needed, and a companion to anyone who has been left alone. I drink to the people we would have given our lives to find and I thank them for the love they bore you. And I bid them farewell."

Across the dining room, Helen stood up. She, too, held up her glass, and in a voice that was quiet yet firm, said, "I drink to Simon, my husband, who left to claim a plot in the Land Allocation Act and never came back. Gabriel will find a new father in you, Michael."

Then Patience. "I drink to Tola, my daughter, lost in the burning lands. May she find me here."

One by one, the people stood.

"To my child Sanjeev, gone without trace in the drowning of Bangladesh. May he, too, find a new father."

"To my grandparents, who ran to escape the second pandemic."

"Tripp, my friend, arrested under the Nazareth Act."

And the list continued. The faces the people had searched for in the bulletins were all given names. The sun set; Emily and her team quietly cleared the plates and the tables. Sounds of crockery being cleaned underscored the recitation.

"Mia, who missed her re-registration."

"Sam, my brother, made homeless by the Possession of Property Act."

"My twin Gill, who went to trade our books."

The moon rose clear and full through the windows; the earth had moved out of her way. The children's eyes became heavy; the grown-ups held them, or settled them in on the carpet with pillows of cardigans and jumpers as the names rolled on.

"Lynde, who lost her card."

"Victor, who went to school."

"Rebecca, arrested in a market raid."

The people had already said goodbye to their dead; in the course of that long night, they let go of their missing. Some, like me, had nothing to say, but like everyone else, I stayed awake all night and listened to the story of the collapse of the world told through a listing of names. Only when the sun had risen again, and the children began to stir, rubbing their eyes and asking what was for breakfast, was the last name committed to the air and set free.

"Let this be the end of longing for what is gone," my father said. "Let our children grow up in safety, knowing that the people who are with them now will always be with them. Think about any mementoes you have brought on board. Do you need them? Or are they holding you back from becoming part of the free, loving family of the ship? Think about why you were invited on board. Think of why you chose to accept. Be worthy. And let us eat!"

Breakfast was curved bits of melting pastry and sweet dark jam. The baskets emptied as fast as they were put onto the table.

"It's a croissant," I heard Helen tell Gabriel. "They used to eat these in France."

"So what?" the little boy said, sticky with pastry flakes and jam, and my father smiled. "Are there any more?"

"Are there any more?" I echoed, wondering how long this bounty could continue. One day, surely, someone would ask the same question and the answer would be no. Where were we going? Would there be croissants there? My father stretched out a hand and stopped Emily in her path.

"Emily," he said, "Lalla wants to know whether there are any more."

"Any more?" Emily laughed. "Any more? Lalla, you could eat croissants every day for a year and there'd still be more. And more." My father's hand was still on her arm and she looked at it, her cheeks going slightly pink. "Would you like to come, Lalla, and see for yourself? Michael, would that be all right?"

"Of course. Unless she'd rather go and help Tom with the football?"

"Football?"

My father smiled. "I've moved Tom to new work. He's going to teach the children to play football. Up in the sports hall."

No wonder Tom had looked so happy. I shook my head, and Emily looked pleased. "I'll tidy away here, then we can go."

"You two go," my father said. "I'll manage here."

"But Father," Emily protested. "I can't let you do my work. I'll take Lalla later on."

"I have to be in the laundry later," I said, with an obscure feeling that I was losing a competition I did not know I had entered.

"There," said my father with amusement in his eyes. "Lalla

needs to be in the laundry later. You'd better go now." He turned Emily around slowly and pulled the ties of her canvas apron loose. As he lifted it over her head, I heard him speak softly into the back of her neck. "Emily. Take Lalla, and help her lose the last of her doubts and fears." I saw Emily's hands trembling as she folded the apron and surrendered it to him.

And so, as the people finished their croissants, and stood up from the tables and made their way out of the dining room, Emily and I went through the wooden doors into the white and steel realm of the kitchen. I looked back through the round window and saw my father holding Emily's apron, gesturing to the tables to be cleared. Emily stood beside me, her hands clasped under her chin.

"It must have been wonderful," she said.

"What?"

"To have lived with him all your life. Just think. There's never been a time when you didn't know him." I stared at her, but she was staring at him. Had I ever known him? He had brought home diamonds and guns and strangers, but he had found tinned peaches, too, and shoes, and had never, ever forgotten to tell my mother to keep me safe. Now he belonged to five hundred people I had never met, and their children were to call him Father.

Somebody tried to take Emily's apron; my father held it out of reach with mock warning in his eyes. The woman—Alice, her name was, an old lady with grey hair and bright eyes—looked disappointed. From nowhere, my father produced a second apron and bestowed it on her, and she took it, beaming, and began to clear the plates.

"Look, Lalla. Michael won't let anyone else touch my apron," Emily breathed.

All I'd seen was that he didn't touch a single dirty plate himself.

"He's *my* father," I burst out. "Mine. What does he want a load more children for? What did I do wrong?"

"I think it's more a question of what you did right," Emily said softly. "Why would he want more, unless he loved the one he had?" And with that she turned, and I followed her, through the kitchens and down, down, down to the stores.

When Emily said she would show me the stores, I'd expected to see something like my mother's larder in London, with its modest piles of tins and packets neatly arranged. But when Emily pushed open the storeroom doors, the comparison melted away. This was no larder, but a warehouse, as big and bigger than the atrium of the British Museum. The tins in my mother's larder could be comfortably lifted between a thumb and a finger. Here, the tins were bigger than my head. They were piled upon great pallets, their black lettering repeated over and over again, to the sides, up, down and back to the distant walls like an optical illusion or a game of mirrors. We walked and walked; the black lettering gave way to pictures of red tomatoes; we walked some more. I stepped backwards and craned my head to see to the top but, like the wind turbines, they were constructed on a scale that one person standing alone could not comprehend. My mother had had bags of dried rice the size of my hand; now we were passing sacks the size of a small child, stacked twenty high and twenty across in layered towers. Like tiny dolls in a giant's larder, Emily and I walked the stores.

She opened another door. Drums. Bigger than the oil drums the street people had used for their fires. "Cooking oil and fat pellets," she said. "Hermetically sealed, fresh until we need to use it." I started to calculate how many there were and gave up. Further on, I recognised the squat white buckets of dried egg, the taller ones that held milk powder, the blue paper sacks of sugar.

"But why is there so much?" I said, feeling more and more like the king who tried to turn back the tides. My feet were aching.

"We've not even finished one of these drums of oil yet, Lalla," Emily said. "Not one."

Another door, more sacks. My legs were tired and I wanted to sit down. More tins, more pallets, more drums, more sealed buckets. I felt dazed. We went down another steel staircase and I sat on the bottom step and rubbed my feet. I had asked a simple question; this heavy artillery of reply was bewildering and exhausting. But one thing I learned—that whatever else happened on the ship, we were unlikely to starve.

"This level is the same again," Emily said, and my mouth fell open. "Want to walk it?"

I shook my head but she had already set off. "Biscuits," she said, gesturing to the left and pointing forwards. "And on this side, cooking chocolate. Milk chocolate. White chocolate. Dark chocolate. Syrup. Crackers. And I can't remember what this is; I forgot to bring the catalogue. I think it's marshmallows. We haven't opened any yet. Do you remember marshmallows?"

I shook my head. "What's the catalogue?"

"It's like the manifest, but for the stores. There's a map in the front and it shows us where everything is. I'm beginning to find my way around now. Sometimes I feel like I'm going down into the depths of the mountains and bringing up gold. At the moment, Gerhard and I manage alone, but one day we'll need a whole team. Do you want to walk to the end? Or shall we go down now?

"Down?"

"Yes, down. All this is just the dry stuff. There's more."

At the foot of the stairs, beside a heavy white door, hung two padded bodysuits, with gloves and hats and face masks. There was a shining silver handle on either side, each one the length of my forearm. Emily felt in the pocket of her dress and produced two keys.

"Here," Emily said, holding one of the keys out to me. "We put on the suits, then unlock and turn the handles at the same time. That's to make sure no one goes into the freezers alone. Ready?" she asked, her eyes dancing. "The freezers are bigger than the storerooms upstairs."

I had had enough. My stomach was rumbling. I thought of the day we had sailed, of Commander Marius threatening to take the ship's stores and distribute them over the city. My father had said that there was no more food than we needed. And I had felt that our stored food wouldn't have made any difference to the city. But Emily said it took one sack of rice to make a meal for the ship. So just the sacks I had seen would have fed the museum dwellers for weeks, let alone the layers of sacks behind those, and the layers behind those, and the layers behind those. We had missed lunch and I had no idea where my father was. But to walk away from the chance to see what the freezers contained seemed to me to be insulting to the people who were still in London, de-registered and dying.

I pulled on one of the suits, and Emily pulled on the other, and as I turned my key and wrenched at the handle, I felt like the Antarctic explorers in my mother's old picture books, back in the days when there was an Antarctic. Lights blinked into shuddering life as Emily and I entered, and my breath rose in a mist. We were in a narrow corridor of wire crates. The ceiling was lower than in the warehouses, but still high enough to need ladders and pulley systems.

"It's smaller than I thought," I said when I realised I could see the back wall from where I was standing.

"Really?" said Emily. She opened another door, which led into another frozen room, and another, and another. I counted seven before I realised I could no longer feel my nose. "Michael partitioned the freezer stores," she explained. "It'll be more efficient when the fuel's completely gone and we start relying on the solar panels."

"So what's all this?"

"Concentrated orange juice, I think. And the next chamber is my favourite."

"Why? What's in it?"

"Look."

I looked, but the racks of wire crates didn't look any different to me.

"It's dough," Emily said. "Cookie dough. You get a great long sausage of dough, and you slice it and put the discs in the oven, and fifteen minutes later there are fresh cookies for everyone." The word sounded out of place, light and frivolous in a serious world. No one was going to die if they didn't get cookies. I couldn't imagine turning up in London and offering cookies to the homeless.

"I've never had a cookie," I said.

"Poor Lalla. They're lovely. Warm and sweet, and when you bite into them the melted chocolate chips ooze into your mouth."

"When did you have cookies?"

"Oh, decades ago. When I was much younger than you are now. And then the other night Father came down and got some dough and we tried it out in the kitchen with Gerhard and Tom and some of the others."

"Tom?" Why hadn't I been there? Why hadn't someone come to get me?

She nodded. "Oh, they were good. I'd forgotten how good. Oh, Lalla, you have so many treats in store for you. Cookies are just the start."

"What about apples?" I asked.

"Oh yes. Dried, tinned, even some frozen—and there are some biscuits upstairs with apple pieces in them."

"No," I said, "apples. Real apples. Like in books."

Emily looked at me as though I was speaking a foreign language, and for the first time I noticed that she had lines around her eyes. "Lalla, sweetheart," she said gently, "apples grew on trees, didn't they?" And for a moment we stared at each other, and the soil sickness seemed to creep right inside me. I thought of the stores I had already seen, their landscape of provision waiting to be mined, and of the ship sailing away from the barren country. And I remembered the film of the last polar bear, swimming and swimming in the empty ocean, in search of a mass of ice that had finally melted away. The freezer chamber felt smaller and smaller and I found myself looking around anxiously for the door.

"What about seeds?" I asked.

"Seeds?"

"Has my father brought seeds? Things we can plant?" I was walking around the chamber but the door seemed to have gone.

"Where would we plant seeds?" Emily asked, bewildered. "Not that way, Lalla, if you want to go back. That door goes to bagels and crumpets." She put her silver padded arm around my shoulders and led me back the way we had come. I didn't protest. I had seen enough, and could barely find the energy to toil after her, back through the freezer chambers and up, up, up through the vertiginous mountains of our future meals.

Emily gave me some biscuits, and I took them to my cabin. I lay on my bunk to eat them and ran my fingers over the scratches I was making to mark the days. Twenty-three days had passed—almost a month, not counting the time I had lost in mourning—and yet five hundred people had not even made a dent in the food stores. I closed my eyes, replaying the sleepless night of goodbyes. How many of those missing people might have been saved if this food had gone to the city instead of into the ship? Tins and sacks and drums rising in great walls, solid and substantial, nourishment for thousands upon thousands for weeks, days, even years.

We have left hunger behind, my father said, and I knew now that he was right. But even as I admired the extent of his preparations, I felt that they had altered the world's balance—that the ship was not so much an escape from hunger as the cause of it. I thought about the women who had been swept into the sea by the flailing gangplank of the departing ship. My father had killed those women, and nothing had been said. Had he also killed others by his actions? His concern for our safety? His longing to get away? I remembered something about a man who'd died the night before we sailed and wondered what had happened. Why had my mother been so reluctant to board? I fell into an uneasy sleep. Then I heard a voice and I froze in earnest.

"Have you ever eaten an apple?"

I could not see. I had slept for longer than I thought, and my cabin was dark. The voice was familiar, but I could not place it. It was musical and confident; it put the question urgently, as though much depended upon my answer. It was not my mother, who would not have needed to ask. It was not my father, who now only asked questions that contained their own answers— *Do we want to return to a life of terror? Who is there among us who does not care, above all, for his fellow man? What are we here for, if not to take humanity to its natural, unfettered destiny?* He would not have wasted a word on an apple, especially now that there was no such thing.

"Have you ever eaten an apple?" the voice asked again, and this time there were breaths snatched between some of the words, as though its owner had been running fast.

"Mother?" I called, but the dark night was silent.

I felt a sudden pain under my ribs, as though my lungs were being forced upwards, and I could not get my breath. I tried to raise myself from my bunk but could not move. I had never eaten an apple, never even seen or held one. *She's here,* I thought, and the words carried such conviction that I knew they were true. I lay clutching my sheet, not daring to move, telling myself that if I stayed completely still, time would not be able to move forwards, and I would not have to live without her anymore.

Mother, I shouted silently, *how could you leave me? What did you want? If the ship was what you wanted, why didn't you come on board when you were well, so that you could have looked after me still? At least in London, I had you. Now I have lost everything, everything. I don't even believe in the ship.*

Child, she said, *child. Good things are happening.* But I could not listen. I lay trapped by my numb and motionless body, and inside I screamed and yelled and stamped my feet until the walkways and the staircases and the metal hull were ringing with my grief and anger. *I do not want to be here. I did not ask for this. Who are you, that you forced me to come here? How dare you leave, when you have not told me who I am? Who am I, Mother? Who am I, and what am I here to do?*

I smelled the fresh, tingling scent of an apple I must have dreamed of in my childhood. Cool, sweet flesh burst over my tongue; my teeth ached at the pleasure of piercing its skin. It was pain, yes, but it was also wanting more, more, and overlying that was the feeling that I would never, never taste that sweetness outside of my dreams. I wanted my mother, and that was impossible, because she was dead flesh tucked around with silk, still floating somewhere beyond the horizon. I wondered if every sensation I would ever have now would be a yearning for something that did not and could not exist.

Have an apple, Lalla.

I ran to my cabin door and pulled it open. The walkway rang, a distant echo of a disappearing footstep. A door closed. I went to follow but there, at my feet, was an orb of bright, vivid green with shining skin. A small stick of a stalk. A springy brown leaf still attached.

An apple.

NINE

The beginnings of my museum ❀ goodnight
meeting ❀ dinosaurs

I brought the apple into my cabin and turned on the light. It sat in my palm, lighter than I had imagined, its green skin smooth, unblemished and cold to the touch. The little leaf bounced slightly when I touched it. I didn't want it to break off and so I put the apple down on my table. I went to my cupboard and took out the velvet jewellery box containing the button my father had given me when my mother died. How many objects make a museum? Eight million? Two? There, on my desk, were the beginnings of a new British Museum, a museum for the ship.

Safe on the ship, I looked at the button, nestled in its velvet box, and I saw how my parents' words to each other were translated in the air, as a beam of light bends when shone through clear water. My mother dismissed diamonds; my father heard ingratitude. My father refused to wait until the people of the museum had formed a plan, and my mother heard him condemn his fellow human beings to death. They were both right, and both wrong. When things fall apart, you cannot save everything. That was the button's story. The man wanted to save his companion from the cold. He wanted to love her, to keep her safe. And the little worn button couldn't cope with the pressure of his expectations. It cracked and fell away. It could have been ground to dust. Instead, it was caught on a tide that brought it to me.

An apple and a button.

Our museum, my mother had said. *Our museum*.

There it sat on the shelf of my cabin. A worn relic of the life before; a shining miracle of life on the ship. I put them together and the sight pleased me. I'd keep these things for someone. And when we got to wherever we were going, I'd build a home for them, and people would come and see them and ask questions and I'd say, *I don't have any answers. Only questions. That's how you learn.*

I was learning now, and the night of the last news bulletin taught me two things. It taught me that, if we were to turn around and go back to London, I would have to find people on the ship who agreed with me, and get them to help me persuade the rest. And it taught me that holding someone's hand can turn them into a stranger. I had not spoken to Tom since the night of the last bulletin. But I watched him move around the ship. I learned him until his face was as fixed in my mind as my mother's. I knew his voice, his eyes, the lines that ran from the edges of his nostrils to the corners of his mouth and deepened when he smiled. The children ran after him all the time, laughing as he demonstrated kicks and turns and bounced the football from knee to knee while they counted and cheered. I began to eat toast and chocolate spread, and to say no to coffee.

But just as real in my mind were the suffocated museum dwellers. Someone, I knew, would say, *Yes, Lalla, you are right. We must go back to London and do what we can to help.* It would be like the moment I threw my card away—just one person speaking the truth would bring everyone else along with them.

We could set the ship up as a clinic, a rescue centre. We could all stay on it, living our happy lives, and no one would have to leave. It was too late for the British Museum. But there were other public buildings. Maybe a community had been formed in one of them. Maybe another mother and another daughter took food from their own stocks and shared it when they visited. We could not have been the only ones in the whole of London. And there were other cities too; who knew what was happening in those? We could save those people.

It was so simple that it was bound to happen. I waited for a while, watching for the resolve I'd expressed at the last bulletin to take hold and spread. But the ship had been invaded by a blissful content. Patience was walking taller, laughing more, even singing as we folded the clean clothes. Doctor Spencer's walk had developed a bounce and the very lines on his face seemed to have smoothed. Helen played with Gabriel, and adults began to join the children in the sports hall as Tom's green eyes flashed among them, chasing his football. There was a small group who met each other in corners, looking over their shoulders, but whenever I approached them they separated and melted away until I convinced myself I had imagined their connection.

In desperation, I defied my father's request that we should not look back. At a goodnight meeting, I talked openly about the sealing of the museum, the pumping in of poisonous gas, the thousands of deaths that resulted. But my words simply energised the community on the ship. Far from depressing them, the horror of the museum gave them a common currency for conversation. It would start with two or more people trying to find a name by which to refer to the deaths. It couldn't be called genocide, because it was not a concerted attempt to eliminate a particular race or religion. Nor execution, which implied that the victims had done something wrong. Elimination gave the impression that something undesirable had been wiped out. Murder was too small, too domestic a word for the sheer scale of what had happened, although it found favour because it was unequivocal in its statement of crime. And as I waited for someone, anyone, to make the connection between the museum dwellers and ourselves, and to declare with me that we should return to land, I realised that they were enjoying themselves. That the people in the museum had become ciphers to the ship dwellers as much as they had ever been to the government on land, and that any doubts anyone may have had about leaving the land for the ship had vanished in the dying breaths of the dispossessed.

Once communication with the land was impossible, people began to live on the ship. Not just to eat and to sleep and to smile at each other, but to live. I was watching and listening, and I noticed the difference. Experiences stopped being calibrated in losses—homes, friends, a parent, a child—and began to be measured in gains: a book discovered, a painting understood, a film watched for the first time. I noticed, too, that my father's way of speaking, his turns of phrases, the words he used most often, became a kind of currency. There was nothing so obvious as a manual of approved words and phrases, or instructions on the screen. Nevertheless, when I woke one morning hoping that breakfast would be croissants and jam again, I didn't say a word. Meals meant wide-eyed gratitude for whatever my father had chosen to provide, and personal preferences were better left unspoken.

Similarly, the conversations in which life on the ship was overtly compared with life on land ceased. For example, I remembered the feeling I had when we came home from the museum having learned something new. There was something about having avoided danger, about having escaped the attentions of the wild people gathered on the streets, about having survived the journey and brought home our precious nugget of knowledge, that had made my heart race and my eyes shine. Now that the knowledge was there, a short deck stroll away, behind an unlocked door, it did not carry the same thrill. But I never said so out loud.

I could not help wondering how many of the books I was reading, how many of the works of art I looked at, would have been created in a life of such pleasant and easy luxury. Here on the ship, the button I had given my mother truly was nothing more than a button. On the ship, Jane Eyre would not have had to escape her evil aunt and cruel cousins by going to a terrible school, or have gone to work in a strange country house, because there would have been no cruelty and no need to escape. The Fossil sisters would never have had to learn to dance, because they would never have needed to earn a living. Macbeth would never have murdered Duncan, because on the ship, Macbeth would have had everything he wanted.

I did not want anyone to be cruel, but I wanted a reason to get up every morning.

I found myself saying less and thinking more, and the girl who had once stood on a deck rail and addressed a mob shrank away, leaving only a person unsure of what and who she was in a world she had not asked to join. And although I never lost my conviction that we should turn around, I stopped saying so, and once I had stopped saying so, I began to understand that it would never happen, and to think more closely about where we were, and where we might be going. My father and Patience had both told me to grow up. I wasn't sure what they meant, but I felt older.

"Why do we need the net?" Gabriel asked me, when he wanted to swim but the net had not been lowered. "There aren't any sea creatures left."

"Maybe not," I answered, "but if there are, you can bet they'll be hungry."

"But I'm bored," he said, and so I took him to the research room and we looked up sea creatures. We found out about sharks that could eat you with a single bite and jellyfish that could wrap you in their tentacles and poison you through your skin and fish that shot darts into your feet that could paralyse you in an instant. But the carbon the generations before us had burned had turned the water into acid, and the coral reefs were gone.

"Isn't it awful?" I said to Gabriel. "Isn't it awful that so many kinds of animals and things have died out?" And when he looked at me puzzled and I said, "Gone. Extinct. Like the dinosaurs," he looked at me anxiously.

"Dinosaurs aren't gone," he said.

"They are."

"No, they're not. I held a dinosaur bone once."

"You didn't."

"I did. I found this big bone in the road, and I took it to mum, and she said that it came from a dinosaur and I was never, ever to leave the holding centre in case the tyrannosaurus rex got me." His eyes took up his whole face.

"But that wasn't real," I said, "it was just a story to keep you safe," and I started to explain about fossilisation the way my mother had explained it to me, about rainwater seeping through the ground and dissolved minerals precipitating in the honeycomb of buried bones, but Gabriel ran off to play football with Tom. I sat alone and thought, and the more I thought, the more I felt that everything was balanced against everything else, and that no one had the right to sail over a dead sea and say, I am not responsible for this.

I began to listen in the goodnight meetings. I knew my mother would have done so, and as I emerged from my grief older, I found that people's stories were a way of connecting with her. Each evening, the people took it in turns to tell their stories, and when they'd finished, my father would tell them to consign their sadness to the past and never look back. It was a kind of ritual. Testimonies, my father called them. I heard my mother say, *Testimonies, or, How Michael Paul Saved My Life,* and could not help smiling, even when the tales were of loss and death and despair.

"I was sentenced to thirty years in prison," Finn said softly, the night he was asked. "Because of the Thursday Project."

"You were the Thursday Project?" someone said, incredulous. "The Thursday Project saved my life."

"It made so much sense," Finn said, the people drawing around him as the moon shone through the ballroom window. "This was decades ago, remember. Before the crash. Before the Dove. The big supermarket near where I lived threw away food every single night. There were people starving in doorways right outside, but the supermarket threw what hadn't sold into these big bins in the car park." I saw Emily nodding her head. "So every Thursday, I took that food from the bins to the people who needed it. And I organised other people to do the same in other places. When they started locking the bins, I started using bolt cutters."

"They gave you thirty years for that?"

"We started raiding farms as well," Finn said. "The industrial ones that supplied the supermarkets in the first place. They threw out all the vegetables that weren't right—crooked carrots, rusty potatoes, all that, they just threw them out. And Thursday Project volunteers used to break in and take all that stuff, and give it away. Because people were starving, weren't they, even then?"

My father said, "But it was already too late, wasn't it?"

Finn nodded. "The soil was already dead. All those chemicals, they were all that was making that stuff grow. Ironic, really.

Making stuff grow and killing off all the insects." He paused, then carried on. "Anyway. After a bit, the big supermarkets stopped using the bins. Army trucks came to take the food straight to landfill, and three of us got shot when we tried to break into one of the trucks. I was arrested."

"For theft?"

"No. For threatening national security and undermining the economy. That's why my sentence was so long."

"No," my father said. "Your sentence was long because you started something with power and passion and momentum. Because you were right, and there was no way the government could argue otherwise. But mostly, they gave you thirty years because you brought others with you. Your goodness made you a threat."

"Are you bitter?" Emily asked.

"I'd only done twenty years before the Prisoner Release Act," Finn grinned. "Prison was full of social criminals by then anyway. The real murderers were all on the outside, running gangs and joining the government troops and that. There wasn't any food left anyway. That's why they set us free, so they wouldn't have to feed us." He turned serious, and as his smile faded the lines on his face smoothed slightly. He looked a little younger, a little less certain. "It didn't feel like much at the time," he said, rubbing at his grey beard, now neatly trimmed. "It was only what anyone could have done."

"But they didn't, and you did," my father said. "And that is why you are here. Now, Finn, consign your story to the past. Move forwards with the ship. Don't look back."

"Don't look back," the people murmured in response. Finn opened his mouth as though he wanted to say something more, but my father held up his hand and Finn bowed his head.

"I won't look back," he said, and the goodnight meeting was

over. As I stood up, I looked at Tom, and he looked at me, and I remembered how he had held my hand as we watched the last bulletin, and I thought of the way the first star appeared over the horizon when the sun set, and that maybe, just maybe, happiness was something I would have to go out and find.

TEN

The people settle ❀ *I spend time in the cinema*
❀ *the boy with the green eyes again*

We could hear nothing of the land, and the land could know nothing of us. I began to wonder what was real and what I had made up, and whether, if the gassing of the museum existed only in my head, that meant it did not exist at all. People sat with their screens reading, or looking at the instructions for some forgotten activity. Alice, the old lady with grey hair and gentle eyes who helped out in the dining room, went to my father, and he disappeared and came back with a bag, which she opened with a kind of surprised and fascinated delight. Whenever I saw her after that she was sitting holding a wooden circle with fabric stretched over it, making patterns in coloured threads with a tiny silver needle, an admiring audience around her.

Tom ran his football games on the second deck and, when I wasn't in the laundry, I wandered up to the sports hall. If the door was ajar, I watched him with the children, teaching, playing, comforting them when they fell over and then giving them water that they gulped down, red from exercise and laughter. I saw him with my father, too, the two of them talking earnestly as they walked along the deck. *You'll make friends on the ship,* my mother had said. And I had—but Tom had thrown the mast into the sea and turned his back on London. My mother had taught me all about fossilisation, but she had never taught me how to disagree with someone who was wrong, and now I was here, and she was not, and when I tried to think of something to say to Tom, I felt myself crumble with missing her.

I spent a lot of time in the cinema. I could hide there; it was dark and you didn't have to talk to anyone. And I loved the films. In them, monsters terrorised ordinary people, eating them, attacking them, driving them to live in underground caves or remote mountains. I found the noises satisfying; I liked the violence, which seemed to answer something in me I had not known was there. I liked the way my heart and lungs seemed to suspend themselves as a head was torn off here, a body torn apart there. In the cinema, and on my screen, I worked my way through the listings for Horror, for Disaster, for Apocalypse, film by film, and counted the forms the monster came in. There were Gabriel's dinosaurs, and men who had been turned evil by power, and aliens from other planets set to take over the world. There were diseases, and people coming back from the dead. There were walking plants and creatures that could change to look exactly like things that were not evil, so that they could win the trust of the innocent masses. There were asteroids about to crash into the earth. But always, always, there were many, many people who died, and a handful who survived. And one day I realised why I was watching these films.

The museum dead were the masses and we were the survivors on whom the future of the world depended.

Perhaps it was because I had so little else happening in my life, or because I had so little control, or because I didn't fully understand what was going on, but I began to love them, watching my favourites over and over again alone on the screen—the portal—my father had given me. They made sense; they gave me a context in which to understand what was going on and permission to stop worrying. The more I watched, the more I felt that

the films were what was real, and that the day-to-day ship life of
meals and smiles and clean water was nothing more than a story.
After all the trials and the threats and the deaths, someone wise
and elderly, one who had been sagely watching events unfold,
would eventually sacrifice himself to save the young hero, who
himself would have already tried to sacrifice himself for the
young heroine, and they alone would survive, ready to replenish
the world. And the earlier in the film you met the character, the
more certain they were to survive.

I began to look at the people of the ship differently. When
Godzilla rose from the sea, or the evil ruler of the Galactic
Empire attacked, I thought of the black-clothed troops, the
screens, the re-registrations. We were the good people who had
escaped from the bad people. It was a comforting way of looking
at things. *Don't look back,* my father told us at every goodnight
meeting, and with the films to think about, I did not have to.
I could think quietly and place myself in the framework of the
story. I had been part of the ship from the very beginning. And
I was young. So whatever threat came to us on the ship, I would
survive. Finn would be eaten, because he was old. Emily would
be eaten, because she was happy. Gabriel would either be eaten to
show the ruthlessness of the beast, or left behind for me to adopt
and bring up as my own, but either way, Helen would be eaten,
because otherwise no one would cry and Gabriel would never
have to grow up. I had a context for my mother's death, too. She
was the prologue victim, the one in the opening scenes who died
mysteriously in order to show that there was a threat, before anyone had understood that there was a threat at all.

And my father. Strong, valiant, truly good, my father would
rush in during the final moments, when the young man was
about to throw himself into the beast's jaws in order to save me,
and use his knowledge and power to defeat the beast, rescue the
young man and die nobly in the process. And the young man

and I would always remember him, perhaps with a giant photograph on our wedding day, or his wedding ring, pressed at the last moment into the young man's hand as he whispered, *Look after her.*

And if I was the young woman, I knew that Tom was the young man. The films, the swimming, Alice and her embroidery, came further and further forward in my mind, and the question of our responsibilities receded. I ate my dried eggs scrambled and my tinned apples baked in pies without thinking where they had come from, never doubting that they would be replaced. I trusted that we'd get where we were going and stopped asking where that was. I stopped dreaming about the gassed thousands in the museum; my lovely apple was more real, still shining greenly on the shelf in my cabin. And as I made more and more sense of the ship, and of my place in it, so my courage grew, and it made less and less sense to avoid Tom.

And so, one day, when the cinema had filled me with pink mist and kissing and brave rescues and a sense that the ship was, after all, a right and proper place in which I had a home, I went up to the sports hall while the football was going on, and I waited, my heart pounding. The outer doors stood wide open but the inner ones were shut. I heard people running and laughing; I heard Tom's voice raised above the others, shouting instructions, and I heard a long whistle blast that meant the game was over. Then the inner door slid open and out they came—adults, which surprised me. I hadn't realised that the grownups were learning too. Finn and Luke and Gabriel, Helen, Jamila who had lost her home in the Indian floods, Ingrid who had lost hers in the Dutch ones. They all looked at me and smiled as they passed, and I felt that they knew something I did not, and that they had known it for a long time, and that they would be glad to see me learn it too. My father passed at that moment, flushed with victory.

"Come for the football?" he said, raising his eyebrows. He kissed me, and although I smiled for him, I waited until he'd gone before I went to the door. It wasn't his kisses I wanted anymore. I stood and watched Tom stacking coloured cones and carrying them to a cupboard. *Hello*, I said in my head, and the very thought of speaking made me blush. What could I say? *You shouldn't have thrown away the mast, but I wanted to be your friend.* And yet I wanted to talk to him. *What's the worst-case scenario?* my mother used to say when I wanted to go out on my own, or walk through the park. In those days, the worst-case scenario was being attacked, killed, catching a fatal disease, and ending up dead. It was her way of saying no. Now, the worst that could happen would be that he laughed at me, or ran away, or never spoke to me again, and suddenly these possibilities seemed like a death in themselves. I turned to leave, but my hard-soled red shoes clicked on the walkway and he looked up. And there it was: hope and apprehension and joy, all shining through those green eyes as he saw me, and I knew that I was welcome.

"Lalla," he said, dropping the cones and running towards me. "I knew you'd come. I knew you would."

And something about his certainty made me almost wish I hadn't. Almost, but not quite.

"You could have come to find me," I said.

"You kept running away," he replied, and his face was so close to mine that I felt his breath on my nose, and I saw that when he smiled, his left eye creased up more than his right eye. And suddenly, I stopped wanting to turn the ship around. The tips of his ears went red and little fires started under my skin all over me. "And I did try," he said. The fabric of his shirt brushed the hairs on my arms, and they stood up as I shivered. "I brought you the apple."

"You gave me the apple?" I asked. "That was you? Why?"

"I wanted to give you something."

"So why did you just leave it by the door? Why didn't you give it to me yourself?"

"I didn't know what to say. I only knew what I felt."

We stood staring at each other and my heart started to beat more loudly. "Would you like to come to the cinema with me?" I asked at last, and my voice was far too loud in the echoing space. He would laugh at me now, I knew it, and I wished I hadn't come.

But he didn't laugh. "I've just got to tidy up here," he said.

"I'll help."

"You don't have to."

But it didn't take much to tidy up. A few black and white balls put into a cupboard, the stacked-up coloured cones put with them and it was done. I couldn't help contrasting it with the work of the laundry; I had ironed seventy-five sheets that day and my arms were still aching. I told myself that this was why I was trembling when he went to the doors; I imagined him shutting them and leaving the ship outside so he could kiss me, here, in the hall where he played his games. But he went out. He doesn't want to kiss me, I thought, blood rushing to my face in shame.

He beckoned me out onto the deck, then slid the inner door shut behind us, and pressed a button in the wall. The main doors began to close. I had not expected them to be so thick, or to move so slowly. "They're hermetically sealed," Tom explained, watching my face. "They have to be left open when we're playing."

"Why?"

"So that we get enough air. You use more oxygen when you're exercising. If these doors were shut we'd all suffocate inside."

We walked together down the stairs to the main deck. Where had he found an apple? Were there more?

It had been my father's suggestion that the people of the ship should watch films together at the cinema instead of alone on our screens, and so Tom and I were not alone when we settled down on the velvet seats. But I didn't see who the others were. Everything I had learned at the cinema seemed to be concentrated on Tom's hand, his fingers curled softly around the armrest between us. Would he take mine? Was I going mad, to think that he might like me? That he went to sleep thinking of our fingers touching at the bulletin? There were thirty-seven marks on my cabin wall. Thirty-seven wasted days.

He drew breath, then leaned close to me and said quietly, "Lalla, I remember the first day I saw you, hiding behind the door of your father's house when I came for interview. When Michael was talking to me, all I could think of was you and the fact that, if he chose me, I would get to see you every day for the rest of my life."

I looked at my hand, now held between both of his, and tried to remember to breathe. His words were hot against my ear. I turned and pressed my lips to his, and felt myself get smaller and smaller at the centre of the picture, as the camera pulled away and our kiss became the centre of the cinema, the ship, the sea itself. And then, with our hands locked tightly together, I think we watched a film. I don't remember. All I remember is my hand in his, the warmth of his skin, the feeling of flesh against flesh and the thought that here, surely, I had found whatever it was I'd been looking for.

"Sit with me at dinner?" he said. I nodded, disappointed. Not because he'd asked me to sit with him—where else would I want to sit, now? But I had sat at dinner a thousand times. My heart was out of control, my body and my blood crying out for more—I did not know what of, but I knew I would not find it in Gerhard's cooking, in the neat place settings of Emily's dining room, in my father's after-dinner speeches.

"What's the matter?" Tom asked.

"I don't know," I said, on the verge of tears. The cinema had emptied. He lifted his hand to my face and stroked his finger-tips along my cheekbone, and although I felt his touch there, it was my palms that burned, my diaphragm that suddenly melted away so that my insides seemed to shift. It was impossible that anyone else had ever felt this way—it was so new, so unexpected. So absolute. It felt like my assertion of my self in this world of my father's creation.

"Do you know?" I managed to whisper, although my breath was coming short, "do you know where we're going?"

He bent his head to hear me; he touched his lips to where his fingers had been, then breathed, "I think we've arrived."

ELEVEN

———

*I want to go back ❀ the fourth deck and what I
found there ❀ Tom and the skylight*

We had not arrived at any geographical place—there was no
quay, no harbour to receive us. But I had certainly arrived somewhere new. I sat with Tom at breakfast; I met him at lunch, and
we always sat together for dinner. I moved away from my father's
table, and people arrived earlier and earlier every day in an effort
to be the one who took my old seat next to him. We both had
our work, but I could usually plan my route through the ship
with the clean laundry so that I saw him in the sports hall at
least once during the day. He was patient with the children and
the grown-ups who were only just learning. But with those who
had played before, he was challenging, tough, setting them ever
harder goals until they all stopped, panting, with their hands
on their knees and their sweat dripping onto the sports hall
floor. They looked up at each other, grinning, and I was envi-
ous of their connection. After dinner, and before the goodnight
meetings, we went to the cinema, or walked on the deck, and
although I hadn't exactly forgotten about the people we had left
behind, they became less and less important. When Tom held
my hand, I didn't want to say anything or do anything that
might make him let go.

I could have learned football with him, but the sports hall was his territory, just as the laundry was mine. If he had come to help me fold sheets, the sheets would never have been folded. And if we'd been together in the sports hall, the football would have been left rolling around like tumbleweed. We needed to be in the same space, because when we weren't, there was a cold gap. But when we were, everything was complete, and the laundry and the football weren't important. There were thirty-eight, thirty-nine, forty marks on the wall in my cabin. Time was stretching in our minds, whole lifetimes passing in single moments. An age. A few weeks. Forty days. What did it matter anymore? We sat quietly in the goodnight meetings, and he stroked the back of my hand with his thumb. I was no longer alone; I had a friend, a friend who would listen. A friend the world felt cold without.

"Don't you think," I would say sometimes, "don't you think we should go back?"

And he would say, "I'll come with you, wherever you want to go."

And the thought that I had an ally made it harder and harder to remember why I wanted to go. I knew I was right, and yet when I tried to explain, the reason bobbed away, like the old days with my mother, when we tried to catch the soap in the bath. And instead of trying to catch it, I would ask again, "Would you really come with me?" and he would say, "Of course. If it's honestly what you want."

But my thoughts about London were changing. Whereas before, I saw the homeless gratefully receiving the food we gave out, now I remembered the mob on the quay and thought of what would have happened to us if we had not given them our cards. I had been so sure; now I had an uneasy feeling I could not explain, like trying to sleep on my bunk when the sea was rough. I had a friend. Was London what I really wanted now?

"You're kind," Tom said. "But don't forget to be kind to the people here, too. What would little Gabriel do back in London?"

"I don't know," I said, and it was a relief to let go of something so heavy, that I had been carrying all alone. "It's not so much that I want to go. But I think we should."

"Why don't you talk to Michael?"

"I barely see him. He keeps saying that the ship was created for me, but if that's true, why won't he turn it around when I want to?" I was starting to cry. "He's all I've got left and I don't even see him anymore."

Tom took my hand and said, "He loves you, Lalla, more than anything in the world. Just look around you, and you'll see how much. And don't forget that you've got me." Tom hesitated, then added, "Your mother, too."

I pulled my sleeve over my hand and wiped my eyes. "I know she's gone," I said. "But I can't feel her anymore. I don't know what she would say. What she would want me to do. It's like I walk the ship, and she's nowhere. I had one single thing of hers—a dress—and it's gone. Sometimes I close my eyes and I can't even remember what she looked like."

He held my hand in silence for a moment, then said, "Can I show you something? Something that might help?"

"Where?"

"Follow me."

I had not been up the infirmary staircase since my mother died. It was near my cabin and I'd never been aware of anyone using it. It was a silent place, half-forgotten, the way we do forget things we no longer need. But when Tom and I got there, we saw Helen with Gabriel, tucked behind the staircase as though they were trying to hide. Tom squeezed my hand and we stepped as silently as we could.

They were busy with something; at least, Helen was. She was holding Gabriel on her lap and he was fidgeting. In front of them, they had a thick book. Not a screen, but a book, like the manifest, only smaller. When they turned the pages, I could see that they were stiff and thick. There were photographs taped to them, photographs of a man.

"Can you see his eyes?" Helen was saying. "They're just like yours. Look." She held up a little mirror, and Gabriel squinted into it. Helen held him more tightly. "He loved us. He helped me to make you, and he was there when you were born."

"I've seen them before," Gabriel said, wriggling away. "Can't we go swimming? You said Michael was my father now. You said Daniel could be my brother. I want Daniel to be my brother."

My shoe caught the walkway. Helen jumped to her feet and put the book behind her back. As I got closer, I saw that she was trembling. She did not say hello.

"What are you doing?" I asked.

"We're looking at my father."

Helen bit her lip and closed her eyes, and Gabriel looked at her with a concerned expression. "Have I been naughty?" he asked. "Am I in trouble?"

"Oh, no, darling," Helen said, trying to kiss him. "No. Not you. Never you." But Gabriel shrank from her, and Tom knelt down and put his hands on Gabriel's shoulders.

"Want to play football later?" he asked. Gabriel nodded, his furrowed little face smooth again. "Remember," Tom continued, "remember that Michael gave you the football? Hey? And the sports hall. And the food that gives us the energy to play. All right?" Gabriel nodded, and Tom ruffled his hair. Helen tucked the book into the gap between the staircase and the wall. I wondered how long she had been keeping it there.

"Why don't you keep it in your cabin?" I asked. But even as I asked the question, I realised what the answer was. I was in and out of the cabins all the time, delivering the laundry. She didn't trust me.

"What was that all about?" I said as they left.

Tom stared after Helen. "She shouldn't be showing Gabriel

photographs. It's not on, and she knows it. Michael told us to let our missing go." I shrugged. I couldn't see the harm in a few old photographs, but if there wasn't any harm, why had Helen been hiding? And if Helen was hiding one thing, maybe she was hiding more. If I could get her to trust me, maybe she would tell me where we were going. If she knew. Then Tom said, "Race you, Lalla," and started running up the stairs.

"Where to?" I called after him.

"Fourth deck," he shouted. He ran, and I ran and Gabriel and Helen and photographs and London, even the dead in the museum, fluttered away in my wake and the staircase rang like bells. Like wedding bells, from the time before.

He got there first; I was panting by the time I caught up.

"Look," he said, pushing open the door onto a dark corridor, lined with doors on either side. The corridor was illuminated with frosted glass circles shining white in the ceiling, shedding regular pools of soft light on the floor. I slipped my hand into his and he squeezed it, and together we stepped from pool of light to pool of light, looking at one another with wide eyes in the dark places in between. Then he put his hands on my shoulders, and I turned to him, and he bent down and kissed me.

My mother told me that all life was contained in the display cases of the British Museum. But now I realised that she had been wrong. What was happening to me now was not about cold stone and history. This was warm and glorious and alive. So alive. Every vital sign—blood flow, beating heart, breathing, sensation—was here, doubled because there were two of us, then trebled, quadrupled, because it felt so good. His breath was so hot, and came so fast. I pressed myself against him and lay my hands flat against his back, pulling him in closer. His body was firm beneath his shirt; I wanted to take the shirt from him and feel his skin, touch it all at once. This wasn't about tomorrow or yesterday. It was about now, this moment, this glorious moment of knowing that Tom liked me as much as I liked him, of my flesh against his.

And then he pulled away. "I'm sorry," he said. "I didn't mean—this isn't why I brought you here."

"But..." I began, then stopped. If he wanted to stop, I wasn't going to tell him that I didn't. I turned back to the staircase and smoothed my dress. My hair was pulled back into an elastic band; I took it out, wishing I had a hairbrush. I gathered it all back up and secured the band tightly, to prove I didn't care, and walked back the way we had come.

"Don't go," he said.

I didn't want to go, but I didn't want him to think I wanted to stay. I turned aside and pushed open one of the doors, and what I saw made me forget I was annoyed. The room was full of great rolls of carpet, propped against each other like the columns of the Parthenon just before the last pieces fell. Behind the next door was a room of tins of paint and varnish. Brushes. Sandpaper. Tools in boxes. Another room, larger this time, full of crockery—endless duplicates of the plates and dishes we used at every meal. I picked up a plate and held it up, white and whole, like a full moon. "What's all this for?" I asked.

Tom was following me. "It's amazing, isn't it?" he said. "This is what I wanted to show you. And there's more."

"More?"

He tugged at my elbow, but I was still holding the plate. "It's all white," I said.

"What?"

"The plates and everything. They're all white."

"What's the matter with that?" he asked. He had found a new supply of energy from somewhere and was striding towards the next door.

I stayed where I was. I was still staring at the white plate when he came back. "What are you doing?" he asked. "Come on."

I looked up at him. "Do any of the plates have pictures on them?"

"I don't think so. They're all the same. Isn't that the point? Does it matter?"

But it did matter. Here on the fourth deck, away from the activity of the galleries and the ballroom and the dining room and the laundry and the cinema, there was silence, and in the silence, my childhood came back to me. I looked at Tom, and he stopped fidgeting and looked back at me. "When I was little," I said into the stillness, "I had a small plate with a picture of lots of little rabbits picking red and yellow apples on it. I loved that plate. And then one day it broke. It must have had a crack we'd never noticed or something, because it just fell apart in my mother's hands. I was really upset. I wouldn't eat from any other plate. My parents were really worried." I remembered my mother and father arguing about it over my head. *I'll find another one, just the same,* my father declared. And my mother. *Don't be ridiculous, Michael. We've got plates. She's got to learn.*

"What happened?"

"I got hungry, I suppose. I don't remember. I just wish…"

"What?"

"I wish I'd known I was eating from that plate for the last time."

I looked at the storeroom, at the plates the same as all the other plates, the cups, the saucers, the bowls, all the same as each other. Gabriel would never stare at the details of a favourite plate, fascinated by tiny paws closed round an apple. Gabriel would never look at the coloured ribbons on the dresses, the many shades of green on the trees, and wonder whether rabbits really did wear clothes and how they cooked the pies with which the checked cloth in the foreground was spread. Our apple pies came ready-made. I wondered whether Helen had thought of this, and whether it would matter to her if I pointed it out.

Tom took my hand and led me into the next room. It was full of deck shoes, the entire population of the world reduced to twenty-three sizes. Fabric uppers, man-made soles, it said inside every single shoe. Most people were wearing them now. But I still clung to the shoes I had worn on land—dark red, hard leather, very scratched, with a bar across and a little silver buckle. I slipped sometimes on the walkways, and everyone could hear me coming, but I didn't want to let them go. Part of me felt that if I were to surrender my red leather shoes and start wearing the blue canvas deck shoes with the white soles and the blue stripe and fabric uppers and man-made soles, I would forget about my life on land entirely. I would forget my mother anxiously buckling the bar across my foot, making me stand straight and walk to and fro across the drawing room while she tried to tell whether they were rubbing my heels. And my father laughing and saying, *Anna, she's got shoes, and that puts her ahead of most of the population these days.*

Where did you get them from, Michael?

It doesn't matter. The point is that she's got them.

(To me) *Do they fit?* (To my father) *Where, Michael? Who wore them last?* (To me) *Do you like them?* (To my father) *Because if they used to belong to someone else, I want to know who, and exactly how you came to have them.*

I would wear them until they fell apart.

But Tom had dropped my hand and was already in the next room.

I followed him. My reverie was giving way to panic; there was too much here I did not understand. I pushed past him, into a room the size of the ballroom, with rails suspended from the ceiling, rows and rows of them, hung with clear plastic envelopes the length of a man, swollen with colours. Each one bore a name, marked on the plastic in heavy black letters. The first six were marked for Diana Aabri. She had dark eyes; I had never yet seen her smile. Then two for Solomon Asprey, the man who'd eaten my dinner when I could not. I wondered whether he had missed me at the dinner table once I'd started sitting with Tom. Five for Garth Britten, who sat on the bench to the left of the stairs down to the galley staring out to sea for so many hours of every day that other people simply never sat there, even when Garth himself was somewhere else. I pushed through to more distant rails. Here were eight for Roger Spencer, the doctor. People I saw every day, lined up in vacuum packs of clothes, arranged in alphabetical order.

Suddenly it struck me. My mother would be here. Was this why Tom had brought me here? I walked through the stiff, heavy packages, pushing them aside as I forced a path between the rows searching for her.

"Lalla," Tom called behind me. "Lalla?"

Here was Hiro Oka. Here was Harry Oz. Here was Lalage Paul, then Michael Paul, then Mercy Perkin. Frantically I went back on myself. There was no Anna Paul. Nothing stood between Harry and me, and for the first time since my mother's death, I felt the chill wind of complete exposure. Buffered on both sides by my parents, I had grown up immune from the cruelties of the alphabet. When we were required to present ourselves for biometric re-registration, to get new food purchase authorisations, or renew our permit to remain in the flat we owned, I would be sheltered between my mother before me and my father behind me. My mother would entrust my card to me for the few moments it took to present it to the officials, but she and my father were there all the while, anchoring me on either side, so my little foray to the tiny opening in the glassed-off window was nothing more than the slight stretching of an elastic band.

And now she was gone. Hiro Oka, Harry Oz, Lalage Paul, Michael Paul, Mercy Perkin. And that was all.

I sat on the hard floor and closed my eyes. The place smelled of new plastic, chemical and unyielding. Once, there must have been a package in my mother's name. At some point since her death, someone had taken it and put it...where? The ship was finite. There were only so many places it could be. But if it was finite, it was also vast, so vast that I could well spend my life searching for it. For them—for if there were eleven in my name and five in my father's, how many would there have been for my mother? *There are clothes, you know,* my father had said before the funeral. *If you wanted to wear something else.* And here they were. Clothes. Clothes for everyone, for a lifetime.

"Lalla." Tom was coming closer, pushing the packages aside.

What if my mother had not died? Would I have come to the fourth deck with Tom? Would I have kissed him? What if I had stayed downstairs? Would I feel so restless, so dissatisfied? I had never asked *what if?* before. My father had asked the *what ifs* for everyone, so that no one else would have to.

What if I am attacked when I go outside?

What if I become ill?

What if I have nothing to feed my child?

I had just taken, taken, taken. My questions had not been *what ifs* but simply *whats.*

What am I doing here?

What is my father?

What is going to happen to us all in the end?

I became methodical. I started at the beginning and I walked the rows. I looked at every name on every package. I thought she might have been filed out of order, that her clothes might have been moved rather than taken away. When the names ran out, the packages carried on; the remaining labels bore the names, not of people, but of ceremonies. Birth. Naming. Coming of age. Funeral. And at every turn, Tom pursued me, calling my name.

I reached the last rail, and when I found the wall behind the plastic packages, I saw twelve flat boxes, all identical, each bearing a small label printed with a black and white picture of a baby's cot.

And that was where Tom found me.

"You see?" he said, coming up behind me.

"See what?"

"All this. Everything on the fourth deck. This is just the start. This is what I wanted to show you."

"Why? Because you thought my mother would be here?"

Tom looked startled. "Your mother's dead, Lalla. Anna's dead. We gave her to the sea, remember?"

"But is that all? She's dead, and she vanishes without trace? Gone? Look," I said, pushing back through the clothes, "she should be here. It's all alphabetical. She should be just here."

"It's all right, Lalla," he said, putting his hands on my shoulders. He began to stroke my collarbones with his thumbs. "Everything we'll ever need is here. And we've got each other. Haven't we?"

Everything, he said. This was it. I thought of London, of the cracks in the walls, the yellowing paint in our flat, cement wearing away between the bricks, so that the bricks themselves could be prised out and taken away. Of rust, and buildings falling. Everywhere bearing the marks and scars of the passing of time. *That house had a balcony once, with plants in pots.* Or, *That was when we had the blue plates with white flowers, remember?* Or things so obvious that there was no point in speaking, such as the fact that the house on the corner would fall if people kept chiselling out the bricks and stealing them. Tom's hands were on my neck, his fingers tracing the contours of my chin, my lips, my cheekbones.

Here on the ship, yellowing paint would be covered with new paint. Rust would be sandpapered into oblivion. A plate broken? Here was the means to replace it—not only to replace it, but to create the impression that the breakage had never happened. I thought of Tom wiping the walls the day we'd met, and realised how blind I had been.

"Get me out of here," I said to Tom, my skin flaming trails where he'd touched me. I ran away from him, pushing past the fifteen million plastic bags to the corridor, looking for a way out. But there was only the corridor, with its round skylights and the storerooms leading from it. I walked its length, searching for ladders or hatches. I remembered how the ship had appeared to me on that first day, the day we came on board, looming over the quay like an old-fashioned wedding cake. Was I walking the top tier now? The small one. The one that people once put away in a box until their first child was born. And even as I was struck at the strangeness of the whole idea of baking an enormous cake and keeping bits of it, and of covering it in sugar and stuff that looked like embroidery, and wondering what that had to do with marrying someone, and what indeed marriage was and why, I suddenly knew that one of these rooms held a white dress and a plastic figurine of a man and a woman. I knew that, if I searched through all the boxes, I would find garlands of artificial flowers and bolts and bolts of white fabric; I'd find green silk leaves wired into long wreaths; I'd find dresses in the same colours as the little cakes we ate after dinner. Pink. Lemon yellow. Sky blue. Lilac.

I didn't bother to look. I didn't need to. I saw my father, his hands tight upon the ropes by which he drove his people. And at the ends of those ropes, I saw, not Emily and Patience and Gerhard and Helen and Daniel and Gabriel, but the things we had left in the broken world. Weddings and funerals and childbirth and books and music. Birthdays and dancing and football and graduations and qualifications. Because all these were milestones that belonged in the place behind us. Not only behind us in space, but behind us in time. My father had reached back, back, past the squatters in the British Museum, past the thefts from the display cases, past the oil drums on the streets and the

rats and the wild dogs and children and market raids, and pulled
things onto the ship from the life that had been his before the
crash. We were not creating, we were simply existing, building
lives upon the flotsam and jetsam of something that had gone.
We were not finding new ways to live. We were living in accor-
dance with some ideal of a former age, which we saw in films,
read of on our screens, but no longer knew or understood.

I pushed open door after door, door after door, and in every
room, there was nothing but boxes and smooth ceilings. No
trap doors, no ladders, no way up. The ship was a tin can, hermetically sealed to preserve us all. The corridor went on and on,
unravelling before me until I had indeed lost all sense of time.
Tom followed me, looking worried. His lips were moving but I
paid no attention to what he said. I needed to get out, not onto
the deck but out, right out, to where there was air and sky and
nothing surrounding me. My body was crying out against this
sterile safety. I was hungry for danger and dizziness. I wanted
mess and sensation; I bit my lip so hard I tasted blood.

I looked again at the fourth deck, so featureless that I felt
utterly lost. I knew that, if we did not go to dinner when the
gong rang, my father would come looking, and that, were we to
hide, he would find us. He would find us without effort, just as
Gerhard's practised hands automatically fell upon the very thing
he needed in the kitchen. My father had created this place. He
had conceived it, filled it, ordered it. He knew where everything
lay; he knew what everything was, and if I were to disappear
myself within his provisioning for the future, he would see what
had been disturbed, and where lay the irregularity of me in hiding. He would see it as surely as I would know if anyone had
interfered with the marks in my cabin, or with the things I had
collected for my museum.

"Let's go back downstairs now," Tom said nervously. "I just
wanted to show you, that's all. To stop you from worrying." I

flapped a hand at him to stop him talking and looked up at the sky-lights. The glass circles had shone white when we had arrived; now they were a yellow gold. This meant that the circles, which I had assumed were electric lights, were actually frosted windows. Where there were windows, there was access to the outside. I thought, if I can get up there, I could prise away a pane, crawl out, even climb up the outside of the ship to the top if I had to. The golden light meant that the sun was setting, and soon it would be dark.

I looked into Tom's anxious green eyes. "Pile up some boxes and take off one of those skylights," I said.

"But why?" I was already hauling boxes. "Lalla, there's no need for this. Michael wouldn't like it. Anyway, there's no time. Look, the light is almost gone. We'll miss dinner."

"I have to get out, now and now and now. I can't breathe."

"If you couldn't breathe, you would be dead."

"I am dead," I said. "We're all dead."

My breath came in short, shallow sobs and my head was spin-ning. I wondered how the wall had fallen, then realised I was lying on the floor. My lungs contracted; hot metal bars snapped around them and gripped so tightly that I gave up trying to draw in air. And then I felt a sting on my cheek, as sharp and painful as if someone had slapped me. My physical body registered its living presence in pain, and I heard my mother's voice. *Stop this at once, Lalage. If I had wanted drama, I would have gone to the theatre. You are perfectly alive. You are also about to faint. Do think things through.*

I shuffled to the wall and pressed my back against it, hard, so that the metal bars gave slightly and I could force air into my lungs. *And again, Lalage. And again.* The voice grew fainter, and was replaced by Tom's anxious fussing. "Are you all right, Lalla? Lalla?"

"I am not dead," I said, and the echoing of my voice down the corridor told me I had spoken out loud.

"No," said Tom, nodding eagerly. "No, you're not. Let's go down. I'll help you. We could walk on deck if you want air."

I stumbled to my feet; my lungs were released, and my mind began to clear. I went over to him and stood squarely in front of him. All the hand-holding and the heart-pounding and the watching him in the sports hall came together in the now. I reached for his hand, and he pulled me up, and I stood so close to him I could feel his breath on my cheek. And then I kissed him, and as I kissed him, he put his arms around me, and he ran his hands down my arms and over my back and I felt my blood rising to meet his hands wherever they touched me. "No," I said as he began to tug at my dress.

"But I thought…"

"Not here. Up there." I pointed up at the skylight. I could see screws holding it up. "Find a screwdriver."

"But Lalla…"

I started to climb onto the boxes I'd piled up. "Find a screwdriver or go to dinner, Tom." I looked down and saw concern mixed with the desire in his green eyes.

"What if you fall?" he said. But I was determined and excited and the danger was all part of it; if I fell off the boxes and hurt myself, I'd know I was alive. And if I got into the open and fell into the sea, maybe I'd find my mother there. I wanted to pull Tom through with me into the open air, and then I wanted to kiss him so hard that I could feel his teeth; I wanted him to crush the breath from my body. I wanted us to cast off all the provision my father had made and set each other alight under the unconstricting sky. I watched Tom, my father pulling him one way, me pulling him the other. The golden light made a circle around me. It would be the difference between learning something at the museum and learning it in the research room.

"You look like an angel," he said.

"I'm not an angel," I said grimly. And then, suddenly, he made up his mind. He pulled boxes together. He fetched two screw-drivers. He climbed up beside me. And together, balanced pre-cariously on our future lives, we took the twelve screws from the skylight and worked on its grey metal rim, pulling on it, using the screwdrivers as levers, until it surrendered with a screech and a crunch, showering us in plaster dust and debris.

"I can get through there," I said, coughing. "I'm sure I can." I reached through with my hands; he pushed me, grunting with effort, his hands on my bottom while I scrabbled for his shoul-ders with my feet. I pushed against him, hard, and as I pulled myself up to my waist and hung on my forearms, I heard a crash below me and Tom's voice crying out in surprise and then, with a final effort that tore my dress and scraped the skin from my knees, I was standing on the top of the world.

"Are you all right?" I called, but I didn't really care. I could not tear my eyes away from the last sliver of the setting sun, laying out a pathway of fire across the sea. And above and behind and all around me stretched the sky. I closed my eyes and reached my arms up as high as I could, standing on my toes and feeling my muscles cry out in celebration of their freedom. And then Tom's head appeared at my feet, covered in dust, a piece of ceiling stuck in his hair, and I laughed.

"The gong will have gone," he complained, and as he wrig-gled his awkward way through the skylight, fighting off debris and muttering about madness, he became mine. Not a boy with green eyes, but a friend, an intimate. Someone I could talk to, for whom I could be Lalla. Not my father's daughter, but a young woman all her own.

"Come here," I told him. I beat the dust from his thick blue shirt. I ran my fingers through his hair and threw the piece of ceiling towards the sunset. I pulled him towards me and pressed my lips against his, and then I pressed my body against him, feel-ing the buttons of his shirt marking circles on my chest and my stomach, and the flap of his shirt pocket pressing a line against my breast. And there was fire, spreading from my nipples to the palms of my hands, and when he stood back to take off his shirt, a cold wind spread goosebumps across my arms and my chest. "Lalla," he said, the gong and the ship forgotten, "Lalla." And he tried to put his hands under my dress, but the skirt was too long and he ended up tangled in crumpled cotton. I laughed, but he seemed annoyed, and so before he could change his mind, I pulled my dress over my head. When he undid his jeans, I could see that his hands were shaking. I unbuttoned his shirt, and he took it off and spread it out so that I could lie on it.

He lay on top of me, and all the breath was squeezed from my body, and he was pushing against me and whispering, "Does that hurt?" And it did, but it was pain I wanted, the pain of something opening and expanding and reaching up to the stars that were appearing overhead, and suddenly he cried out, his back arched, his body tensed. And then he simply lay, his body limp against mine, his head on my shoulder, and I thought, whatever it is, we have just done it, and wondered whether it would always hurt like that. Under his shirt, the top deck was cold metal, and it began to bite through the fabric as night fell. The hairs on my arms and legs stood up and I shivered, trying to make sense of what had just happened. Was this rebellion or just a way of catching pneumonia? I wondered if I was bleeding; certainly I was sore. What was I now? A girl? A woman? Tom was staring out, out over the dark sea; I put my hand on his arm and he came back from wherever his thoughts had taken him.

"I'm cold," I said, and he jumped up and pulled on his jeans, and then he wriggled through the skylight and came back with blankets. I put my dress back on, and he tucked one blanket around my shoulders and another around his, and we sat a little way apart from each other. All the diamonds the world had left had been ground like flour and spilt across the sky; if I reached up, I could write my name in them. I remembered searching for a blanket to cover my father once, and a button that had fallen from a coat.

"What do you think would happen if we stayed up here all night?" I asked.

I waited for him to say, *I don't think Michael would like it*, and braced myself to send him away. But he didn't. "We'd get hungry," he said.

"There'll be breakfast."

"I can wait till breakfast."

I moved closer to him, and we wrapped both the blankets around both of us. It was warmer that way. He stroked my hair, and I rested my head on his shoulder, and we fell asleep. As I drifted off, I heard Helen saying, "It's hardly subversion, is it?" But this was subversion. I had found a place of my own, a way to get to it, a way of being with someone way beyond my father's control. *There's a conversation we'll need to have when the time comes*, my mother had said the first time I bled, but the time had never come. Now I had grabbed it and dragged it to me. It was mine now. My time. I had found my freedom with a pair of green eyes. Perhaps it wouldn't always hurt—and oh, the wanting. The wanting had been sweet.

When we woke up, the sun was rising. It was rising in front of us, exactly where the path of fire had been the night before. We put the blankets back into their plastic wrapping, then squeezed through the skylight. We didn't replace all the screws, just six of them, enough to hold the skylight in place, and we put all the boxes back. I put the spare screws in the pocket of my dress, where once I had kept my card. There were only five; I could not find the last one.

"We'll find a ladder next time," Tom said. Only the dust on the floor and a little tiny crack in the glass of the skylight showed that we'd been there. I liked looking at that dust. The ship was

so clean. But dirt told stories, too. I liked that I could smell Tom
on my skin as we climbed back down to the main deck, and that
the smell was not of soap, but of sour milk and the warmth of
the iron.

We said goodbye by the infirmary stairs. And as I walked to
my cabin, I held the precious secret of my freedom inside myself.
Where there had been only me, now there was me and Tom.
And the sunrise showed that, wherever we were going, we were
on our way. We had provisions enough to last until we arrived,
and to give us a good start when we got there. Tom was happy. I
could be happy, too.

The spare screws were for my museum. I put them in the jewellery box with the button. The apple was there too, still shining
as brightly as the day Tom had left it for me. It showed no signs
of withering, and I was glad. We were on our way. My mother
was dead, but I was no longer travelling alone.

TWELVE

My secret ❀ *shell eggs* ❀ *the mystery of the missing sunset*

There is nothing like having a secret to make you see secrets in others. As I walked to the dining room—I was extremely hungry by this time—I saw people talking in corners, walking to breakfast tables together, or slipping away from them, or catching other people's eyes and then smiling and looking away, in a way I had never noticed before. I remembered Tom pushing himself inside me and caught my breath. A trickle of warm fluid oozed from me and dripped down the inside of my thigh. I could feel a new story traced all over my body; surely these people could see it? Did everyone have a secret? What other thoughts were going on in all these people around me? For a moment I felt almost sorry for my father, with all this subversion going on under his nose. But there he was, eating an omelette and smiling, and my pity was drowned out by elation when I met Tom's eyes across the dining room. I wondered what my father would say if he knew, and whether he was going to tell me off for missing dinner last night. But he just waved at me across the dining room. It was Emily who frowned, Emily who raised her eyebrows and pursed her lips.

But Emily I could ignore.

I took my omelette. Patience had told me that you could hold a shell egg comfortably in your hand, and I held my hand out, trying to imagine what an egg might have felt like sitting in my palm. Crack, you broke them and they flooded out. Crack. Had I broken Tom last night, or had he broken me? *You can't make an omelette without breaking eggs*, my father had said to my mother too many times for me to count. But the omelette in front of me had been made without breaking any eggs. How could it be otherwise, when there were no eggs left to break? The only eggs I'd ever known were dried. What was this place, and where were we going?

"Meet me on deck for sunset," Tom whispered as we left the dining room, and my cheeks flamed again.

I was due in the laundry after breakfast. Patience was already there, pulling sheets out of the big machine and tumbling them into the dryer. I stuffed the machine with more sheets and set it going.

"When did you last see a real egg?" I asked.

"In my omelette this morning," she said shortly. She was busy over a pile of sheets and didn't look at me. I fetched the basket from the chute—it was a plastic crate really, but we called it a basket—and started sorting the clothes. There was a long silence, but we often worked that way. I drifted away, thinking about Tom, the weight of his body on mine. Why had it taken me so long to go to him? Why had my parents kept me so enclosed, so safe? What else had they been keeping from me? They had kept me a child for so long. I smiled.

"So, you are enjoying yourself now?" Patience pulled out a dry sheet and flapped it straight, ready to fold for ironing. The smell of washing powder wafted over, so strong that it masked the human smells of the used clothes I was sorting. Her voice came from behind the sheet, as though she was playing ghosts.

"You found a good thing, yes, and you are your own woman now?"

I felt my face go scarlet. I took the basket of dark clothes and pushed them into another machine, hiding my face behind the door.

"You be sure you keep right. There's a right way and a wrong way. You stay right and you'll be right."

"What do you mean?" I asked from behind the door.

"I mean it's time to stop asking about eggs, Lalla. If you going to grow up now, you need to ask better questions."

Lalla? Patience had always called me *child* until now.

She finished folding her sheet, and I couldn't keep the machine door open for ever. I shut it and stood up, and realised that I was taller than she was. I had never noticed it before.

"Like what?" I asked.

"Like how to knit."

"How to *knit*?"

"Or sew. How to sew would be a good question."

"But I don't want to know how to knit. Or how to sew."

"Then you got no right to call yourself your mamma's girl. You and me, we used to talk, Lalla, and I worried about you then, losing your mamma like that. But we here now."

"Where are we?"

"Here. Like Michael says. Right here, exactly where we are. And this right here's where you got to start living. Your mamma didn't keep you in dresses by fretting over eggs."

I sat on an upturned laundry basket and stared. She looked at me and I felt that she could see everything, from the redness between my breasts where Tom's stubble had scratched me, to the wet patch on my thigh, to the sweet-tasting swelling on the inside of my lip where we'd kissed too hard.

"Do you know where the ship's going, Patience?"

"What're you asking me for? I've arrived where I'm going. If you listened more to Michael and less to what voices are in your head, you'd know that. I'm not clever. I never went to a museum with my mamma. But I know that we in a good place, and that you asking the wrong questions. You want to be a woman, you got to grow up. Now. Not in a while, but now." She paused, considering, then added, "And go see the doctor."

Grow up? I grew up last night, I wanted to say, and there's a pile of dust and a cracked skylight to prove it. As for the doctor, I hadn't spoken to him since the night my mother died and had no intention of doing so now. Patience turned back to her sheets and I looked at her stiff and frightened back, and I imagined myself in a film, running towards Tom as molten lava exploded around us and bits of falling building rained down, and saying, *We have to get out of here! Now!* But I was still sore and the dust in my hair was making my scalp itch. The wetness between my legs was cold now, sticky and uncomfortable. Already the monster films seemed a world away, the preoccupation of a child with nothing more important to worry about. But the thought stayed with me. We have to get out of here, now.

"I only asked about eggs," I said at last.

Out of here to where? There were no windows in the laundry, so it was easy to imagine worlds beyond its closed walls. I imagined a house surrounded by grass, flowers growing out of the ground, a chicken laying an egg. But even before the collapse, these things had belonged to picture books, not to London, and as Patience would not talk, my imaginings were colourless. I found my mind drifting to Tom and his hands and the top of the world, a dream of freedom I had touched for myself. We worked the rest of the day in silence. I didn't bother with lunch and by the time I had taken the clean sheets to Leyton, who coordinated the making of the beds, I was exhausted.

The light was goldening through the windows. It was sunset time; I wanted to stand with Tom and see the fire on the water and pretend we were on top of the ship. Knitting, I thought. Sewing. Alice and her embroidery hoop. Rows upon rows of clothes in plastic bags, so many for each person, but none for my mother, who was dead. Twelve flat boxes with babies' cots printed on them. A sprinkling of plaster dust. A crack. I pushed open the doors and stepped onto the deck, mindful that the golden light was already fading. There was a strange heaviness in the outside air, and it was hot; I found that I was sweating just walking along the deck.

Under the darkening sky, a group of people walked past me towards the dining room. The gong rang out and I moved with them. I had come to watch the sunset, but where was the sun?

"Coming to dinner, Lalla? Hasn't it turned hot?" It was Mercy, a woman I'd noticed because she looked about the same age as my mother, although Mercy's hair was fair rather than dark and I'd never seen her pink, round face frown. Mercy never disagreed with anyone. She was smiling now. "Or is there somewhere you would rather be?"

"I missed the sunset," I said, too distracted to notice that I was being teased.

"Too busy in the laundry?"

"No. I was here, but..." *But the sun wasn't.*

Mercy patted my shoulder kindly, as though I'd turned up for breakfast at the wrong end of the day and was asking for a croissant. I could feel her hand damp through my dress and dodged away. "You need to go to where the sun is if you want to watch it set."

"But it should have set here. On this side."

She looked at me strangely. "It'll be this deck again," she said comfortingly. "Soon. Maybe even tomorrow."

"How do you know?"

She gazed at me with radiant confidence, tempered with just a little pity, and shook her head. Mercy, I wanted to say, Mercy, there are five packages hanging in a storeroom on the fourth deck with your name on them.

"You do a lovely job in the laundry, Lalla. My clothes always feel like new." She looked almost shy as she offered her compliment, and whereas before I was sure she was approaching fifty, now she could have been forty, or thirty, or even younger. Too young to be my mother. I wondered how I could ever have seen anything in common between them.

"What if they wear out before we arrive?" I said suddenly. She looked startled, but I didn't stop. I was hot and troubled, and the heavy air was hard to breathe.

"What do you mean?" she said. "I've got more clothes in my cabin, more than I've ever had before."

"But they'll wear out too."

"I'm going to learn to sew," she said eagerly. I rolled my eyes in exasperation, but before I could speak she went on. "And if the knees of my trousers tear, I'll ask Alice to embroider a square for me and she'll sew it over the hole and the trousers will be even better than they are now."

She looked at me. "Lalla," she said more gently as she pushed open the dining room doors, letting out a blessed draught of cooled air, "there's no need to be angry. Michael has thought of these things. Just trust, and everything will work out."

"But," I began, but Mercy had already left me then and gone to her table. Finn pulled her chair out for her and I looked around me, my damp blouse cooling against my back. Five bags for Mercy. Eleven for me. Three for Finn. Ten for Tom. And I knew that Mercy was right. Of course my father had thought of these things. There were packages of clothes for everyone, the more packages the younger you were.

But why so many? Were there no clothes where we were going?

"Where were you at sunset?" Tom asked, bringing me a plate of quiche and peas. "I waited."

"How did you know where to go?"

"Michael told me."

Think, Lalla, think. Look around you. What can you see? What does it tell you?

We finished our quiche and peas and now I saw four hundred and ninety-eight people eating chocolate tart and cream. I knew their names, I knew most of their stories, but I could not see one single person of whom I could say, *You. I trust you to tell me the truth.* Even Tom didn't seem to have any questions.

I pushed my chocolate tart away, and one of the children grabbed it. I wasn't hungry anymore. I wanted to run up to the fourth deck and look again, to tear open one of the packages and check inside. I was sixteen. Maybe I would live to be sixty, or seventy. That meant one package every four or five years. And the sun. I had watched the sun rise that morning in the same place as it had set the night before. And I had been on the wrong deck to see the sunset; this had amused Mercy and annoyed Tom. We were clearly heading somewhere. But where? Where was this place to which we were travelling, that was so far away, yet made everyone so happy? Why would no one tell me? The behaviour of the sun was as real as the little golden chariot drawn by the little golden horse in the British Museum, even if it had been stolen.

Then I saw Helen. Gabriel sat next to her. Helen alone had not accepted my father's offer to be a father to all the children; she had hidden away with Gabriel to show him all she had to show of his real father. I could not articulate why, but I felt that her determination had something in common with the questions I was framing so badly. *Look, Lalla. Look carefully, because that's how you learn.*

"I need to talk to Helen," I said.

"Be careful, then," Tom replied, making little ravines in his chocolate tart and filling them with cream. As I waited for everyone on our table to finish, I saw Roger beckoning to Abigail, and Abigail exchanging words with Vikram. Perhaps it was just that I had a secret myself, but I was sure that they were looking over their shoulders. Tom was the last to finish; he begged the others to carry on to the meeting without waiting for him, and we were left at our table alone.

"Why should I be careful of Helen?" I asked.

"Because Helen's still got a lot to learn," Tom said. "She shouldn't have been showing Gabriel those pictures of her husband."

I couldn't help laughing. "They were photographs of Gabriel's father," I said. "Why shouldn't she?"

"You've got a lot to learn too."

We heard my father's voice coming from the ballroom. The goodnight meeting had started, and we were together in the empty dining room. He grinned and kissed me so quickly that only the taste of chocolate on my lips showed it had happened. There it was again—that wanting—and the soreness became an ache. We crept silently to my cabin, and this time he kissed me very, very slowly. I forgot about Helen, and the goodnight meeting happened without us.

"My Tom," I whispered to him, and he was. My rebellion, my growth, my discovery. My proof that I was alive.

THIRTEEN

"Time no longer" ❋ *Tom's story* ❋ *Tom asks a*
question and ends the film

Tom and I proved that we were alive all over the ship. We found each other in our cabins, the sports hall, the laundry. Wherever I was, whatever I was doing, I found myself thinking of him, and all the energy I had once put into wondering and remembering went into him. I was confident that we were going somewhere, even if no one would tell me where; when we got there, there would be other work to do, and so the time I spent helping Patience to make sure that everyone had clean clothes and clean bed linen seemed important, because it was limited. Some days I was so busy I didn't see Tom at all, which was why we went to the goodnight meetings. Even without clocks or watches, we could be sure of seeing each other there. When my father announced at a goodnight meeting that we had heard the last testimony and that we could now set ourselves free from the past altogether, we were looking at each other, and later we could not even remember whose the last testimony had been. When my father called triumphantly, "There shall be time no longer," I cheered along although I had no idea what he meant. We read the same books; we laughed at poor Garth, sitting staring out to sea, and at Emily, for whom a clean white plate was the most important thing in the world, and at Finn, who seemed to say, *Yes, Michael, Yes, Michael,* more than he said anything else. We tried to find a way of spending the nights together, but my father watched everyone return to their cabins after the goodnight meetings and then turned out the lights. Tom's cabin lay in one direction and mine in the other, and the nights were far too dark for roaming.

More than anything, I wanted to go back to the fourth deck. But the ship kept us too busy. Tom was wiping the walls again now as well as teaching football, and a girl on another laundry shift sprained her wrist so the piles of washing were bigger. I stayed until they were done. I didn't exactly mind. Not being with Tom was almost as seductive as being with Tom, because the fact that I loved him created a secret place that had nothing to do with my father, nothing to do with the ship. I didn't bother with the research room or the galleries, or even the cinema, anymore. I lost interest in food. The menu card would say confit of duck, creamed potatoes, petits pois, raspberries and ice-cream. Or casseroled chicken, sweetcorn, peach melba. Or beef and dumplings, green beans, sticky toffee pudding and custard. But whatever the card said, it all tasted the same and left a dull, metallic aftertaste. I played with the food on my plate, imagining myself with Tom. When I wasn't working or making snatched love or forming patterns with tinned sweetcorn and rehydrated potato, I lay in my cabin, staring at the scratches on the button or the shine on the apple, and listening to the sounds of busy people busy about the business of keeping the ship clean and comfortable. I knew it all so well by then that I could see what was going on with my ears. The heavy, regular stride was Gerhard Goltz, the cook, trekking to the stores. The lighter step that clipped alongside was Emily, come to help with her soft skin and bouncing curls. The doctor's footsteps always slowed as he reached the infirmary stairs, then clanged as he took them two at a time. When I was mourning for my mother, footsteps had come in single sets. Now they came in rattling collections, as though the feet themselves were chattering along with their owners. There were fewer slow, contemplative strides and more quick ones, as though people had places they wanted to be, as though there were things to be anticipated, looked forward to, raced towards. Tom raced too, and sometimes, the footsteps I heard would be his, and his face would shine with delight when I opened the door to him.

I watched the sun, too, and sometimes it rose over the prow and sometimes it rose over the stern. Sometimes it rose in the place where it had set. People asked my father where the sunset would be and gathered where he said, and he was always right. Sometimes I asked, "Where are we? Where are we going?" But no matter who I spoke to or when I spoke, the answer was always, "Right here, Lalla. We're right here, right now." Once, Tom asked me at breakfast whether I would watch the sunset with him that day, but I hated the thought of having to check with my father first so much that I said no and went to bed early. I sat on my bunk with the apple in my hands, its surface smooth and cold, and stroked it against my cheek pretending it was Tom's hand.

The marks on my cabin wall became more and more important to me as time began to count for less and less. In the beginning, I had known time in other ways—hunger, tiredness, the rising and setting of the sun. Time just was, like death and the sun. And of course, in the beginning, I'd known time through the tenderness of my breasts, the aches in my belly, the dull passing of unnecessary blood. I don't suppose my father had even thought of that.

But things were different now, and the marks were all I had.

Even the bleeding had stopped. I knew this meant I needed to eat more—it had happened once before, in London, when my father was still refusing to use ship stocks at home. My mother had told him that I had to eat; more food came into the flat and the blood came back. But I had no mother to make me eat now. I worked hard, I went to my cabin, and from time to time I walked aimlessly, staring around at the people running about, living their cheerful lives with their white teeth set in their delighted smiles. I looked at my museum, and I waited for Tom, and the fact that I felt light-headed for much of the time felt right.

What I wanted from Tom changed too. I loved his body, but I wanted more. I wanted him to take my hand and lead me to some rust, or dust, or a worn-out cushion he had saved from the ballroom. He wanted me to stop making the marks on my cabin wall, but I wanted him to watch them mounting up. I wanted him to show me something—anything—and say, yes, Lalla, of course there is time, and however much of it passes, I will stay with you and love you as I do now.

Oh, the ship was a busy place! So much joy and hope and anticipation that there really wasn't any space for the grumbling cloud I carried around. Gerhard had small teams going into the kitchen, learning how to bake. My father produced tins in different shapes, and for a while we ate crescent moons and ellipses decorated with tiny stars in pink and blue and green and yellow, and hats and shoes and coats of shaved chocolate and swirled cream. Something different, people said delightedly, while my father smiled on. But they weren't different. They were the same things in different shapes. The same flour, egg powder, fat pellets, sugar, mixed to make the same cake. Whether it was shaped like a hat or a shoe, or a cone or a chair or a dinosaur, it tasted the same. It was the same. There was nothing new, and while everyone in the ballroom exclaimed delightedly and laughed as though something extraordinary had happened, I wondered what was missing in their minds that they thought these cakes were anything to be pleased about. What is being alive if it is not to grow? And what is it to grow, if not to make something new? But they ate the cakes and left nothing to show for the time that had gone into their making.

Patience began to knit. My father gave her needles and wool, and soon she had a circle around her, learning to follow patterns. No one except me ever seemed to wonder why, when Gabriel was the youngest child on board, they made toys and baby clothes. They knitted and knitted and knitted, and as I watched the booties and sleepsuits growing on their knitting needles, I wondered whether Patience might be my ally after all. Because if there were four pairs of booties where once there had been none, there was proof of the passing of time. But before I could speak to her, they all unravelled the little clothes and wound the balls of wool up again to be knitted into something else. Whenever anyone wanted to join in, my father gave them knitting needles, and the unravelling meant that there was always wool. "The point is the process, not the product," he said, offering me knitting needles as I walked away.

The weather grew warmer and the winds grew less. My father gave us clay. We all made little models, then left them to go hard. I looked at them—a cat, a fish, a pot that looked like something from the British Museum, and the shapeless lump that I had intended to be a copy of my button—and thought, now there is a time before we made these models and a time after. But after a while, they were all put into a bucket of water, soaked into shapelessness and made back into clay for others to use.

I heard a plate break in the kitchen when I went in to dinner, but there were no fewer plates at the table when we sat down.

I called up the library list on my screen. There was more

material there than I could read in my lifetime. Was this the
answer? Could time be measured in the books you had read
and the books you had not read? I took my screen and scrolled
through every single book title available in the library, the titles
passing down the screen so quickly I could not read a single one.

But after three hours, during which Tom knocked twice and
went away without an answer, the titles came to an end. The
library was a vast, stagnant pond. I might as well just sit and
re-read *Ballet Shoes* until the day I died. The only fresh and unexpected thing was Tom, and even so, I was beginning to know
exactly where he would put his hands, and when, and to feel less
desperate for him to do so.

"Where are we going?" I asked, again and again.

"Why does it matter so much?" Tom answered, every time.
"We're here, now. Isn't that enough?"

But it wasn't enough, and for three days I punished Tom by
avoiding him, angry that he would not share my anger. But I
missed him. When I lay in my bunk at night, I thought of him.
My fingers were not his hands, and without the weight of his
body against me, I could not lose myself as I longed to be lost.
I kept my tally of the days, hating him for wanting me to stop,
yet hating the marks too, which could not love me as he did.
Patience looked at me with pity, but I did not talk to her. I did
not talk to anyone, and I tried not to notice them staring at me
as I went about my work.

"It's a process," I overheard my father saying to Emily on the
way to dinner, and I shrank into a doorway. "Tom will explain
it better to her than I can. She'll catch us all up, and then she'll
overtake us. You'll see." I didn't see, and I didn't follow them into
the dining room. I lay on my bed and listened to my stomach
growling, and imagined the house I would build for myself when
we arrived, and how far it would be away from everyone else's.
It was hot—I found myself thinking of a book called *Robinson*

Crusoe, of a picture of a beach and a tree that only had leaves at the very top. I would collect branches and build a hut.

On the third day—the seventy-fourth mark—I went out onto the deck in the hope of a breeze, and as I stood staring into the warm sky, Tom came to me. His hair was floppy over his eyes; he brushed it back and his forehead was damp. "Lalla," he said, and his face was so serious and his hands so still that I knew something was about to change. He's going to tell me where we're going, I thought, and my heart began to beat faster. *The fear is part of the love*, my mother had said. Looking at Tom, and looking through him to the rest of my life, I felt that I was touching the edge of what she meant. Would we be going back to London and hunger and pain and chaos and yes, maybe death? Would it be Robinson Crusoe's island, and this heat? Whatever it was, it would be us, together—and that would be life. I burst into tears and clung to him as though he was the one who'd been running away.

"Lalla," he said simply. "Why are you so angry?"

"Are we going back to London? Are we looking for an island somewhere? Has my father sent you to tell me?"

He shook his head. "We're never going back to London." He took a deep breath. "Listen to me, Lalla. Michael says that we shouldn't think about time anymore. That if we let time go, then everything happens together. Like the knitting wool and the baby suits. They're the same. The wool is the sleepsuit, and the sleepsuit is the wool. And I didn't really understand. But when we went up, when you pulled me through that skylight and we did—what we did—I did understand. I understand every time we're together." He took my hands in his and we stood facing each other on the deck. "I'm everything, Lalla. My parents, my grandfather, the Land Allocation Act. Michael saving my life and coming here and meeting you and being with you. It's all concentrated here, in me, whether I'm wiping the walls on the deck or teaching football or wanting to be with you."

"And tomorrow? And the day after that? And the day after that?"

"Tomorrow's already happened. That's the point. Nobody's frightened anymore, because everything is here. Why won't you see? It doesn't matter how long the journey is, if we've already arrived."

I tried to pull my hands away, but he held them tighter and pulled me close. "What do you want, Lalla?" he said, and his breath was urgent against my ear. "I want you. I want to stop hiding, and be with you, openly and for always. I want us to tell Michael, and to get his blessing."

"I want…" I began, but I did not know what I wanted, and before I could find any words his arms wound around me, more confident than before. He kissed my lips, my cheeks; he swept my damp escaping hair from my face and kissed my ears. He pressed the length of his body against me and I could feel him growing hard. I felt my face burning. The cracked skylight and the pile of dust beneath it appeared in my mind like the answer to everything, all surrounded by light. The dust. I wanted the dust.

"Come upstairs with me," I said.

"Now?" He smiled. "Your cabin's closer."

"Upstairs. Now," I said, and took his hand.

We ran to the infirmary stairs. The thought of the skylight drove me on; I barely noticed that the photograph album had gone. Tom ran behind me, setting staircase after staircase clanging. My work had made me fit, for this time I took the stairs with ease. There would be a pile of dust, and a cracked skylight, and we would fetch a ladder and go out onto the top of the ship, and wherever the sun set, we would see it without having to ask.

That would be freedom. And if we were free, we could choose each other, and that would be love. And then Tom would be right; it wouldn't matter how long it took us to find our island and start again.

I burst onto the corridor of the fourth deck and stopped. Tom followed so eagerly that he ran into me. We fell onto the floor and he lay on top of me, kissing my face, stroking my hair so hard it felt like he was trying to wipe it off. I pushed him away and went to the skylight.

"It can't be this one," I said, "there's no crack."

"Does it matter?" He stood firmer now, his feet planted solidly on the floor. He was undoing the buttons on his shirt.

"Where's the dust?" I demanded. He walked towards me. "Where's the skylight with the crack in it?" I walked along the corridor, looking up, walking in and out of the pools of light.

"Stop it, Lalla," he said, and his voice sounded older, less hesitant. But all I could see was the clean floor.

"The dust," I said, starting to run, "the dust. I want the dust."

"Dust?" he said, catching up with me. "Life, Lalla. That's what we want. And it's what we've got. All of us. Life. Come on." He grabbed my hands and pulled me around, breathing hard. Where was his softness, his hesitancy, his uncertainty? "What's dust got to do with us? Have I got to fetch a ladder, Lalla?"

I jerked my hands free and faced him squarely. Everything about him that had made him a boy had gone. Here was a man, a man like my father. Telling me what to do. So certain of himself that there was no room for anyone else to breathe.

He looked at me. "What's wrong with you, Lalla?"

"What's wrong with you? With all of you?"

He laughed then, and it wasn't a kind sound. "We're happy," he said. "We all enjoy our food and our work, and we play games and care for each other. You're the one who skulks around, avoiding the people who love you."

"But you're all mad. Nobody cares about where we're going, or how long it'll take us to get there."

"Because it doesn't matter! Don't you listen to anything Michael says? Or me? We're here, together, you and me. Why are you forcing us to hide? You act as though we're doing something wrong."

He was pleading now, and reaching for me, and the trouble with love is that it shuts off the part of your brain that wants to understand, because there is nothing to understand about the burning under skin that longs to be touched, and your lips and your stomach going soft and the centre of the universe gathering to be exploded under his hand.

I pulled away. "Tell me something you miss," I demanded.

"I miss you when we're not together."

"No. That doesn't count. Something you miss from before. From before we sailed. That's not on the ship. That can't be hidden behind one of these doors."

He looked over his shoulder. I heard the humming of the solar panels, sending the sun to the desalination unit, the ovens, the engine room. I thought I felt the throb of the engines through my feet, but they were in the bowels of the ship and we were on the fourth deck. It must be my blood, then, I thought. It must be my blood.

"Nothing," he said. "There's nothing."

My blood pounded harder. "Not your father?" I was goading him now, willing those blazing green eyes to burst into flame. "Not your mother? Your home? Come on, Tom. There's something you miss. Something you'd go back for. Something you'll never, ever have again. Like Helen and her husband."

For a moment I thought he was going to hit me, and I almost wished he would. But as I pushed harder, the tension went from his body and he leaned against the wall.

"You don't get it, do you?" he said, and his eyes were soft

again. "We all miss things. People. But it doesn't matter any-more, because all those things, everyone we've ever loved, are part of where we are now. We don't need to go on about them. Or show our children photographs of them."

I didn't say a word. I sat in silence, wishing I had a photo-graph of my mother. It wasn't that I couldn't remember what she looked like; when I closed my eyes and concentrated I could see her eyes, her skin, the pale blue veins that pulsed over her col-larbones, the thousands of different smiles that betrayed her true feelings, whatever her actual words. But a photograph would have let me show her to other people. I suddenly wanted to go to my father. Not to talk, not to ask where we were going, but sim-ply to breathe the same air as someone else who had loved her. Who could see her face as clearly as I could. I stood up, but Tom grabbed my hand.

"My mum had relatives in Shanghai, in China," he said. "She used to message them all the time before the borders closed. And then one day, right out of the blue, they sent her all these pictures. Bodies lying in the street. Bodies piled in factories. Hundreds, thousands of them, like they'd just fallen where they stood."

"I never saw that on the bulletins."

"No. Almost as soon as she'd opened the pictures, all commu-nications from Chinese servers were deleted. Gone. And there was a Dove warning that anyone retaining messages from China would be in contravention of closed borders. That was a death penalty, Lalla. We deleted everything. Even the message her parents sent when I was born. My dad said that all the Chinese people must have lain in the streets to make everyone think they were dead, so that China could just get on. But my mum cried. Oh, Lalla. She cried and cried. I couldn't get anything on the bulletins. It was like China never existed. But I'd saved one of the pictures onto my own screen."

"Wasn't that illegal?"

He nodded. "I thought it would be all right. They weren't de-registering minors then. I waited. And after a couple of days, when nothing had happened, I put the picture on my blog. And the stats went wild. Hundreds of thousands of hits. After a couple of hours, I got scared, and I took it down. But it was too late. The troops came on the same day."

"The troops? Did they de-register you?"

He shook his head. "They de-registered my parents. Said they should have controlled me." I stared at the floor, as though I could make the dust reappear if I looked for it hard enough. De-registered. I remembered the way my parents looked at each other when they said the word, the fervour with which the people on the quay had scrambled for our cards.

"My grandfather said it was time to use the Land Allocation Act. He remembered growing things in the ground. He talked about apple trees and carrots, and planting clover in the first year to make the soil safe again and bring back the insects."

"What's clover?"

"Something you plant, I suppose. I don't know."

"Did you go?"

"My grandfather got his allocation code. We left my parents with the last of our provisions and promised we'd go back for them. My grandfather and I walked out of the city, and what we saw...oh, Lalla, what we saw. It was frightening. You don't know who anyone is. We hid more than we walked. And no matter how far we walked, there was nothing green. Nothing growing at all. And we were so hungry. My grandfather got slower and slower. He just kept saying, tomorrow we will find a garden. I was so scared. We got to a shelter, and when we signed in, Michael was there, waiting for me. He'd been tracking me through my screen, ever since the blog. I've never been so glad to see anyone in my life, never."

I leant on the wall next to him and we slumped down side by side, our backs against the wall, our legs making four mountains, our toes pointing at a storeroom door.

Tom spoke to the floor. "Michael told me that my parents had been executed. They'd tried to use their cards at a food drop. He said he wanted me for the ship."

"And your grandfather?"

"Michael told me I had to decide. He said that a man in love with the soil would always long for the soil. He said that my grandfather could never be happy on the ship. We were still citizens then, so we were allowed to sleep one night in the shelter, and in the morning…" He looked at me as though he was trying to make up his mind about something, and then took a small piece of paper from the pocket of his shirt. "In the morning Michael gave me this." I unfolded the paper. The writing on it was small, faint and shaky, and by the end, the words were so close together it was hard to read them at all.

Dear Tom, it said, *I give you to Michael Paul, who will be your father now. I am going to find a garden for I am sure one is there. I will tend my garden knowing you are safe and happy and that one child on this broken planet we called earth may live to see his family's prayers for him answered for this is no place now and you are so young this is no time in your young life to die or see such deaths. I hold you in my heart and let you go. Your loving Granpa.*

Tom took the note back and held it between his fingers, turning it around and around, a soft, regular rustle of a beat, counting seconds, minutes, time itself until we spoke again. Such a simple thought, to place a seed in the soil and watch it grow.

"I shouldn't have kept it," Tom said. "Michael said to get rid of our mementoes. I can hardly blame Helen for keeping hold of those photographs when I'm just as bad." He looked down at his hands. Strong hands. I could see his tendons moving beneath his skin as he turned the note.

"You're not bad," I said. "Or if you are, I am too. If I had a letter from my mother, I'd never let it go."

"But that's the trouble, isn't it? Not letting go. That's why you make those marks in your cabin."

"I'm scared of stopping."

"If you stop making the marks, I'll give up my grandfather's letter. We ought to be raising each other up, Lalla, not holding each other back. I love you. I love you so much."

I took the letter from him and read it again. *I hold you in my heart and let you go.* How could Tom honour his grandfather's wish for him unless he did the same? How could I live the life my mother wished for me, unless I forgot her?

"Maybe we're on our way to China," I said at last. "We could be. We could have a life there. Start the factories again, make things. Grow rice."

"The photos looked like a pandemic," he said. "Like they'd all just dropped dead where they stood."

"Maybe we're going to go and see."

He rested his elbows on his knees. "A country full of dead people behind closed borders? I don't think so."

I shut my eyes, and leaned my head back against the wall, and thought about the survivors in my monster films. I thought about how people lived and died and made love in films, and how different it was in real life.

"Did you ever see anyone smoking?" I asked eventually.

"I saw a pile of bodies being burned. Just outside a village on the way to Oxford."

"No, I meant cigarettes. Like in the films. If we were in a film right now, we'd be smoking cigarettes. You'd light the cigarette, and then you'd pass it to me, and we'd be sitting here talking just like this."

He laughed. "You're funny, Lalla." I moved closer to him and rested my head on his shoulder. He kissed the top of my head and we stayed like that for a while. I don't know what he was thinking about, but I was thinking about my mother.

"The worst thing is . . ."

"What?"

"Michael thought I was so brave, putting that picture on my blog. He thought I was telling the truth to the world at my own risk."

"And weren't you?"

He shook his head. "I just wanted to see if anyone knew what had happened. So that I could have something to tell my mother. Instead I killed her."

"You didn't kill your mother." But maybe he had. Maybe that was what drew us so closely together, whether we knew it or not.

"I'm an imposter," he said. "Everyone else here has done incredible things. I'm scared too, Lalla. I'm scared Michael'll find me out. He's told everyone I'm some great truth-telling hero. But I was just an idiot."

I loved him more at that moment than at any other since I'd first set eyes on him.

"Let's go down," he said at last. "You should eat something. You're so thin, Lalla."

"I can't help it."

"It's just not . . . It's like there's not enough food or something. Like you're rejecting everything Michael's given us."

I said nothing, just sat and looked for non-existent cracks in the wall opposite.

"Let me talk to Michael," he said. "Let's stop being a secret."

"I need a secret."

"No, you don't. Not now." He stood up and gave me his hands, then pulled me to my feet. He kept his arm around me as we made our way down the stairs, and although it was a bit awkward at the turns, it was nice. By the time we reached the bottom, I had made up my mind. I stopped and turned to face him.

"We're not the only ones with secrets," I said. Tom raised his eyebrows and I went on. "There's a group of people—a small group—I see them meeting and whispering. But I don't know what they're saying. And there were clothes upstairs once, clothes for my mother. There must have been, but they're gone. And the sun never rises and sets in the same place. Ever. There are never any lights on at night. The ship's full of secrets. It's not just us."

Tom laughed, and then his face softened and he put his hand to my cheek. "Your mother's gone," he said softly. "Like my grandfather. You miss her. And I wish I'd known her. She loved you so much."

"How do you know?" I asked, my voice shaking.

"Because she was part of the ship. Part of what made it happen. Because she was part of what made you. But she's here, Lalla. Like my mum and dad, and my grandfather, and Patience's daughter, and Roger's baby. All that has been and all that is, all that will be. Right here, right now. If you need to ask where we're going, then you haven't learned to trust. Secrets just hold us back. And looking for secrets in others—that's worse."

I shook my head; a tear splashed onto his hand and he kissed my wet eyes, very softly. "That's for you," he said as he kissed the right one. "And that's for the people we lost, who are here with us now," he said as he kissed the left. "Do you really love me, Lalla? I love you. We could get married."

Married? The shock of the word brought on a wave of nausea, and I took deep breath after deep breath, trying to quell it.

And yet why was the suggestion such a surprise? What was marriage, except two people who loved each other and wanted to be together? What more did I want than what I already had?

Marriage. It meant that things had worked out. That the film was over. I felt as though I was back in the museum, staring at a shapeless lump of stone while my mother told me how exciting and interesting it was. What was wrong with me, that I saw only a shapeless lump of stone? The world should have been tinged pink and gone misty, and I should have been happy.

I made Tom go into the dining room ahead of me. I wasn't ready to give up my secrets. I hadn't answered his question and I certainly didn't feel like eating.

FOURTEEN

Helen's trial ❀ *Tom's confession* ❀ *what I want*

I ate what I could of my dinner, and Solomon Asprey ate the rest. I wondered what would happen to the packages of clothes if I grew too thin for mine and he grew too fat for his.

Tom kept catching my eye and smiling. I smiled back, but my attention was focused on the doctor's small group. They came together at the table where the water jugs stood; they passed each other in their quests for cutlery, for napkins, for second servings. Why don't they just sit together? I asked myself, but when they saw me looking, they separated as though they'd burned each other. I sat over a glass of water until everyone else had left, including Tom, borne away by a chattering group I didn't care about.

I left the air-conditioned dining room and went out into the heated air to walk to my cabin. Most people walked through the ship to get from place to place; it was more comfortable, especially in the heat, and usually quicker. But I liked to watch the sea, to feel a connection with where we were. I hadn't intended to go to the goodnight meeting, but as I passed the ballroom I heard a noise, soft whispering overlaid with something harsher and more urgent, like a high wind. Curious, I pushed open the doors, and the first person I saw was Helen herself, white-faced and slumped at the desk on the raised podium where once my father had checked the manifest. The people, instead of being sat on the blue velvet benches, stood surrounding the podium talking at her. Helen's eyes were red, and although I was half a room away from her, I could see her lips forming the single word, "But," over and over again. But... but... but. No one gave her the chance to finish, and no one met her eyes. They fell silent when they saw me, and shifted uncomfortably.

And then I stopped dead. There, on the desk, sat the photograph album. All around the room, people were looking at the album, then at Helen. She looked at Finn, at Greg, at Alice, at Mercy, but they all turned away from her. Then the doors opened and my father came in. Everyone turned towards him, and I slipped quietly onto an empty bench.

My father looked at where Helen sat, sobbing and shaking her head.

"Sit, friends, sit," my father said, and as he walked to the podium, they moved to the benches, as though the sea itself was making way for him. I bit my lip and wiped my palms on my dress.

Look carefully, Lalla. That's how you learn.

My father stepped onto the podium. Helen concentrated on him, her eyes wide and adoring. He surveyed the room slowly then asked, "We have no laws on the ship. Why do we need a courtroom?" He stood next to Helen and put his hand on her shoulder.

"Where is Gabriel?" he asked.

Finn stepped forwards. "It was better that he didn't come tonight," he said. Several of the people nodded. But Emily did not nod. The doctor's head was still. Was there a division among the people of the ship? The exhilaration of thinking I was not alone brought my mother before me with startling clarity. I felt a hand on mine and saw that Tom had slipped onto the bench beside me. His hands were hot and damp; he must have been walking outside too.

My father frowned. "You think Gabriel is better without his mother? Did his mother agree?"

Finn stood up. The air he displaced pressed heavily on my shoulders. "Michael, you said we must not look back. You said there should be time no longer. And we threw away the mast and we said goodbye to the people we left behind."

My father nodded, gesturing at Finn to continue, but he did not take his hand from Helen's shoulder. Finn's voice rose in pitch, filling the ballroom with unease. "You became the children's father. So Gabriel is your child. Our child. But Helen's keeping him from you. From us. How can we be family to him, when she keeps showing him photographs of a man who's dead?"

"He's mine." The voice that broke across Finn's rising pitch was so thunderous that I thought it was my father who had spoken. It was not until I saw Helen standing, shaking, her hands clutching at the desk for support, that I realised that the words had been hers. Finn stepped away, staggering on the edge of the podium as he did so. The ballroom pulsed with the collective instinct to steady him, but he saved himself and kept his feet, staring at Helen. Helen stood still and white, the blood completely drained from her lips. I willed Finn to say nothing. We had all seen fights in the time before, people so driven by one need that they forgot everything else. And it was that single-mindedness—the single-mindedness that forgets humanity and community and all thoughts of tomorrow in the pursuit of bread, or blankets, or shelter—that we saw suddenly flash before us in the challenge the mother threw down before the old man. The sky beyond the ballroom was black and oppressive, pushing at the windows.

Finn and Helen were looking at each other, breathing hard.

"Helen?" my father said.

"Simon was my husband, Michael. I loved him, and we had Gabriel together. I brought the photographs to the holding centre, and I brought them onto the ship. And I show them to

Gabriel. But I've never spoken against you, Michael, or the ship. Never." My father's expression did not change and Helen's voice tailed off. "Michael, have I done wrong?" she asked him, her eyes damp and wide.

My father shook his head. "You've caused a storm, that's all." He pulled the photograph album to him and turned the pages slowly. "So this is Simon?" he said. "He looks like he was a good man."

"He was. He left just after Gabriel was born, to claim land under the Land Allocation Act."

"And he never came back. What did you do when he didn't return? Did you give up and wallow in your misery?"

"Everyone's already heard my testimony."

"Everyone except you." He was speaking as he spoke to the children, with soft encouragement. "I wonder whether you've ever really listened to your own story."

"I didn't do anything," she faltered. "Everyone else did incredible things. But I...I didn't do anything. I don't deserve to be here. I'm not like all the others."

"Is that why you cling to what is gone, because you don't believe in your own worth? I didn't choose you because you loved Simon. I never knew Simon. Neither did Gabriel. I chose you because I saw the stories of the children you saved. People wrote about you, Helen. Do you know how far some of them travelled to find you? The hope you gave to parents who thought everything was lost? I read about you, and I saw at once that you embodied not motherhood, but ship-motherhood."

"All I did was feed the babies," Helen whispered. "That was all. I was lucky. I made so much milk for Gabriel, and so many of the babies were starving. And Gabriel loved it. They held him while I fed their babies, and—oh, he was so loved."

"Can't you see that it was a heroic thing to do, Helen? That the ability to let others love your child was what marked you out for the ship? Have all the testimonies, all the time we've spent together, taught you no more than that? It's not just Helen." He turned to the room, frustration verging on anger etched across his forehead. "Every single one of you—every single one—was chosen. No one slipped onto this ship by mistake. If you doubt yourself, then you doubt me."

Tom sat beside me, his gaze fixed on my father, his eyes wide.

"All this *I'm not worthy* rubbish. It has to stop. It's dangerous. If everyone had acted as you did—each one of you—then the ship would never have been necessary. Think about it. If every nursing mother fed a starving child alongside her own. If every able human took the food they did not need and gave it to one who did. If every witness of injustice, or cruelty, or exploitation, or murder, stood up and said, *Here is something happening that is wrong.* If everyone put another's ease ahead of their own pain. I'm not talking about other people." He looked around the room at the upturned faces, the clasped hands, the tears. "I am talking about you. All of you."

"But what about love?" Helen cried out, and I saw my father flinch. He turned to her slowly, and I saw a dangerous light in his eyes that made me wish she had not spoken. "Simon loved Gabriel. Why is it wrong to keep that love alive?"

"I had photographs of Debbie," Luke called out, speaking very fast. "I threw them overboard. After that night we all said goodbye." Other people spoke in agreement; Michael had said to get rid of mementoes, and they had done so, and they felt better. Relieved. Lighter. Helen could feel better too. Misery was unnecessary.

My father crumpled slightly, as though something had tugged painfully at the very centre of his being, and all of a sudden I felt that, little as we seemed to speak these days, there was nothing I would not do to save him that pain. Emily, braver than I, walked over and laid her hand upon his arm, and he put his hand over hers and pressed it for a moment. Helen looked at Emily, and two red patches flamed on her pale, pale face.

Patience stood up, but before she could speak, there was a movement at my side and Tom was marching to the podium. He stepped up on to it and raised his hand, and for a moment I thought he was going to strike Helen. "Because love is where we're going!" Tom cried, bringing his hand down onto the desk so hard that the drawer handle rattled. "The ship is the important thing now. If we all sit around loving what's gone, we might as well have died in London." He looked across the ballroom, straight at me, and I was overwhelmed with piercing green and longing. "If you don't let go of the past, you'll never find the love that's here for you. On the ship."

My father fell on Tom, hugging him so hard I could barely see him. The entire room burst into applause, and my father let Tom go and joined in. I looked at Finn, expecting to see him triumphant, but he seemed younger, uncertain, and he looked at Helen as though he was hungry. I saw a *but* rise from Helen's heart to her throat; I saw her swallow it; her face cleared, and I knew that I had lost her.

The meeting broke up. The people made themselves into smaller groups. Helen and Finn ran to each other as though they'd been joined by elastic, and my father stayed with them, and although I could not hear what they were saying, a golden glow seemed to come from them. Tom was there too, looking over and beckoning to me. He did not come and fetch me. He wanted to stay with the laughing, touching, happy people, inside their magic circle. Eating cookies. People who were a shining example to the world. I was no shining example. What would the world have been if everyone had done as I had done? Exactly what it had become.

My father's shadow fell over me.

"Lalla," he said. "It's so good to see you at a meeting. I'm glad Tom brought you."

"Tom didn't bring me," I said. "I heard the noise and wondered what was going on. That's all."

My father nodded. "And what do you think?"

"I think you're all wrong." I spoke louder than I meant to, and the people near us fell silent. "You can't stop Helen showing Gabriel photographs of his father. I think Helen should be allowed to teach Gabriel anything she wants."

"But she can." My father called to Helen, who came hurrying over to us. "Helen," he said. "Lalla's worried about you. How are you now?"

Helen held out her hand so we could all see it trembling, and she laughed. "It's like being found all over again," she said. "I was so worried I couldn't think straight. And there was no need to worry. No need. Simon will always be a part of Gabriel, but Gabriel needs a mother who's with him now. And a father who's able to give him what he needs." She turned to Finn. "And new friends," she said quietly, and he took her shaking hand and squeezed it.

"Michael," Tom said. "Michael, I have a confession."

My father inclined his head.

"Shall I leave?" Helen asked.

Tom shook his head. He spoke very fast. "You know my story," he said. "But what you don't know is that I've been worse than Helen. I've been clinging onto something that I should have let go." He felt in his shirt pocket and took out his grandfather's letter. I leaned forwards to stop him, but he held it out to my father. My father stood aside and gestured Tom towards the podium.

"Michael," Tom said, "everyone." The room fell silent. "This is the last letter my grandfather wrote to me. I have kept it until now. Please forgive me. I'm giving this letter up, in the hope that might help anyone who's still struggling. I didn't think I was worthy either. But Michael thought I was, and I'm glad. And I'm going to do what my grandfather told me, and look to Michael as

my father, because he believed in me enough to bring me here."
He looked straight at me. "And by being happy on the ship, as
my grandfather wanted, I'll be keeping him with me." My father
strode over to the podium. He put his arms around Tom and
held him as close as he had ever held me. The applause broke
out again, stronger this time, and I thought that if the applause
went on for long enough, I would be able to tell who else was
still keeping mementoes of the life before simply by studying the
force with which they clapped.

"Let it all go!" my father cried over the noise. "If it happened
before the ship, then it didn't happen at all. Life starts here!" I
joined in, hoping to keep the applause going for longer, and I
saw Roger and Abigail exchanging looks, and glancing across to
Vikram and Luke, and I knew then that this small group, who
met secretly, were like me. They saw no threat in the last words
of a grandfather to the child he had loved, or a photograph of a
father who was dead. I would find them, and I would join them.

My father and Tom left the meeting together, and I looked the
other way as they passed me. I stayed in the sticky air of the ballroom until everyone had gone. When the ballroom was empty, I
rescued the abandoned photograph album. I took the letter, too,
and I put them on my desk and lay staring at them through the
long humid night, sweating where the sheets touched me. I did
not sleep, and went to breakfast simply for the air-conditioning
in the dining room.

The British Museum had been full of objects, and every single
one of them had a story. I had five now. The button, the apple,
the photograph album, the letter and the screws. When I looked
at them, I was filled with a sense of what we had lost. Not just my
mother, but our connection to things. To people. Without con-
nections, there was no learning. Without learning, there was no
journey of discovery. And without discovery, there was nothing
but a full plate at dinner and a soft bed at night.

It wasn't that I cared much about Helen's Simon. I'd never known him. But he was part of a past that was part of our present. Helen's trial and Tom's confession had crystallised my thinking, although not in the way Tom had hoped.

I loved Tom and he wanted to marry me.

But I did not want to marry Tom. Not now. I wanted to be with him for ever, to love and fight for him, to give my body up to his and to take him into me. I wanted to fear for him, and need him, and ache when he was gone. I wanted him to stand with me on the deck rail and declare with me that the sun rises in the east and sets in the west, and that its journey across the sky is called a day, and that many days together make a lifetime. I wanted the people to hear us, and cheer, and take the ship as quickly as possible to our tropical island, or China, or even back to London, and start again.

FIFTEEN

———

The storm breaks ❦ *the temptation of Tom
Mandel* ❦ *the message of Alice's tapestry*

The weather broke; it rained for an entire night, fat drops slamming against the portholes like stones, and in the morning, the world was new. I stepped through the puddles on my way to the laundry, and in the clean, vibrant air, I realised that since I was the only one for whom it existed, time was on my side. Someone knew where we were going, even if I didn't, and when we finally got there, Tom would begin to understand me, and the stores would give us a good start. He might even be glad, then, to have his grandfather's letter back. And so I relaxed a little and began to enjoy myself once more. It was no challenge to get Tom to take his clothes off; the real excitement began to come from getting him to break my father's unwritten rules by talking about the time before.

"Do you remember the Nazareth Act, Tom?" I would ask, pulling him into my cabin and pressing him against the wall with the full length of my body.

"No."

I untucked his shirt. "What about the Dove?"

"Nope."

"Money," I'd say, undoing the buttons on his trousers one by one. "Do you remember money? Actual notes and coins you held in your hand?"

"Nope."

"Did you ever go to a restaurant?"

"A what?"

In my cabin he was on his guard, and I rarely won. The conversation usually ended with him grumbling, "Why do you keep all that useless junk?"

But in the safety of the fourth deck, just sometimes, I triumphed, and we would talk, and that was when I loved him most.

"My mum would have loved all this," he said once. "The cookery and the crafts. The book group. You."

"Your mum would have liked me?"

"Well. She'd have worried about your obsession with dust."

I hit him then, and he grabbed my wrist and stared at me until I thought I'd melt. "Why won't you marry me, Lalla?" he asked.

"Because I'm alive."

"What do you mean?" He loosened his grip, but I didn't take my wrist away.

"I mean that nothing's allowed to happen."

"Then make something happen," he said, and his green eyes sparkled through his fringe. "Marry me." I moved away from him and stood looking up at the whole, perfect skylight with its new full complement of shiny screws. Then he laughed. "Anyway, there's so much happening. Take a look around. There's the cooking, and the swimming. And all the books in the library to read. You could learn how to play football. Come on, I'll show you."

"I don't want to play football."

"Tennis, then. On deck, even, while the weather's like this." The storm had given way to clear blue skies that felt as though they'd last for ever. "Michael's got all the things."

"What's tennis?"

"We'll find out. Or knit."

"I don't want to knit. It all gets undone anyway."

"Learn Latin."

"What?"

"There's a Latin class starting. Charles is going to teach it and then he's going to show us round the Roman Galleries of the British Museum on the screens and we're going to recreate Pompeii in one of the empty rooms next to the sports hall. It's all right," he said hurriedly as I felt my mouth fall open, "Michael says it's all right. It's not looking back because it was so long ago and none of us have ever been there. It's honouring our heritage."

"The Heritage Restoration Act," I muttered, but he didn't hear me, or chose to ignore me. One or the other.

He stood up and joined me under the skylight. "Shall I fetch the ladder?" he said hopefully. But I didn't feel like it. His enthusiasm had driven mine out of me.

"What will it take?" he asked me softly, one finger stroking the nape of my neck. "What will it take to bring you with me? With the rest of us?"

I looked up at him. "What will it take to bring you with me?"

"You've got me, Lalla. Look, I'm here with you, aren't I? I'll get the ladder, we'll make more dust if that's what you want. Tell me what it is you need and I'll find it. We've been happy, these last few days, haven't we?"

"I want to be somewhere. Do something."

"The ship is somewhere. And there's loads to do."

"I know that. I know. But none of it's important. Helen fed all those babies. Finn had the Thursday project. Patience helped loads of people."

"But you're the reason any of us are here at all. You should be proud."

I tried to think of another way to explain. "Look at the library here," I said. "If you did nothing but read, and lived for long enough, you could read it all."

"Of course. But who does nothing but read?"

"That's not the point. There's nothing infinite here. There's nothing that doesn't have an end." I paused, then realised that, for once, I had said what I meant. "Everything on the ship," I said carefully, for Tom deserved that I should try, "everything, every single thing, contains its own ending. The cooking, the knitting, the clothes, the library. Pompeii. Whatever you look at, you're also looking at its final point. Its end."

I looked at him, waiting to see a flash of illumination on his face. But the only light there was, was pouring over him through the skylight. And I understood that, even if we went through that skylight and joined our bodies together and brought the stars down all around us and became one with each other again, I would still be alone.

"Why can't you be happy, Lalla? Why must you worry? Is it because of your mother?"

I shook my head. I missed her. I missed her every minute of every day. But that wasn't a worry. It was a sadness, a misery, a visceral longing for a world in which she had not died. But not a worry. Why, then, was I worried? Food? I had seen the towering stores in the holds. Health? We had a doctor and dentist and more medicines than we'd ever need. Occupation? We hadn't yet scratched the surface of the playthings my father had provided for us.

And then I realised. I was worried precisely because everyone was so happy. Everyone was so content. No one seemed to care when we were going to arrive, or be worried about what we would find there. No one was making plans. We were learning to play tennis, not learning to build houses. They didn't even mind that they were no longer counting the days and the weeks and the months. It was a relief to them not to have to. And more and more, it became borne upon me that we simply could not go on. We needed to arrive. Who would listen to me? Not Helen; I had lost her in the ballroom. Not Tom, who was looking at me with adoring incomprehension. He had given me an apple, but even now I was not sure what that meant.

What were the secret group doing while I was trying to explain myself? Maybe they had a map, a compass, and were charting our location. Maybe they were creeping into the engine rooms and speeding up our progress. Once, I thought I heard a dog barking, and became convinced that they had a pet somewhere. But whatever they were doing, they were my allies.

"Lalla," Tom said suddenly, his eyes alight, "if I could show you something that was growing and developing on the ship— if I could show you something that will be different tomorrow from what it is today, and different the day after that and after that—then do you think you might be happy?"

I expected him to fetch a ladder and a screwdriver. I could tell he wanted to by the way he kept touching me as he was talking—my hair, my face, my arms—as though he needed to be sure I was really there. But he stayed beside me, drowning in sunlight.

"Something that hasn't come from my father?"

He raised his eyebrows at me and I gave up.

"Follow me," he said.

He went back down the stairs, and I followed him, dreaming of subversion and dissension and somebody other than me standing on a blue velvet bench and saying, "The sun rises in the east and sets in the west, and this is called a day," and everybody cheering. They'd cheered me once before, when I'd made it possible for us to leave. If I could only make them see what was so clear to me, they'd cheer me again, for making it possible for us to get to land.

But I had to give Tom his chance. I loved him. Maybe there

was a garden on board, a secret space of grass with an apple tree
in the centre laden with fruit. A farm, a pig, a rolling field, a
horse to ride, a house made of red bricks with a garden and a
child's swing moving to and fro in a gentle breeze.

A place where he and I could live and be together until we
died.

We clattered down the stairs together. He pulled me through
the ballroom and up to the gallery and the research room. I was
all ready to tell him that these places didn't count, that there was
nothing new in them, only thousands of things we hadn't looked
at yet, but he didn't stop. I was wondering how much further
he was going to take me when he pushed open a door and said,
"There, Lalla. What do you say to that?"

And, sitting on a chair in the middle of an otherwise empty
room, with the sunlight streaming through the windows behind
her, was an elderly lady surrounded by a sea of silk. I had not
seen Alice's embroidery since the early days, when she worked
with her hoop on a single length of silk in the ballroom. Now
the silk filled a room that was three times the size of my cabin.
Here and there were patches of colour, but for the most part
the silk was bare, except for a grey outline of the ship itself. The
patches of colour were people. I was there, a little figure standing
on the prow of the ship, reaching up my arms to the sky. I knew
it was me because I was wearing the orange dress I'd been wearing the day we boarded, but I looked like a little girl still, with
two plaits sticking out of my head. Helen was there, watching
Gabriel swimming in the net. I would rather have been in the
net with Gabriel, but this was Alice's work, and I had no choice
but to stand where Alice had stitched me. There was Roger, resting his hand on the forehead of a prone figure in the infirmary.
The figure was wearing green and blue, and I realised it must be
my mother. I looked up at Alice.

"Do you mind seeing her there, Lalla?" she said, and I shook my head. Finn was there with his grey beard, screen in hand before a group of listening people, and the engineers, clustered together, tools in hand. And there, in the centre, was my father. He was ten times the size of anyone else and he stood on the deck of the ship, his arms outstretched, outlined in gold, waiting to be filled in with millions of tiny stitches. More gold stitches outlined a rope coming from his right hand, and at the end of the rope was a circle. I wondered how long all this had taken, and how long there was left until the tapestry would be complete. But there was no doubt that there was time, time, time, stitched into it as securely as the lengths of coloured thread that made the picture. I looked at Tom; he met my eyes in challenge and I was the one who looked away.

"Why is my father bigger than anyone else?" I asked.

"Because he is," Alice said, putting blue stitch after blue stitch into a section of the sea.

"What's he holding in his hand?"

"If you can't tell," she said, "you'll have to watch and wait." She fastened off the blue and took a reel of silver. She held the end of the thread and drew it away from her body, setting the reel spinning between her fingers, then cut the thread and held the cut end in front of the eye of her needle. She made a few attempts to thread the needle, screwing up her eyes and holding it up to the light, before the thread finally went through and then she began to stitch again. With the blue thread she had made a solid block of colour; we watched as she made a silver upside-down V-shape on top of the blue.

"Is that a wave?" Tom asked.

"No," I said, "it's the ghost of a shark."

"Oh, there are still sharks," Alice said, looping the silver around her needle and pulling it taut. "There were sharks before there was almost anything else and there'll be sharks long after we've gone."

"How do you know?" I asked.

"I just know."

"Why don't they come after us when we're in the net, then?"

Tom cut in. "Why do you think Michael thought of providing the net?"

I looked at him and this time I did not look away. "Do you think that there are still sharks?"

Tom shrugged. "I don't think there aren't. I don't know if there are. All I'm saying is, whatever is the case, Michael thought of it."

"But if a shark came, the net wouldn't stop it. They're really fierce. They've got never-ending rows of teeth that never stop growing and they can detect one drop of human blood in a million parts of water."

Alice and Tom laughed. "You've spent too long in the cinema," Tom said.

"It can be the ghost of a shark if you like," Alice said, her eyes kind. "That's the thing about work like this. You make of it what you will."

"But I don't want to make of it what I will. I want to know what it really is."

"Then you will never be happy," she said quietly.

No one spoke after that. Alice stitched at her silver shapes. Tom stared out of the window at the original of the sea. I watched Alice's fingers as she made one stitch, two stitches, three stitches, just as once upon a time I might have watched the second hand on a clock. Time passed here and could be measured. Eight, nine, ten. Twenty-one, twenty-two, twenty-three, and another ghost shark was complete and she went on to the next.

"Better than dust, isn't it, Lalla?" Tom said. I nodded. Maybe by the time Alice finished the sea, we would find a better way out onto the roof of the ship. Maybe by the time she finished the sky, Tom would understand me. Maybe, by the time she'd finished the ship, we'd have arrived and started building our home. There was a measuring stick here, and that was something I wanted. I felt content flood through me, and I moved closer to Tom.

Then I realised.

"It's the sun," I said. "That circle at the end of the rope in my father's hand. It's the sun."

"Indeed."

"Is that really what you think? That my father holds the sun on a rope?"

"It's what I see," said Alice. "I embroider what I see."

I felt my content seeping away.

"It's not true, though." I looked from her old face to his young one, her pale to his golden. "You know it's not true."

Tom smiled. "Shall we meet up and watch the sunrise in the morning?"

"But we never know where the sun is going to rise."

Tom and Alice laughed. "Michael knows," they said, and I felt sick. I went to the porthole and tried to open it, but there was no fastening, no handle. I stood still and tried to breathe, long slow breaths. I wanted rest and tranquillity; for a brief second I had found it, and now here was something else. I seemed destined to a constant struggle.

"What will you do when you've finished, Alice?" Tom asked.

"Oh, I'll never finish this. Look at how long it's taken me to get this far. If I've done before I die, I'll be lucky. I'll spend the rest of my days looking at it. And if I don't, well, my days will have been filled with something good. And someone else will have to take it on. There'll always be unfinished work, and there'll always be someone left to finish it. That's the way."

But it wasn't the way. It was the way for tomorrow, maybe, and for the day after, and the day after, and the day after that. But not for ever. Everything anyone said seemed to point to some kind of collective blindness, as though the whole community had taken sleeping pills from the infirmary and swallowed them together with our evening coffee.

Tom turned to me. He never could sit still for long. "Come on, Lalla. Alice wants to get on. We've disturbed her enough. And I bet people are waiting for football."

"Michael has taught us to wait, Tom," Alice said. "I am enjoying your company, and Lalla is enjoying mine. Michael would tell you to leave if you want to, but don't put the responsibility for your actions on the shoulders of others."

Tom bowed his head and said, "Thank you, Alice. Please excuse me." Alice nodded a benediction, and I stared at them, amazed.

"Are you coming, Lalla?"

I shook my head.

"See you at the gong, then." He went to the door, grinning as though he had done something clever.

"Alice hasn't answered your question," I said, but Tom left the room and closed the door behind him.

Alice picked up her needle again. "We are too quiet here to contain such energy," she said. "Let us be thankful for Michael's provision, that Tom and I may both be happily occupied."

"What will happen when you've finished?" I asked.

"I told you, Lalla. I'll be dead before that happens."

"But I won't be. And neither will Tom. What will happen to us?"

Alice smiled at me, a warm smile right from her eyes. "Tom, is it?" she said. "I did wonder. Well, Lalla, mankind has been asking that question for millennia. The first moment that there was man, there were questions. Who am I? Where am I going? What happens when I'm gone?"

She was working on a figure now. It wore blue deck shoes, so it could have been anybody. She selected some deep red and rethreaded her needle.

"Well?"

"They told stories that explained what was going on around them. They said that the dark was a dragon that ate the sun every night, that the sun itself was a flower that grew when his back was turned."

"Is that true?"

"As true as that the world was created when a god sneezed, or that winter came when the king of the underworld took the goddess of the harvest's daughter away with him. Or that thunder was because of a god who worked as a blacksmith."

"A blacksmith? Like from the olden days?" My mother had told me about men who, once upon a time, had heated metal until it glowed red hot, so that they could bend and shape it. She had said they made gates, fences, tools. She'd also said they made shoes for horses, an idea so unlikely I'd never bothered to ask for details.

I asked now. "Did horses really have shoes?"

"Yes. Horses had quite soft feet, so they used to make curved pieces of iron and nail them to the feet so that the horses would be comfortable walking for long distances."

"Is that true? Or is it like the god sneezing thing?"

"It's true."

"How do you know?"

"I went to school, remember. I read books."

"You didn't have a screen?"

"There were two. In the corner of the classroom. Fixed to the wall. We used to take it in turns to use them. But it was better to read a book."

"There aren't any books here."

"No." She took her scissors and snipped off the red thread, and I thought, well, no one will ever use that thread again. Then she chose a new colour, a lighter, golden orange, like a tinned peach. She cut a length, then unravelled it, so that instead of one thick thread, there were six thin ones. Her needle threaded with one bright strand; she made tiny knots with the point of her needle against the silk, each knot so close to the next that the stitches became a living, shimmering mass of curls, catching the sunlight as they moved. Emily. Emily with red hair, who was never still.

"Alice?"

"Yes, Lalla?"

"The way you've done my father, with the sun on the rope like that. Do you really think that's true, like the horse shoes, or is it like the dragon eating the sun?"

Alice put down her needle and looked at me. "What is it that you see, Lalla? Where does the sun rise in the morning? Where does it set at night? Who made that happen? Look, Lalla, and decide for yourself." She bent her head over the embroidery threads and I knew that I had been dismissed.

I could not resist. I went close to her and whispered, "You know it's not true, Alice. Help me tell the others. Help me to get us to our destination."

She spoke softly, moving her hands through the colours.

"My hands have work. My body is nourished. I sleep, and I am not afraid."

"But Alice..."

"I will be dead before I have finished, Lalla. Before your father found me, I was finished, but I was not dead, and it was hell. Now, I look out of my porthole in the morning and I see the sun. I look again in the evening, and I see it again. It is a better world, Lalla. Let it be. What harm?"

So, I thought, here it is. My father stands on the deck of the ship, holding the sun by a golden rope. He swings the rope over his head, and the sun arcs over the ship. He transfers the rope to his left hand and rests. Once we have all slept and restored ourselves, he swings the rope back. And the sun passes over us all once more, and his right hand resumes control, and we rest, and he brings forth the sun once more. Our world was not sneezed out, or created in six days to end an eternity of loneliness. Ours was salvaged from decay and destruction by one who was part of it, and saw where it was leading. And he chose those who were worthy and carried them with him, and thus birthed life from death, hope from despair, love from fear.

And the sun shifted to illuminate the new centre of the universe and submitted itself to my father.

And the evidence was there, every single day. Twice a day. As long as people like Alice could look out of their portholes and say, *This is what I see,* I would be unable to say, *Yes, but it is not what you think.* Because they knew. They already knew.

At dinner that night, I watched Alice cut her food with the same grace as she made her stitches. What harm, she had said. What harm. But to me, the harm was clear. If there were eighteen thousand tins of pineapple in the stores, then they would one day be gone, the same as if there were a hundred thousand, or a hundred, or only one. Alice would reach out her hand for a skein of coloured thread and it would not be there. First the blue, then the grey, then the gold would run out, and there would be nothing left but the outlines of a child's colouring book, made of the shadows of thoughts and ideas that could never be brought to life. The longer we took to get to land, the fewer resources we would have to start our new lives.

Tom's green eyes danced in front of me, and I knew that if I were Alice, and the tapestry she was stitching was the story of my life and thoughts, it would be the green thread that would run out first, because everywhere I looked, all I could see was the green of his eyes. It was for him I had to act. For him, so that we could know time, know ourselves, and be truly together. We could not lose ourselves in each other until we knew where we were. After all, if you do not know where you are, you are lost already, and how can you ever hope to find anyone else?

For Tom, because I loved him.

I went over to her table. "Thank you, Alice," I said, and I kissed her soft, wrinkled cheek. She put down her knife and fork and squeezed my hand.

"Try to be happy, dear," she said. "It's much the best thing."

I would go to the goodnight meeting and I would listen with all my heart. And then I would go back to my cabin and wait for the dark.

It was time to talk to my father.

SIXTEEN

My plan to save the ship ❋ I go to find my father,
but my father finds me ❋ I fall

I sat in the goodnight meeting and looked from face to face. At last I had a plan, a way to prove to the people that things were not as they thought. My father did not control the sun. It rose in the east and set in the west. That was the truth, and whether they admitted it or not, they knew it. I would force them to admit what they knew to be true. Helen, I thought, when I bring my evidence, you will be free to teach Gabriel as many truths as you please. Patience, you will knit for a purpose. I will find out where we are going, and when we are going to get there, and that knowledge will set you all free.

And Tom. Tom. When we know where we are going, we can marry. Make plans. I had come to the goodnight meeting intending to listen, but I had been so lost in my own thoughts that the discussion was underway before I realised it had started.

"Of course we should write," my father was saying. "But let us consider why. In the time before the time before, any words that were to be heard by more than a few people had to be written down and published in a book, printed on paper. And because this was a process that cost money, the mere existence of a book meant that someone, somewhere, thought that what was in it was worth reading. That is why only pre-published works were authorised by the Dove. A reminder of a nobler time."

"But, Michael," Finn said, "without the raven routes, you would never have known of me."

"Or me," Tom agreed.

"For every one Finn Johnson," my father said, "for every one Tom Mandel, there were hundreds of thousands of people pouring words into the ether, words that meant nothing. An hour with a book expanded understanding; an hour with the screen contracted it. Since you had the strength and the wisdom to cast away the mast, the danger of suffocating yourselves with irrelevances is significantly diminished. The portals I gave you are tools. Just tools. A way to access important things that have stood the test of time. Cast aside ephemera. And before you dare to write, make sure your words are worthy of standing alongside those that have gone before you. Read. Before you write, read."

"Read everything? All the books on the screen?" Finn asked, his face reflecting his struggle to understand. He owed his life to the very thing my father was dismissing—an unrestricted flow of words, pouring from him to anyone reckless enough to access them, unfettered by paper and ink and someone else's controlling mind. Unreliable, uncensored and illegal as the raven routes were, they were the only way of circumventing the Dove. People like Finn had hacked, decoded and tampered to pass on what they had to say. Now there was no Dove, there was no risk, or danger either.

But I was going to find my evidence, and then talk to my father. In the morning, we would be on our way; the risk and danger would be back and Finn would be free to write again.

My father smiled and he held out his hands, just as he did in Alice's tapestry. I had never seen him stand like that before; now, he drew himself up and held his hands out with his palms towards us. It was as though he had seen an idealised version of himself in Alice's work, and decided to become it.

"You are my books," my father said, and I knew that this would be all I would hear from anyone for the next few marks on my cabin wall. *We are Michael's books. I am a precious book, belonging to Michael. I am a glorious book that Michael has written.* He continued, "You are my library of the best of twenty-first-century man—of all man, across all time, all ages. What need have we of more books, when we have each other?"

Your mother will always be a part of you, Lalla, so what need I weep when you are with me?

That night, I did not change into my cotton nightdress. I stayed in my clothes, and when the night noises of running water and creaking bunks had subsided, I slipped out of my cabin door. The dark was more than dark; it was black in a way London nights had never been. It made no difference whether my eyes were open or shut. I could see nothing. I felt my way forwards, along the corridor of cabin doors, until I reached the bigger doors that led out onto the deck. When I pushed them open, the thick air took me by surprise. The days had been cooler since the rain. But the dark seemed to have brought back the heat, and in any case, the night was a strange place to me. There was a wind too, a hot stifling breath that brought no relief. I blinked as air blew into my eyes. I felt tears forming, swelling, spilling onto my face and I celebrated them as a purely physical reaction to a purely physical thing. My body had a reflex with which to protect my eyes from wind. Self-preservation, not preservation by the father.

And the night had a different smell, too. In the day, the smells were of food, washing powder, the warmth of an iron on rumpled cotton. Soup. Soap. Now, those smells were gone, and there was only salt and emptiness, with a warm dank undertone of neglect. After all, when had any of us really acknowledged the presence of the sea? If there was anything still living there, it would not come in the daytime, when everyone was busy, but in the night, when we slept. I felt for the metal wall and stood with my back to it. In the dark, there was no horizon. The ship, the sea and the sky were one expanse of black, less than an arm's stretch away, or miles and miles beyond me. It was impossible to tell. And because I could not see its edge, the sea ceased to be a vast barrier, a cage without bars, and became one with the ship and the sky and the land.

I could leave just by putting my foot over the side.

I thought of going back to my cabin and trying again when there was a moon, or at least replacing my clothes with my cool cotton nightdress. But I had no way of knowing whether there would ever be a moon, and it had taken me long enough to inch my blind self this far. It had to be now. A fat drop of water fell on my hand and I heard thunder, far away. I felt like yelling, *You didn't see this coming, did you, Father?* I left the security of the wall and took a step towards the deck railings opposite. I could not see my feet upon the deck or my hands stretched out in front of me; I was blind, and the sense of possibility made me dizzy. I took another step, and another, following the smell of the sea, expecting at any moment for my fingertips to meet the deck rail. Warm, heavy drops splashed onto my reaching arms and the thunder rolled closer. But the further I travelled, the more remote the deck's edge seemed to become, until I was surrounded by nothingness, turning this way and that, groping above the unsteady deck for a fixed point from which I could navigate. Then the rain came in earnest, great sheets that were draped over me by the winds. It felt as though the sea itself was pouring onto the deck; I was soaked in an instant, as thoroughly as though I had fallen in. The infinite union of the ship, the sky and the water enfolded me, and in that infinite and terrifying blackness, I heard my name.

"Lalla."

The walls and bars sprang back into being. I turned towards the voice, but I had no idea where it was coming from, or whether to seek it or hide from it. The thunder was all but drowned out by the noise of the downpour, hammering on the deck, the walls, the window. Through the chaos the voice came again. *Lalla*, it said, *Lalla*, and I panicked. I ran towards the dissolved edges of my world. My hard soles slipped on the water-coated deck; I fell, and cried out as my face hit something cold and hard. White lights exploded inside my head; my mouth flooded with warmth. I put my hands to my face then got to my knees, struggling for breath. A flash of lightning ripped through the sky. I saw my hands red and shining, with bits of them dripping onto my shoes. I saw a figure in the doorway, silhouetted by the light, its shadow falling so close to me that only a shard of light separated us.

"Lalla."

My father had called me; now he had come for me. I scrabbled along the wall, my bloody hands slipping, trying to find a hook or a handle I could use to pull myself up. The metal was smooth, and the rivets had been beaten into perfect hemispheres. My legs refused to act. I crawled away from his shadow as though it would burn me if it touched me, but my strength was gone. I was wet and shaking, and when hands closed around my ribcage and pulled me up, I could not break away.

"What do you want?" I demanded, but the words were slurred and indistinct in my damaged mouth.

"You came looking for something, Lalla, and you have found me. So the question is not what do I want, but what do you want?"

What did I want? I remembered my mother, lying in the infirmary with her green and blue dress tucked over her.

"I want to know," I shouted over the rain, while the wind whipped my sodden hair around my face.

"Then you had better come with me." I could not move without his help. I pulsed and throbbed where my skin had broken, and I wondered how I could possibly have done myself so much damage. It was as though the ship itself had slammed into me, the full force of its tonnage crashing against my fragile human frame. *I am bigger than you are*, it said. *I have been created by a brilliant mind, a mind that saw the future; I am knit together, not of metal and rivets, but of dreams and ideas. Mine is the power; you are a mayfly, a gnat, a minor irritation. You are rusting; I am eternal.*

I limped beside my father, dependent on his arm. The next flash of lightning showed me the deck rail, strong and silver, the sea and the sky beyond still as black as each other. I tried to remember that, for a fleeting moment, the sea had been, not an insuperable eternity of dead water, but simply so much space, at one with the land. For a moment, the darkness had been my friend; now I could only feel pain and trembling.

"It's all right, Lalla. I'm here. Feel me. Everything is all right now. You know it is."

Did I? Did the fact that I was stumbling alongside the man who had brought me into the world mean that everything was all right? His arm was strong, his flesh beneath the soaked shirt warm; as I surrendered to its support, tiredness stole over me. My aching body was no longer my own. The pain receded as I leant upon him, glad to feel that he had strength enough for both of us. What was thought, after all? Only a means for self-torment, self-doubt.

"Lalla," he said into my hair. "My Lalla, at last."

I heard the sound of a key in a lock, and my father passed before me into a room full of screens, lights, control panels. I saw books. I saw maps. I saw something that looked like a clock, but it had only one hand and just four numbers. I looked more closely and realised that they were not numbers, but letters.

N, E, S, W. North, East, South, West. A compass. I had last seen this one in a museum, inside a glass case, and wondered how it had come to be here. I saw two chairs, padded in dark blue, on wheels. My father led me gently to one, then sat on the other, his right arm leaning on the arm rest, his shirt stained with my blood. I wondered how long it would take me to get the stain out. He disappeared briefly and came back with towels, soft white warm towels, and wrapped one around me. He closed the door behind him and the noise of the storm ceased completely.

"You wanted to know," he said. He leaned over and kissed me on my temple, where there was no blood and no bruising. "Are you ready, Lalla? Are you ready to learn?"

I was tired. I wanted my mother. I wanted Tom. My face hurt. My eyes burned with the pain in my nose and I could feel the cuts in my mouth with my tongue. I sniffed, then coughed as the warm metal taste of blood oozed into the back of my mouth. The blood dripped onto my clothes, onto the carpet, and I dabbed stupidly at it with the towel, which clung to me damply. My father produced a handkerchief and I sat holding it to my nose.

Then he reached for a switch and the overhead light went out, and with the blackness came clarity.

In the darkness, leaving seemed possible, because everything was one. If infinite is truly infinite, then it is as close as it is distant, and as far away as it may be, you can reach out and touch it with nothing more than an outstretched hand.

A green light flashed on a screen as a green line swept over it. Bleep. Bleep. Bleep. "There we are, Lalla. That's us, that dot. You're always asking, and now you know."

"Where are we going?"

"Didn't Tom tell you? I told him to tell you. We've arrived. This is the ship, my darling. When you get to where you are going, you stop."

"What's that?" A solid green patch appeared in one corner,

with an uneven edge, like torn paper. "That's land, isn't it? Is that where we're going?"

"Keep watching."

I watched, leaning forward and using the handkerchief to stop the blood dripping on the instruments. The green dot went bleep, bleep, bleep. And as I watched, the solid green corner receded until the little dot was once more bleeping in a circle of nothingness.

"Why are we sailing away?" I asked. "That was land. What are you doing?"

"Look at the charts, the radar, the patterns of the sunrise and sunset. Look at the compass. You know what I'm doing. You only have to look." He paused. "Your mother would have worked it out weeks ago."

"You're turning the ship," I said at last. "You take us so far, and then at night you turn the ship around and go back the other way. That's why the sun never rises and sets where it should. We're going round in circles." I paused for a moment. "The people will kill you when they find out."

"Why would they do that?"

"Because they think we're going to a place where we can make a new start, where we can leave the misery behind..."

"Which is exactly where we are."

And I thought, and my thoughts all ran into each other like toppling dominos. The gangway, released to the sea, never to be used again. My mother, so reluctant to leave the land. Alice's tapestry. And Tom. *I know where I am, Lalla. I'm right here, right now.* The stores. The readiness with which the people knitted and used clay, all the while knowing that their work would be undone. Photograph albums.

"The ship is where we're going?"

"The ship is where we're going."

"The people knew?"

"The people knew."

"We're not heading to an island somewhere, or a place that still works?"

"There are no such places. There is nothing left."

"It's madness," I said, the enormity of the truth breaking at last. "You'll kill us all."

I expected him to be angry, but he simply cocked his head as though he found me interesting. "How so?" he said.

"The engine parts will give out. They'll wear away and stop working, and then you'll have no control at all over where we're going. The solar panels will break off and fall into the sea. The bolts under the water will rust through, and they'll fall away, and the sea will pour in and the ship will sink. Like the Sinkers back in London, remember? Or that village Jamila lived in, that ended up under water. Or else someone will get ill and it'll spread. We'll run out of food." I stopped, astounded at having to explain. "It's just not sustainable," I concluded lamely, and even in the darkness I could hear my father smile.

"The Sinkers were deliberately scuppered by troops. And Jamila's village was at the mercy of a world that didn't care about it, that could barely be bothered to acknowledge it existed. Her village was under water once a year for decades and nothing was done. The warnings were all there. But they weren't acted upon, and that was it. One year, the waters didn't recede. That was the end of her village and everyone in it." He paused for a moment, then added, "It was the end of most of Bangladesh, actually."

"I know."

"But the ship isn't Bangladesh. The ship is cared about. Maintained. If something is wrong, it is sorted out. If there is a problem, it is solved. What do you think the engineers do all day? The world was destroyed by blind eyes. We of the ship will never be blind to her needs."

"It's a machine. A machine. It's not a person, it's not a country. It's not organic."

"Listen to yourself," said my father. "Sustainable. Organic. You should have been born fifty years ago." He paused. "What was your next thing? Illness?"

"The people will get sick," I said, remembering Tom's parents and China, feeling the pain in my face. "There'll be a virus and it'll spread through the ship."

"Ah, yes," he said slowly. "The pandemics. The warnings were all there too. New strains of bacteria, new viruses, vaccines made from the very sources of the infections and pumped into populations across the globe. People visiting places thousands of miles away and bringing the new strains home, taking antibiotics like sweets. How did they think it was going to end?"

"I suppose they thought they'd make a new antibiotic."

My father nodded. "They didn't, though, did they? Science had come to the end of what it could do." He nodded towards my nose gravely and spoke in a doom-laden voice. "If we don't get that cleaned up, it'll get infected and you could die." I cried out—I could not help it—and he laughed at me. "It's all right. This isn't some poverty-stricken tent city. There's no new strain of disease waiting to unleash havoc upon us here."

"Your radar will stop working and we'll drift to land."

"There's the compass and the maps. And the stars haven't gone out yet."

"You stole that compass," I said, suddenly certain. "Just like you stole the people."

"Better to fulfil your purpose than to rot behind glass."

"The food will run out, or the freezers will stop working."

"You've seen the stores. Or some of them. You could eat and eat and eat and not make a dent in what there is. If we all ate like you, we wouldn't need the food at all." I think I was meant to laugh, but the green line kept up its bleep, bleep, bleep as it swept across the green dot, and in the green light my father's smile looked ghoulish.

"The football will fall to pieces," I said. "The knitting needles will break. Alice will run out of thread."

"There are other footballs. Other needles. More thread."

"The people will get bored and end up fighting against you." He laughed out loud then, and the next bleep showed me green teeth and the green whites of his eyes. "You don't even believe that yourself."

"They meet in secret," I said in spite of myself. "I've seen them, giving signals to each other after dinner."

"You have?" he said, faintly amused. "You don't think they might be—I don't know—discussing something they've read? I trust my people. What else do you have for me? You've threatened pestilence, famine and war. Isn't there another one?"

"Death," I said.

"Oh, death." He sounded impatient. "We are all going to die. We were always all going to die. No one has ever lived who has not died. Death is…"

"I know, I know. Death is the only thing all living things share. That doesn't mean we have to go out and invite it in."

"How else would you suggest we live? Cowering away from death as we did in the time before? Thinking we were immortal because we had seven hundred channels on our televisions and thousands of friends we'd never even met?"

"You wouldn't have found all these people without all that."

"That's what I keep saying. That's what I'm trying so hard to make you understand. The ship is where human life has been leading, ever since mankind walked upright. It doesn't matter what happens now."

"It's just a thing," I said impatiently. "And things wear out." I thought about the dresses my mother had cut down for me, my red shoes.

"Perhaps. But this is all new. This is a new way of working, a new way of being. We no longer simply exist, waiting for the next new thing to come and replace the previous thing. We've found rightness. And when something is truly pure, nothing can taint it. It heals where it touches. The ship is healing, Lalla. It has healed the wounds of the people, and the people care for and maintain it. It's perfect, in concept and execution, and nothing will ever need to supersede it." He paused, and as the green line swept across the dot again, I saw how much he was enjoying himself. There was a spark in his eye and I remembered how he had argued with my mother. Her opposition had helped him, given life and substance to his plans, helped him grow and be purposeful, just as playing football kept Tom's body fit and taut. She had been his discipline and he had loved her for it. But I was not my mother. I lacked her intelligence, her courage, her restraining hand.

Even so, I felt a tiny fluttering of power in my stomach. My secret love, my woman's body. No, my father did not have it all his own way. How could he, when I had Tom?

"I'm not a child," I said.

"You are. I've lived forty years longer than you have. I remember things you have never even heard of."

"And I am looking at a future you won't be a part of. You'll be dead and I'll still have forty years to go."

"Why do you think that I show you all these things? Why do you think I talk to you, allow you to speak to me in this manner? I recognise youth. I recognise idealism. I see myself in you, and I've done everything I can to give you a future." He stopped and looked around. The screens, the maps. The bleep, bleep, bleep, louder in the silence. The little green dot in the middle of the blank screen. "You cry about things running out as though it's news. But it's not news. Of course things will run out. But we're stocked for at least twenty years, probably more. And that's twenty years for you, Lalla. Twenty years for you to learn and create and decide your own future. The future of the next generation."

The green light on his face. The blood on my hands, the searing pain behind my nose, which struck me anew each time I took a breath.

"I don't know what you'll do," he said. "Perhaps there'll be fish again. Or you'll work out how to make cultures in which you can grow proteins. You haven't even started to explore the resources on the fourth deck." He smiled. "You could build a rocket ship and fly to the moon to harvest green cheese."

I drew breath but he cut me off. "The point is this. You need to think. You need to take responsibility and stop waiting around for everyone else to solve things for you. I've given you at least two decades. I got the ship together in less than half that, with no help at all, in a world that worked against me at every turn. But you are not alone. You've got me. You've got scientists on board, engineers, you name it. Win the people's trust. They want you, Lalla. They want to trust you. You are my heir."

"Trust, yes. But not blind trust."

"The people are not blind."

"They are. Look at Gabriel and the photographs of his father. Helen let them go, because you said she must. Look at eggs. At apples."

"Apples?"

"Have you ever eaten an apple?"

"Of course." He looked at me as though we had just met. "Haven't you?"

"No. I've had apple out of cans, in pies, sauces, things like that. But I've never had a real fresh apple."

He looked pensive. "Time goes faster than you think," he sighed. "I knew you'd never had an orange. But I thought apples would have been in your time. It was a pity about the bees."

"Bees?"

"It doesn't matter now," he said quietly. "What matters is this room, these displays. The compass. The people. You."

He looked out of the round window and rested his hands on the desk. It was a beautiful desk, made of wood that glowed warm and red with polish and care. It had drawers with metal handles that looked like gold, just like the desk on the podium in the ballroom. "It was a lonely thing, getting all this together," he said slowly, and I felt sorry for him in spite of myself. "There were times I thought I might die from the loneliness." I thought of my mother, her feet tucked underneath her as she sat on the sofa saying, *Not yet, Michael, not yet.* "But I persevered. We have escaped destruction, and disease, and degeneration. We have taken on the guardianship of the things that made humanity beautiful. Friendship. Peace. Love. Trust. Suppose—just suppose—that you're right, and all you threaten comes to pass. We'll seal ourselves in the sports hall and breathe our last together, and all these beautiful things will survive until the end."

"But there are people out there!"

"Out there? There's nothing beautiful out there." He gestured out across the waters. "If there's any life there, it is a life of blame and hunger and misery. Anyone alive out there is dead, even if, at this moment, they still breathe. But the death I suffered has been rewarded a thousand times."

"What death?" I said. Because even though I was falling into his every word, I still had a ledge I could cling to, a jutting place where I could rest my feet and keep myself from complete surrender. And it was this: Tom and I had found each other. We were young, we were in love, and we had a life of passion and desire that was truly our own. His body, my body. His heart, my heart. Together we had stood on the deck rail and thrown away our cards; together we had balanced on boxes and climbed out of the ship.

"There are many kinds of death," my father said simply.

And for a moment, my certainty wavered. I saw my father as the others on the ship saw him, as he saw himself. A man for whom humanity was more important than self. A man whose love for others surpassed all else. "The joy of my life now," he continued, "is that I have saved you, my daughter, from all but one of those deaths, and that one is the one we all have a right to, that everyone on the ship may now anticipate, and welcome when it comes. Natural death, good death, a calm goodbye amongst friends to a life truly lived. It may never come. It may come tomorrow. But here, on the ship, we are ready." I felt tears coming to my eyes. Because what he was offering was so easy. Did it matter that we were all going to die? Everyone has died, always. And if death was the end of everything, what was wrong with living a life in which nothing would attack me in the dark, a life in which I knew what would happen, tomorrow and the next day and the day after? A life of which I was in control?

No one has ever lived who did not die.

My father spoke softly. "You're stuck in the time before, Lalla, when the sea was the enemy, and ships used tonnes of oil to fight its currents and winds. The sea is our ally now. It bears us up. It shares with us its glorious expanse, gives us space to breathe. It and the ship are as one. There are no destinations, once you have arrived."

"But Helen's husband?" I said, struggling to hold on to my certainty. "Why must she forget him?"

"So many people died. Would you have their loss—or even Anna's—define our life on the ship? We move on. We honour our dead by living well."

It was as though a mist was emanating from my father, a

scented, warm mist that covered my skin and entered into my brain, so that his thoughts and mine became one. As I breathed, I tasted the life he had poured into the ship, so that I could be safe. And I realised that the reason he had dedicated his life to creating the ship was because he loved me. Not my mother, who had always argued with him, but me. I was flesh of his flesh. I was made from a part of him; from that part, I had grown under his care and guidance; because of that part, he had planned and created a new world, brought it into being, made it concrete. Because of him, I could weep for the dead in the British Museum, mourn for the drowned in India, feel the luxury of horror at my recollections of the rats chewing on the homeless in Russell Square Gardens. Because of him, the crater in Regent's Park was just a crater in Regent's Park, neither closer nor more relevant to me than a crater on the moon.

"And Tom?" I breathed softly, forgetting the pain for a moment as I readied myself for his anger and gathered myself up to fight. If he denied me Tom, I would be able to hate him. I would find the energy to tell the people what was going on, and to defy him.

But there was no anger in him. He looked younger, and I saw the face my mother had loved before I was born. "I would not have my children be alone," he said softly. "And if a generation yet to come retreats into the sports hall and seals the door—well, it is good to know they will be together, and fulfilled. But that moment won't come. I believe in my people. Their creativity, their ingenuity. I believe in you. I can't tell you what the future looks like, my darling, but I know that it will be beautiful. How can it be anything else, with this as its beginning?" I saw Tom's green eyes looking down on me, and I saw his gentleness with the children, felt his hands upon my skin. Was there really no destination? Were we to glide along for ever, uncomplaining in a field of plenty?

But I wanted more. I wanted to be with Tom, to share everything I was with him. To hold his heart in mine and defend it; to share our stories and determine our own future. That was my hope.

And I understood, suddenly, that it was this hope that had allowed me to leave food on my plate for the walnut-faced man to finish, this hope that had kept me apart as others had wept at my father's speeches. Hope that there were still choices to be made, that my future was not set out in tiny stitches in Alice's tapestry. Hope that whatever miraculous agency had connected Tom and I existed somewhere beyond the ship, and that by being together, we would find it. Hope was the danger. If I threw hope overboard, there would be certainty. Without hope, oranges and eggs would become historic curiosities, like jade axes. Apples would not bother me, and I would never have to worry about where the sun rose. With hope gone, I would have space in my mind to wonder about the glories my father had hidden away in the storerooms, and to dream of the people of the ship all looking at me with love and pride as I fulfilled my father's plans for me.

To give up hope would be to give up Tom, because Tom was my hope, and I could not live without him, no matter what I owed to my father. *I'll go back to London with you*, Tom had said once upon a time, *if it's really what you want*. Tom, not my father, was where my trust resided now. For all his talk of death, my father had not died. It was my mother who had taken a bullet and had her body invaded by poison from the infected wound. My father was alive, adored, standing before me, and he knew nothing of the woman I had become. But Tom did, and together, we would work out what to do with the truth I had discovered.

My father switched the overhead light on again. He stood before me, tall and powerful and smiling, his torso outlined by his rain-soaked shirt, stained with my blood. Only surrender hope, and I would have the universe at my feet. The world beyond the ship would no longer exist, and therefore no longer matter. I could ask my father for deck shoes, throw my old shoes into the sea and consign them to a fantasy world that may never have existed. Hope. The cruellest thing in Pandora's box. Disease, death, destruction, misery, pain, loss; terrible though they were, hope was the worst. Because it was hope that made humanity bear the rest.

And that was what the ship was. A life without hope.

I looked down at my cracked red shoes, felt them press against my feet. My mother had given them to me. They were a part of the life I had lived before, and if I threw them away, they would still exist, and become shoe-shaped coral beneath the sea. For as long as there were my red shoes, for as long as I could remember the British Museum, for as long as my mother's voice still sounded in my head, for as long as I loved Tom, I would have hope, and my life would be hard. The pain of my broken nose reasserted itself and my father's cabin began to swim.

"Lalla," he said, coming towards me with his arms outstretched, "I love you."

But it was too late for that.

SEVENTEEN

———

My broken nose ❀ *the doctor's tale* ❀ *stupidity*

I had wanted to know, and now I did. We were going round and round in circles, stimulated, loved, learning, too dizzy on plenty to see. Part of me was aghast that I had not realised what was going on. And yet how could I have realised? My father claimed to have created the ship for me. His chosen people had brought their children on board. They were not cruel, or self-ish, or unkind. I could not hate them for their decision; indeed, when I concentrated on today, or tomorrow, or even the day after that, I could understand. Already I was so used to the motion of the ship that I didn't notice it. But we would grow old. We would stumble about, scraping the remains of the preserved foodstuffs into each other's mouths, throwing each other's bodies into the sea with the rubbish as old age or illness claimed us. And when we lost the strength in our arms, the bodies would lie on the deck as they had lain in the streets of London, and those who were just little children now would step over them as they went to the stores, anxiously calculating how long the food might hold out. How different would life on the ship be from life in London then? The passing of time would return us from whence we had come, for as long as we chose to do nothing. How the children would curse us. My father held out the sealed sports hall as some kind of last resort, but slow suffocation seemed a poor sort of future to me, no matter whose hand I might be holding.

My father left me in the infirmary, in the company of the doctor once more. The doctor set about cleaning the blood from my face and injecting my face with something that made it go numb. He pressed white tape over my nose with a grinding crunch that I sensed rather than felt. He stroked cotton wool over my hands and put some cream from a tube onto the cuts. He did not ask how I had come to be injured.

"Michael wants you to stay here until your face has healed a bit."

"No," I said. I could not bear to think of the last time I had been in the infirmary. "Take me back to my cabin."

"I need to keep an eye on you."

"I'm fine." There was a tingling sensation around my nose; it would become painful as the anaesthetic wore off.

"You need to lie still. You can't traipse across the ship every time I need to check up on you. And the infirmary certainly can't come to you."

"I'm not staying in the infirmary on my own."

He picked up the clean sheets. I had delivered those sheets only the day before, when I had been a different person. "All right," he said. He held out his arm and helped me off the bed. I was aching all over—my hands and nose had been the main casualties of my encounter with the ship, but I had bruises all over me. "It's time you and I had a talk anyway. My cabin's next door. I'll make tea."

I had never seen the doctor's cabin before; his clothes and sheets went to the infirmary and he collected them from there. It wasn't like my cabin, or like Tom's, or like any of the cabins I delivered laundry to. The doctor had two big leather armchairs and an infirmary bed instead of a bunk; the floor was covered in red carpet, and there was an intricately patterned rug between the chairs. I leaned on the back of the chair nearest to the door, trying to look as though I belonged.

"You can sit down."

I sat.

He put teabags into two mugs and poured water onto them from a kettle. They weren't the white mugs from the dining room. One was red and one was blue, and they had gold patterns on them, swirling over and over, like the swell of the sea. These mugs had not come from the fourth floor. Was this man, whom I had avoided for so long, to be my ally? Was this why he had brought me here?

"Have you always been a doctor?" I asked.

He nodded. "It was all I ever wanted to do."

"Why?"

He stirred the tea. "I thought that people were essentially good. I thought I could help us all to stay alive, stay sane, keep it together so that we could get through. Because humanity's been in crisis before. And it's always survived."

"Even Regent's Park? The British Museum?"

He shrugged. "It wasn't the first time bodies have been flung into handcarts."

"So why didn't you stay behind and help?"

"The thing is." He stopped and stared out of his porthole, as though the thing might be floating in the sea. I willed him to say, *I was waiting for you to come and find me, because I knew I could not turn the ship alone.* But he didn't. What he did say, though, was the next best thing. "In the past..."

"I thought you weren't allowed to talk about the past."

He gestured dismissively and my heart raced. "In the past," he continued, "no matter how terrible the atrocities, no matter how many lives were lost, there was always a group doing the inflicting, ready to be toppled or challenged or assassinated, or even just to die out and be replaced by someone else. Time goes forward and things change. But that's not true anymore. This wasn't a dictator pounding a people into dust."

"What was it then?"

"Stupidity, mostly."

"Stupidity?"

I remembered one of the very few times my mother was angry with me. We'd been to the museum, looking at the mummified cats in the Egyptian galleries. I can only have been eleven or twelve, maybe even younger, because the cases were still quite full. We had just finished eating lunch, and I said, "Why can't we have a dog? Or a cat?"

My parents both looked at me, eyes wide, a mirror of each other's surprise.

"A pet?" my mother said. Normally her voice was like a soft hand. This time it was a fist and it hit me in the stomach. The pain was sharp and as it faded, I felt the desire for a dog blossom in its place, until I wanted one so badly that I could feel its fur, wiry under my hand, and its breath hot against my skin. I was a lonely child.

"Yes," I said. "A dog. It could be my friend. I could take it for walks and look after it. You wouldn't have to do anything. It could sleep on my bed."

"Lalla," my father began, but my mother interrupted him.

"A dog," she said. It wasn't even a question. It was a statement, a flat, bald statement of impossibility.

"Yes." I could see it. It had big dark eyes, and it was looking at me, wagging its tail against the floor. A shaggy brown and white tail, the length of my handspan.

My father spoke with reason and authority. "We can't have a dog, kitten. Someone would eat it. It might get sick. And there aren't any dogs around anymore, except the ones that have gone wild." His voice tailed off as the futility of explaining the obvious overtook him. "You're being silly, Lalla."

"She's being stupid." My mother was shaking.

"OK, she's being stupid."

"It was a stupid thing to say. What was she thinking about, to ask such a thing? What are we working for, to have a daughter who understands so little? A dog?"

"She didn't mean it."

"That's even worse. Why ask for what you don't want? We give you everything, everything, and you understand nothing." Her face was quite white, and I knew that the little brown and white dog with loving eyes I had conjured up in the face of her anger would never return. I had pushed my mother far enough; more than anything, I feared being the reason that she cried.

"She was stupid. That's all. There's no charge. It's all right, Anna."

"It is not all right. There is a price for stupidity. And it is never the stupid people who pay it. They lumber about like elephants, trampling all over the things other people have planted, then complain when the plants don't grow. But they don't go without. Oh no. They want what they want, no matter what has gone before or what will come after."

"I know, I know."

"And that's what stupidity is. Wanting something because you want it. It's not enough, Lalla. It's not enough to want something. You have to need it. To need it with your whole heart and soul, and with every last atom of your being, because everything you get is at a cost somewhere. If people had stuck to that, we'd still be living in beautiful places, surrounded by trees, eating food from the earth." The image calmed her; her breathing was easier now, and I knew that if she cried, it would not be because of me. The dog retreated across the room and the door closed behind it.

The doctor passed me the red mug, its handle towards me. "Careful," he said, "it's hot."

"Did you talk to my mother about stupidity? When you were interviewed for the ship?"

He nodded. "Anna and I agreed that the only thing to do with stupidity is to escape from it. To get away, somewhere where the decisions it makes cannot affect you. She knew it, but she could never make up her mind to go. We were all sorry about that. We talked about Anna in the holding centre, often. But Michael refused to force her. He is a truly great man, your father, and you are a very lucky young woman." He pulled up his sleeve and looked at his watch. A watch. He had a watch.

"I'll have to go soon," he said.

"Why?"

"There are some people I said I'd meet."

"Can I come?"

"No."

"You're doing something," I retorted. I thought of all the times I'd watched him in the dining room. "You and Abigail and Vikram. And that man with the grey hair down to his ears and lots of stubble. Luke. You meet up secretly." There. I had said it now, and my little piece of hope drew breath and shook out its wings. I watched it fly, sparkling and golden, to the doctor, and willed him to give it a home in which to grow. I plunged on. "You do know what's happening, don't you? We're sailing round in circles and that's all we're going to do for ever. There's no island waiting for us. But you're trying to take the ship somewhere, aren't you? To land somewhere. I can help you."

The doctor stared at me and I felt the tape across my nose, the tenderness around my eyes, the scrapes on my palms. The room seemed to turn grey. He closed his eyes and put his forehead in his hands. "Little girl," he said into his palms, shaking his head. "Don't do this to yourself."

"Do what?"

Hope folded its wings and settled on the desk to wait. The doctor lifted up his head. "Do you know how I came to be here?" he asked.

"You had a wife called Sarah and a baby who died," I said. "That's all I know."

"Then listen," he said. "I knew the baby might die. I knew the moment that I told my Sarah to push, and she said that she was pushing, and I felt the bump and it was hard and frozen and the head was in the wrong place. I had to get our baby out quickly. Really quickly. Don't talk," he said as I drew breath. "You need to stay still, so that dressing can set properly."

I put my grazed hands around my hot tea mug and focused on the pain.

"I needed to cut her open. It was routine once, back in the days when there were proper medicines and all doctors had to do was call for them. But my Sarah was too late for that. Hospitals didn't have anaesthetics and clean blood anymore."

"What happened?"

"I waited. I don't know what I was waiting for. Some miracle, I suppose. Anaesthetic to fall from the sky. But it didn't. Sarah was screaming, and when I finally got on with it, she passed out with the first cut. The hospital generator was working for once, so I put her on the ventilator. I rummaged in her belly. It was like looking for a working pen in a drawer full of junk. And the baby I pulled from her—a girl, blue and purple, covered in a layer of white wax and her mother's blood—made no sound. I took her, I held her, I breathed for her. I told her I loved her. But I'd waited too long. I couldn't save her. I laid my baby on her mother and left the room, so that they would not hear me howl."

I sat absolutely still.

"There was a monitor and when I went back in, I could see Sarah's heartbeat growing weaker and weaker. I took our daughter in my arms and sat beside my dying wife, watching. And then Sarah opened her eyes and stared at the baby, and I saw that she was terrified."

"What did you do?"

"I told her not to worry. I told her that the baby was fine."

"But that wasn't true."

"No."

"And?"

"And then I turned off the ventilator."

"Why?"

"So that the last thing Sarah knew before she died was love and not despair."

"Why are you telling me this?"

"Because you're looking for something, Lalla, and you won't find it in me. Or in anyone here. I was truly sorry I could not save your mother. And Lalla—think of this. If I'd acted more decisively, I could have saved my baby, if not my wife. And if I'd had the infirmary and all its resources, I could have saved them both..." He let his sentence trail away and I hung onto it with all my might. But he didn't finish it. He took a breath and started again. "Your father and I..." An agonised look crossed his face. "Try and understand, Lalla. Try and understand what the ship cost, and what it means. I thought I would die with missing Sarah and my baby. But now—now that all time is the same time, the world in which I could have saved them is the same as the world in which they died. So when I look at the ship and all that we have here, I don't see a prison. I don't see a trap. I see love."

"So do I," I protested, but he took no notice.

"I see a place where Sarah and my child are with me. Not

where they could be with me, or where they might come to me, but where they are. And I love it for that. I love Michael for bringing me here, to live out my days with my family, in comfort, with purpose. And I know what it cost, and that it was a price worth paying."

"What did it cost?" I asked, but he ignored me.

"Think of the ship as humanity's last song," he said. "I've found what I'm looking for, and as far as I know, so has everyone else on this ship. I've told you my story. Everyone else's may be different, but they all come down to this. We are where we want to be. And we thank Michael for that."

It was a warning. My nose was pulsing and my eyes beginning to droop. But I could not let go. "What about your secret meetings?" I said.

He pressed down the tape on my nose a shade too firmly; my eyes widened and watered. "You have secret meetings too, Lalla. You keep yours and I'll keep mine, and we'll respect each other as Michael asks. Now, will it be the infirmary or your cabin?"

The message was clear. I could hide where I liked, but I would not find what I was looking for in the doctor, and I would not be welcome in the community of the ship until I had properly surrendered to it.

We walked to my cabin in the dawn light. The doctor turned his back while I changed into my nightdress, then helped me into my bunk. He held out a couple of pink pills for me, and when I did not take them, he pulled a vial from his pocket, put the pills into it and put it on the shelf above my basin. As he left, he stood in the doorway and said, "Take some advice. Skip the bit of your life where you have to rebel and go straight to the part where you embrace what your parents have done for you. Skip the part where you throw everything away and cut straight to being happy. I mean it, Lalla. Especially now."

"Why now?"

"You and Tom need to come and see me. Together. You need to listen to me, and to yourself, and you need to eat. Will you do those things, Lalla? Do you promise?"

I felt my eyes narrow and my face go hard. Who was the doctor, to tell Tom and me what to do? "Does my father know about your watch?" I sneered. "And your mugs?"

He turned his back on me and shut the door behind him.

EIGHTEEN

I bite the apple ❧ the fourth deck and what I found there ❧ Emily's story

I made a mark beside my bunk; now there were eighty-one. Eighty-one sunrises. In the time before, that would have been eleven weeks and four days. More than two months and less than three. On the ship, it meant nothing, but I would not let the counting go, no matter how uncomfortable it made Tom or how much it went against my father. We had been too quick to throw the mast into the sea; the fact that it lay there, being eaten by whatever creatures there were, or simply rusting alone in the junk and poison that had been thrown there over the decades, did not mean I could forget the bulletins it had once broadcast.

The doctor had forbidden me to work until my face was healed. I was to lie in my bunk and rest until he gave me permission to get up. All around me, I heard the sounds of the people waking up and preparing for the day. I heard water running in the cabin to my left; that was the woman with the long grey hair cleaning her teeth. The clunk that followed shortly afterwards was the tap being turned off. Another such clunk came from the cabin to my right; subconsciously, they had synchronised their teeth-cleaning. Oh, we were all so safe, so safe, wrapped in our soft down duvets with our shining white teeth and clean clean skin, gradually becoming one.

But the toothpaste would run out.

We are better nourished than our forefathers, my father said. *Their bread was only made of wheat; ours is fortified with vitamins and proteins. Their vegetables rotted after a few days; ours will last for ever, their flavour and nourishment locked in until we need it. We are deficient in nothing; if we were, we could take a tablet from one of the millions of little bottles with which we are equipped. We want for nothing. Nothing.*

I gripped my duvet and decided not to clean my teeth. I would never clean them again. If they rotted, the rot would give the ship a marker of time that could not be ignored or banished. My healing bruises would mark time for a while, but when my face healed, I'd smile every single day, so that the people could see my teeth turn yellow, then black, then fall out one by one. The walls might remain white and the crockery unchipped, but they would all remember that Lalage Paul once had teeth.

My mouth was dry. I thought about getting up for water, but my head ached and I lay back on my pillow. The noises were not only those of my neighbours heaving themselves from their bunks, making their beds, slipping their deck shoes on for breakfast. No, the very ship itself seemed to wake up at this time. The rings and clangs were the metal plates of which the ship was constructed expanding as the sun rose, just as we all stretched our bodies to the new day.

I heard Helen's voice shepherding the children to breakfast. Helen's school was now a regular part of the ship; my father had given her a huge touchscreen, and the children sat around it, watching as she showed them how to form letters, read words, navigate the research room and the gallery. I'd seen them going from breakfast to lessons, then tumbling out like so many bread rolls from the basket at dinner, and bouncing to the net to swim, or to the sports hall, where Tom took their football lessons.

My father had created it, and they were happy.

I waited for silence. My duvet was light and warm, the way I always imagined a cloud would feel when I watched them floating across the blue sky, their edges tinged with sunlight. My mother, perhaps, was sitting on such a cloud, looking down on me and wondering whether I was going to be all right. Maybe Tola was with her, laughing at the way some people worried about whether there were going to be any pink cakes left when it was their turn to choose. Maybe there was a cloud big enough for all of us, and we would climb to it slowly as the ship sank underneath us, and we would all sit there, comfortable and warm, eating fruit. *Here, Lalla,* my mother said, *this is for you.* And she put something cold and hard and round into my hands, and I smelled sweetness and sharpness and my teeth stung as I pierced its skin and juice flooded my mouth. An apple, an apple, and the eggs had shells.

I sat up sharply. A sound, not of settling metal but of wood, hard yet forgiving, close to my head. The sound came again, a dull, dense thud, and I realised someone was knocking at my door.

It could only be Tom. *Love Tom, and let it be.*

I was naked under my nightdress. As I raised myself from my bunk, the cotton brushed the backs of my knees and my stomach and my breasts and sent blood rushing to my face. Where the cotton touched, I burned; where it did not, the skin was cold, and the hairs upon it lifted in anticipation.

Tom had come.

Maybe the ship could be my home. We could tell my father, have a cabin together, make a home among the boxes on the fourth deck, install a ladder and make love on the roof of the world. Love, everyone kept saying. Love. Tom had missed me at the breakfast table and run to find me when he heard I had been hurt. Love was the biggest thing after all. If we loved each other, everything else could rot.

Except my teeth. I would clean them after all. There was toothpaste enough for now.

I took a deep breath, steeled myself against the pain in my head, and opened the door. There, on the threshold, was my breakfast on a tray.

I hated them all. I hated Emily and Gerhard and Patience and the doctor and Tom and his green eyes and Helen and the school. I hated my father for living and my mother for dying. I hated myself for being so sure that Tom would come to me, and for giving myself away to the doctor. And most of all, I hated this life, this death, this timeless place of plenty that I had not chosen and over which I had no control.

I kicked the tray, scattering bread and jam and tea over the corridor, and went back into my cabin, slamming the door. I picked up the apple Tom had given me, green and shining, and I thought, what if this is the last apple in the whole world? I clung to Tom; Tom had brought me the apple. This apple is mine, I thought, and I will have it. I brought it up to my mouth; I bared my teeth; I brought them down on the apple as though it was the last thing I would ever do. My teeth cracked; my broken nose jolted under its dressing; I breathed dry dust into my lungs and choked. The apple fell to the floor with a puff of plaster dust, its shining green coat of wax cracked and falling away. For a moment I thought, if that was an apple I'm not missing much. Then pain blossomed through the anaesthetic. I held on to it, and as it receded I refused to let it go. My cabin went dark and I slipped into a place that was something like sleep, where my mother was calling me.

I lay in a haze of pain and followed the sound of her voice, past the infirmary, past the pharmacy. It was dark, but somehow I knew what I was looking at and where I was going, because she was leading me. On the second deck I peered into the games stadium, where a line of footballs waited for breakfast to be over. *No,*

Lalla, you must keep going. So I did, onto the third deck, where I opened doors into empty rooms while my mother called, *Come further up, further up.* I climbed up to the fourth deck, where a delicious smell came from behind a closed door. I pushed it open and sunlight poured over me. There was a tree, covered in little pink flowers from which petals fell like rain. I stepped in, and felt grass beneath my feet. *Shut the door behind you, Lalla, and you need never go back.* I could see the grey metal of the ship through the open door behind me.

I opened the next door, where row upon row of floured rounds of dough rose gently in front of an open oven filled with logs of brightly burning wood. Behind the next door, an old woman sat in a rocking chair with a little child on her knee and a storybook in her hands. Behind the next was a garden in which rows of feathery leaves stuck out of the ground; an old man in muddy blue trousers pulled at the leaves and there, dangling from his hand in a spray of earth, was a carrot. The man held out the carrot to me; his eyes were green. "Are you Tom's grandfather?" I asked, but my mother was still calling.

If you come far enough, you will find me.

The corridor stretched before me lined with doors on either side, hundreds of doors; I could not see their end. I saw a man painting in fat strokes of blue and yellow with a bandage over his ear. A woman in a long lace dress held her hair in a knot on the top of her head and gazed into a mirror; seven or eight girls floated across a wooden floor in pale pink dresses that stuck out; a whole orchestra played something that touched me below my ribcage and made me feel that I could listen for ever. Music. I would love to play music, I thought, and wondered if someone in this orchestra would teach me if I closed the door.

A man wrote with a pen on sheets of paper that he threw over his shoulder as he filled them. Another raised an axe and cut the head off a chicken; the chicken ran around headless for a few seconds, spurting blood from its neck. And behind the next door were thousands, millions of people. At first I thought it was a riot, because so many people were gathered together, but I noticed that they were staring at a patch of green with men running about on it chasing a black and white ball.

The football made me think about Tom. Tom, with his strong hands and green eyes and his desire for me. Tom was not behind any of these doors. Even as I tried to choose between the music and the dancing, the garden and the bread slowly rising, I knew that what I was looking at was as distant and illusory as the idea of my mother coming back. They were images from other people's dreams. That was all I was. A part of other people's dreams. The entire ship was a dream that my father and mother had conjured up for me.

Only Tom was real. He had not come yet, but he would, and if I wasn't there, he would go away. The thought of Tom pulled me back, away from the corridor and the doors, back to my cabin, where the sun was shining full through my porthole and my nose was bleeding and I felt blinded by the pain in my head and my nose and my torn cheek. My hand was being held, and when I opened my eyes, I saw Tom hovering over me, his green eyes wide with concern.

"Lalla," he said. "Oh, Lalla, what have you done to yourself?"

"The ship did it," I said, struggling to sit up. He arranged my pillows and helped me settle back. It was easier to settle when he was with me. "I went out in the storm. But Tom, listen. I know what's going on. And I know what we should do. I'm sure now."

Tom sighed, but before he could answer me, there was a knock at the door. He jumped to open it; it felt as though he was avoiding what I had to say. Emily stood there with my breakfast tray at her feet. The tea-soaked bread and broken jam pot had all been gathered neatly together. In her hands she held another tray, this one with two bowls on it—one of soup and another of tinned pears. She gave the tray to Tom.

"The doctor says Lalla needs to eat," she said as she stepped over the ruined breakfast tray and came in. The little cabin was crowded now.

"I'm not hungry."

"You're hurt," Emily said carefully. "You need to rest and eat and give your body a chance to recover." She took the soup from the tray and offered it to me but I kept my hands by my sides. "Lalla," she said, "I'm trying to help you. Everyone is." She put the bowl back on the tray and motioned to Tom to put the tray on the desk. "What's this?" she said, as a bit of the wax and plaster apple crunched under her deck shoe. "Honestly, Lalla, you make more mess than everyone else on the ship put together." I looked at the white and green shard in her hand. She was turning it over, touching the sharp edges.

"That's the apple I gave you, isn't it?" Tom said. "What happened to it?"

"It wasn't an apple," I said, my voice wavering.

"You didn't try to eat it, did you, Lalla?" Tom looked as though he was about to laugh, and then he sighed. "Oh, Lalla, you are an idiot. Why can't you just let things be what they are?" I turned away from him, but the cabin was so small I ended up looking at the wall beside my porthole.

Emily sat beside me with her arm around my shoulders. "We've got apples, Lalla. I've told you before. Apple pie, apple crumble, apple pancakes, apple strudel, apple cake. Tell me what you want, Lalla, and we'll get it for you. Won't we, Tom?"

Tom stood awkwardly by the door. "She doesn't mean apples like that. She means, you know—a round apple, off a tree. But what's the difference? Lalla? Really?" I kept staring at my bit of wall, angry that he was speaking for me, angry that he was belittling something I'd cared about. "I'd better get to lunch," he said when I wouldn't answer. "And then I've got work. But I'll come and see you later, all right?" I wouldn't answer, and he was gone.

Emily smiled after him. "He can't sit still, that one," she said as the door closed. She stroked the hair away from my face and wiped the tears from my bruises very, very gently. "Your poor face, Lalla. What were you thinking of?" She took my hands in both of hers.

"We're floating round in circles," I said, sniffing, tasting blood at the back of my throat. "No one will listen to me, and I don't know what to do. We're not allowed to talk about the past. We don't know what's going on back on land. And I've broken my apple, and Tom called me an idiot."

Emily looked around my cabin and saw the pink pills above the sink. "When I was a teenager," she said, walking over and picking up the vial, "I thought the world would end when the law against the manufacture of new clothes was passed."

"I don't remember that."

"No, you'd have been a baby then. Maybe not even born. But the point is that the world didn't end. We had to change our ideas of what new meant. And you need to do the same. You've got this idea of what it means to be alive, and you won't even try and accept that this is it. I can't bear it, Lalla. I can't bear to see you turning your back on all this. On Michael. On Tom." She held out the pills. "Do you want one of these? Does it hurt?"

"You all knew," I said, shaking my head. "You knew we weren't going anywhere, and you didn't tell me."

"We all told you a thousand times. Alice. Tom. Roger. Even Michael. You just wouldn't hear." She looked ruefully at me as she put the pills back, and I thought of the doctor and the way he had lost his wife and child.

"What happened to you?" I asked.

"It doesn't matter. I'm happy. I live right here, right now, and Michael is—oh, Michael's wonderful. He's everything. Why would I talk about the past? The ship is just…it's like Heaven. Made with love."

"I missed your testimony."

"Whose fault was that?" She knelt on the floor, gathering up bits of broken apple in a cupped hand. She put the apple pieces on the breakfast tray and brushed the plaster dust from her hands. "All right. I'll tell you. But then I'm never going to talk about it again. Do you understand?" I nodded. "Do you remember Tube trains? Before the stations were all sealed up?"

"I remember the boarded-up stations. I don't remember the trains."

"Well. This was eight or nine years before the ship, just after the Dove. People risked the Tube if they had work to get to. The gangs down there were at war with each other, after all, not with ordinary people. So when the screen said there was work in Uxbridge—a government distribution centre being built—my husband decided to go."

"You were married?"

Emily nodded. "We'd just found a flat," she said. "You remember the Possession of Property Act?"

"A bit," I said, although I didn't.

"It came in just after the Nazareth Act. Any property that had belonged to the banks reverted straight to the emergency government. If you found an empty property and stayed in it for seven days, you could live there. But if you left it, there was always the risk that someone else would take it. And we wanted to have a baby. So Peter went to Uxbridge alone. We'd saved enough food for five days; we didn't think it would be that long."

"My mother and I went out sometimes," I said. But even as I spoke, I thought of the locks, the bolts, the keypad whose code we changed as regularly as we checked the government updates on our screens.

"It was a good flat," Emily said, "and I had my screen, and the next biometric re-registration wasn't for a week. I was quite pleased to stay. I never really liked the outside. But Peter was different. Peter liked adventure. He liked challenges. Tom reminds me of him, actually. He took a rucksack and went to the Tube station. Covent Garden, it was. We used to laugh, because we'd never have been able to live in Covent Garden if it hadn't been for the crash. It was Peter's idea. He used to see the best about everything. Even those foul government-issue water-sterilising tablets."

"My mother used to boil my water."

Emily nodded. "Lucky you. Peter just said that at least the taste told us that the water was safe. The second night he was away, the bulletin went live to Covent Garden station. I thought it was a new act, or maybe even a feelgood story about a gang defeat or something. And then the screen showed the lift doors opening."

"I thought Tube stations had moving staircases."

"Covent Garden had these great big lifts. And on the bulletin, the lift arrived in the station, and the doors opened, and the floor was covered in dead bodies. One man stood alone in the middle, still alive."

"Peter?"

"I could see the terror on his face. And blood—oh, the blood. Shining on the floor, filling the gaps between the bodies." She looked at the floor, where the blood from my nose was congealing. "The troops arrived and I was glad, because I thought they'd help him." I held my hand out to her and she gripped it without looking at me. "I thought they'd bring him home. We had an oil stove for emergencies and I lit it to make him a hot drink, even though I knew he'd tell me off for wasting the oil."

"What happened?"

"The troops arrested him."

"Arrested Peter?"

Emily nodded. "When the bulletin was repeated the next hour, they said he'd been found guilty of exploiting the instability of the transport infrastructure to murder fellow travellers for food. They unpacked his rucksack live on air and put the case to a Peoples' Jury."

My mother and father had never allowed me to participate in a Peoples' Jury, but it was impossible to use the screen and not see them. If your card was valid, you could vote—the red button for execution, the green for a peoples' pardon.

"The rucksack was full of food. Powdered milk, flour, dried egg, pasta, tinned vegetables. A sponge pudding in a tin. Sugar. And with each item they took out, the red bar kept going up and up. Peter said he'd been given the food as wages, and that the bodies had been thrown into the lift after a gang fought with troops on the platform. But the screen displayed the comments people sent in, and all anyone wrote was that if Peter was telling the truth about the gang, how come the gang hadn't taken the food? I kept pressing the green, over and over, but I only had one vote. Peter was executed, and the next day they announced that the Tube would be closed. Permanently."

She released my hand and I watched her rocking gently on my bed.

"What happened?"

"I had—" she clutched at her stomach as though she was in pain—"this burning rage. His face, staring down at those dead bodies, so terrified—it was all I could think of. They used him. They just wanted to close the stations so they wouldn't have to worry about the gangs. He was set up. I had to do something."

"What did you do?"

"I disabled the Dove and got on the raven routes. I knew I

was risking my screen and my registration. I didn't even know what I was looking for. At first it was just obsolete stuff—tonnes of it. Supermarkets, holidays, all that campaign stuff about saving the insects. Insurance. Everything for sale in a place where there was nothing left. But I kept at it, and when I finally accessed the restricted stuff, I was sick. Lalla, it was horrible. People—and animals—and children. And I couldn't even close my eyes in case I missed a pop-up. I had to go through it all until I found the blogs. But I found them, and when I did, I posted and posted. Anywhere I could find. I wrote about Peter, and about the trial, and about the look on his face and the rucksack full of food that had got him executed. I told the Peoples' Jury voters that they were cowards and fools, and that they deserved to lose the Tube. The longer the Dove was disabled, the higher the risk, but I could not stop. And then there was a knock at the door."

"What did you do?"

"My screen began to burn. Some virus. It was amazing it had held out for as long as it did."

"Did you have another screen?"

She turned to me and her eyes were huge and shining. Her face was pale; she reminded me of my mother, and I stopped listening for a moment. I was thinking about my mother's face, frowning with impatience, or pale with determination, and finally, purple and strangled with pain.

"Do you think I had a stack of screens behind the door?" Emily demanded. I said nothing. We had had a stack of screens. "My screen was dead," she told me, her eyes dry and blazing. "Peter was dead, killed by the people who were supposed to protect us, and our dream of a family was over. I'd lost everything. Can you understand that? Of course not," she continued before I could speak. "You got given everything you wanted, didn't you?"

"I want my mother," I said.

Emily's face softened again and she put her hand to my cheek. "I want a child."

I pushed her hand away from my face. I didn't care about her story anymore. Emily was not my mother and never would be. I wanted my mother. I wanted something of her, something she had touched, worn, owned. I pulled my clothes from the cupboard, tossing them across the room while Emily hopped about, flapping her hands and begging me to stop, but there was nothing of my mother left. My orange dress had never been returned. Even the marks on the broken button had been made by someone else. I called up books we had read together on my screen, but they flashed across the screen exactly as they had the first time, the second time, every other time. There were no pencil marks, no crumbs or stains, none of the million telltale creases and folds we had made in the pages of our paper books. And our paper books were still in London. Was my mother with them, a collection of crumbs and creases? A crumb or a crease was all I wanted.

I ran to the lower deck, ignoring the pain. Emily's voice followed me, calling, "It was your father at the door. Your father, Lalla, come to save me." But it might as well have been the troops she'd feared for all I cared.

I stood where I had stood when my mother's body was released into the sea. I watched the part of the sea where she had gone under for a moment, then floated back to the surface, her dress swirling around her in mockery of my father's plans. But as long as I stared, I could not see the swirls and eddies repeated. There were no scars on the water. My mother was dead. The water had covered her over. That was our existence on board ship. It was what my father meant by time no longer. A life of the moment, a life of now, with no yesterdays and no tomorrow. There would be hunger and tears, even death, but the water's surface would never be marked.

What was I to do? Return obediently to my cabin? To accept that this was my life now, and take what sweetness from it I could? To take my place, love Tom, and let Emily love me?

Or to take all the pink pills I could find and hope that my mother would take me to the fourth deck once more, where I could choose a door, and shut it behind me?

Footsteps came up behind me. "Lalla?" said a voice, and it was my father's voice, and Emily was tripping along behind him, worry written all over her face. But the hands that were placed on my shoulders were his hands, and the face that looked into mine when I turned around was his face.

"I want my mother," I said.

"She's dead."

"But I can't feel her. I can't hear her." My voice wobbled out of control. "I can't even remember what she looks like."

"Darling girl. Darling, darling girl."

I rested my swollen face on his shoulder. "I broke my apple," I sobbed. He kissed my cheek. "It was made of wax. Wax and plaster."

"Oh, Lalla. I never imagined you'd think it was real."

I stopped crying. "How do you know about it?"

"It came from a museum, before we sailed. I was going to give it to Anna—*have an apple, Michael*, she used to say, do you remember? But she died, and when Tom came to see me, asking if I could suggest a present for you, of course I thought of the apple."

"You gave it to Tom? To give to me? It was your idea?" He nodded and I felt my stomach drop to the deck.

"Where is Tom now?" I asked.

"He's probably busy. The ship carries on, you know. We can't just stop everything because one person gets hurt. Have a shower. Choose something pretty to wear. Don't just sit and wait for him."

The pain was creeping back. My eyes were watering and my nose pulsating under the dressing. I could feel blood seeping through the bandages and trickling down my face.

"Why can't I find my mother?" I whispered.

"Because you're looking in the wrong places. You should think of the things you loved most in her, and find them in other people."

But what I had loved most in my mother was the way she stood up to my father. And that was the one thing I could not find in any other person on the ship.

My father led me back to my cabin and I consoled myself by imagining Tom longing for me, missing goal after goal because he wanted me so much. I dreamed up scenarios in which he got into trouble and had a trial like Helen's, where he stood up and told everyone that the ship could sink for all he cared, because he loved me, and he was going to help me take the ship to land.

Emily brought my supper on a tray. Mashed potato and gravy, carefully selected so that I would not have to chew. I gave the tray back to her untouched, and she rolled her eyes and went away.

Grow up, Patience had said. So had my father. Even Alice had told me to try and be happy, which meant the same thing. But we were speaking different languages. To them, growing up meant acceptance of the world around me. I did not yet know what it meant to me.

What was on the other side of my door that I wanted, anyway? Food made me feel sick. I had no desire for book group, or football, or tennis, or swimming, no urge to learn to knit, or embroider, and no reason to sit quietly and count my blessings as the others did. The ship had taken my mother and my father from me, and although it had given me Tom, the balance would not be even until Tom and I were together, and on our way somewhere. It didn't have to be London. *I would not have my children be alone*, my father had said, and yet here I was, alone. I could not trust him. I had my portal, but there was no facility on it for sending messages now that the mast was gone. We were all flesh and blood friends, my father said; if we wanted to tell someone something, all we had to do was knock on their cabin door.

But Tom clearly thought the football was more important.

I turned my portal on and wandered the galleries of the British Museum, but the photographs were meaningless. I wanted to press my hands against the glass; to be tantalised by the possibility of touch. I tried to read, but my screen wasn't working properly—*Ballet Shoes* had frozen at Petrova longing for a moving staircase and I could neither read on nor load another book.

Emily came back with a mug of warm milk and some biscuits on a tray. It was getting dark, and I wondered if she had left it so late on purpose, so that she would not have to stay with me.

"I want *Ballet Shoes*," I said.

"Ballet?" she said eagerly. "I'm sure..."

"No, the book. *Ballet Shoes*. I can't get my portal library to scroll."

"Take it to Christopher," she said. "He'll sort it out. Do you want me to do it for you?"

And suddenly, I was gripped by a panic so real that I struggled to breathe. The room swam around me, and I forgot about Tom, about being shut up, about not being allowed to work. I drew breath to scream, but instead found myself sobbing.

"What's the matter, Lalla?" Emily said, putting down the tray on my desk and coming to me. "Lalla, talk to me. Let me help you." But I was crying too hard for words, and my breath came in gasps.

"Is it your mother?" she asked, putting her arms around me. I found myself clinging to her. Salt tears set my cut face stinging. What if *Ballet Shoes* was gone for ever? I tried to explain, but fear made me inarticulate, and I found myself sobbing, gulping for breath, until I wore myself out. As my sobs subsided, I became aware of Emily's arms around me and wriggled away.

"Drink your milk," she said as I hugged my knees. "If you dip the biscuits in, they'll be soft enough for you to eat." She went to my desk and fetched the tray. "Shall I send Tom to visit?" she asked.

"No." I looked at Emily and wanted to hurt her like I was hurting. "He'll come if he wants to. You only come because my father makes you."

"That's not true."

"It is. None of you care about me. You just want me to be like you. Forgetting what's gone. Forgetting the dead. All of you just want me to be what you want. Not one single person on this ship gives a damn about me or what I want."

Emily threw the tray. Milk splashed across the wall; biscuits, mug and plate shattered together. The tray fell with a flat crash. The light of my desk lamp caught the fragments of plate as they exploded from the wall. Almost immediately, she knelt and began to gather the pieces together. She held one up for a moment; it was pointed and sharp. If she drives that into me, I thought, I will not flinch. I will bear the pain, and my scars will tell my story.

But she did not stab me. She put the pieces on the tray and spoke slowly and carefully. "Lalla," she said, then took a breath. "Love works both ways. It's not enough to love someone. You have to let them love you, too." She brushed the biscuit and china crumbs from her hands onto the tray and spoke as though she were reciting a lesson. "Love is patient," she said. "Love is kind. But all you've ever done with our love for you—Tom's, mine, Patience's, even Michael's—is to turn it into some kind of weapon. Tom doesn't know what you want. None of us do. Michael told me to bring you round with love, but my goodness, you don't exactly make it easy." She nodded towards the milk, its translucent tear tracks marking the wall. "I'll have this cleaned up. Get some sleep and sort yourself out, Lalla, because I can't take any more of you." She took the tray in both hands, stood up, and walked away.

The night was black, but I knew Emily would find her way. She would not be left to fall in a storm, to break her face on the ship. She was loved; she let people love her, and neither the ship nor my father had anything to prove to her.

NINETEEN

Oranges ❁ *panna cotta* ❁ *subversives on
the ship*

That night, my thoughts circled and clashed and made noises I could not bear. Tom and my father, and Emily, and Roger, all tumbled around in my aching head until I didn't know what to think. Less than three months ago, my biggest challenge had been to remember the code on our keypad. Now my mother was dead, my father had adopted five hundred other people and my lover said he wanted to marry me, then walked away. When the first rays of sunrise came through my porthole, there was a knock on the door. I lifted my head to see, not Tom, but my father, standing in the doorway. He looked at the milk marks on the wall, the blood on the floor, and at me, crumpled and bruised on the bed. I expected sympathy, but he was not sympathetic.

"Emily was in tears most of last night," he said. "You can't go round upsetting people just because you're angry." He sat down. "You were lucky, compared with other people."

"I know."

"I think you forget. Do you know what Diana was doing when I rescued her for the ship, for example?"

"No," I said, resisting the temptation to say that I didn't care.

"She was standing over her brother's dead body with an iron bar."

"Why?" I asked, interested in spite of myself.

"She was fighting off poachers. People who came for the freshly dead." I felt sick. "There's a lot of meat on a human being. We spared you a lot. Cannibalism. Chlorella." I shrugged my shoulders. "It's an algae. You grow it in human urine and eat it to keep yourself alive. Anna never taught you that, did she? It's time for you to stop wallowing and wake up. I've spoken to Gerhard and you're going to the kitchen. You will work there for a while, and as you work, you will look at the food that is provided for you here. You will eat it, and you will stop obsessing about apples. Of course there are things you don't have. But there is so, so much more that you do."

"You never ate chlorella."

"How would you know? You have no idea. Literally no idea of what I went through to keep you and your mother safe. Of what the world had become."

I left him in my cabin and stalked off to the kitchen immediately, so that Tom would not find me if he came. *Accept things for what they are*, he had said. But to do that, you had to know what they were. Otherwise, you would accept something, and then find it was something else, and then you'd have to accept that, and no one would ever know what anything was. How could that be life?

Gerhard nodded as I walked in. He told me to take over making up the orange juice. He and Emily brought up concentrate from the freezers after dinner and put it into plastic buckets to thaw overnight. He showed me the jugs and the proportions and I began. As I did so, I watched the people through the kitchen doors. They drifted in, and I watched the patterns of their groupings. I watched Helen. She had been reabsorbed, forgiven for the photograph album. I saw Diana, and thought about the people who would have eaten her brother. Frozen orange juice didn't seem so bad, when that was the alternative.

Tom came in. I watched him smiling at people who were not me. Was he looking for me? Was my father keeping him away from me, or did he simply not want me anymore? I couldn't tell. Gerhard and Emily hugged him, warm, encouraging touches for which they were rewarded with sighs. This is an orange now, I thought, poking at the ice rock as it turned into slush. This is what an orange means. It is all an orange means.

"This is an orange," I said, jumping as my words bounced back at me from the walls. Gerhard looked around from the bucket of egg powder. Scrambled eggs for breakfast. Scrambled eggs and orange juice. Those were eggs, these were oranges. Eggs, oranges, eggs, oranges, Eggsoranges.

Tom, I love you. I stared into the bucket. Was it true? If I forgave him for the apple, I would be accepting this world.

"Are there any oranges left?" I asked suddenly, my heart pounding. "Real ones?"

Gerhard stared at me. *Please,* I begged silently, *please please don't tell me that these are oranges.* I leaned towards him, feeling sick with a struggling maggot of hope inside that, even now, refused to die.

Gerhard looked over his shoulder. We were alone in the kitchen, and he sighed.

"Tom loves you, you know, Lalla. We all do."

I refused to answer. He looked over his shoulder again, but we were alone, and I stared at him until he said, "I had oranges once. Long, long ago."

"Did you have the last orange? The last ever orange?"

"I don't know."

I hesitated over the enormity of what I was about to say, then pointed at the slush and said it anyway.

"This is not an orange."

Gerhard looked sharply at me. Then he shrugged. "Oranges were a nuisance. Most of the orange went into the bin and the rest you had to wash off your hands." He pointed at the plastic bags of concentrate, the cartoon oranges on its label round and bright. "This is the way to eat oranges. No skins, no pith."

"Pith?"

"The white, bitter part under the skin."

I could no more stop than I could produce a fresh orange from the sea. I remembered the petrolheads on the streets. *I can stop any time I like*, they used to yell at us as we passed. *Any time I like.* "An orange had white parts? It wasn't just orange all the way through?"

"No. The very outside was the brightest part. It was filled with tiny little sacs of oil."

"Sacks?"

"Little bubbles under the skin, that burst when you squeezed them. The only way to start peeling an orange was first to pull some of the skin off with your teeth. And the oil would spray out and sting your lips. And then you tore off the skin, and you'd be left with bits of white pith clinging to the orange, and you'd have to tear each bit off, and nine times out of ten you'd go through the membrane into the orange, and the juice would start running out onto your hand and down your sleeve."

"Through the membrane? But you'd already taken the skin off."

"No, the individual segments were separated by a membrane. Oranges came in segments. The orange was spherical. But the sphere itself was made of segments—portions—separate parts, each covered in a thin skin of its own. That was what contained the flesh and the juice. You pulled each segment free of the others, one by one, and ate them."

Any time I like. This was better than a picture. I'd seen lots of pictures. But for the first time, I felt I was learning what an orange was. "Did you eat the segments whole?"

Gerhard smiled. "My brother did. One segment, one mouthful.

All gone at once, and the juice dribbling down the sides of his mouth. Me, I used to bite the end off each segment and suck out the insides. And my sister used to slide her fingernail under the segment skin and try to pull it away without bursting the little tiny globules of juice underneath, and then she'd lick the surface under the skin until she couldn't wait anymore, and then she'd bite."

"What globules?"

"The tasty bit of the orange..." He suddenly broke off and grabbed a saucepan from the huge metal grid that took up one wall of the galley. All the utensils hung from it, on hooks shaped like the letter S, and when he snatched the saucepan, the handle caught on the edge of the hook. Gerhard yanked it free, and the whole grid started ringing, as though a hundred people in hard-soled shoes were running up the metal staircase.

"What about the tasty bit of the orange?" I insisted.

He slammed the saucepan onto the range. "It's not important."

"It is to me."

He rummaged on the racks, trying to drown me out. But if my father had not managed to drown me out with the vastness of the great seas, Gerhard and his saucepan lids stood no chance. *Any time I like*. But I did not like.

Apples.

Shell eggs.

Oranges.

Life on the ship meant many things. I would never be hungry. I would never be bored. I could make love with Tom for the asking. But I would never be able to decide how I would eat an orange. I would never crack an egg. I would never know how it felt to press my teeth into an apple. How could I feel such a sense of loss for things I had never had?

As though he had heard me, Gerhard said, "You'll never see an orange. And okay so that's a shame. But you'd never have had one on land either. If all that mess was so great, why did your ancestors work so hard to get rid of it? What's the point in Michael giving us the essence of oranges if you, his daughter, cannot throw away the rubbish that has gone?"

"My father said the same thing about pineapples."

Gerhard did not answer. He stared at me across the galley in silence. His eyes were grey; I suddenly saw him floating in the net, with holes for his eyes and the sea showing through. There were five packages upstairs with his name on. This meant that he was forty-five years old. His hair was dark, but there was grey in it too. Then he crashed the pan lid back into the rack, then hooked the pan back onto the wall grid and set all the utensils jangling again.

My father had brought him home. That was the difference. My home had been a flat in London, near the British Museum, with a mother and a father and a plate with rabbits on it. I had lost my home in coming here, and although I had never eaten apples or oranges there, my consciousness of their one-time existence was connected to it. Everyone else on the ship had had their home wrenched away, leaving them floating, rudderless, on an ocean vaster and more terrifying than the one we were floating on now. Gerhard belonged here, feeding five hundred people on frozen concentrated orange juice, making tiny fancy cakes from sugar paste and imagination. I looked into his eyes, and the ship floated there, reflected from his heart.

"Why are you so cross with me?" I asked.

"Because I love Michael."

"I don't know what he wants from me."

"He doesn't want anything from you. He doesn't want anything from any of us, except that we should be happy. And if you are lucky enough to have someone in your life whose only thought is of your happiness, then you should be happy." He paused for a moment and then added, "I am," as though that simple statement would change everything for me.

And in a way, it did. I knew that I would never be able to ask questions of Gerhard again. He had gone the way of Finn, of Helen, of Patience, of Alice. Of Tom? Tom had to come to me. If he did not, I would know I had lost him too.

I looked at the rows and rows of identical white mugs, lined up on the shelf. And two mugs came into my mind. Mugs that were not white. A red one and a blue one, that could not be replaced when they broke. The doctor wore a watch. He said he was happy going nowhere, but he was still hiding something. Why else would he meet with others in secret? Suppose he, too, remembered three women who had been swept, broken, into the sea the day we sailed? Suppose the dead in the British Museum were reaching out to him, too? Maybe he sat around with the others, discussing how they used to eat oranges. And if they did, I wanted to be there.

Clover, Tom's grandfather had said. Clover, to clean the soil and make it safe. It could be done.

I crumbled some toast onto a plate in the kitchen and sipped some orange juice. I watched the doctor through the door; I watched the people he spoke to. I observed and deduced. Vikram, Abigail. Luke. They didn't sit together but they spoke to each other, fetching cutlery, taking a second serving, or bringing empty breakfast plates to the hatch. I was not imagining the connection between them. I was more certain of it than I was of Tom's love for me.

I watched the kitchen team bringing in the dirty dishes and processing them through the steel washers, sliding in rack after rack, locking down the great handles and bringing out sparkling white plates and bowls. I wanted to help, but they were so efficient that, although they smiled at me, I knew I'd only get in the way. And then they were gone, and it was as though breakfast had never happened, and I was sitting in the kitchen alone, watching the white frost slowly disappear from the sides of the silver trays that held our thawing dinner.

I tipped the orange juice out of my glass and rinsed it out, and as I filled it with fresh water, I heard someone calling Gerhard's name. The door crashed open. "Can we have some biscuits?" Tom said, and stopped when he saw me. "Where's Gerhard?"

"I don't know."

"What are you doing here?"

"I helped at breakfast. I did the orange juice." I couldn't help but feel a little pride as I said this, but it soon turned to bitterness. "I'm to stay here until I've learned that apples aren't important."

He looked past me to the cupboards. "I wanted some biscuits. The children need something; they've been running around for ages."

I got up and we opened doors and rummaged in crates until we found a hoard of bright packets. I pulled one out.

"Not those," Tom said. "Emma likes the ones with the smiley faces on them. The others don't mind, so we might as well go with Emma." I knew Emma; she was one of the younger children, with a row of tiny, white, even teeth and freckles. She worshipped one of the older boys, a boy called Fillipo, who was slightly older than Gabriel. And Fillipo, in his turn, wandered around after Tom, his face tilted up to catch Tom's every smile. I looked through the cupboard again, and sure enough, there was a red cardboard packet with a cartoon picture of a smiley-faced biscuit on it. It had arms and legs; it seemed to be dancing. I handed it over and turned away, but Tom put his hand over mine and wouldn't let go.

"Come with me," Tom said. "Come with me now and see their faces. You never saw children smile like this in London." I hadn't seen many children in London at all. But I remembered the ones on the bulletin, being held up to the windows of the British Museum.

"Where have you been?" I asked.

Tom looked over his shoulder and spoke quietly and very fast. "Michael said I should give you some space. He said to stop crowding you. He's cross with himself. Angry for making your life so easy that you can't see how lucky you are. I don't like seeing Michael angry with himself. I wish you'd just let yourself be happy. I wish that you could be happy with me. But Lalla, if it's me, if I'm the one making you unhappy, I'll leave you alone, I promise, even if it kills me. You need to decide."

I pushed aside my glass of water. "You're the only reason I want to be here," I said.

He stroked my bruises so gently that it didn't hurt. He kissed my forehead. "Be with me, then. Let me look after you. It'll be all right, I promise."

"Is the ship really all there is?" I asked him.

"You've heard the stories," Tom said. "You saw what you saw in London. It's not just London either. The ship is our universe, and it's a good one. Let's guard it together, you and I. We can, you know."

I let his arms surround me. My body began to melt. If I was wrong—if the doctor had no secrets and this was all there was— then there were worse things than being with someone you loved, for ever.

"Can I come to you tonight?" he whispered. "You won't tell Michael? He told me to leave you alone." I shook my head. I wouldn't tell my father. He had tried to keep Tom from me, and I was never going to tell him anything, ever again. Tom was mine again, and the day went faster in the excitement of knowing he was waiting for me.

Dessert that night was a thing Gerhard called panna cotta, which I had watched him ease out of tall tins with a long knife—a thick, fat snake of opaque white jelly that gave a monstrous sucking sound as it slid from the tin. He cut it into slices and I put a frill of red jelly around each one with a giant tooth-paste tube as the kitchen team whisked the plates into the dining room. Gerhard had let me empty one of the tins, but the white snake would not ooze out for me. I had to dig it out with a spoon, and when Gerhard saw what I was doing, he rushed to me in consternation.

"No, Lalla, no. You are ruining, ruining dessert." And he cut the other end of the tin open, and the snake slimed out, whole and perfect except for the concave part where its flat head should have been. "You see, Lalla," he said, "this is why I am the chef and you should go back to the laundry." But he was smiling when he said it.

When the panna cottas went out to the tables, everyone gave sighs of appreciation, but I could only think of the fat snakes and wonder if being a chef had always meant knowing the most efficient way of getting stuff out of a tin. I couldn't eat it, and while I was busy not eating it, I looked out of the kitchen into the dining room. And I saw Luke raise his eyebrows at Roger, and I saw Roger raise his hand to Abigail, and I saw Abigail turn and look over her shoulder at Vikram, and my breath came faster and my heart beat in my ears, because I knew that if I watched them now, I would find out where they were going.

Vikram left first, going towards the doors that led to the toilets. I could not follow him without being noticed, because the men's toilets were on one side of the dining room and the women's on the other. Abigail left through the main doors into the ballroom. I moved away from the doors as Emily came in. She looked disapprovingly at my untouched plate, and by the time I had shrugged at her and smiled, Abigail was gone.

"Lalla," Emily said, "you've got to eat. You know you've got to eat." I looked back into the dining room but Luke had gone. Only Roger was left.

I walked slowly towards the women's toilets. I could feel Roger watching me. He was waiting for me to go, but I couldn't follow him if I left before he did. Then I saw Vikram, walking past the dining-room doors. Roger's shoulders relaxed as he watched me; I glanced over my shoulder as I opened the doors and saw him pushing back his chair. I almost laughed. Vikram was walking fast and I was behind him. Emily was nowhere in sight. I was safe.

I ducked behind pillars and hid behind cabin doors as Vikram went up the infirmary stairs and doubled back, down a cabin corridor and through to the research room. This was clever, I realised, because anyone watching him leave the dining room would have assumed he was going to his cabin. I saw Abigail approaching the research room from the other direction, and heard voices coming from inside. I waited until she'd gone in, then ran down the corridor and threw open the door, expecting to see them all gathered together. But the research room was empty.

I stood still and listened. I heard footsteps and hid under a table; Roger came in. A door opened and shut and I crawled back out. I scanned the wall with my eyes and saw a door set into it, not steel or shining wood but painted, the same colour as the wall. I had never noticed it before, although I could not say it was exactly hidden. I had simply never looked. I walked over and put my ear to it. Yes, there were voices. I had tracked them down at last.

I pushed open the door. There were no windows, no lights, and all I could see were faces illuminated by the revolving colours of a screensaver. As I edged in, I heard Roger's voice say, "No, no. Regent Street went all the way down to Piccadilly Circus, and then Leicester Square was just beyond that."

"That can't be right," said Luke. "I used to walk that way all the time. Piccadilly Circus was where the statue of Eros used to be. Right in the middle. And there was a theatre on the opposite side."

"And Leicester Square was just down from there."

"You're thinking of Trafalgar Square," someone else said, and then they all noticed me and fell silent.

"Hello," I said, because I could not think of anything else. There were six of them. The five I had followed for so long, and one whose presence surprised me so much that I couldn't say anything else. She looked at me through her red snake-hair fringe and paled.

"I just…" I began, but the words dried in my mouth and I did not know how to continue. I was there, they were there, and neither party had the slightest idea what the other was doing. But the fear was tangible. Emily was white and Abigail's hand shook as she withdrew it from the table. Roger's eyes were the only ones that met mine, and they seemed to be burning from the inside.

"How much did you hear?" he asked finally, his voice rasping and dry.

"Piccadilly," I told him, "and Leicester Square. That's all."

They looked at each other, and at the lace tablecloth on the desk, which I supposed to be another fourth-deck novelty introduced by my father. I wanted to reassure them that I had heard nothing they did not want me to hear. But that would not be enough. If there was nothing going on, why did they all look so afraid? I wanted to know what they were doing so that I could become a part of it, because I needed to be a part of any activity on the ship that was not being dictated by my father. I wanted them to have something to hide.

"Does my father know you're here?" I asked Emily.

"Does he know you are?" she retorted, staring at me.

"Sit down, Lalla," Roger said. There was no spare chair and so I moved towards the desk. "Not there," he said, but it was too late. I had already touched the tablecloth, and I recoiled at a strange sensation on my hands—something dry and soft which made my skin crawl with its unfamiliarity. I could see their faces clearly in the light from the screen; they were exchanging desperate looks. I moved away from the desk; the dry softness came away on my fingers, and when I looked at them, I could see by the light of the screen that they were covered in white powder. The entire surface of the desk was covered in it. There was no lace tablecloth, only narrow lines traced painstakingly through a dusting of white, with a great dark emptiness where my hands had been.

"What are you doing?" I asked in a whisper, not daring to raise my voice in case I disturbed more of the pattern. They were all staring at my hands, and as the revolving coloured patterns of the screensaver changed from white to red, they became one great wound, with someone else's lifeblood staining them. I held them out and they all shrank away. My palms were sweating, and little clumps of powder fell to the floor as the red turned to green. No one spoke.

"What have I done?" I asked, scarcely able to hear my own voice.

"That," Roger said in a voice devoid of any emotion, "was the National Gallery."

"And most of Trafalgar Square," added Emily bitterly. I turned to the desk and looked more closely. And as the colour on the screensaver changed from green to yellow, and from yellow to a bright, turquoise blue, I studied the lace tracery. The delicate patterns resolved themselves slowly into streets, squares, buildings. If I had obliterated the National Gallery, then this was Oxford Street. I remembered it so well, thronged with desperate people trying to secure supplies from people with things to sell, hundreds tightly packed around little folding tables, grasping with outstretched hands, then spreading like an explosion when the sirens came, only to regather as the sirens passed on. Crossing it was Baker Street, which figured in the stories on my screen about a detective called Sherlock Holmes. *From your hands, Lalla, I can see that you have intruded into a place where you have no right to be.* And Baker Street led up to the vast expanse that was Regent's Park, which my mother swore had once been green and open, but which I had only ever seen covered in tents. Blue and purple and green and black and orange, some big enough for families, some so small that only one person could ever have crawled inside.

There was a time when life was an adventure. When the springing up of tents in Regent's Park made walks with my mother more interesting. When eating tinned peaches for tea was exciting, because it was different. When the horrors of other lives falling apart happened somewhere else, on the screens, or in whispered conversations between my parents that I was not supposed to overhear. As I stared at the powder tracings that marked out Regent's Park, what I remembered most was the way the tents had been arranged in streets, the way some people had even put little fences around the front of their tent, like a garden.

I turned back to the six frightened people before me. I realised that I was still standing; I was looking down on them, whereas they had to look up to me. It felt wrong, and yet there was nowhere else for me to go.

"It's London," I said. "You're drawing London." Roger came and stood behind me. I followed Oxford Street up Tottenham Court Road, where a dusting of powder spread to the edge of the desk, untouched. I pointed. "If you put a road there, it would be Great Russell Street, and then the British Museum would be just there." I kept my hands well away from the desk surface. "And there was a theatre there, on that corner. And there, opposite the main entrance of the museum, there was a cafe once." I was still trembling, but this time I was trembling with life. I could feel blood hammering around my body; I had found people, people who were not confined by the parameters my father had set out, but who were reaching out with their minds and memories, back to the past, back to the way things had once been. To the out-lawed, forbidden time before.

"How did you know where to find us?" Roger asked at last.

"I've been watching you all. I've been following you." I had nothing to lose. "I wanted to know what you were all doing. Who you were, why you kept meeting up secretly."

"And what were you planning to do when you found out?"

My heart raced.

"I don't know," I said weakly. "I just thought... if I wasn't alone. I don't know."

Emily broke in impatiently. "Are you going to go to Michael about this?" she demanded.

"I'm not going to say anything," I said. That, at least, I was sure of.

Luke spoke up. I had not heard him speak since Helen's trial and it seemed to me that his voice had become slower. His hair was longer, too; he wore it in a ponytail now, and his stubble had become a beard that made it hard to guess his age.

"I don't think she will tell Michael," he said. "After all, she's part of it now. Those are her fingerprints on the desk. If she went to Michael, she wouldn't be able to prove that the whole thing hadn't been her idea."

"What whole thing?" I asked.

"Nothing," Emily said. "I split a bag of flour and they came and helped me clear it up. What else is there to say?"

"I don't know, Emily." Roger's voice was harsh, and his face, washed with blue light from the screen, seemed frozen, immo-bile. "What else is there to say?"

"Nothing," she said, and before the others could stop her, she had pushed me out of the way and started brushing the flour to the floor, making great sweeping strokes with her sleeve stretched over her arm, the cuff held so tightly that her knuckles were bright white, green, blue, red in the screen light. "Nothing," she repeated, and I could not tell whether her voice was cracked with anger or with tears. "This was madness. It was stupid, bloody-minded madness. What possessed us? Who cares what London used to look like anyway?"

It was definitely tears. They spilt as she demanded, "What possessed *me*? I love Michael. I love him."

"He doesn't know, Emily. Calm down. He'll never know."

"What if she tells him?"

"I won't tell him," I said. "Why would I tell him? I've been looking for you all ever since we boarded. I knew I couldn't be the only one." Anything seemed possible now. Tom would join us, and we'd find land. Go back to London, even. Five faces stared at me, expressionless in changing colours of the screensaver. Only Emily was turned away, and a tear shone on her cheek like a leftover sequin from Alice's tapestry. "What are you all going to do?" I went on. "Have you got a plan? I thought we could look at the maps, find out where we are. There's a machine in my father's study that shows the position of the ship. I'm sure I saw land on that. We can find it again. That thunderstorm the other night, I think it meant that we're near land. We can check." I drew breath. "He turns the ship, you know. At night. With the electricity from the solar panels, or something. The engineers will know. We can chart a course. If he won't let us use the machines, we can steal the compass. There's one in his study, I've seen it. We can find land."

"You think?"

I nodded. Were they going to exclude me after all? Did they think I was too young for subversion? But I had been up to the fourth deck with Tom. I was not too young.

"Stop it, Lalla," Roger said. He sighed. "I wish you hadn't come."

"But I have. So you have to let me in."

"Into what?"

"Into whatever you've got planned. Were you making that London map to work out how to distribute our stores?"

Vikram put his arm around Emily, who had started sobbing quietly. "Tell her, Roger," he said. "Go on."

"She won't believe me. Us. I've told her before, but she won't stop. She just keeps banging on and on. Patience won't have her in the laundry anymore. She's driving Gerhard mad in the kitchen. Breaking Tom's heart. And now she's here."

"I don't believe my father controls the sun. But I'll believe you. Of course I will."

Roger looked at me. "You won't. You'll believe what you want to believe. But I'll tell you the truth."

I nodded, open-mouthed.

"We meet up because we thought it would be fun to see how much of London we could remember. We didn't want to leave a permanent record, so we got creative. Hence the flour, rather than paper, or the touchscreen in the school, or canvas." He paused. "That's all, Lalla. We're just smoking behind the bike sheds."

"What does that mean?" I asked, as the floor beneath me turned to water.

"Michael's told us not to look back," Luke said, as though I was stupid. "And we thought it better to be quiet about this. We can handle it—we're strong enough to know the difference between a game and a dangerous exercise. But not everyone is."

"I am."

"No you're not," Abigail cut in as the screensaver washed her red. "You're just a silly, pampered little girl. You know nothing, you see nothing, you appreciate nothing. You barely even eat. How ungrateful is that? You make Tom creep around after you, when all he wants to do is stand up and tell us all how much he loves you. He barely eats either, but that's because he's waiting for you. Waiting for you to choose to go to him. You're a spoilt, spoilt, selfish brat. And then you march in here and claim membership of some kind of conspiracy..."

"You all know about Tom?"

"Oh, please."

"Did he tell you? Does he talk to you? Did he tell you that he promised to come back to London with me?"

"Be quiet, Lalla. No one's going back to London." Roger took a handkerchief from his pocket and wiped Emily's face with it. She took it from him and scrubbed at the reminder of the desk, tears and flour making a sticky paste on the surface. Regent's Park, Oxford Street, the little secret alley and square that was once St Christopher's Place, Baker Street. The space that was waiting to become the British Museum. All blotted out in seconds by misery and shame. The delicate lace, the beauty of memory. Gone, all gone. They were no more plotting to turn the ship around than I was planning to take my father's place.

And that was how I learned that the people who break the rules are the ones who are least interested in changing things.

"Cowards," I said, my voice thick with disappointment.

Roger turned on me. "What did you expect? Really, what did you expect? Did you want us all to be making bombs and strapping them to ourselves? To march on your father with guns and force the ship back to where we came from? We've been de-registered, thanks to you. We'd be dead before we got off the ship."

"Land, then," I said. "Just land."

He shook his head. "This is what friendship looks like. It's not a life-changing plot. It's just people who like each other sharing something particular to them. We were trying something out. It didn't work."

Emily sank onto a chair, the floury handkerchief hanging stiffly from her hand. "Michael's right," she said. "We shouldn't look back. He's always right."

"I think so." Roger took the handkerchief from her.

They stood up, straightening their clothes, and filed away together. Abigail and Vikram were holding hands. They left me alone with the doctor and the handkerchief.

"Thank you, Lalla."

"What for?"

"Bringing us to our senses. It was a silly, pointless thing to do really. I don't suppose we'd have realised how pointless if you'd stayed away." He looked at me curiously. "Did Michael know? Did he send you?"

"No. I followed you. By myself."

He looked at the handkerchief, the sole reminder of the map in flour. "There is nowhere for us to go," he said. "There's nothing left."

"But..."

He put on a high-pitched whining voice and screwed up his face. "*I want to go back, I want to go back.* If you want to be heard, say something worth listening to." He sighed. "Beautiful things are happening here. Right here, right now."

"To you?"

"Yes. But to you too. You have the potential to bring us all happiness beyond anything we've dreamed of."

"Me? How?"

"Because you've never suffered. Because you're young and healthy. Because you're Michael's daughter. Because of Tom."

Tom. I was meant to be meeting him in my cabin and I'd completely forgotten. I hoped he had, too.

"I broke my nose the other night," I protested. "I know about pain. I do know about being hungry and all that."

He shook his head. He seemed about to say more, then he changed his mind. "You'll see, Lalla. I hope so, anyway, for your sake as well as ours." He held out the handkerchief. "Would you slip this through the wash?"

"I don't work in the laundry..." I began, but then I nodded. Perhaps this was a gesture of faith; an invitation to friendship. Patience would be glad to see me, surely, if I stopped asking her about eggs? I could wrap the handkerchief in a shirt, or a sheet, and bundle it into the machine so that no one else could see. I'd have to whip it away at drying time, and sneak it into Patience's ironing pile, or do it myself. And then, and only then, would I be able to return it to Roger's cabin, white and fresh and folded, so that no one would ever be able to tell that it had been used to wipe out London as we once knew it.

TWENTY

Tom is angry ❀ *the museum of the ship*
❀ *how do you know you exist?*

When I got back to my cabin, there was a note on my pillow, written on the back of a biscuit box. *Where the hell were you?* The dancing, smiling biscuit on the reverse mocked me. Tom had not forgotten; he had come to me. He had disobeyed my father's injunction and I had not been there. How long had he waited? I told myself it was too late to go and find him now; I would talk to him at breakfast. I knew I ought to feel guilty, but I had other things to think about, and very early the next morning I went back to the little research room. It was completely empty. Just the desk and the screen and the gently shifting colours of the screensaver. I passed my hands over the surface of the desk, where I had wiped out Trafalgar Square and the National Gallery, and I understood why they had come and traced the roads and the monuments with their fingers instead of just looking up a map on the screens. Great Russell Street, I thought, tracing a path with my fingertip. Bedford Street. Russell Square Gardens. Bloomsbury Street.

All my father had done on the ship was to reinvent the Dove inside our heads. Our admiration and gratitude was a filter that made the creation of a map in flour into a crime. And yet, only my presence had turned their activity into something forbidden.

I wondered if they would ever forgive me. *What harm*, someone once asked me, and I had grown less and less sure of the answer.

As I reached the end of Goodge Street, my fingers met something hard and irregular, like a small stone stuck to the edge of the desk. I pushed at it with my thumb and it snapped off. I placed it carefully on my open palm and looked at it in the changing colours of the screensaver. It was a lump of flour paste. There was London in it, and Emily's tears. It was smaller than the button but it held a story just the same. I wrapped it in Roger's stiffened handkerchief and put it in my pocket.

I found an empty room on the third deck, above the infirmary, and carried the little lump of flour and tear paste there. I took Helen's photograph album, too, and Tom's letter, and the skylight screws and what was left of the broken apple. And I took my button in its velvet jewellery box. It wasn't a real museum, with an atrium and glass cases and more galleries than could be visited in a lifetime. But it was a museum of our lives, and I didn't want Emily to throw it away. Six objects. The British Museum had held thousands, millions, and when I thought of the significance of my six and multiplied it by those millions, the world began to spin around me with the sense of what had been lost, and with what I had saved.

I was late to breakfast; Tom had already gone. I thought about going and finding him in the sports hall, but I had a handkerchief to wash. I bustled about the laundry work, and as I was careful to keep my questions about anything other than sewing or knitting to myself, Patience began to look kindly on me again. She didn't ask whether I had my father's permission to be there, and I didn't tell her. Tom was not speaking to me at lunchtime. I understood what it had cost him to go against my father, and I owed him an apology I did not know how to give. Every smile he shared with someone else made it harder and harder for me to find words. At dinner I took my old place at my father's table, and stared at the pink, pale slices of gammon ham. There were rings of pineapple on the top; they reminded me of my first meal on the ship. Eighty-three marks ago. Eighty-three marks.

"I saw you'd tidied your cabin," Emily said as she sat beside me, glowing, and my father looked happy: I felt as though I had come home after a long absence and that everyone apart from Roger and Tom was pleased to see me. Was it really this easy? I thought. Were they really so ready to see what they wanted to see? And yet I liked it, too.

I never saw the people who'd made the London map in flour together again. Emily took her place at my father's side, a penitent shadow, looking up at him with wide eyes and an open face. Roger avoided me; at first I thought it was coincidence, or my paranoia, but as the marks grew in number it became clear that he did not want to be alone with me any more than Tom did. He was never in the pharmacy when I delivered the clean towels, nor in the infirmary when I went in with the laundry. I left the handkerchief in his pile of clean clothes, and looked and looked for an answering nod or smile over the dinner table that evening, but he looked away whenever he saw me, and I am sure I saw him frown with frustration as he did so.

Luke started helping Tom with the football, and Patience told me that the two of them were teaching each other tennis now too, and that soon we would all be able to learn. I feigned delight to make her happy, then found that I was actually looking forward to the first lessons. Helen spent less and less time with Gabriel; she had given him up to the ship, and when she saw him she smiled briefly and let him go back to whatever he was doing. I took him swimming, half expecting him to comment on the change in his mother, but he talked only about the next thing he intended to do. He sang a song that Helen had taught all the children in the school. Helen had written it herself, he told me proudly, and it went *The ship has saved us all, grown-ups*

and children small, and life is new. Happy and future-proof, borne
on by trust and truth, safe under Father's roof, Father we love you.

The tune was familiar, although I couldn't place it, and
although I found the words ridiculous, they wormed their way
into my mind, so that I would find myself singing, "The ship
has saved us all," as I folded laundry and took it to the cabins.
The tune was a dull one—there were thousands, millions of
better ones that we could listen to just by summoning them on
the screen. But it was hypnotic. It floated just below the surface
of my conscious mind, and whenever I thought, I must stop
singing that song, I'd find I was already doing so. *Happy and*
future-proof. I wasn't alone. Before long snatches of the children's
song could be heard all over the ship.

Future-proof. It was printed on the Dove-governed screens,
although I didn't mention that to anyone. Mentally, I consigned
the Dove to my third-floor museum; like the other artefacts, it
had no place in ship conversations. It was in my museum that
I let my memories roam; I went there most days, and because
I was smiling and eating and had stopped asking questions, no
one seemed to mind, or want to know what I was doing. Like
Roger and his friends, I'd learned that obeying the rules means
you can break them. Eight days after I'd found them out, I sat
on the floor of my museum, staring at the dried-up ball of paste
that was all that was left of their London map. I remembered
watching the bulletin after the bombing of Regent's Park, and
the announcer's sorrowful voice announcing fifty-four deaths.

"Fifty-four?" I'd said to my father. "Did all the others escape?"

"Yes," my mother said at exactly the same moment as my
father said, "No." My mother had a way of arranging her face
with her eyebrows slightly raised and her eyes wide, with the corners of her lips turned up but no warmth in her eyes. It meant,
There are things Lalla does not need to know. There are things I will
not discuss here, in front of her.

"But there were thousands of people living there," I said.

"Only those fifty-four existed," my father said; as he spoke my mother turned away from him and bit her lips together so hard that it looked as though she had new, thin, white ones.

"But I saw them," I said, puzzled. "They existed."

"How do you know anyone exists?" my father asked me. "How do you know you exist?"

I was fourteen years old when Regent's Park was bombed. I had never thought about how I knew that I existed. How could I know such a thing? It wasn't something to know or not to know. It just was. I remember looking at the challenge in my father's face and thinking of all the other things that just were, like water, and air, and food when I was hungry and the fact that I could walk and run, and that there were clothes for me to put on to keep my body warm, and that my mother and father and I lived together in a flat in a place called Bloomsbury.

And I remember how I thought, even then, about the number of things that had always just been, and which were no longer. Books. Shops. Restaurants. The fact that I had once been able to walk around the display cases without tripping over foul-smelling people in sleeping bags, and that the cases themselves had once been full. I thought about the objects, and realised that they, too, had once just been. The iron spoons had once carried food into the mouth of a living, breathing person who lived and loved just as I lived and loved now. The necklaces had been worn; the pots had held valued possessions; Lindow man had walked and talked and held some-one close. Once upon a time, they all *just were*, and somehow they came to be shut behind glass, hundreds, thousands of years later, until their only existence was as part of someone else's *just am*.

"I breathe," I'd said at last, and when neither of them stopped me I continued. "I feel pain when I fall over, or when I burn myself on the fire. I get cold. I get hungry."

"And when the tent city you live in is bombed to oblivion?" my father asked. "What happens then?"

"But I don't live in a tent city," I said.

My mother turned to me and the blood rushed back into her lips so quickly it looked like she was returning from the dead. "That's right," she said quickly, and as my ship-self relived the conversation I winced, because I realised now how important the conversation had been. "She doesn't live in a tent city. So that's fine." She clapped her hands, as though celebrating the departure of an unwelcome guest. "What shall we have for dinner?"

"A roast chicken, I think," my father had said dryly.

"There isn't any chicken," I said.

My father shrugged.

And my ship-self watched my long-ago self take the final step inwards as my thoughts pulled in once more, to the central circle, the smallest one, which was also the biggest because it encompassed absolutely everything else.

"But doesn't the fact that I remember roast chicken mean that I exist?"

My father kept his eyes fixed on mine. "Try that the next time we go to re-register. Leave your card here, and tell the official that you remember roast chicken."

My mother laid her hand on my father's sleeve. "She's right, Michael," she said softly. "If she remembers roast chicken, she exists. That's all right. Once upon a time, we thought we existed just because we thought. Let's leave it now. There's corned beef."

My father's laugh was harsh and short, more like the coughs that came from the sleeping bags in the museum than a laugh. He had invented the Dove to bring fairness, equality, hope into a desperate situation, and it had not worked. "The tent people remembered roast chicken, Anna."

"Corned beef," my mother repeated, emphasising the words

in an attempt to puncture my father's thoughts. "Good protein. And fat. For energy. Lucky we got to the food drop quickly."

"Only because we knew where to go." Now, on the ship, as I remembered the conversation, I could see that my mother was playing into my father's hands. By trying to get away from the subject, she was bringing him back to it. From the safety of the ship, I could look back and see that my father was right. I was there now. Ninety marks into our voyage, I had arrived.

"How did we know where to go for the food drop?" my father had asked.

"The screen told us."

"Now think of yourself with no card," he said to me. "How do you get your food?"

Two days before, the screen bulletin had given the address of the food drop. An hour before it was due, the drop address changed. And as we went to the new address, we passed the old one, and the queue there wound around the building, down the street and around the corner, so long that we could not see its end.

"Shouldn't we tell them?" I had asked. But not even my mother said yes. That queue, hundreds, thousands of people we did not know, became the left behinds. In the hour since the change in the food drop location, they had fallen from the government list. They had re-registered late, or searched for something out-lawed on the screen, or not renewed their identity cards. Perhaps the internet hot spot they relied on had gone cold. They would starve. Or be bombed. And no one would count them.

We killed those people, Father, I thought, straightening my stiff-ening legs. My ankles were beginning to swell. I looked around at my exhibits. What was the difference between the Nazareth Act and the manifest?

My mother had never been able to commit to the ship. *The ship will be the last thing we do*, she had said. Every additional day we stayed in London had been a chance she was giving me to find a way of my own. But she had never had the courage to turn me loose, and I had never learned enough to leave. She had loved me too much, and she had failed. I knew now. I had begun to understand.

I had been kneeling on the floor of my museum for too long; my legs had gone dead. I forced myself to stand up and it hurt to do so. The light was fading; I had missed dinner, but I found that I wanted to go to the goodnight meeting. I wanted to see my father, to look at him, to study his face and see if there was any trace there that he, too, remembered where we had come from. I pictured myself apologising to Tom, too, and the prospect of reconciliation was soothing. Being in trouble all the time was exhausting, and I was very tired.

I slipped into the ballroom and stared around me. Pleased, confident, shining faces, all turned towards him. Michael Paul, father not only to me, but to all the children. No longer challenging his own child about her existence, but bestowing existence generously, lovingly, openly on everyone. The only things that mattered now were the ones which were in front of us every day. Rivets were metal and round; bolts were metal and hexagonal, but the stars were made of diamonds, or kitchen foil, or light bulbs, or holes punched in a vast swathe of black velvet. And the sun bounced over the ship, controlled by a rope in my father's hands, and the ship was the centre of the sky and the entire world was nothing more than a plate of water.

Father, we thank you.

What, after all, was I fighting for? The world was gone. There were no apples, no oranges, no eggs. I saw Tom, sitting with an empty place beside him. There was a place for me here. Gerhard put a hand on my shoulder in greeting. Would I, like Helen, be forgiven for my childish questioning, my doubts?

But my father was speaking, and I sat still to listen.

"The glitches with our portals may be irritating," he was saying, "especially if you were halfway through a good book. But glitches remind us of what we have gained. I know, Chris," he said, as a man in a dull green jacket put his head into his hands, "you've tried to sort them out, and I know you'll keep trying. I also know you'll succeed." So it wasn't just *Ballet Shoes*, I thought, then put the thought away. "What I'm saying is that it doesn't matter. We're not defined by screens and cards anymore. Now we exist because we learn." He looked at Helen, who smiled and pulled Gabriel a little closer to her. "We exist because we play together, eat together." He held one hand towards Tom, the other towards Gerhard, palms upwards, as though he were offering them something. "We exist because we create." Here he bowed towards Alice, who blushed and looked at the floor. "We exist," he said, lowering his voice so that we all had to lean towards him, "because we love." I wanted him to look at me so badly that I turned my head away, but when I looked up it was Emily who was pink-cheeked, Emily who attracted tender, approving smiles, Emily whose head was inclined to the side in prettiness and pride.

And then, before I could feel jealous, he looked at me. "We exist, my darling, because we remember roast chicken."

My father had won. This, then, was the end, the triumph of humanity, the final destination of mankind. No mast, no screens. Learning, playing, eating and loving. It was sweet of him to remember the roast chicken, but it really didn't seem to be important anymore. I looked at Tom, and my heart contracted. Tomorrow, I promised myself silently. Unless the ship sinks tonight, I'll join it tomorrow. I'll apologise to Tom, and I will never go looking for anything beyond what I am given, ever again. I slipped away to my cabin and lay in the dark, my body aching for my lover. Sorry, Mother. I was not strong enough, and I am in love.

I lay awake and I thought about the water. All around us, bearing us up, supporting us. But threatening us, too. My mind raced. Water will not be stopped, I thought. Hold it in your hands and it will seep through your fingers. Hold it back with chains and it will trickle through the links. Hold it back with a walled dam and it will burst through, all the more powerful for having been contained. My father dictated, and my mother broke away from him, went to the window and threw open the curtain. If she had not broken away. If she had not...

I remembered the shot, and a figure in faded black running away. I lay in the dark and I suddenly realised there was one place I still had to look. There was one final question to be answered. One place where, even now, I might find what I was looking for.

TWENTY-ONE

I search for the truth and find a stranger
❀ *an engagement*

Four or five hundred years ago, people walked the streets with oranges stuck with cloves held to their noses, or little posies of sweet rosebuds. They believed that terrible diseases were carried by terrible smells, and if they could not smell the smells, then the ghastly rashes that marked the dying would never blossom on their own skin. They were wrong, my mother said. But we had no oranges, no cloves, no scented flowers, so I don't know how she could have known. It wasn't as though we could do what she always told me to do, and find out for ourselves. Do things really change? Four hundred years. What did it mean? Four hundred years on, we were no further on than we had been. They had oranges stuck with cloves; we didn't even have oranges. And in four hundred years more, the ship would be at the bottom of the ocean with the mast; my museum would be gone; everyone would be dead.

I felt my marks with my fingertips. Ninety of them. I thought of going on my quest in the dark, but it was another moonless night, although there was no storm in the air now. I tried to sleep, hoping that my mother would lead me to the fourth deck again. But the things she had shown me there had been her dreams, not mine. The things Tom and I had found, the cots and the clothes and the crockery and the paint and tools, were my father's dream. And wrapped in my father's dream were the dreams of everyone else on board. Roger dreamed of healing the sick; here he was, healing the sick. Helen taught the children. Gerhard provided food. That was why my father had interviewed so carefully, searched out the people he would save. That was why no one argued with him, why the little secrets I had uncovered had, as Helen said, hardly been subversion. What would you subvert, if everything was as you wanted it? Tom's grandfather had wanted something that my father could not provide; he had not been allowed to come on board. Those who were here had all been chosen, not just for their good deeds, but because they, too, had surrendered hope.

We are every human being that has ever lived, has ever thought, has ever created. We are the ultimate expression of humanity, and it is humanity that we celebrate here. Every kindness that has ever been done in the name of humankind, from the first man who reached out his hand to a crying child, to the last person back on land who broke his sole piece of bread in order to share it, is here, in us. In our floating home, we contain all that has ever been. Let us savour, and enjoy.

Let us savour, my father said, and enjoy. The difference between his chosen people and me was simple. They could rush forward, immediately, and throw themselves headlong into the riot of learning and experience my father had put before them. The only prospect before them was of better things, wonderful things, a richer, more beautiful, more profound life than they had had any hope of before. There was no risk.

But my inclusion had been automatic. No one had made sure I was starving before they set a feast before me.

Savour, and enjoy. Perhaps I could have done. If my mother had lived, I thought, we would have walked together, to the library, the gallery, the music room, and embarked upon a sweet,

clean journey of discovery. We would have walked without looking over our shoulders, looked at paintings and artefacts without
the weight of my father's warnings pressing us down, experi-
enced the wonder of learning without the fierce oppression of
guilt. I saw us walking down Great Russell Street together, she
in her floating dress, me doing double skips to keep up with her,
only this time the street was safe and bright, and the bodies were
gone, and the sun shone on green trees and white buildings, and
the blue plaques on their walls were the colour of the sky. We
would have had the past to live again, and live differently, for
however long we were granted.

But what was I, now that my mother was gone? Who was my
father? The man who had once loved my mother? Or the man
who had created this world for me, and in so doing, had made
sure I would never be able to find out who I was?

At first light, then, I left my cabin. My hard red shoes set the
gangways ringing; I stepped as softly as I could, but I could not
help the noise. Eventually I took my shoes off and dangled them
from my hand. The cold metal impressed itself on the soles of my
feet. Was this man, sailing his people in circles with no thought
for the future, also the man who had rushed back from his trips
just to be able to kiss me goodnight, who had scoured London
for my red shoes and said nothing of their origin? Just how great
had been his desperation to sail? Around me, behind the cabin
doors, the people began to stir. When I got to my father's cabin,
I hid behind the stairwell. I watched the sun rising; when he left
for his breakfast, I slipped inside.

There was nothing in the instruments, or in the map I found
in the top drawer of the great wooden chest. There was nothing
in the green dot that still went bleep, bleep, bleep as the circling
green line swept over it, although I studied these things carefully.
Nothing in the telescope I found in a corner cupboard, or in
the compass that lay beside it. I looked quickly and thoroughly,

because I wanted to be at breakfast if I could. I searched the surface of the desk, the floor, and the padded cushions of the chairs. And it was while I was searching the chairs that I finally found something important, sitting on top of the little table beside the leather armchair. It had not even been hidden.

The manifest.

I opened it. I was struck once more by its texture, dry and yet solid, the smooth surface on which we had inscribed our names. I turned page after page, trying not to tear them in my anxiety to find what I was looking for.

Harry Oz. Round, fat letters, carefully formed.

Lalage Paul. My own signature, a little shaky in the middle.

And between them, my mother's page. There was no signature. She was gone. No more present in the manifest than she was in the clothes store upstairs. I sat on my father's chair, breathing hard. It was not enough. She had been too ill to sign the manifest. The fact that her name wasn't there proved nothing.

I kept searching. I didn't know what I was looking for, only that I would know what it was when I found it. In one drawer, there was a notebook. It fell open at the ragged remnants of a ripped out page. I did not need to go back upstairs to know that Tom's grandfather's letter was written on the missing page; I recognised the paper, the pattern of the torn edge; I could see the words indented on the page beneath. And I wondered how my father could have borne to watch the old man writing those words. *I love you, and I let you go.* What more had my father been prepared to do, to ensure our departure? The notebook gave no further clues; my mother was not there. *I was terrified that one of you would be hurt before she would agree to come away. I am only grateful that it was not you.* But we had both been hurt. She by a bullet, me by her death. Where had that bullet come from? I pulled out every drawer, searched in every cupboard, but could find nothing more.

I went back to the manifest. In my head I heard my father's voice. *Anna's gone.* Fine. I would look beyond her. I turned the pages of the manifest one by one. I read the summaries my father had written at the top of each page. I looked at the names; I studied the signatures. And there, just seventeen pages in, I found it. Neil Bailey. Engineer, twenty-seven years old. Used scavenged items to create rainwater savers; distributed them without charge to those without access to water. There was no Neil Bailey on the ship. But here he was in the manifest. A man, a history, and no signature. What had happened to him? Where was he now?

I marched out of the cabin and into the dining room.

"I need to talk to you," I said to my father. "Right now."

"We're just about to eat, Lalla," Emily said, walking behind me with the toast basket. "Surely it can wait."

"Sit down," my father said patiently. "You're so hungry you're forgetting your manners. Eat something. And then afterwards, if you still want to, we'll go to my cabin together and talk for as long as you like."

I looked around at the people, all so familiar now. At Emily, eyes wide with love for my father. At Patience, head inclined in pity or despair. At Roger, whose frown still held a secret. At Tom. Roger, Patience, Finn, Luke, Helen, Gabriel, Mercy with the embroidered patch on the left knee of her trousers. Alice. Emily. My father. Tom. All here to die. Tom was going to die. And something in me broke, and the nausea I had been feeling for weeks became a vast, all-consuming hunger. I burst into tears, and as my tears emptied out, the void inside me grew, and I wanted to eat and eat until there was nothing left in the stores.

Tom got up from his table, and the people around us began to clap and to cheer, a sound that started small but that spread over the whole dining room like spilt water. Was this what it all came to in the end? Floating aimlessly, waiting for certain death, saved by love?

I had thought he was my rebellion.

He smiled at me, and I tried to smile back, and after all it was quite easy to whisper, "I'm sorry."

He held my hands in his, and went down on one knee in front of me. "Lalla," he said, "you know I love you. Will you marry me?"

And the room went silent, and every person in it held their breath in a joyful pause. My tears stopped. I looked around and saw the floodtide of happiness that my next word would bring forth. All the people who had cared about me, who had been angry or frustrated with me, who had argued over and over again that they were happy and that I could be too, were gazing at me with approval. I felt loved. I felt enfolded and included. We were all going to die. Where was the harm in enjoying ourselves first? What harm? I felt utterly drained.

"A wedding!" Gerhard shouted, his deep voice booming in triumph over the general delight. "A feast." And the people shouted and laughed, and I stood in the middle, a little tiny dot, sheltered by Tom as I stood inside the circle of his arms without saying a word.

And as I stood being shaken to bits by all the people who came rushing towards us, hugging and kissing our cheeks and kissing each other and waltzing around in each other's arms, I saw my father look at Roger, and Roger look at my father, and something hit me from the inside, and I knew that my happy ending had been as carefully orchestrated as the existence of the ship itself.

TWENTY-TWO

Preparations for the wedding ❀ Ballet Shoes
and the Art Trials ❀ *my mother's last chance*

I meant to ask more questions before the wedding. I meant to
stop everything, and ask how they dared to dictate the course
of my life in this way. I meant to demand the full history of
Neil Bailey, whoever he was. But for the first time since my
mother's death, I felt loved. And it was not just Tom who loved
me. Everywhere I went, people smiled at me. I started going
to book group again, just to feel the warmth of people celebrating the engagement. My father offered to release me from
laundry duty while we planned the wedding, but I refused.
I liked going into people's cabins and have them say lovely
things about Tom, and about me, and offer their congratula-
tions. And I liked it when Patience, having smothered me with
kisses, held me at arm's length and said, "Child, you are so
beautiful when you smile." Just as the first time we went up
through the skylight on the fourth deck, time had condensed
into a single moment, so being with Tom, thinking with Tom,
spending time with Tom, stopped other thoughts from growing and developing. The sun rose and set unencumbered by my
concerns; if I didn't accept Alice's tapestry, I was at least happy
to watch with everyone else and admire the way the universe
had shifted to accommodate us.

In any case, the tapestry was no longer an issue. Alice put it aside to embroider a wedding veil. Gerhard disappeared into the stores for hours on end and came back with menus which he pored over with my father. I went with my father to the fourth deck, and I tried on the dress he had chosen for me. "You saved us at the start, Lalla," he said to me, "and now you are saving us again." Saviour. It had quite a ring to it, and I stopped wondering why everyone seemed to love me so much. He offered to take me to his cabin and answer my questions, but every day, I decided that tomorrow would do, until at last it seemed too late to bother. Maybe Neil Bailey had just missed the boat. And the dress was so beautiful.

I learned to be happy. I thought of my early days on the ship as a troubled night that had given way to dawn, and the dawn was so bright that I could not see the darkness beyond. I had Tom and I had the ship. I had my father and I had myself. I was a new person, a happy person, and to be that person I had to let go of anger and doubt and enjoy each moment as it came. I stopped feeling that the weight of the world was on my shoulders and my shoulders alone. The children were a creative lot, and would surely think of something if the time ever came that they'd need to. I did the laundry and joined the knitting circle and danced about the ship as the others did. I put my red shoes in my museum and asked for deck shoes. I ate and ate, and got fatter every day, and if I could not quite give up making the marks, at least I made them on a different part of the wall, for I was in a different place now, and it was better.

And then one day, thirty or so marks later (although I could not be sure; I did not always remember to make them), I came back from swimming too tired to walk up to the sports hall and find Tom. We shared a cabin now, and I went to it, and as I sat on our bunk, I thought that I might like to read again. I picked up my portal and found that my library was still frozen on *Ballet*

Shoes. Petrova, the only one who hated ballet, stuck at a station, forever longing to travel on a moving staircase.

I had always loved *Ballet Shoes*. My mother read it to me, from a paper copy that had been hers. Later I read it myself, from the screen. The world of the Fossil girls had always been impossibly exotic. They descended into the depths of the city as though it was the most normal thing in the world. The Tube, where tunnels and corners could hide anything, where a power cut would plunge you into pitch dark, where a cry for help would echo for so long that there was no way of telling where it came from. Once the gangs had been smoked out, the petrol dealers moved in, and the sealed entrances swarmed with muttering people who carried the petrol smell with them. I loved the way that smell sent my mind circling above me and set me slightly dizzy where I stood, and I would pretend to have forgotten something, or seen something, so that I could go back and smell it again. The filthy, incoherent people did not frighten me then. They seemed to belong to a different world, and held no more threat than if they were already dead.

"How can they still be selling petrol if it's all gone?" I asked my mother.

"This is the end of it," she told me. "The bits left. The last drops in the bottom of tankers, of storage tanks. They scoop it up and sell it to kids."

We had a Tube map at home, and I followed the familiar names—Russell Square, Regent's Park, Oxford Circus—to the outmost edges. Amersham. Uxbridge, where Emily's husband had gone to work. *Here be dragons*, my father said when I asked him what was there, which made my mother laugh, although I never understood why. And, safely on the ship, sitting in my cabin with my frozen portal in my hand, I finally realised that I had read *Ballet Shoes* for the last time.

The British Museum was all about last times. Every object in there had been used for the last time. Did the person who used the iron plough know that it was the last time he would prepare his fields with it? Did the person who wore the silver buckle know, when they took it off, that they would never put it on again?

You change. You move on, and life where you are becomes the only life that is, until it changes, and the next new reality becomes the only one. For the Fossil sisters, going to dancing school was so normal that they could complain about it. For me, school had been as impossible as eggs, as tantalising as oranges. And travelling daily by Tube—three girls and an old lady, unarmed, with no guard—was an idea from another world. The frozen page contained the illustration of the girls asleep on the Tube. No matter how many times I stared at it, they were never attacked. Not once. No petrol dealers approached them, and in the picture they all wore shoes and socks and coats. They looked so clean.

And the illustration itself had been drawn by hand, not digitally generated. Painting and drawing had still been legal when *Ballet Shoes* was first written, but I could not remember it. It was just another thing that belonged to another time. The Optimum Resourcing Act as I knew it simply stated that what resources there were, were needed for important things, like eating. I didn't remember the act coming in—like the Seasonal Food Act, it predated the collapse—but I did remember The Art Trials that started just before we sailed.

"If this man was working today," the screen bulletin said, "his working methods would have destroyed acres of rainforest. If this man were alive today, the oil in the paints he wasted could have been used for fuel. The canvas he ruined would have made blankets, clothes, tents. It is criminal waste, and has been a factor in the shortages we experience today." They were talking about an artist called Van Gogh, who had been dead for hundreds of years. I was fifteen; even I could see that this was a way of placing responsibility for the shortages in the past, where no one could do anything about it.

"Why now?" my father asked, staring at the screen, where bright yellow flowers were overlaid with the words recounting Van Gogh's crimes. "Why outlaw dead artists now?"

"Because the Optimum Resourcing Act got rid of all the living ones." My mother shrugged. "We're the dinosaurs, thinking that it matters."

"But of course it matters!"

"Why?" My mother threw down the word like a challenge, and I remembered that there had been bread on the table at lunch, actual bread, soft, with a crust that crunched as I bit into it, not dried biscuits. Had my father been trying to persuade my mother onto the ship with luxuries? At the time, I'd just been pleased to see the bread. "Why does it matter?"

"Anna," my father said, looking at my mother as though she was a stranger, "why are you asking that?"

"Because I want to know the answer." My mother's cheeks were pink, and her eyes were brighter than usual. "It matters, you say. It matters to have paints in many different colours and brushes, and canvas, for the sole purpose of putting down a picture that could easily be created on the screen?"

"But it couldn't," my father said, his tone at once hesitant and exasperated. "You know that. No screen can match the image I might create with my hands if I had the chance. Anna, what is this about?"

"I'm just saying. You have—what—fifty metres of canvas at the dock?"

"Five hundred and three."

"Whatever. And outside our window are at least that many people with nowhere to live. You could distribute that canvas, Michael. They'd have something to sleep under."

"But our people will need it. There'll be another Van Gogh on the ship. Another Titian, another Michaelangelo. Another Leonardo da Vinci. You should be grateful to these Art Trials, not picking fights with me."

"Grateful to them?"

"The hoarders will lose their nerve now they know that the Optimum Resourcing Act will never be rescinded. We'll be able to get clay, oils, pigments, remember?"

"I remember," my mother said, but my father was riding the wave of his enthusiasm and didn't react to the dryness in her voice.

"They'll give me the stuff for nothing if I time it right." He paused and looked at her. "It means I'll be away for a while," he said gently, and stepped towards her. She moved away, towards the window, and shrugged his hand off when he placed it on her shoulder. "I'll be back for Lalla's birthday," he said. "Don't be like that."

"Like what?"

"So cold. At least say that you'll miss me."

"But I won't," my mother said, staring out of the window with her back to him. "Not in the slightest. Why don't you leave Lalla some paper and pens, so that she can draw a picture for you while you're away? You've got a lovely fat blank book there. Leather bound. That would do."

I started up, ready to protest that I could not draw a picture, hardly ever got to hold a pen, but neither of them was looking at me. They threw me into the debate as a way of challenging each other's ideas. If they were the knives cutting through the difficulties of the world in which we were living, then I was the whetstone upon which they sharpened themselves. No wonder I had remained a child so long.

My father opened the door to leave. "I need that book for the manifest."

"But Lalla needs it to express herself creatively. That's just as important, isn't it, Michael? After all, a human being deprived of the means of self-expression is nothing better than a slave to the undignified mechanics of physical survival. That's right, isn't it? That's what we said."

"I'm thinking of the ship."

"And I'm thinking of the people we're leaving behind."

"Anna, please."

"Please what? Please just accept what you say without question? Please stop expecting you to live what you preach? Please just let you take a vision we used to share and change it until I don't recognise it anymore? Please what, Michael?" And there she stopped, as though she had been walking a tightrope and had just looked down.

My father's face clouded over. His eyebrows drew together, and I saw a glimpse of something dark in his eyes as he drew a deep breath.

"You'll never let us leave, will you?" he said. He stood over her as she sat on the sofa, her legs curled beneath her, her dress pooling over the balding velvet. Her face was tilted upwards; she was looking directly at him. Their eyes were locked together. The waters were pressing relentlessly at the dam. Her eyes fell, and the dam held. Right up until the day she died.

TWENTY-THREE

The thing about museums ❀ I am married
❀ Van Gogh and Lalla Paul

I shouldn't have tried to read *Ballet Shoes* again. It sent me up to the fourth deck, to my neglected museum, to fetch my red shoes on the morning of my wedding. If I hadn't thought about Posy's ballet shoes, the ones her mother left her, such sentimentality would never have occurred to me. But my mother had given me those shoes and no one would see them under the long white dress my father had chosen for me.

And the thing about museums is that they set you to thinking. There was a button, scratched and worn. There was a wax and plaster apple, broken by my desperate teeth. The screws from a skylight, from back in the days when I had thought freedom was important. Now, nothing was forbidden. Tom and I did whatever we liked, and it wasn't the same. A photograph album and a letter, whose stories I had almost forgotten. A lump of pastry, turning greyer and greyer. And my shoes. My red shoes.

I shut the door on my museum and walked slowly down the infirmary stairs. I let myself into my old cabin, which stood empty now, to add the final scratch to my tally of the days and to change my shoes. There were ninety marks in the original section, sixty in the new, but I was getting married now and it was time to stop. Tom was right.

I went on to the ballroom where my father was waiting with his people. The dress was made of heavy, smooth satin. The shoes my father had given me had high heels, but my red shoes were low, and the skirt puddled around my feet. I gathered it up so that I wouldn't trip, but the fabric simply slipped through my arms like so much water and I gave up. I moved more slowly these days anyway; there seemed to be more of me. Had my body expanded as my brain surrendered? Once I'd have asked. Now I simply accepted that the dress only just met around my waist.

Tom was there, waiting for me outside the ballroom door. He took my arm and we walked through the ballroom together. There was music, and the people smiled on either side of us. My father stood on the podium, behind his desk. The manifest sat open and the trumpets finished as we came before him.

"We have won," he said, and even then it seemed a strange opening for a wedding speech. "Every battle that humanity has ever fought, every cause that any man or woman ever felt was worth fighting for, or dying for, we have won. There is not a man or woman in history who struggled for a cause that has not triumphed here, on the ship. There is not a dream that has not been realised here, on the ship. Tom and Lalla stand before us as the expression of what we have achieved."

I looked at Tom. But he was looking at my father, and they were as radiant and proud as each other.

"We know what wealth means now. We know that wealth is living for and in each other. That every stroke of paint on a canvas, stitch of a tapestry, kick of a football, is an investment in our lives. We know that every meal shared, every activity enjoyed, is an investment in humanity itself. We are everything man was ever intended to be. We are creatures of love, of togetherness, of creativity.

"So, Tom and Lalla, take the legacy of the millennia that have brought us here, and live. Live! Love each other. Till the end of all our days."

I barely heard the people cheering. At that moment, as though my father had called it into being with his words, I felt a movement inside me, a bubble in my stomach that could have been hunger. I looked at my father, who was preparing his pen to write in the manifest. I looked at Tom, who was grinning around the room, nodding at the people as they shouted our names. I saw Patience holding out her arms in blessing; I saw Finn wiping away tears and Gabriel calling my name while Helen made a pretence of wanting him to quieten down. And then I saw Roger. He was looking at me, and I felt another bubble burst inside me and a soft fluttering, as though I had swallowed a butterfly. And suddenly I knew.

Where had my father been standing, the moment that he made the decision to buy the ship and offer five hundred good people the chance of a perfect death? In my imagination, he was on the top of a mountain, looking down on a mighty city, or sitting on a golden throne in a room filled with oil paintings and marble statues. But he was probably doing nothing more than walking down a road. Certainly, when I realised what was happening to me, my body just carried on, while my mind wrapped itself around the revelation and stared at it. My father put the pen in my hand and I signed the manifest for the second time. I passed the pen to Tom, and then my father joined our hands and we were married.

The people bore us off to the dining room, where Gerhard had prepared a feast. Emily stood smiling and crying beside a vast arrangement of artificial flowers. They were everywhere, and when my father told me that I should throw the bouquet I was holding, it was Emily who caught it. She looked so young. So full of hope. And I realised that this would be neither the last wedding, nor the last birth.

The dining room was decked in bright colours, not only the flowers but the clothes people wore, the little cakes, the decorations that were everywhere. I thought about Jamila's tales of Bangladesh before it had been drowned, of the spices and the heat and the way that rain turned everything a bright, vivid green and of a pink and gold sari she had once worn. I thought of Patience, tending to ripening watermelons, deep green on the red earth of her homestead, and the pale bleating of her goats. I thought of the tulips of Holland leaving their scarlet kisses on the ocean floor when the dykes gave way. And my mother, her green silk dress floating about her, at one with the sea.

Yellow sunflowers in the paintings of Van Gogh.

I'm having a baby, Mother, I whispered silently, and I saw her, sitting on the balding velvet sofa in London, picking at its arm. My father had just set off his expedition to secure now-outlawed art materials for the ship; the sound of the locks being set behind him was still reverberating in the air.

"Van Gogh killed himself," she said quietly, dropping her hands. "He created a thousand paintings, but still he died, mad with his inability to show what was inside him. Your father hasn't got enough canvas for even one Van Gogh. Not one. Vincent would clean him out in a week if he came on board."

"But Vincent's dead."

"We're all dead," my mother said, looking out of the window onto the square. "All of us."

We're all dead, she said into my wedding celebrations, breaking her silence at last. *All of us*. And I knew what I had to do. It was not a decision I made over time. It was sudden and absolute and irrevocable, like the moment the overhanging cliff falls into the sea, or the moment my child was conceived.

I think my father knew too, because he watched me leave the

dining room without a word, my long white satin skirts trailing behind me. I don't know what Tom thought; he was a dream from a place I should never have visited, and he wasn't even looking at me. I left them celebrating with their people, and I thought, maybe this is what has happened to me. I am going mad with the inability to express what is inside me, and my father has run out of canvas.

TWENTY-FOUR

—

Tom and Roger ❧ *the speeches at my wedding*
❧ *Tom and my father*

I went to my cabin and picked up a bag, and then I went down
to the stores and filled it so full I could barely drag it to the little
boat, from which I had learned to swim. The people were busy
singing and dancing in the dining room; the rest of the ship was
deserted, and no one saw me heave the bag into the boat. The
solar panel showed that the engine was fully charged. I went
back for some clothes, although I did not stop to change, and the
gown swept after me, rippling over the diamond pattern on the
walkways. It was but the work of moments to release the pulley
and lower the boat into the sea, where it bobbed cheerfully at the
end of its rope, like an image from a holiday picture in another
world.

The ladder was fixed to the hull; it would not take long to
climb down to the little boat, even if I went slowly.

I saw my mother's body floating away from the ship. The sea
had borne her up; it would do the same for me. The canvas was
still on the fourth deck, waiting for my father's Van Gogh. I had
never tried to paint a picture. If I stayed, he would give me canvas. He would give me paint, and brushes, and I would paint my
pain onto the canvas, even though I did not know how. People
would look at my painting like they looked at Alice's embroidery,

and there would be a point to existing. There was no canvas on the little boat, which looked pathetically flimsy now. I imagined the next great rainstorm, my slowly swelling stomach and I hunched in the cabin as the sea and sky became one. And I knew that my mother had been afraid of the ship, just as I was now afraid of the world beyond it.

I heard the door behind me swing open.

"Lalla. Where have you been?"

He had come. Tom had come. And when I saw his face pink and his green eyes alive with concern, I wanted to stay. If his heart beat like mine, if his hopes were wrapped in me as mine were in him, then we could live and love and die on the ship, and the future would be for our baby to sort out. He had come for me. I could do it. I could brave the degeneration of the ship. I could eat from tins and packets of powder until they were exhausted, and then I could starve with him and say nothing of my hunger. I could stand between him and my father, and take one of their hands in each of mine and press them to my growing belly, and see them look at each other with pride, and their love for me would make our inevitable descent to the ocean bed as nothing.

I could do this, if Tom loved me.

"What are you doing, Lalla?"

"I'm leaving," I said, and as soon as the words were in the air, I knew that they were true, and that I could no more stay on the ship than I could change my father. Tom followed my eyes to the little boat.

"You're what?" he said, his voice constricted. "Just—please, Lalla. Don't even joke about it." My hands were shaking in his. I held his hands more tightly.

"I love you," I said, and my voice was steady. He tried to take me in his arms, but I could not lose him now.

"Lalla," he said.

I looked at him, and I saw how we had changed. This was not the face of the boy who had jumped eagerly at the gift of a football. The sun had coarsened his boy-skin; there were tiny red veins in his eyes and lines on his forehead. And I—I was no longer the grieving child who had come on board, so needy, so lonely, so desperate to be liked. We had grown together on the ship, and now it was time to leave. "We're married," he said, this man who held my hands. "You don't mean this. You're ill, Lalla. I'm going to fetch Michael, and Roger, and we'll help you. All the excitement—it's sent you a bit mad. That's all. I'll get Michael."

"Don't," I said. My husband. My lover, who was going to be a father.

But of course, he didn't know. Did he know? I took his hand and pressed it flat against my belly. "This is why," I whispered. "There's a tomorrow now. We can't be right here, right now anymore, and the ship won't let us be anywhere else."

"I know."

"You know?" I said, and the colour drained slowly out of my world.

"Roger said it was possible. He said to keep an eye on you. How long have you known? Why didn't you say anything?"

"I've only just realised," I faltered. "You sound angry."

"I'm not angry. But you've got to stop saying stupid things now. You just ruin things. This ought to be the happiest day of our whole lives." He pulled me towards the ballroom door, just as he had once pulled me onto the top deck. "Let's go and tell Michael. He ought to be the first to know."

"Stop it," I said, and I held myself hard and would not be pulled. "It's our baby. Yours and mine. Not his."

He stopped pulling. "Of course," he said. "But he'll look after you. I'll look after you. I said I'd always be with you, and I will." He put his hand back on my stomach, but the baby was still.

"Roger said to take you to the infirmary as soon as you said anything. Just to be certain."

But I was certain. I didn't need Roger, and I didn't trust him.

"Have you said anything to my father?"

"Of course not," Tom said indignantly. He paused as though he expected thanks.

"Let me go, Tom," I said.

"Go where, darling? Tell me, where?" He came and stood beside me at the deck rail, and the warmth of his hands on mine made me waver as his words had not.

"Just away. Away over there," and I gestured at the horizon, beyond which was land or death. Or land and death.

"No," he said. "I won't let you. How can you even ask me? There's nothing out there. I saw it. I know. Trust me." And I could not hold myself apart from him anymore. "Come back," he said. "Eat. Cut the cake. Dance with me." He smiled and wiped his eyes with the back of his hand. "Would that be so painful?"

I shook my head. No, it would not be painful. If dancing with Tom had been painful, leaving would have been easy. "You said you'd come with me," I burst out.

"We'd starve."

"So will the ship."

"We'd die on the sea."

"So will the ship."

Tom let me go then, and stepped backwards. "What if you die, like Roger's Sarah?"

"Then you'd have our baby."

"What if the baby dies?"

"You'd have me."

"And if you both die?"

"You'd have yourself. Free. And maybe none of those things will happen. We might find land. You have to choose, Tom."

"There is no choice," he said. I felt a terrible tearing in my own breast, as though a part of me was being clawed apart. "I'm going to be a father. Do you know what that means? It means not breaking your promises. It means putting your children first."

"Did my father tell you that?" I asked.

"He's done better. He's shown me. All the plans he made, the provisions he stored. For you. Do you know what frightened me most when I came on board, Lalla? Do you know?"

"What?"

"That I wouldn't be worthy. That I could never be what he wanted me to be for you. He loves you so much, and he trusts me. He chose me for you. It wasn't the China pictures I posted on my blog. It was his plan for you. That was why he told me to give you space. He needed to know that you'd chosen me for yourself. And you did. You love me, and I love you. He was right."

"He chose you?"

He nodded eagerly, and the last fibre holding me to the ship strained, and snapped.

"You say you love me," I said quietly. "But you don't. You love the girl my father sold you. And I've tried to be that girl. But I'm not."

"And the girl you are can't love me?"

"Not on the ship." The baby moved. "Tom," I said, "if there was ever a moment when you loved me for myself, then you have to come with me."

He put his hand in his pocket and there, held between his thumb and index finger, was one of the skylight screws. "I wanted to give you this instead of a wedding ring," he said. "But Father had the ring ready, and..." He put it into my palm and folded my fingers over it. He pulled me to him and kissed me, and I clung, not to my father's creature but to the boy who had followed me out through the skylight and into the world.

The ballroom door opened and the people spilled out onto the deck. They were laughing, and when they saw Tom and me, kissing on the deck, they began to cheer. Tom put his arm around me.

"The cake." I heard my father's voice through the open door. "Where's the happy couple? We should cut the cake."

I put my lips to Tom's ear and whispered, "Let me go. Now."

Tom hesitated for a moment, and in that moment, my father appeared in the doorway, all smiles and pride. "Tom," he said. "Lalla. Come back inside. Cut the cake. You'll be together all your lives. Today you have to share each other with the rest of us."

Tom put his arm around my shoulders and pushed me forwards, back through the doors into the ballroom, smiling to left and to right. My red shoes had no grip and I slipped along, propelled by his strength. "I'm sorry," he said quietly, guiding me up onto the podium. The clapping and the stamping that greeted us drowned out the music and made it impossible for me to reply. He bent down and kissed me again, and the ballroom exploded in cheers. And I liked it. Oh how I liked it, even though I was furious. There was nothing simple here.

Patience and Mercy bustled over with the cake knife, its handle tied with ribbons and flowers. Tom took it and offered it to me, and I ran my finger down the flat of the blade. The cutting edge caught the light; it looked wickedly sharp. Patience and Mercy looked at each other, delighted, as though they'd overheard me saying something lovely. I held the knife, and Tom put his hands over mine, and together we pushed it through the smooth white icing and into the cake below.

"Speech," someone called out, and the word was taken up. "Speech, speech." Tom grinned and held up his hand as though he was reluctant to comply. But I could see his eyes, and I could see his pride in standing where my father had stood, speaking to

the people as my father spoke to them. My father was there, standing with his people and gazing at me. He took in my dress, my
veil, the tiara in my hair. But he could not see his compass, tucked
inside the bodice of my dress, warm against my skin.

"Speech," the people called, but not until my father held
up his hands and joined in the cry did Tom lean over to the
microphone.

"Is this on?" he asked, and it clicked into life. "I just wanted to
say one thing. Only one. And it's this—that I really, really wish
Lalla's mother were here." Silence fell, broken only by murmured
agreement. People looked at Tom, and at each other, and at the
floor. Only my father continued to look directly at me. "Lalla
loved her mother, and I know we all lost people, but Lalla actually lost her mother here on the ship, and I think that's why it's
taken her a bit longer than the rest of us to be happy here. But
Lalla's happy now, aren't you, Lalla, and I'm going to make sure
she stays that way."

People began to clap, but I leaned across to the microphone
and said, "Wait." I spoke louder than I had meant to, and the
word echoed slightly. Hundreds of pairs of eyes followed my
father's and fixed on me.

"What are you doing?" Tom asked, frowning.

"I've got some things to say." I tried to say this to him quietly,
but the microphone was on and Tom was leaning over me, so our
words were picked up and broadcast across the ballroom.

"We're going to tell Michael first," Tom said quietly. I shook
my head. My father raised his eyebrows. The unconditional joy
that had reigned only a few moments before dissipated, and in its
place was an air of unease.

"Let Lalla speak," my father said, and Tom stepped aside. I
could see the satin of my bodice pulsing with my heartbeat and
wondered whether I was going to be able to say a word. The bride
did not normally make a speech, my father had said casually

as he brought the flowers down from the stores. But I had not planned the wedding. I had not chosen to be standing where I was. They had no choice but to listen.

"I've got some things to say," I repeated, my voice unsteady. "It can be my testimony, if you like. I never got to say what brought me here, like the rest of you did." Tom shifted nervously beside me. "I wish my mother was here too. But she isn't. And there's someone I wish was here even more than my mother." My father was looking grave, and Emily's hand tightened on his arm. "Tom had a grandfather. Tom's grandfather was the only family he had left. The only family. And he took Tom into the country, to find a plot of land to grow things on."

Tom hissed in my ear. "This is an old story, Lalla. Everyone knows it already. We've left the past behind, remember? The testimonies are over."

"Mine isn't," I said. "The point is that Tom's grandfather wasn't allowed to come on the ship. It's not that he was dead. It was because he wanted a garden. And what I wanted to say is that I wish he had been allowed to come, because he had a right to be saved too. You can't just pick and choose. Not people. Because people aren't things. You can't just store the ones you like, as if they were tinned tomatoes or cooking chocolate."

My father removed Emily's hand from his arm and strode up to the podium. "Let's talk later, Lalla," he said. "Stop this now. Say thank you to your guests, and go and dance."

"I won't be dancing," I said, and I could feel my smile tight and false. "I'm going to leave now. I'm going to find apples. Real ones." I gathered my skirts. "Thank you," I said as I got to my feet. "Thank you for looking after me, and putting up with me for so long." There was an uncertain smatter of applause as I stepped down from the podium and began to walk towards the doors.

"What are you doing?" Tom called.

"I told you," I said, and the room was so quiet that I didn't need the microphone. "I'm leaving. You won't let me go, but it's not your decision to make." The wedding was crumbling; people looked around at the flowers, the cake, the clothes they were wearing, as though they expected these things to melt. I kept walking, and the people stepped aside. When I reached the door, I heard my name echoing around the room, and I knew that my father had taken the microphone.

I spoke to him without turning round.

"Tom doesn't love me enough," I said. "Do you?"

Patience began to cry, and her sobs cut through the set air. Mercy held her. I looked at Mercy, her wide soft eyes turned pleadingly towards me. But I could not stay just because Patience wanted me to.

"Close the doors," my father called, but no one moved. I kept walking.

"Close the doors," came another voice, higher, more desperate, but still the people hesitated, scared to do at Tom's command what they had failed to do for my father.

"Look at me, Lalla," my father ordered. "Look at me." His voice was cracking and I knew I had to get out of the ballroom before he began to cry. I remembered my mother, how she had stalled and stalled and stalled the sailing of the ship. If she had not been shot, we would still be in London. I knew this now, and I had a suspicion of the lengths my father had gone to, to create the world he wanted.

I heard the desk drawer open and shut.

There was a scream, and another, and I knew what I would see when I turned around as clearly as though it was happening in front of me.

"I can't let you," my father was calling, his voice choked. "I won't let you. Where do you think you'll go?"

I was trembling so hard that I wasn't sure I could turn without falling. *Let me be wrong*, I begged to nothing. *Let me be wrong.* But I remembered a figure in faded black running through the crowd and my mother collapsing to the floor. I was not wrong.

I turned around. My father was holding a gun, and he was pointing it at me. The room was so still people did not seem to be breathing. He held the gun steadily and said, "I would rather kill you myself than have you suffer what you will suffer before your death in the world beyond the ship."

"And I would rather die out there, looking for a future, than die here, knowing there is none."

"Michael." Emily stepped forwards, her hands held out. She kept her eyes on my father and walked towards him. "Lalla is your daughter. You love her. We all love her. This is not the way. We convince her with love, remember?" But my father was not deterred. His gun was trained on me and he did not flinch, even when Emily joined him on the podium and touched his arm.

"What will you do?" I said, turning to the ballroom in general. "Will you leave your children to sink with the ship? Will you live this glorious life of plenty, knowing that your children will starve because of it? Or will you help me take the ship to land?"

"The ship is for the children," my father said, and for the first time I saw a tremor in his hands.

"And their children?"

"A beautiful life makes a present of death," my father said. "I gave my daughter a beautiful life. I have given you all a beautiful life."

I looked around at the people, frozen in dismay, in shock, in fear. "Tell him," I said to them. "Tell my father to take the ship back to London. Or anywhere. I've seen the radar and the charts. There is land. Let's find it, and go there, and start again. We can

use the stores to give us a good start. We'll grow clover." I looked
at Tom and willed him to join his voice to mine. But no one said
a word.

Then Helen spoke. "No," she said. "I'm not going back. If you
make me go back, I'll throw myself into the sea and take Gabriel
with me."

"Me too." Patience pushed Mercy from her and got heavily to
her feet. "Lalla, child. Africa's burned. India's drowned. China's
dead. You saw London. There's nowhere. Nowhere but here."

"And even if there was somewhere else, why would you go
there?" Mercy joined her voice with Patience's. "We've got everything here." She looked around shyly, the guardian of a secret.
"Michael told me there's pianos. We're going to learn to play
music."

"Things may have got better," I said. "How will we know
unless we go and see? You threw away the mast."

Tom looked at me, and for a wild, glorious moment I thought
that he was going to tell the engineers to storm my father's cabin
and set a course for the nearest land. I would not have to leave.
We would be together, and find a future for our child.

"But it's safe here!" my father cried, the gun now trembling
in his hands. "That's all I ever wanted. To keep you safe, to keep
you nurtured. Why are you doing this to me, Lalla?"

I looked at him. "Who was Neil Bailey?" I asked.

My father's self-command was gone. Emily cradled his head
in her arms and he cried, gripping the gun as though it was the
only thing stopping him from falling. "No," he cried. "No." I
looked at Emily, waiting for her to shout at me. But she did not.

"It was an accident," Emily said. "You need to understand
that we were in the holding centre for a long time. Years, some of
us. We wanted to sail, but your mother would never quite agree.
We had food and shelter and the guards—we were all right as far
as your mother was concerned. She was more interested in the

street people. I wanted her to bring you to meet us, but she never did. Michael said she was scared we'd hold you hostage until she agreed to sail. We were so insulted by that. We said too much to each other, got ourselves too wound up. And one day, Neil disappeared. That same night, Roger got the message from Michael that we were to sail at last.

"When Neil came back, we were singing and dancing. Only Roger wasn't joining in. When I asked Roger why not, he showed me the rest of Michael's message. Anna had been shot in the stomach. She was barely breathing. Roger didn't think she could possibly survive. And Neil—when he realised what he'd done— he went outside and shot himself."

"Where did he get the gun from?"

Emily didn't answer.

"Did you give it to him?" I asked my father. "Did you tell Neil Bailey to shoot my mother?"

"No," my father sobbed, his face contorted. "Not to shoot her. A broken window, that was all. She was sleepwalking into hell and she was holding your hand. A warning. To wake her up. To save your life."

"Is this the same gun?" I felt myself drawn to it; I imagined taking it in my hands. My father was cradling it like a child. *No, Lalla, never a gun. Just my toothbrush and my wit.* I had been so naive.

"We didn't know what to do with it," Helen said. "It all happened so quickly. Neil died, then you arrived, and we sailed. We couldn't just throw the gun into the sea, not with all the government troops, and the mob on the quay."

Gabriel clung to Helen and began to cry, "I don't like the gun, Mummy. I don't like it."

Helen held his hand. "No one likes it," she said, keeping her eyes on me as though the gun was my fault.

"But thank goodness we've got it," Roger said grimly.

He took the gun from my weeping father and aimed it at my skirts, and the tilt of his chin and the light through the ballroom windows told me the truth. Roger, who had red and blue mugs and made maps in flour. Roger, who broke the rules and changed nothing. A broken window wouldn't have been enough to persuade my mother to board. It had been Roger's idea to shoot her. An arm, he would have said to poor Neil Bailey. A foot. I imagined Neil Bailey's trembling hands, his fear. I could forgive him. But I couldn't forgive Roger. I couldn't forgive my father.

I walked backwards towards the deck doors, facing Roger and the gun. Any moment, I would hear a shot and feel the searing pain of a bullet in my foot, or my leg. The train of my dress caught under my shoes. I tripped, and as I struggled to my feet, I saw that Finn and some of the engineers were blocking my path to the deck door. The internal door—the door into the ship, through which the doctor had carried my mother one hundred and fifty days ago—stood wide open. I could escape into the ship, I thought. I could live in my museum and sneak down to the stores at night, the hidden, ghostly conscience of the ship. And I knew, as clearly as though I had seen it happen, that one day, someone on the ship would do this.

But I had a life of my own to find, and another to protect.

"Please," I said to Finn. "Move aside and let me through."

"We can't do that," he said. "You're not well. You've never really been well, not since we sailed. Isn't there something you can give her, Roger? To help her a bit. She doesn't know what she's doing."

I looked at Tom. Did he think I should be winged, like a captive bird, or tranquillised, like the zoo animals in screen documentaries? Is that what I was to him now—a sick elephant, incubating his heir?

But Tom did not speak. Instead, he reached over to Roger and put his hands gently over the hands that held the gun. "This isn't the way, Roger," he said gently. "It's not what Michael's taught us, or what he wants." Tom took the gun, and spoke softly and calmly, using a monotone that made me think of lullabies. Emily looked at Tom gratefully; Tom looked at my father. "We are your people, Michael," Tom said. "We will be with you, and be grateful to you, for all of our lives, and our children's lives." For one wild, ridiculous moment I thought Tom was going to shoot my father. But he didn't. He called to the engineers, "Let Lalla go." My father was shaking now. Tom carried the gun towards me. My father shrank into his chair, like a speeded-up film of a man growing old.

Emily knelt in front of him, holding his hands. "Are there any more guns?" she asked him. He shook his head, and a great cry rose from him, involuntary and animal. Tom stood next to me, holding the gun, facing into the ballroom.

"Stay there," he said. "All of you. Stay where you are." He stepped backwards through the ballroom doors, motioning to me to go through first. I went through to the deck, and he came with me, bringing the gun. The doors shut behind us, and we were alone.

"Lalla," he said. "Don't do this."

"I don't have a choice."

He took the gun in both hands; he looked at it; he looked at me. Then he raised his hands high over his head and, with all his strength, he threw the gun over the deck rail. It flew in an arc and plummeted into the water near the little boat, and the splash it made caused the little boat to rock.

"You do now," he said.

I wanted to kiss him. I wanted to hold and hold him, and never, never, never let him go, but I knew that if I felt his lips against mine, I would decide that tomorrow would be soon enough, or the day after, or the day after that. I had to live, even if I died as a result.

I could neither live in a grave, nor birth my child into one.

Tom looked at me. He waited. He waited a little longer. And then he went to the ballroom doors, opened them and looked back at me. I stayed still. He stepped into the ballroom and pulled the doors shut behind him.

TWENTY-FIVE

What happens in the end

And so I climbed, and my red shoes made the deck rail ring. I pulled myself up and swung my legs over, so that I balanced like a child on a swing, gripping the rail until my palms were numb. My satin train hung heavy below me.

If I let go and threw myself forward, I would hit the water. I could push off from the deck rail with my feet, and launch myself away from the ship, beyond the little boat, to the true unknown that awaited all of us. It would be quicker that way, and my mother would be waiting for me.

But no. The end was not going to be so easy. I gathered up my dress and felt the little boat rocking beneath my feet, even though the deck rail was still pressing cold into my thighs. It would be firm and solid decades after the little boat had fallen apart and rotted away. On the ship, I lived and worked with hundreds; the little boat was barely big enough for just me. The ship stored food for years to come; the little boat held only what I'd been able to carry, and a map from my father's study. If time on the ship was running out, on the little boat it had practically gone. And yet I was going to take myself—take us—from big to small, from plenty to dearth, from the known to a place I had no power to predict.

I felt with my foot until I found the first rung of the ladder. I wondered whether Tom would betray me at the last. I looked back at the ballroom door, half-hoping for a tall shadow, a foot-fall. But there was nothing. Tom had chosen, and he had not chosen me.

For you, Lalla, my father always said about the ship. I did this for you, for your future, so that you could be safe.

For me, Father? I thought, remembering his arm slipping softly around Emily's waist. For me? I remembered the cots waiting on the fourth deck. The looks of adoration on Alice's face as he presented her with more silk, more beads, embroidery threads in ever brighter colours. The bewilderment in Tom's green eyes as I reached for his hand in the sunlit air, and the sudden clearing of his face as my father showed him the way forward. *I think this is what Michael would want, Lalla. I think this is what would make him happy.*

When you are born, little one, I will never say that I did this for you. I will never place that burden upon you. These are my feet climbing down the ladder. Mine is the heart that longs for another way, mine the eyes that have seen the emptiness in the way we are living. You, as yet, are nothing. But even now, even before I am certain that you will ever draw breath outside my body, I know that I cannot, I must not, feed you for ever. You will be mine for a time, and then you will feed yourself.

On what?

Mother, you are out here somewhere. Mother, look after me. After us.

There is land. I have seen it on my father's maps. And on that land are people. I will find them, or drown. My child will not be born into the safe, dying world of the ship, but into the desperate, shifting world of the living. My child will be born in a place I do not yet know, among people I have never met. They will welcome me, because I have given everything I have, everything I am, to find them. I will steer my little boat on the high seas, and one day, if I am lucky, I will see the vast trunks of the wind turbines towering above me, their giant arms reaching for stardust in the air, and I will know I am almost there. Maybe my hands will be the ones that reconnect the wires. Maybe, little one, those hands will be yours.

I had my father's compass. I was leaving my museum to the ship; it was a fair exchange. They could read my story there if they wanted to.

I climbed down the ladder, my train weighing on my arm, each foot secure for a matter of seconds before taking its turn to bear my body down.

The ship was not the beginning, but the end. In a day, or a year, or a decade, or a century, the food would run out. The ship itself would rust and sink. And the people upon it—these people whom I knew, or their children, or their children's children—would die. Burnt out, like night's candles.

I was seized by the desire to know where the thought of night's candles had come from. Maybe it was not too late. I would find out in a moment if I went back. I felt the cold of the metal rungs pressing into my palms, their solidity beneath my feet. Now that I was leaving, the certainty of the ship seemed very precious. I longed for it, for the knowledge that there would be food, that there would be shelter, that there would be meaningful work for me, a life in which I could flourish, love, grow. And yet, it was this very certainty that made it essential to leave. Because there is no such thing as certainty, and in creating it, we lose the very thing that keeps us alive.

I stepped into the boat and released the pulley ropes. The boat shivered on the surface of the vast sea.

I blinked away the tears that were clouding my vision, and I saw a halo of bright rust surrounding the rivet that held the ladder to the hull. Like a sunrise trying to burst through, or the creeping orange embers on a paper's edge before the paper bursts into flame. Or a sunset, or a dying fire.

ACKNOWLEDGEMENTS

My agent, Jonny Geller, who understood the apple, and my editor, Arzu Tahsin, who bit into it.

Anna Davis, Kirsten Foster, Alice Lutyens, Jennifer Kerslake, Sophie Hutton-Squire and everyone at Curtis Brown and Weidenfeld and Nicolson.

My supportive and talented writing friends Emily de Peyer, Emma Sweeney and Rachel Connor, my long-suffering non-writing friends, in particular Ali Jezard, Rebecca Singerman-Knight and Julie Walther, and my sister Carissa Honeywell.

Everyone I've been taught by or alongside, with particular thanks to Maggie Gee, Katharine McMahon, Louise Doughty, Andrew Miller, Helen Dunmore and Erica Wagner.

All who read and gave feedback on the manuscript, including Jessie Burton, Geoff Curwen, Laxmi Curwen, Lucy Eyre, Emma Haigh, Daniela Haller, Sue Harris, Sarah Hooker, Tim Jordan, Rosie Pearson, David Salmon, Rose Mary Salmon, Ruth Shabi and Gillian Stern.

Helen Lappert and the wonderful women of Amersham A Cappella, who know why.

Kate Honeywell, Maureen Hancocks, Howard Hancocks, Jane Diduca, Charlotte Yeoman and Jane Davies, who have given me time.

My children. OK, so I could do it quicker without you, but the thought of doing so takes away all meaning.

And James. I thank you from the bottom of whatever it is that drives me to write. My heart belongs to you already.

extras

orbit

meet the author

Photo credit: Chris Honeywell

ANTONIA HONEYWELL studied English at Manchester University and worked at the Natural History and Victoria and Albert museums in London, running creative writing workshops and education programs for children before training as a teacher. During her ten years teaching English, drama and film studies, she wrote a musical and a play, which was performed at the Edinburgh Festival. She has four young children and lives in Buckinghamshire. *The Ship* is her first novel.

READING GROUP GUIDE

IN CONVERSATION WITH ANTONIA HONEYWELL

Q Where did the idea for *The Ship* come from and how did the plot begin to take shape in your mind?

A The idea for *The Ship* began to form when I married but in many ways the novel has its genesis in my childhood. I was an odd child—I didn't make friends easily and used to spend school playtimes wandering round the playground writing notes to the ladybirds in chalk. Then came an apocalyptic divorce when I was thirteen. The legacy of that divorce and the bitterness that led up to and away from it meant that I walked through life on eggshells. Relationships were a snare and a delusion; arguments were like the molten lava beneath the earth's crust, showing the seething dangers beneath. I became a skilled mediator and peacekeeper, but those skills came from a genuine doubt about my right to inhabit the space I took up. I also became a constant observer of other people—the way they talked to each other, influenced each other. I began to understand that lack of self-confidence—constant reliance on other people—can be a form of tyranny. I couldn't just wait around to be rescued by some insightful teacher, or doctor, or handsome prince—I had to become an island in order to join the mainland. And when I married, I wanted to keep my hard-won happiness safe—but how could that be done without shutting out the flawed and damaged aspects of the world? And that got me thinking about the ways in which the hugely privileged defend their privileges, and the ultimate consequences of that. The financial crash in 2008 sharpened my nebulous ideas, and then I saw Lalla, a bored and angry teenager, through a display case at the British Museum and began to write.

Q   *The Ship* is set in the near future in a world which is unfamiliar to us. How did you create an alternative history for Lalla? Did you plan a timeline from the present day to the time of the book, and if so, do you think the world into which Lalla is born could become a reality for us?

A   I think we're living in it already. What are the people found dead in lorries, or drowning in fishing vessels, or relying on food banks, or dying of exposure on the streets, but an expendable underclass? How fully are you able to participate in modern society if you have no access to the internet?

Q   Lalage is an unusual name. How did you come across it and does it hold particular significance for you?

A   I first came across the name Lalage in John Fowles' novel *The French Lieutenant's Woman*. I was thirteen when I read it, and it had a powerful effect on me. Sarah Woodruff is a woman whom society has defined in a particular way. She is powerless to reject the definition, but maintains her sense of self in spite of it, and becomes a pariah. I don't want to spoil the novel for people who haven't read it—suffice to say that a small child named Lalage appears in its final pages, and that the outcome, not just for the individuals concerned but for the progress of society as a whole, depends entirely on the über-Victorian Charles' reaction to her. My Lalage is John Fowles' Lalage, a fair few decades on.

Q There are a number of religious references in the novel, for example the Nazareth Act, the symbolism of the apple and the ship, and the way those on board start to call Michael Paul, "Father." What value does religion have in *The Ship*?

A There is no religion on board the ship—not overtly, anyway. But by choosing the people he will save, Michael creates a bond between them, and nurtures their very human desire to believe that their good fortune is due to more than mere luck. Their elevation of him is necessary to them—without it, they would have to challenge his decisions, and their own. They'd have to answer Lalla's questions. And it's necessary to Michael, too, because without the people's unwavering, uncritical faith in him, the ship would be torn apart. They create a pseudo-religion that suits them. Religion can be a deliberate anaesthetic for your conscience, or a means of finding it. Look at the Church of England's struggle to embrace equal marriage, for example, or the strength with which huge swathes of avowedly religious people clung to slavery. It's Lalla, at the end, who faces the true conundrum of faith.

Q Have you considered writing a sequel to *The Ship*? How do you respond when readers ask what happens to Lalla?

A I love questions from readers—one of the main joys of being published is meeting readers and grappling with their questions, particularly in a book group context where we don't have to worry about spoilers. Lalla belongs to anyone who reads her story and every reader brings something new to her decision. I've had readers draw parallels with their own lives—one spoke of Lalla's story resonating with his own struggle to come out to parents, for example, and another talked of the pressure to take on the family business her parents and grandparents wanted to pass down to her. Readers have talked about divorce, about facing infertility, about end-of-life treatment and assisted dying. Every life contains a Ship moment—a time when a particular course of action becomes the only possibility, regardless of what happens next. Some people commit everything to an idea and succeed beyond their wildest dreams—which is wonderful—but I feel that we're living in a world where success is seen as an inevitable consequence of total commitment, when in fact it's no such thing. I'm interested in the no-man's land between commitment and success. Suppose *The Ship* had never achieved publication? What about the young people who give their lives to developing their tennis or swimming, yet never win Wimbledon or an Olympic gold? What about the couple who've sunk all they have into IVF but never become pregnant? It's an underexplored area, and *The Ship* is about the decision Lalla comes to, rather than its consequences. Any sequel would have to respect those stories—the ones that look like failure, but which contain sacrifice and devotion equal to any success.

Q You have four young children. Do you find it difficult to find the time to write? Have you developed any strategies for balancing the demands of parenthood with your writing life?

A It's impossible. It could be made possible by a full-time nanny, or boarding schools for the children, I suppose, but...but...It's not just money. We wanted the children. And for reasons too complicated to explore here, it's a complete miracle that they came and were all healthy. They'll grow up and leave us soon enough, so for now I juggle and contrive and cry for help, and maybe when they fly away, the time and space to write will soothe the pain. It might help aspiring writers in the same situation to know that these replies have been written a) in the kitchen while the porridge bubbles b) in the café at a local activity centre and c) hiding in the bathroom. I have to look hard at how I spend my time, and ruthlessly cull the non-essential. Some activities are easy to let go— like dusting, ironing and clothes shopping. Others are harder, particularly where the children are involved. It takes a good deal of discipline. But it's right that the children should see that I work. And that writing is my work is a privilege in itself.

Q Who are your favourite writers and how have they influenced your work?

A I love to read. I always have. Benson Village Library featured largely in my childhood and I read indiscriminately. I had no idea whether a book was well-written or improving or *suitable* for a child; I absorbed the lot. The insidious erosion of our libraries is a terrible thing. When I was eleven, my English teacher suggested I try some classics. I started with *Jane Eyre* and just kept going. At sixteen I discovered Thomas Hardy and fell heavily in love; by eighteen I was boasting that I didn't read living authors. I wore long full skirts and lacy blouses with high collars and wondered why I didn't get invited to parties. But literature was so much easier than real life. Now I read living authors constantly and despair at the impossibility of reading even the novels that were published yesterday. But those classics are part of me—Lucy Snowe, Dorothea Brooke—women who reject the narrative they've been brought up with and reach for a creed of their own. (But not Maggie Tulliver or Tess Durbeyfield; pre-death self-actualisation is preferable. I'm working on it.)

DISCUSSION POINTS

"I think he was a little bewildered that his great triumph, the Dove, had not saved the world, and so he set about saving his own world— my mother and I—another way." Is Michael Paul a bad man? Do you feel any sympathy for him? How difficult are moral judgements in a world in which civilisation has collapsed?

How fine is the line between caring for children and controlling them?

The Ship has been described as a coming-of-age novel. What does Lalla learn during the course of novel, and can you see any differences in the choices she makes at the beginning of the story and at the end?

"Eat. Smile at me. Be happy." Why do you think Lalla struggles to follow her father's instructions?

If you found yourself on board the ship, what would you miss most about the world you inhabit now? Do you think you would be more or less content than Lalla?

How many religious images or references can you find in the novel and why are they significant to the narrative?

"*Have an apple*, she used to say when I asked for the impossible." What does the symbol of the apple represent in *The Ship*?

Lalla and her mother are walking home from the British Museum when they see a button fall from a man's coat as he wraps it around a woman. While Lalla's mother thinks the button is a token of love that should be in a museum, Lalla's father sees it as a "broken button... not worth anything." Discuss the differences in their ideology, and who you think is right.

What contemporary political, social or environmental parallels can you find within this novel?

"And that was what the ship was. A life without hope." Do you agree? Is the overall tone of *The Ship* hopeful or pessimistic?

Discuss the tension between love and freedom in the novel. Consider Lalla's relationships with Tom and her father. How well do they know Lalla really?

Why does Antonia Honeywell include phrases at the beginning of each chapter? Do these affect the way you approach the story?

"We honour our dead by living well." Do you agree? How does Lalla experience grief?

Do you think that the five hundred people on board the ship are worthy of salvation? How do you feel about their willingness to forget those left behind?

"*I don't have answers, Lalla. Only questions. That's how you learn.*" How are these words brought out in the novel?

SKETCHY BEHAVIOR

Amy Patterson :)

SKETCHY BEHAVIOR

Erynn Mangum

ZONDERVAN®

ZONDERVAN.com/
AUTHORTRACKER
follow your favorite authors

We want to hear from you. Please send your comments about this book to us in care of zreview@zondervan.com. Thank you.

ZONDERVAN

Sketchy Behavior
Copyright © 2011 by Erynn Mangum O'Brien

This title is also available as a Zondervan ebook.
Visit www.zondervan.com/ebooks.

Requests for information should be addressed to:

Zondervan, *Grand Rapids, Michigan 49530*

Library of Congress Cataloging-in-Publication Data

Mangum, Erynn, 1985–
    Sketchy behavior / Erynn Mangum.
        p. cm.
        Summary: As part of an art class assignment, high school junior Kate unwittingly
        sketches a wanted murderer, propelling her into instant celebrity and extreme
        danger while her parents fret and police provide constant protection.
        ISBN 978-0-310-72144-4 (softcover)
        1. Murder—Fiction. 2. Artists—Fiction. 3. Police—Fiction. 4. Celebrities—
        Fiction. 5. High schools—Fiction. 6. Schools—Fiction. 7. Family life—Missouri—
        Fiction. 8. Missouri—Fiction. I. Title.
    PZ7.M31266532Ske 2011
    [Fic]—dc23

                                                                                    2011013223

Cover still-life illustration: Connie Gabbert
Additional cover images: iStockphoto.com and Shutterstock.com
Interior design and composition: Greg Johnson/Textbook Perfect

Printed in the United States of America

11 12 13 14 15 16 /DCI/ 22 21 20 19 18 17 16 15 14 13 12 11 10 9 8 7 6 5 4 3 2 1

*For my sweet little family—my husband, Jon,
and my son, Nathan. I love you both more
than I can put into words.*

Chapter One

GUESS IT WOULD MAKE SENSE THAT SOMEONE LOOKING death in the face would be shaking violently. I just always figured suicides were a little bit calmer.

My friend Madison Hanson was perched precariously on the edge of the one and only bridge in South Woodhaven Falls. And while the name sounds impressive, the Falls, I think, refer more to the direction gravity flows than any large quantity of water. A river about five feet in depth and about thirty feet across was directly below us.

Enough to get her wet. Not enough to kill her. Which was why I was more concerned about Madison's essay — which counted toward a fourth of her final grade in English and was most likely in the backpack strapped onto her — getting washed away in the muddy water than I was about her imminent end.

"Maddy, what are you doing?" I asked as casually as I could. I kept walking at a nonthreatening pace toward the railing. She was on the other side, hands behind her holding on to the rail.

"It's over, Kate." She sniffed and I saw tears coursing down her freckled cheeks. Madison, in any other circumstance, was really cute. Coppery-red hair, almost-violet blue eyes, on the tall-ish side.

"What's over?"

"Me and Tyler." Her voice was trembling almost as much as she was.

Figures.

I have this theory about guys and it goes like this: Until they reach the age of about thirty-two, they're not even worth associating with, much less dating. All you get is a bunch of tear-soaked Kleenex, awkwardness for everyone around you when you pass in the hallway after your inevitable breakup, and apparently, suicidal tendencies.

This was where I would like to have started the "I told you so" monologue, because I did tell her so, but I didn't have time for that.

Madison was still on the wrong side of the railing, after all.

"Maddy, Tyler's a jerk."

She sniffed. I got a little closer.

"But even if he wasn't a jerk, no one is worth you jumping into the Falls." *And ruining your A+ in English.*

Blinking like crazy, Maddy croaked out, "I know."

"So why are you about to jump?"

She shook her head. "I didn't know what else to do, Kate. I hate feeling like this."

My dad is an engineer. And as such, he has very few spontaneous emotions left inside him, because they try to breed those out of potential engineers freshman year. Deep down, I thought this was why nerds are so often picked on — God knows that someday one of them will have to make a life-or-death decision about leaving a man on the moon, or how to dig out a town covered by an avalanche, or whether or not to nuke a communist country, and they'll have to do it all with zero emotions and a hundred and thirteen percent logic.

All that to say, Dad has a little saying that he told me from the time I was six years old: "Basing a decision on a feeling is like trying to balance an egg on your head while you're on a pogo stick. It doesn't turn out well for you or the egg."

Which was when my mom, who has a psych degree and bases everything on feelings, would say, "No, if you base a decision off of a feeling, it's like holding the egg steady in your hand while on the pogo stick. All you're left with is the feeling of accomplishment." And then my parents would argue for the next ten minutes.

My childhood was interesting.

I wasn't sure if Madison would benefit from either of my parental unit's sayings, so I came up with my own.

"Maddy, life is like an egg."

She frowned and looked at me for the first time. "What?"

"When life feels broken and the heat gets turned up, just remember: You're being made whole again."

"What are you talking about?"

Okay, so it was a bad saying. I'd have to work on that.

"Could you just come back to this side of the railing?" I asked her. "It's cold, school starts in twelve minutes, and you need a Kleenex."

She rubbed at her nose with the back of her hand, which was quite disgusting. "If I go to school, I'll have to look at him all day."

"No, you won't. You don't even have a class with Tyler."

She sighed. "But he comes by my locker every break."

"That's because you were dating, not because he had classes down that hall."

Her shoulders fell and the tears started again. "But we're not anymore, are we?" Her voice reached an impossible decibel level at the end of that sentence. A beagle started wailing in the distance.

"Please just come with me? I'll guard you the whole time. You won't even know he existed. Besides, you need to make Tyler think that you're even better off without him than you were with him."

She looked at me again. "Better off?"

"Vindication, Madison Hanson. Let Tyler know that he can be the big mean football player all he wants. You are better than him."

Slowly, she climbed back over the railing. "Better off," she mumbled again.

"Much better off." I wrapped an arm around her shoulders and tried to push our speed a notch faster. I hadn't been late to class in exactly six days. Considering that the principal, Mr. Murray, has had it out for me for the entirety of my two and a half years at SWF High, it would be in my best interest to be on time.

We made it by thirty-four seconds. The bell rang just as I gave Maddy one last hug. "You're better without him."

"Right." The red splotches on her face were still tattling her breakdown this morning, but her eyes looked clearer. As clear as bloodshot blue eyes could look.

I turned to run to my locker down the hall.

This year being my junior year, I got to pick from a better-rounded list of electives. Which is why I dumped my backpack in my locker, grabbed my sketchpad and pencils, and hightailed it to art, my preferred elective. I'd always been good at drawing and SWF High's art teacher, Miss Yeager, was probably one of the best teachers at the school. She was twenty-six, extraordinarily attractive, and liked to push us to be more detailed.

I plopped into my seat right as the second bell rang. There were fifteen of us in art class, all gathered around four tables that faced the front of the room.

"Good morning, guys." Miss Yeager had a balding, middle-aged man with a paunch seated in front of us. His only redeeming physical quality was his emerald-like green eyes.

"This is your test subject," Miss Yeager said. "I want you to draw him how *you* see him. You'll have the entire class period for this. Work quickly. Begin now."

I set my sketchpad in front of me and pulled out a soft-leaded pencil. To my right, Allison Northing was scraping big, dramatic strokes on the page. She drew the way she talked. On my left was Justin Walters, who has never spoken to me once in all of my life, but whom I'd been sitting next to in class for the last two months had this big pink tongue that just lolled all over the place. She still did.

It was gross, but we all still loved her anyway.

"And Kate?" Mom called, as I dumped a big cup of food in Lolly's bowl.

"Yeah?"

She came around the corner and looked at me. "I want you to keep the doors locked whenever you are at home by yourself. Apparently, there's some guy they're calling John X who has committed three murders. One in Warren County, one in St. Charles County, and one in Franklin County."

All surrounding counties to St. Louis County, where we lived.

"Statistically, the odds are outrageously low that he would pick our house for his next target," I told Mom.

"Statistics or not, keep the doors locked."

"Yes, ma'am."

My family had dinner at 5:32 every single night.

My dad liked it because three and two make five, so he found it funny in his weird engineer sense of humor. My mom tried for 5:30 every night but always ran two minutes late.

We sat at the table, and it was just the three of us. We still left a chair there for my older brother, Mike, but ever since he moved to California for school he'd been home twice.

But his chair was still there. "Just in case," Mom always said.

"In case what? He flies home in the middle of a semester?" I asked. Mike was following in our dad's footsteps and becoming an engineer. He was not going to leave in the middle of classes that intense.

"Just in case."

And so we left the chair.

As was the custom she borrowed from my grandmother, my mom held both hands out for the prayer. Dad grudgingly put his fork down. "God, bless the food. Amen," he mumbled. "Kate, what did you do in school today?" he asked immediately after.

Mom sighed.

"Well, we drew a guy."

"I meant math. What did you do in math today?"

"Algebra. Same as yesterday."

"Are you understanding it?"

"Yes."

He nodded. "Good girl. See, Claire? Both kids are well on their way to becoming engineers. Keep the Carter name going."

"I thought reproducing kept a name going, not becoming an engineer," I said. "Some people might consider those mutually exclusive, actually."

Dad rolled his eyes. Mom laughed.

"However, this one is sarcastic," he said, pointing to me.

I hated it when Dad talked like I wasn't there.

Dad had this grand illusion that I wanted to be an electrical engineer. When, in all reality, I wanted to be an artist. But *artist* is on the same playing field as a car wash worker or a gift wrapper in the mall as far as my dad is concerned.

We finished dinner, and I started my three hours of homework. I closed my last book just in time to change into my pajamas.

I snuggled under the covers, turned out the light, and sighed. Same as always, always the same.

If I'd known then that my life would never be the same again, maybe I wouldn't have been so depressed by that thought. I drifted to sleep slowly.

Chapter Two

CRISPIX HAS TO BE THE BEST CEREAL EVER. IT IS LIKE A race to see who wins breakfast — will you get them all eaten before they get soggy? Or will they win out when your dumb dog puts her giant head on your lap and slobbered all over your brand-new skirt?

"Lolly!" I shouted, mashing at her head until she finally moved her big drooly face. "No!" I looked down and there was a big huge patch of slime oozing on my skirt.

Fabulous.

"What's wrong, Kate?" Mom asked, running into the kitchen. It was nearly eight and Mom was trying to put in her earrings while simultaneously pouring her coffee into a travel mug.

It didn't work out too well.

"Crumb!" Mom said, which is her version of swearing. She swiped at the coffee blob on the counter before looking at me. "Sorry, Katie-Kin, I have an appointment at eight fifteen."

She kissed me on the forehead and left, yelling, "Lock the doors!" behind her.

The house was completely silent. And there was still a big slimy splotch on my skirt.

When I was a kid, I once read a story about this little girl who was an only child. Her parents worked and she had to walk four miles home from school every day by herself, and she made up all these adventures.

Mom said that the little girl must have had some version of schizophrenia brought on by the stress of being six and having to stay alone all the time. Dad said that instead of having "adventures," she could have been doing her homework so she could have skipped a few grades and left her loser parents behind while she went to college sooner.

I said, "Hey, Dad, I'm home a lot by myself."

And Dad said, "I think I still have some of my old calculus textbooks in the garage."

I never said another word about being home alone after that. Dad has been known to bring flash cards to the table.

So I cleaned up my bowl of soggy Crispix and decided to go hungry rather than pour another bowl. And I exchanged the slobbery skirt for jeans.

This was why I never looked cute at school.

Not like it really mattered whether I looked cute or not. We had to run three miles every day in gym. Our crazy gym teacher, Mr. Hannigan, told us that the most responsible thing we can do for our human bodies is run. And when he said run, he meant run until your feet were bleeding and you were coughing for mercy.

But when we pleaded and cried for mercy, he just told us this story about a woman who was saved from some horrible avalanche or mudslide or whatever because she was like this long-distance running champion. And then Mr. Hannigan told us we would all die in the mudslide.

I might die in the mudslide, but when they uncovered my preserved body thousands of years later, they wouldn't find calluses so deep on my feet that they hadn't even started decomposing.

I got to school with a few minutes to spare, so I headed on into art. It was so early that Miss Yeager wasn't even in the room yet.

How come our principal, Mr. Murray, couldn't see me now?

I sighed and plopped into my seat.

Silent Justin was already there. He was sitting there with his sketchpad and pencils all laid out on the table and two erasers on each side of the pad.

"Good morning, Justin," I said.

I thought he grunted, but I guess I'd never know.

Supposedly, Justin didn't always used to be silent. I've heard that all freshman and sophomore years, he was like the school chatterbox. But then this year he walked through the doors to SWF High's first day of school without saying a thing, and nobody had heard a word from him since.

Maddy said that she thinks Justin joined some cult during the summer that made him take a vow of silence.

And then my friend Aubrey said she heard that Justin went to Bosnia or somewhere all weird like that and he ate the food and his tongue got all infected and they had to amputate it.

I'd seen him lick his lips in art class, so I was pretty sure he still had a tongue.

I looked over at him and watched him stare at his sketchpad, at the chalkboard, at the lights, and back at his sketchpad.

"So did you hear about this John X guy?" I asked.

Allison Northing slid into her seat just then. "Hi, guys. Oh my gosh, I heard that the school board decided to repaint all the lockers a horrible green color next year, can you believe that? I mean, green. Green? Our school colors are black and red! It totally doesn't fit."

She pulled her sketchpad and pencils out while she talked. Allison has always been slightly fascinated with the lockers. Every time we had to draw something freestyle, she drew a row of lockers.

Everyone went through an "Awed with the Lockers" phase when we first got to SWF High, because our one and only junior high did not have lockers, but still. It had been three years — maybe she could start finding other stuff more interesting.

Justin just looked at her. I opened my mouth to be polite and respond, but Miss Yeager walked in right then.

"Okay, class, get settled." She had this super-excited look on her face and her cheeks were all flushed like she just made a homemade organic face mask with strawberries. My mother said that the antioxidants in strawberries could do wonders for your skin.

Miss Yeager said, "I have a very important visitor here today. We're going to be discussing how art can be used in the real world and so I asked Detective Masterson to share a little bit about the field of criminal sketches."

She turned and nodded to the doorway, where a tall guy who looked vaguely like a tougher and less-girly-looking Orlando Bloom stood.

That explained the strawberry face mask.

"Uh, hello," Detective Masterson said. He stepped all the way inside the classroom and took the seat of horror in front of the class. Pete Faraelli picked up his pencil to start sketching him and Miss Yeager told him not to.

"We're not sketching Detective Masterson, Peter. You can put the pencil down."

"Right, right, right," Detective Masterson said. "Don't draw me." Only he said it like *don't drawl me*, because Detective Masterson was apparently not from around here.

Missourians had their own weird way of saying things, but we didn't stretch words out that weren't meant to be stretched.

"So I'm supposed to, uh, talk about criminal sketches. I'm a detective with the SWF police, but I actually spent my first five years with the force doing criminal sketches. Kelly ... uh, I mean, Miss Yeager, asked me to come down here and give a little example of what a criminal sketch artist would do."

He looked nervously at Miss Yeager, and she smiled too brightly. Miss Yeager was very passionate and excited about art, but she was not usually overdramatic about it.

"Yes," she said. "And today we have a special exercise, so everyone get your pencils ready." She looked expectantly at Detective

Masterson. "Would you like to explain a little bit of the nuts and bolts of this procedure?"

"Yeah," Detective Masterson said. "Forensic sketch artists, or criminal sketch artists, are usually part of the interview team when we are talking to witnesses. Uh, you need to know how to ask good questions, because usually the witnesses are so emotionally battered they can't really think straight."

"Wow," Miss Yeager said.

Allison raised her hand. "You mean questions about the bad guy?"

Detective Masterson almost flinched at the words *bad guy*. "Yeah. Uh, so, I'm going to show you a quick demonstration, and then Miss Yeager is going to have you guys do an exercise, I think."

Miss Yeager nodded. "Yes, that's right."

Detective Masterson picked up a Sharpie and walked over to the huge sketchpad that covered almost one side of the classroom. "Typically, you want to start with the gender and an approximate age. Next, work your way down from the forehead to the chin, ending with the details."

He wrote each point out on the paper. "If you're observant and you're skilled at drawing, this can be a great job. Uh, I had a lot of fun with this back when I was forensic sketch artist. You feel like you're really contributing to the case, you know? I once helped slam a guy who used to be a pharmacist and then sold drugs on the black market."

I raised my hand. "Better money?"

Detective Masterson nodded. "Fewer hours too."

"More nights and weekends, though," I said.

"True." He gave me kind of a half-grin. "So, I think you guys are going to do some kind of a practice of this."

"Yes, you are going to have a chance to practice this." Miss Yeager picked up a folder from her desk. "I want you all to pay attention and do your best. This is a very valid field for those of you who are talented at art."

"Definitely valid field," Detective Masterson hummed.

Miss Yeager started reading. "Male. Around thirty-five."

Allison immediately started drawing.

I kept listening.

"Short dark hair, widow's peak. Wide forehead. Wide eyebrows. Brown eyes. Five o'clock shadow and a square chin. High cheekbones."

Silent Justin began sketching.

"Nose is long, but not skinny. Lips are thin, but not too thin." Miss Yeager looked at me now. I glanced back, but mostly I just kept staring at the floor in front of Detective Masterson's shoes, listening.

Miss Yeager continued. "Eyes are small in comparison to the rest of his face. Wears wire-framed glasses."

Allison began erasing.

Miss Yeager looked around the room and everyone was already sketching. Except for me.

"Do you need to know anything else, Kate?" she asked.

"Teeth. Are they straight?"

Detective Masterson looked at the paper Miss Yeager was holding. "Doesn't say." He looked back at me. "But they didn't mention the teeth either when it came to the pharmacy school guy."

I nodded. "Pharmacy school is expensive."

"Nothing compared to braces." He shrugged. "So I imagined straight teeth. Think about the guy's face and then see what comes to your mind."

I closed my eyes.

Pharmacy school was stuck in my head. Mike had a friend who wanted to go to pharmacy school. He was a little straggly guy who looked for all the world like he would blow away with the next windstorm. He always had his hands in his pockets and he talked with a permanent *um* sound. "Um-hi, um-Mrs. um-Carter, um-Mike um-invited um-me um-for um-dinner."

It got annoying.

Dad told Mike that if he ever brought "Um-Chris" back to dinner, we would need a full day's warning.

I started sketching.

I decided to start with his chin. Square chin. Not too many guys have square chins anymore. I like square chins.

I snuck a quick peek and, yup, Silent Justin had a square chin.

For a person to have a square chin and high cheekbones, they would need a seriously dramatic jawline. So I gave the sketch a dramatic jawline. And sprinkled it with some of the five o'clock shadow Miss Yeager mentioned. Sort of à la Matt Damon.

The bell was ringing way too soon.

"Okay, class, please turn in your drawings before you go," Miss Yeager said. She and Detective Masterson spent the whole class quietly whispering.

She still looked like she had on the strawberry face mask.

"So cute," Allison hissed, nodding toward Miss Yeager before she left to go turn in her paper.

I packed up my pencils.

It wasn't that I *didn't* think it was cute. It's just I thought it was overrated. Look at what happened with Maddy and Tyler. Detective Masterson could have been over the age of thirty-two and therefore dateable for Miss Yeager, but still. Was it really worth it?

I had no good luck with guys. My one dating experience was labeled "Do Not Speak of Ever Ever Ever."

So. I didn't speak of it. Ever.

I handed my paper to Miss Yeager.

She smiled at me. "Thanks, Kate."

"You're welcome, Miss Yeager. You are the best teacher at this school. I appreciate your honest desire to teach us the proper techniques for art."

Miss Yeager narrowed her eyes at me, but flushed more. "Compliments don't buy A's."

"But they might buy lunch," I said, nodding to Detective Masterson.

She blushed even more, and this time the detective joined her.

"Kate!" Miss Yeager gasped as I left.

The hallway between classes is always packed. South Woodhaven Falls was quickly becoming one of the best, albeit smallest, suburbs of St. Louis.

I pushed slowly through the throng and finally ended up at my locker. All around me people were talking on cell phones or laughing with their friends.

I grabbed my algebra book.

My mother was always concerned that at school I was a loner. I told her that there were not very many logical people left in my school to talk to, which was when Dad busted into the hallelujah chorus. When I was a freshman, I hung out with all of the juniors and seniors.

Now I was a junior, and all the seniors were so wrapped up in what the theme of prom was going to be, we had nothing in common.

I told Mom that I knew Maddy.

Which was why Mom sent me to that church camp last summer. She said I needed to "make more friends" and "spend a week in a wholesome environment." Really, I thought Mom and Dad just wanted the house to themselves for a few days and the only other camps I could have gone to were for kids with eating disorders or disabilities. Both fine and good purposes, but I didn't fit into either one of those categories.

The Christian camp wasn't bad. I didn't make a ton of new friends. The guy who led it kept harping on all of us to read our Bible more and stuff like that. I read my Bible the camp handed to us every day for a week after I got home.

It didn't make very much sense. I didn't really know where to start, so I started in Leviticus, because I thought that was a weird-sounding word.

I was hoping it was just a poor choice on my part, because if the whole Bible was written like that, I didn't understand why there were so many churches around.

Mom and Dad weren't really religious, per se. It wasn't that I didn't believe in God. I just didn't know what to believe. Some people claimed "God is love" and all that jazz so He sounded like a heavenly Santa Claus, but then others talked about "God is just" and "God is everywhere" and "We are all gods."

It got confusing. And to be honest, I didn't spend that much time thinking about it.

Kyle Barlett bumped into me right as I was walking through the door to algebra.

"Oh," he said, like he just hit a brick wall. He started rubbing his arm like he was going to get a bruise or something now. I was not that solid — I thought he was being a little dramatic. But I kept my mouth shut.

"Sorry, Kate. Didn't see you there."

Then he looked at me real quick in the eyes and darted out the door.

Kyle Bartlett was in that category of "Do Not Speak of Ever."

Actually, he was a major player in that category.

But, like the category title said, I didn't speak of it. Ever.

Chapter Three

MADDY CAUGHT ME AS I WAS DIGGING IN MY BACKPACK for my car keys. When I turned sixteen, Mom and Dad bought themselves a car and they let me borrow it. It was a 1962 Volvo and was a puke greenish-yellow color.

Dad said it was so boys would like me for who I was rather than what I drove. Mom said she didn't know Dad was buying that car, and she thought it would be a horrendous blow to my self-esteem.

I didn't really mind the car as long as it started. So most of the time, I didn't mind it. But I'd had to catch a ride home with Maddy four times in the past two months.

"So, Kate, I told Tyler that, like, if he wanted to break up with me then whatever, because there was totally someone better out there for me," she said. She flipped her copper hair over her shoulder.

Maddy was one of those friends who sometimes intimidated you as far as looks went. She was tall, had the gorgeous hair, the perfect complexion.

Me? I broke out at least once a month, my hair was supposed to look like Reese Witherspoon's hair in *Sweet Home Alabama*, but it flipped out all weird, unlike hers. And I was five foot one. And my hair was probably the most boring shade of brown there is.

She liked to tell me how lucky I was to be shorter than all the guys at school and how I never had to worry about running into things with my head.

Ever noticed how people who give advice about being short are never short? Sorry, but if you've never had to call the dorky bagging boy at Tim's Grocery to help you with the Fritos on the top shelf, you should keep the advice to yourself.

I found my keys and looked up at Maddy. "Well, that's good."

"Yeah."

I tossed my backpack over to the passenger seat.

"So, can I come study with you this afternoon?" Maddy asked.

I looked up at her again as I started to climb into my car. This would be the third time this week.

And it was only Wednesday.

Maddy was one of those students who didn't even need to study and could still pull straight A's. Evidenced by her lack of studying capabilities. When she came over to study, she would spend the whole time talking, watching E!, and filing her nails.

But the house did get quiet with just me and Lolly before Mom and Dad got home, so I always said okay. "Okay," I said. I slid into the Volvo. "See you at the house."

"Great! Thanks, Kate!" She ran to her brand-new, jet-black Tahoe.

The differences between us just kept getting more and more glaring.

It took three tries, but the Volvo started and I drove the few minutes back to my house. Lolly was barking and turning in circles when Maddy and I walked in.

"You really need to see more human contact," I told Lolly.

We settled on the couch. Maddy grabbed the remote and turned on the TV to E! like I knew she would.

I dumped my books and notebooks onto the coffee table.

"Want anything to drink?" I asked her.

"Is your mom still on the health kick?"

Unfortunately, yes. I nodded.

"I'll have water then. No offense to your mom, but that green tea lemonade or whatever it was, was pretty nasty."

I didn't disagree with Maddy. The green tea lemonade tasted like leaves. When you swallowed, there was still this powder-coating stuff all over your tongue. Mom said it was all the vitamins from the green tea. I said it felt like my tongue had a shower cap on it.

I got us two waters and sat down on the floor, pulling my algebra book over.

"Here," Maddy said. "I brought contraband." It was a package of Nutter Butters and I grinned.

"Thanks!"

We sat there crunching. I was focused on reading the homework assignment. Maddy was focused on Ryan Seacrest, who was rattling off the day's "news."

"Michelle Moriega celebrated her birthday last night with two hundred of her best pals at one of the swankiest nightclubs in New York City ..."

I tuned him out after that. I was concentrating on finding x.

Maddy sighed. "I wish I could have my birthday in New York City surrounded by my two hundred closest friends."

"I don't," I said, scribbling down the problem in my notebook. "Two hundred closest friends implies there are more, and I think Michelle Moriega is just a lonely girl who doesn't know how to deal with her fame. So she makes friends and parties."

"Gosh, Kate." Maddy rolled her eyes. "What do you want to watch instead? The news?" She flicked the remote to the local news station, KCL.

Ted Deffle, the highlighted anchor with the entirely-too-brilliantly-white teeth, was talking. "In other news, yet another victim has been claimed by the man known only as John X." The view switched from somber Ted to a crime scene. "In Chappell today, located in Jefferson County, authorities found the body of Linda Summers, a forty-seven-year-old preschool teacher, outside of a Chappell grocery store."

Maddy grimaced. "That's scary. Jefferson County is just south of us."

"I'm sure it's nothing to be worried about," I said. There are sixty miles of woods between South Woodhaven Falls and Chappell.

"I know. Still ..."

Ted continued to talk. "This is the fourth life taken by the still unnamed and unknown killer, currently called John X. Police warn to take extra caution when going in and out of public stores and to keep your doors locked at all times."

"Are your doors locked?" Maddy asked.

I rolled my eyes. "You worry too much." I went back to finding *x*.

Little did I know *x* would find me instead.

Another morning, another bowl of Crispix. Only that morning I was up a good thirty minutes too early, thanks to a slobbery face washing by Lolly.

I glared at her as I took my first bite.

Mom saw the look. "Oh good grief, Kate," she said, pulling her two slices of whole wheat toast from the toaster. "Lolly loves you. Don't fault her for that."

Dad was halfway through his power breakfast of eggs, bacon, and a half of a grapefruit. Dad claimed power breakfasts were what made him successful. "I would just like to restate that I was completely against getting a dog in the first place," he said.

Lolly's head drooped.

Dad had the TV going in the background, half listening to KCL and half reading the paper. Mom was lazily thumbing through a book about boundaries or fences or something relational; I was hurriedly eating the Crispix before they got soggy.

"A case that baffled law enforcement and terrorized the public is now officially at an end," the cheerful blonde reporter said on the TV.

All of us looked over.

"John X, the notorious killer who claimed four lives in four counties surrounding St. Louis, was apprehended today in what authorities say was a 'miraculous link.' The one and only witness to John X's third murder, who wishes to remain anonymous, was able to correctly describe John X for the police."

"Wow," Mom said. "That's great!"

"It's about time." Dad nodded.

I slurped up a few more Crispix. They were just starting to get soggy, so I needed to eat fast.

"However," the reporter continued, "a criminal artist who works for a Missouri police department was not the one credited with John X's arrest."

A picture flashed up on the screen and a half-chewed, soggy Crispix fell out of my open mouth and back into my bowl with a tiny splash.

"As we showed you last night on our six-o'clock show, here is the depiction of John X. This is the sketch created by a local South Woodhaven Falls teen, our brightest new criminal sketch artist."

There, very plainly visible in the corner under John X's perfect square chin, was the scrawl that had been perfected over the years. *Kate Carter.*

There was dead silence in my kitchen for all of about ten seconds. Then Mom started screaming, "What? What?"

Dad just looked at me. "Kate Carter. You Kate Carter or a different Kate Carter?"

It was hard to hear him over Mom's screaming. I kept watching the TV, where the drawing I did yesterday in art class was still plastered.

"Authorities say that this drawing of John X is a near photo-quality match of the killer of four. We're hoping to go live to South Woodhaven Falls' very own Kate Carter's house and get a statement from her soon. I'm Candace Olstrom, and this is KCL."

Mom and Dad both stared at me now. The silence was back— this time it lasted a full two minutes.

"How did you know what he looked like?" Dad asked first. Logical question.

"It was a drawing assignment," I said.

"You were assigned to draw a criminal?" Mom gasped.

"Apparently." Detective Masterson's appearance yesterday in art class was more than just to see Miss Yeager's blush, I guessed.

Again, silence.

The quiet was shattered by a knock on the door and Mom whirled to look at Dad. "What if it's John X?"

"He was caught," I said.

"Not now, Kate." Dad said, standing. "Claire, take Kate to the back bedroom and stay there." He was in his protective state. Which, on most dads, was very sweet.

On my dad, it usually involves a gun.

"Dad," I said.

He ignored me and looked at Mom. "Claire, now."

Mom grabbed my elbow and apparently the Crispix were going to win the battle of sogginess this morning. Mom hustled me to the back bedroom, aka the Guest Room. Lolly followed us happily.

"But Dad," I started again as we passed in the hallway.

"Hush," Mom told me as I opened my mouth to protest further. She pushed me down into a sitting position on the bed. "You cannot be too safe. Not mentally, not emotionally, not physically."

I opened my mouth again.

"I mean it. Not a word."

So I sat there on the guest bed. Mom paced the floor, wringing her hands and muttering things like *art teachers* and *lawsuits* under her breath.

A couple of minutes later, Dad walked into the room, a 9mm gun holstered to his hip, escorting a pale and open-mouth-stricken Maddy. "She came to give Kate a ride," Dad said, lightly pushing her toward the bed.

"That's what I was trying to tell you," I said.

Maddy's eyes were the size of snow cones. "What. Is. Going. On."

"Sit," Mom commanded, standing from her spot on the bed. "Neither of you are going to school today."

Maddy gaped at her and then at me. "But what about — ?"

"No excuses," Mom said, staring Maddy down. "Your personal safety is of more concern than a couple of grades."

Maddy just stared at her. "Wait. What happened? Personal safety? Did Mr. Hannigan threaten to put you on the track team again?" She turned to me.

I opened my mouth.

Dad beat me to it. "No, Madison. Kate drew a picture of John X."

Maddy's eyes became snow cone sized again and turned to me. "You what?"

"And it got put on the news," Mom said.

"It's on the news?" Maddy's mouth was still open.

"He got caught, there is no danger," I said.

Dad glared at me, one hand on his 9mm. "I've never trusted that Candace reporter girl. Nobody's voice is really that squeaky. Who knows if he really got arrested?"

"Dad."

He held up a hand. "And I'm going to have more than a word with Miss Yeager or whatever her name is who made you draw a known criminal. What kind of art teacher is she? This isn't *CSI*, these are high school juniors!"

Mom was nodding through Dad's whole sermon. "I am going to talk to her as well. She obviously was not thinking clearly about the damaging effects to the kids' psyches."

"Claire, write a note. We need to contact Pete What's-His-Face and see how we need to go about correcting the school on this."

I sighed. I assumed Dad was talking about Peter Colligher, the attorney they met at the last Parent's Night Out at school. Mr.

Colligher said he specialized in copyright law, so I'm not sure how he was going to help them.

The doorbell rang right as the home phone started ringing. I reached for the handset and my elbow about came out of socket when Mom whacked my hand out of the way and grabbed it herself.

"Dale?" she said, nodding to the entryway and stepping into the hallway with the phone.

"I got the door." Dad nodded and left.

Maddy and I stayed on the bed.

She stared at me. "You drew John X?"

"Well. I didn't mean to."

"How did you know what he looked like?" she asked.

"Detective Masterson told us when he was making Miss Yeager blush," I said.

Maddy's eyes popped even more. "Miss Yeager blushed?"

I nodded.

Mom came back into the room, gripping the phone. "Channel Six wants an interview," she said to me. "I told them by all means, absolutely not."

Dad walked in right then too, carrying a huge bouquet of red roses, followed by a wagging Lolly. "This is from the sheriff's office and Channel Eight has a news crew out there."

Maddy and I were off the couch before he finished talking. We ran to the living room and peered through the cracks in the now-closed drapes.

A news van was parallel parked on the curb in front of our house. About ten people were gathered on the front lawn. Maddy's jet-black Tahoe was in the driveway next to Dad's pickup and my Volvo.

Another news van, with "Channel Two — The News You Can TRUST!" emblazoned on the side drove down the street.

I stepped back and stared at Mom and Dad.

Then at Maddy.

31

Then at Lolly.

I looked at the TV as the doorbell rang again.

On the screen, there was Candace Olstrom standing on my front porch. "I'm here at the heroic Kate Carter's house, the girl who saved who knows how many lives and brought four victim's souls to justice."

And all I could do was sit down and stare at the TV as Candace continued on about how John X had been terrorizing the four surrounding counties for two months.

I *drew* John X.

I drew John X.

On the one hand, I felt kind of proud that I helped the SWF police in one of the biggest crimes this year, but on the other hand...

I just knew it. Life was never going to be the same again.

Chapter Four

THE REST OF THE MORNING PASSED IN A BLUR OF THE phone ringing, the doorbell chiming, Maddy's endless questions, and Lolly's head sogging my lap. Dad and Mom both took the day off and Dad was pacing around the house, 9mm still strapped to his waist. He'd allowed us to move to the couch in the living room, but only so he could watch the news and us at the same time.

"So, it was an *assignment*?" Dad asked again, for the fourth time that hour.

I was still watching the front of our house, now being broadcast on Fox News. "Yeah," I said, for the fourth time.

"For drawing class," Dad said.

"Miss Yeager wanted us to see how art as a career could work in everyday life," I said. "I think it was the start of a series."

"A series of criminals?"

"A series of careers." I shook my head.

Dad grumbled something under his breath and continued to pace. Mom was now clicking around on her laptop.

"Kate, listen to this. Criminal sketch artists, or forensic sketch artists, are usually one of the top careers to have mental breakdowns and panic attacks, and of all of the careers available to an artist, they are foremost in needing psychiatric help." She looked up at me, eyes wide. "I do not like this."

Maddy elbowed me in my ribs. "At least you might get a discount," she whispered.

I grinned.

Mom frowned.

Dad noticed my grin, then frowned and launched into lecture-mode. "There is nothing funny about this situation, Kate Carter," he said sternly, one hand on his gun. "This was a dangerous, stupid move for a teacher to have a student make, and you can bet that I'm going to have a very long talk with Miss Yeager or whatever her name is."

I opened my mouth to stick up for Miss Yeager, but the doorbell cut me off.

"Now who is it?" Dad grumbled, sneaking over to the door and peering through the peephole.

We had been instructed that under no circumstances were Maddy or I allowed to look through the curtains, answer the door, look through the peephole, or basically move off the couch unless we were otherwise ordered by Dad.

Dad squinted through the peephole and then growled. "Police guy." He unlocked the door, opened it three inches, reached his arm through, and yanked a uniformed man through the crack before slamming the door shut and locking all the deadbolts again.

"You," Dad barked to the poor guy, who was now trying to smooth his wrinkled and squished uniform. "Start talking."

I still had yet to see the man's face, but then he turned toward me and Maddy sitting on the couch and I waved. "Hi, Detective."

Detective Masterson squinched a half-smile at me and then looked at Dad. "Do you have a permit for that weapon?" he asked.

I was pretty sure this was not the time or the place to ask that question.

Dad seemed to agree with me. He started sputtering so badly that Detective Masterson had to wipe off his cheek.

"My ... my daughter is on Fox News ... and you have the *audacity* to come here and ..." Dad couldn't even finish his sentence, he was so mad. Anytime my very logical, thoughtful father used words like "audacity" and slobbered, I knew it was bad.

"Sir, I'm going to need you to calm down," Detective Masterson said quietly, holding his hands up surrender-style.

Mom was glaring at the detective from the couch. "How do you know my daughter?" she asked icily.

Even Mom was royally ticked. By this point I was starting to realize that the parental units were not going to be cheering me on toward a career in forensic sketching.

If anything, they might be wrapping my hands in a permanent plastic wrap so I'd never be able to draw again.

Detective Masterson turned very slowly away from my dad and faced my mom. "I was present on the day that Kate drew John X."

This did not endear him to my weaponed, spittle-encrusted father. "You encouraged this?" he demanded.

"Sir, ma'am," the detective said, looking at both my parents. "Your daughter has supreme talent in this field and I believe that it was no accident that she was instrumental in helping us apprehend John X."

Maddy elbowed me again when Detective Masterson said "supreme talent."

I was suddenly very hungry for pizza.

Very hungry and very flattered. I peeked over at my dad to see how he was taking this, considering the Master Plan was for me to follow in his mathematical, engineering footsteps.

He was still sputtering.

"Now, all that being said, I do need to formally apologize for both having Kate draw John X and for the way the sketch was leaked to the press. When Kate's art teacher came to us to have us discuss the career of criminal sketching, she and I both thought it could be beneficial for the students to attempt a sketch of a known criminal." Detective Masterson winced. "I didn't, however, anticipate your daughter having such a natural talent. Nor did I anticipate that the sketches would be taken off my desk and shown to the witness who saw John X." He nodded at me. "But it was no accident."

Mom was still glaring at the detective. "You believe in fate," she said.

"No, ma'am. I believe that God orchestrated this."

Oh, now this was just getting better all the time. I felt my eyes widen. Dad tolerated Mom's attempts to get this family to be more spiritual, but I was imagining that mixing religiosity with his daughter's safety was not a smart move for the detective.

Even though we were faithfully in the church pew every year at Christmas thanks to my mother, who wanted us to experience a "spiritual" side of life, Dad did not go willingly. If anything, he was dragged there purely from the desire to sleep in his bed that night instead of on the couch. And Mom, who pretended to listen intently, was not that interested in Christianity.

"It's just good to keep our names on the list," she would tell me. "Plus, goodness knows you and your father need something to balance your logical bones."

I doubt she'd still call me logical at this moment.

"God?" Dad gasped out the word. I was waiting for "oh, kill me now" to follow his exclamation, but the doorbell rang yet again, saving the detective from a nice verbal lashing.

Dad peered again through the peephole. "More of you," he announced to Detective Masterson.

The detective nodded. "We are going to take Kate to the police station."

Dad started sputtering again, and this time Mom joined him.

Detective Masterson quickly hurried up and finished his thought. "We need to question her, and we also want to be mindful of her safety right now. As well as all of your safety." He looked at Maddy.

Maddy leaned back against the couch. "I wonder if I'll still have to take that geography exam," she said quietly.

"We will be certain to arrange things with the school," the detective said, obviously overhearing Maddy.

"Absolutely not," Dad finally got out.

"But Mr. Carter, my geography exam counts for a third of my final grade," Maddy protested.

Dad didn't even spare her a glance. "We are not going down to the police station."

"Sir," Detective Masterson said.

"Dad," I said.

"Dale," Mom said.

"You already had my daughter draw a murderer. What could you possibly need her to do now? Draw a gang leader? A drug lord? The guy who piloted the plane in *Con Air*?" Dad was ranting now.

And Dad didn't even like that movie. He said that no guy with Nicolas Cage's hairstyle would have ever ended up with a woman who looked like his wife.

I have to admit, I had to agree. And Mom just told us to hush because she had a thing for Nicolas Cage — scraggly, long hair or not.

Maddy elbowed me yet again. "What is *Con Air*?" she whispered.

"Sir, this really is the best option," the detective said calmly. The doorbell rang again. "Actually, it's the only option. Our primary responsibility now is to keep you and your family safe. And we only want to question Kate, not hire her." When Dad didn't budge, Detective Masterson nodded. "You really have no other choice, sir."

"Dale," Mom said. "We need to go."

Dad shook his head and walked down the hallway. We all just looked at each other for the next thirty seconds. Was he on his way to get the rest of his arsenal? Was he calling Pete What's-His-Name?

Dad came back with a coat a minute later. "Kate, what are you doing?" he barked. "Get your coat and shoes. We're going with Detective Masterson or whatever he calls himself."

I ran down the hall to my room and found my Chuck Taylors. I glanced in the mirror as I was about to leave. I never thought I'd be on TV, and I especially never thought I'd be on TV while wearing my least attractive pair of jeans. They were ripped on the right knee and shredded around the hemlines because I'm short and most of my pants aren't.

I shrugged and grabbed my favorite red hoodie jacket.

Maddy was waiting with my parents and Detective Masterson by the front door. She was still wearing her backpack and a wide-eyed expression.

"We are going to be on TV!" she hissed in my ear when I joined them.

"I know," I whispered back.

"I didn't curl my hair very well today," she moaned.

"Okay," the detective said. "Here's what will happen. We will surround you and try to get you into the police vehicles with minimum amount of camera exposure. So stay together, and stay close to us."

He opened the door and nodded to a bunch of uniformed guys on my front porch.

Immediately, we were all surrounded and shoved en masse toward a couple of police cars parked right smack in the middle of my father's front lawn. Yet another occurrence that had him bristling.

Mom and Dad were stuck in the back of one police car, and Maddy and I were put into the other one. Meanwhile, there were cameras and flashes and microphones and people screaming, "Kate! Kate! How did you know what John X looked like? What is it like being the town heroine? Kate!"

I didn't get a chance to even answer them because the door was slammed the second my feet were out of the way.

Chapter Five

DETECTIVE MASTERSON RODE IN THE PASSENGER SEAT and another policeman drove.

"Girls, this is Officer Walker," he said.

"I guess that's fitting," Maddy whispered to me as we drove off the curb, leaving some nice tire marks there for my dad to stress over. "You know, the whole Walker name and him being a ranger and all."

"But he's an officer," I said. "And I'm pretty sure he's not from Texas."

"Yeah, but he's still into the whole keeping-the-law, protecting-people bit. You never know, maybe that guy has almost been run over by an unmanned plane before."

"Walker was almost run over by an unmanned plane?" I asked.

She shrugged. "I don't know. I usually watch E!"

The police station was only three miles from my house, so it didn't take too long to get there. There were reporters there too, though, so once again we got surrounded and hustled inside while people were yelling at me and waving cameras in my face.

Once we got inside, there was a huge room, filled with tons of cubicles.

I'd never been to prison, but I kind of imagined it would look more like Alcatraz than the set from *The Office*.

Mom and Dad joined us in the entrance of the big room, and

Detective Masterson waved for us to follow him down one of the outside aisles and into a small room that was off to the side.

There was a table, six chairs, and a pitcher of water in there.

"Wow, is this where you interrogate criminals?" Maddy asked the detective, her voice all hushed for the souls gone before us.

"We have concentrated staff meetings here," Detective Masterson said, nodding to the chairs.

I guess there was no need for the hushed voice.

Right then a tall, heavy, older-looking guy wearing a business suit walked in and closed the door behind him.

"Please, have a seat," he told us and we all sat. Mom and Dad sat on either side of me, and Maddy and Detective Masterson sat next to the older guy across the table from us.

"I'm Gene Slalom, the deputy chief of police here in South Woodhaven Falls," he said, all deep and booming voiced. He didn't sound at all like I thought deputies sounded. But maybe that was because my entire basis for deputies was founded on Barney Fife from *The Andy Griffith Show*.

We all nodded.

"That's Kate," Detective Masterson said, pointing to me.

"Ah." Deputy Slalom said, looking at me without smiling. "Hello, Kate."

"Hello, Deputy Slalom."

Awkward silence. I almost wanted to ask if he skied or not, considering his name, but I held my tongue. They brought me here, they can talk.

"Nice conference room," Maddy said.

Or Maddy could talk.

"Thank you." Deputy Slalom nodded at Maddy. "We recently updated the paint. It used to have wallpaper."

I looked over at the neutral tan color while Maddy smiled. "Good choice. Wallpaper is very out of style."

She would know.

He nodded again and looked away from Maddy. "Kate, Mr.

and Mrs. Carter, we brought you here because Kate has done her city, her state, and her country a service that can never be repaid."

"What kind of danger is my daughter in?" Dad asked.

"Do you have any idea what this type of situation will do to a young girl's psyche?" Mom said at the same time.

Deputy Slalom held up both of his hands. "Trust me, we will get to all of your questions." He leaned across the table and looked at me. "But first, Kate Carter, I wanted to extend a hand of thanks."

He reached across the table to shake my hand, and I have to admit, I've never been given a hand of thanks before.

"Thanks," I said.

"No. Thank you."

"Oh. Well. You're welcome."

Handshake dispensed with, he turned to my parents. "Okay. Danger. Kate is in a significant amount of danger. John X was not believed to have any accomplices, but then we won't know for sure until we are able to extensively question him, and we have been unable to do so for the past twelve hours."

Dad glared at Detective Masterson.

"That being said, we will have around-the-clock protection for Kate. She will take one of my officers to school with her and we will also have at least one, if not two, officers in your home night and day."

"Two," Dad said. "I don't want even the chance of something happening."

"Understandable, sir. And while this is a regrettable situation to be in, it is also one that will bring a tremendous amount of relief to many people in this state, you do realize. Your daughter is a hero."

"Heroine," Maddy corrected.

"What about *her* mental state?" Mom asked. "You do realize how much stress this puts her under, don't you?"

It is definitely a huge pet peeve of mine when people talk about me in front of me like I'm not even there.

"We do realize," the deputy said. "And we have a staff psychiatrist that has supervised many a witness case and will be working with Kate as well."

I raised my hand. "But I can still go to school?" We were covering how to multiply and divide fractions in algebra. And knowing my dad's teaching skills, I'd rather learn from my algebra teacher than Dad.

"Yes, you can still go to school." He raised a hand to cut off my parents' immediate rebuttal. "Accompanied by an officer, of course."

A lady knocked on the door and then opened it, sticking her head in. "Sorry to interrupt, sir, but the mayor is here and wants to meet Kate."

Deputy Slalom winced slightly and then nodded. "Send him in."

A minute later, in walked Arnold Walinski, who was arguably the biggest schmoozer you could ever meet. I was pretty sure he prided himself on having the most handshakes of any mayor in Missouri — and coming from such a small town, that said a lot.

"Kate Carter," he said warmly to Maddy.

She pointed to me and Arnold didn't even skip a beat. "So nice to meet the girl who saved our town from disaster!"

And here I thought that disasters were typically made up of those mudslides that our gym teacher liked to tell us about.

"Hi, Mayor," I said, shaking his outstretched hand. "I don't think I saved our town from anything. Was John X even around South Woodhaven Falls?"

Detective Masterson shook his head. "Ballwin," he said, naming one of the neighboring suburbs.

"Regardless," Arnold said. "Kate, it would be my honor and privilege to have you and your family join me and my wife for dinner at the mayor's house Saturday night." He was grinning in a way that I thought was supposed to be welcoming, but it ended up just looking toothy and cheesy.

And I was now going to refer to my house as "the Carter's house."

"Um," I said, looking at Mom.

She shrugged. "Sure," she said after looking over her shoulder at Dad, who nodded rather stiffly. Dad was not one for hobnobbing with politicians. He said they got annoying and that while most of them could talk circles around a band of turkeys, they couldn't hold one straightforward conversation to save their lives.

I wasn't sure that turkeys ran together in bands, but whatever.

"Fabulous, fabulous!" Arnold started crooning. "I'll not interrupt your conversation with these fine gentlemen any longer. See you this weekend, Kate and family."

He left whistling.

Deputy Slalom waited until the door was closed and latched before he started up again. "Where was I? Oh yes. School." He nodded to me. "You will take an officer to school with you tomorrow."

"Are you sure it's safe for her to be returning to school so soon?" Mom asked.

"She'll be fine with Officer Kirkpatrick." The deputy nodded to Detective Masterson. "And if the need comes up, I can send Detective Masterson as well, just to monitor the situation."

Judging by the slight redness to his cheeks, I was thinking that Miss Yeager was contributing more toward the detective's presence at school than my imminent danger.

"I ... I guess if you think it's safe ..." Mom stumbled.

Dad was resorting to silence. Meaning he didn't agree.

"Wonderful," Deputy Slalom said. "Now, if you and Maddy could wait outside, we have some questions we need to ask Kate alone. Margo out there can get you some refreshments."

My parents got up and left, looking sadly at me as they walked out the door. Maddy whispered, "Remember everything!" and then followed them out.

And then it was just me with the two policemen.

"Kate," Deputy Slalom started. He had his hands woven together and sitting on the table. Detective Masterson looked more at ease, lounging back in his chair.

"Yes?"

"Kent here has told me that you are a remarkable artist," Deputy Slalom said, angling his head toward the detective.

Kent. Awkward name, no offense to the detective.

I shrugged. I don't take compliments well. Mom said that's a reflection of a lack of self-confidence and one of the top three signs of a loner, but I said it's just because I don't get them too frequently. Practice makes perfect. I'm barely over five feet tall. There's not much here to compliment.

Which is when Dad told me that I had nice earlobes.

"I have to admit, when Miss Yeager came to us and asked if we could help explain the forensic sketch artist career field to a bunch of high schoolers, I was less than enthusiastic," Deputy Slalom said. "I guess we can see who was wrong. Anyway, I have something I want to ask you, but I don't want an answer today. Actually, I don't want an answer until all this insanity with John X is over and done with."

I was trying not to cringe in my chair, waiting for the word *babysitter.* I wasn't sure what it was with adults, but I tend to attract potential babysitting jobs like Lindsay Lohan attracts miniskirts.

I was not a babysitter. I didn't like kids. I did not like the way they smelled or the way they had some weird fascination with Dora. Any show that makes little kids think it's perfectly normal to talk to and interact with a television set was breeding future clients for my mother, if you ask me.

I waited for Deputy Slalom to finish his thought.

He leaned across the desk. "Kate, you are a very nonthreatening person."

"Please don't tell my father that." He would send me back to that self-defense class again.

"You're very nice, you seem to listen before you speak," the deputy continued. "And I already mentioned the artistic talent."

Maybe he wanted me to draw pictures of his kids.

"Kate, I'd like you to consider joining the police force as a junior member."

I just blinked at him.

"I really feel like we need a female forensic sketch artist and witnesses need someone who is nonthreatening to talk to, especially women and children."

I opened my mouth to protest, and he held up his hand.

"I told you to think on it, Kate. It's just a thought. Though, I think it's a good thought, and Kent here agrees with me."

I did not know why hearing the word *Kent* kept throwing me off.

The deputy smiled very briefly and very tiredly at me. "Thanks again, Kate."

I nodded.

We all stood, and Detective Masterson opened the door for us. Outside, there was a redheaded police officer talking with my parents.

"This is Officer Kirkpatrick," the deputy said. "Get used to him, he'll be around."

"Hello, Kate," the officer said. He couldn't have been more than about twenty-five, and he was tall and kind of on the skinny side.

He didn't look very menacing. I think my dad was thinking the same thing as he sized him up.

"Hi," I said. "So you are following me around now."

He did one of those little smiles that was half friendly, half pained. I guess I couldn't blame him, considering it did mean going back to high school for him.

"We'll take you guys back home. If anyone requests an interview, please refuse it for the time being. And Kate, you will probably receive a lot of offers for various things ... just turn them all down," Detective Masterson said. "Shall we?" He motioned to the door.

We got back home and it was just me, Mom, Dad, Maddy, Lolly, and Officer Kirkpatrick.

And it was silent.

Mom looked exhausted and went into the kitchen. I could sense a vanilla-laced bath in her near future. Dad was still strapped to his gun and followed Mom into the kitchen. Maddy sat on the couch and reached for the remote.

Officer Kirkpatrick stood in the doorway, pensively. And I had to wonder how much of the pensiveness was because Lolly wouldn't stop smelling the guy.

"Lolly. Cut it out," I said, patting my leg.

She didn't cut it out.

"Lolly."

Maddy whistled, not taking her eyes off the TV. "Lolly, cheese!" she yelled.

Lolly immediately bolted toward Maddy on the couch.

"Good girl, good girl," Maddy crooned to her.

"Where's the cheese?" I asked. "You can't promise something and not give it to her then. Now she won't come the next time."

Lolly, depressed because of the lack of cheese, slumped in front of the couch in a dog heap.

"Hey, Officer Kirkpatrick," Maddy said, ignoring me, angling her head toward him, but waiting for the story about some star's new love interest to end before she moved her eyes.

"Yes, Madison?"

"What's your first name?"

Officer Kirkpatrick squinted at her. "Darrell."

Now I looked at him. I was not sure how a couple could look at a scrawny little redheaded baby and name him Darrell. Judging from Maddy's expression, she agreed.

"Your name is really Darrell?" I asked.

"It's a family name. My great-uncle's name is Darrell."

"Well, my great-aunt's name is Olga and my parents were kind enough to forgo family tradition," Maddy said, going back to Ryan Seacrest's rundown of all the top "news."

Seriously, since when did seeing Sienna Miller sans makeup on her way to the gym become news?

Darrell Kirkpatrick shrugged at me. "He didn't have any kids, and my dad was always pretty attached to him."

I asked, "So you go by Darrell?"

"I go by DJ. My middle name is Jefferson."

I wanted to say that was a big name for a little guy, but for some reason, I didn't think our friendly officer would like that. And considering he was going to be following me around for the foreseeable future, I wanted to be on his good side.

"So, should I call you Officer Kirkpatrick or DJ?" I asked.

He thought about it. "DJ. At school, I'm going to be dressed in plain clothes."

School.

I really needed to study for my test tomorrow. I nodded. "Well, it's time for me to get to studying."

Madison looked at the still-closed blinds on the front windows. "I don't think I'm going to go home until my parents will be there," she said. "If it's okay with you, I'm going to stay here and watch TV."

"Fine with me."

I went to my room and shut the door. It was the first time all day I had been alone.

I took a deep breath and closed my eyes.

Which is when someone knocked.

"Yes?" I yelled, quietness shattered.

"It's DJ. You need to leave your door open, Kate."

I opened it and looked at him. "How am I supposed to use the bathroom or take a shower or get dressed?"

He nodded. "The bathroom doesn't have any windows. You can shut the door when you are in there. But not in your room."

He smiled a friendly smile and then moved to the hallway where he could see almost all of the house.

I was going to have to have a very serious talk with Miss Yeager tomorrow.

Chapter Six

FRIDAY MORNING. APPROXIMATELY FIFTEEN MINUTES before the bell was scheduled to ring.

School looked normal enough. I was peering out the windows of the unmarked police car that DJ had driven me to school in. Apparently, me driving by myself was a definite no. DJ did swap the uniform with a pair of jeans and a Polo shirt though.

Still. So much for all the privileges that came with that hard-earned driver's license.

DJ, who looked as refreshed as a man could look after sleeping on an air mattress in the hallway of my house, was looking out the window too. Another policeman, Officer Colton, came at night as well, only he stayed awake so DJ could sleep.

"Let me get out first and you follow. Your first class is drawing. You are to be no more than five feet away from me at any given moment. Understood?"

I wondered if this is what the daughters of the president had to go through and I immediately was overcome with despair for them. Dad always said that pity is pointless. Mom said it's only pointless if we don't do something to help.

Aside from kidnapping the first daughters and showing them what life outside of a security detail was like, which I imagined was a federal crime to the highest degree, I couldn't think of a way to help them.

So I stopped pitying them and glared at DJ instead.

"Hey," he said, holding his hands up. "I didn't draw John X."

"I didn't mean to."

Good thing art was first. Miss Yeager and I were about to have it out.

DJ got out of the car and I followed him as instructed. What I didn't expect was that all the news crews that had been parked outside my house for half the night would be at SWF High.

"Kate! Kate!" one lady yelled incessantly at me as DJ hustled me into the school.

I would think there must be more exciting news in South Woodhaven Falls, but surely there was not. One of the perks and apparently curses of living in a small town.

I remembered when Dusty McSweeny, the local grocer, put up the very first "Handicapped Parking Only" sign in all of South Woodhaven Falls in front of his store. That was the only news we got for the next three nights. People were getting their picture beside it and making bad jokes about it like, "Hey, did you see the new sign outside of McSweeny's? It's pretty handy!"

Suddenly, I found myself wishing for another natural "disaster" like the Great Tornado of 1993 that took out a woman's leaning storage shed and knocked over a couple of other people's grills. That story lasted on the local news for about three weeks.

DJ and I made it inside, barely, and then the real chaos started.

"Hey, it's Kate Carter!" one guy I'd never seen before in my life shouted.

"Kate Carter?" another girl I did not know repeated.

"Kate Carter?"

"Kate Carter!"

Suddenly, my name was being repeated so consistently and on such a good beat that I was waiting for the music to start and my personhood to be sung about like what happens in *High School Musical*. DJ kept pushing me toward my locker.

"Wow, that was really brave," one guy said as we passed him.

He was actually kind of cute, so I wouldn't have minded talking to him, but DJ didn't seem to care. It was all for the better, anyway. We already know my history with guys.

I grabbed my pencils and sketchpad from my locker and then heard another rousing chorus of "Kate Carter!" and "Wow, that was amazing what you did!" as I was rounded into art class.

Considering my history of tardiness, I wasn't even sure what to expect as I pushed open the classroom door at ten minutes until class time. Miss Yeager was busy writing instructions on the board, and no one else was there yet.

She turned when she heard the door close and at first she smiled. "Kate!" she said excitedly. Then I guess she noticed the man behind me and the firm set to my jawline.

"How are you?" she asked all hesitantly, putting the dry erase marker down and walking over slowly.

"Well," I started, ready to unload on her.

Which of course is when Silent Justin walked in. I almost growled in frustration. I couldn't lambaste Miss Yeager in front of a classmate. It's like the highest form of insult to get mad at an authority figure in front of her subordinates.

Or so I thought. My knowledge of authority and subordinates is completely from movies like *The Guardian* and *Remember the Titans*. Which was about the only thing I took from those movies, other than a fear of boating or swimming in the ocean.

"Good morning, Justin," Miss Yeager said to my classmate. She got a grunt of recognition before turning back to me.

"Miss Yeager," I said, carefully, keeping one eye on Justin as he started arranging his pencils on our table. "Were you aware that we were sketching a nationally known and state-feared criminal when you had me complete the last assignment?"

Miss Yeager looked at me and then at DJ.

"Kate," she started.

"Did you know we were sketching John X?"

She took a deep breath. "No, for the record, I did not know it

50

was John X. I knew it was a man who had committed a crime and hadn't been caught, but I was not aware it was him."

Which placed the blame squarely on the good Detective Masterson's shoulders.

"I see," I said. I went to my table and sat down.

"Kate," Miss Yeager said again, apology reigning in her tone.

"Miss Yeager, I can barely even go to the bathroom by myself now. My dad's constantly got his 9mm strapped to his chest, my mom is on the verge of a mental breakdown, and I'm constantly shadowed by *him*." I jerked my thumb toward DJ.

He smiled and waved at Miss Yeager. "Officer Kirkpatrick. Pleased to meet you."

"Likewise." She was smiling back at him.

I really hoped I wasn't interrupting the moment. Oh wait, yes I did.

"Seriously, you guys?"

"Okay, okay," Miss Yeager said, coming over and putting a hand on my shoulder. "Listen, Kate, I'm very sorry about the sketching assignment. But, if it makes you feel better and it should, you are the person to thank for protecting our state from a very dangerous man. And you wouldn't have gotten that opportunity without the detective providing you with that assignment."

Justin was sitting directly to my left, and he made a tiny noise in the back of his throat like he agreed.

That sent me over the edge. "Look, instead of grunting like a caveman, why don't you just speak? We all know you can. Gosh!"

"Kate Carter!" Miss Yeager exclaimed, only it wasn't in the adoring way that everyone outside in the halls was proclaiming it.

"Sorry," I mumbled. I rubbed my head. I hadn't even taken a good shower this morning—I was so weirded out by the fact that DJ was standing in the hall waiting for me. I could feel the start of several zits along my hairline.

Fabulous.

I held my head for a few seconds and then looked over at Justin, who was flipping through his sketchbook. "Sorry," I said.

He nodded.

Wordlessly, of course.

Miss Yeager sighed. "Listen, Kate, I understand that you've been through a lot of emotions in the last twenty-four hours. In fact, I really wasn't even anticipating you being here today at all."

"I've got a geography exam."

She smiled at me. "I think Mr. Walsh might have let you take it later, all things considered."

I just blinked at her. If I didn't come to school, what would I do? Sit on the couch with DJ and Lolly and watch E! reruns?

All last night, I dreamt about some shadowy figure sitting in a jail cell and carving *Get Kate Carter* over his cell door like the poor man in *The Count of Monte Cristo*. Only that man was carving the name of the woman he loved.

I was fairly sure that John X did not harbor feelings of affection of any kind toward me. Even though my dad said that prison these days was better than the outside world, because apparently they get cable, no taxes, basketball games, and pot roast. Dad said that if he weren't an upstanding citizen, he would have hoped to get into prison years ago.

Part of me thought my dad was just kidding because I've seen some of those documentaries on the Discovery Channel about life in the slammer. I've never seen anyone playing basketball in the yard. All the clips they ever show are the ones where the guards were breaking up one of the daily fights with tear gas and bean bag guns.

No, it was better to be at school. At school, I have to concentrate on art and math and what the population in the capital of Brazil was. At home, I would be researching prison and worrying.

"I'm fine," I said, pretty much lying through my teeth, but trying to look calm as I wove my fingers together and set my hands on top of my sketchbook.

Miss Yeager didn't look like she believed me, but she nodded. "Fine."

She walked back to the board, DJ moved to the back corner of the class, and the bell buzzed once as a flood of bodies came through the door.

I felt Justin looking at me, but when I looked over at him, he snapped his head around so fast I heard his neck pop.

Then again, he wasn't the only one looking. Everyone was craning their heads as they sat down, gawking at me and whispering.

I will never stare at babies in McSweeny's Market whose mothers dress them in horrendous clothing again. I know now what it feels like.

"Okay, everyone, stop staring at Kate," Miss Yeager said finally, as the second bell rang.

Allison Northing dropped into her chair beside me right as the bell finished. "Oh my gosh, Kate, I cannot *believe* you are here today!" she tried to whisper but didn't really succeed. "Oh wow, did you know who we were drawing? Did you get like an award or something? Holy cow, you should *totally* hang it in your locker!"

"Today, we are going to continue with our discussions on how to use art in the career world," Miss Yeager started and, thankfully, Allison quieted.

I tried to focus on what Miss Yeager was saying, but honestly, the word *career* just reminded me of Deputy Slalom's job offer yesterday.

Now, granted, I had told Mom and Dad that I wanted to look into getting a job over the summer. Something with casual work attire, nice hourly pay, and good benefits. I was thinking about maybe working at Kelly's Creamery and serving ice cream. For every ten cones you sold, you got one free.

That sounded like good benefits to me.

Dad wanted me to consider working at the local hardware store. I figured he wanted some discounts for when he finally built that shed he'd been talking about building for years.

I didn't like the smell of sawdust, however, and the hardware store always smelled of sawdust and wood glue. Which also made me worry a little bit about the architectural integrity of the store.

But working as a forensic sketch artist? With the police?

I was willing to bet there was no free ice cream with that job.

"... makes it one of the best choices for an art major's career," Miss Yeager said, and I shook my head slightly, trying to bring myself back to the present.

I raised my hand.

"Yes, Kate?"

"I'm sorry. What's one of the best choices for an art major's career?" I asked, feeling dumb but not wanting to miss what she was talking about. Justin wouldn't have answered me if I'd asked him and Allison doesn't know the meaning of whispering.

Miss Yeager smiled faintly at me. "Freelance artistry," she said. She looked at the class. "I have several friends who make a very good living contracting out with people to design their restaurant menus, drawing the winter art you see on store windows, and painting creative pieces on people's walls. You have to be willing to keep very unusual hours and have very good self-marketing skills, but it can be a great line of work."

She told us that we would now spend the rest of class designing a menu. "I want you to use your creative brains and come up with a restaurant, a good description of the kind of food they serve, and a sample menu for me. I need it in color and finished on my desk by Monday morning. Don't worry about putting prices on there."

She walked around handing out huge sheets of paper that had been pre-folded into a menu with three sections.

Allison immediately started working on hers. She'd only had her paper for seventeen seconds before *Allison's Awesome Appetizer House* was written across the top of the front page.

Justin was lightly sketching a few lines here and there, making what looked like a vine wrapping around the edges of the menu. I was willing to bet his was going to be an Italian restaurant.

Everyone around me was working and sketching. I stared at my blank piece of paper.

All I could think about was John X whiling away time in prison by cutting my name into the rubber sole of his shoelace-less shoes, listening to a basketball game outside his window while the smell of pot roast wafted down the barred hallway.

"Kate?" Miss Yeager said softly.

I jerked up. "Oh. Yes?"

She just smiled one of those sad, sympathetic smiles at me. "You don't have to be here," she said.

I nodded. "Yes, I do." I picked up my pencil.

I worked quickly and I worked hard. By the time class was over, I had a halfway decent menu about halfway done.

Granted, it was for a restaurant called *Jailbird's* and the main thing they served was pot roast, but it was done very tastefully in an art-deco design.

The bell rang and everyone stuffed their pencils, menus, and sketchpads into their backpacks. "Have a great weekend everyone, see you on Monday!" Miss Yeager yelled over the chaos.

DJ waited for me while I gathered up my supplies. "So," he said as I shrugged on my backpack. "Jailbird's?"

"DJ," I said, walking into the loud hallway and trying to ignore yet another chorus of "Kate Carter! Kate Carter? Kate Carter!"

"Yes, Kate?"

"Do they serve pot roast in prison?"

Chapter Seven

SOMEHOW, I GOT THROUGH THE REST OF THE DAY WITH minimal visions of John X in his cell and only hearing my name shouted another eighty-seven times. Maddy caught me in the hall right before lunch and warned me to just give her my lunch money and she'd meet me by her car to eat it.

So Maddy, DJ, and I ate school cafeteria lunches in her shiny, black Tahoe. I don't believe I've ever eaten something that disgusting in something so nice. Our cafeteria excels in only two lunches — pizza and soft tacos with Spanish rice.

Today's lunch was cold chicken nuggets and congealed macaroni and cheese.

Needless to say, both DJ and I were starving when we got home.

Mom, still on the verge of a nervous breakdown, apparently cancelled her afternoon appointments so she could worry over me when I got home.

"Kate!" she cried as soon as I walked in the door.

"Hi, Mom," I said as she grabbed me into one of those almost-painful hugs, it was so tight.

"Oh, Kate, I worried about you all day today. School was uneventful? People were kind to you? The pressure wasn't too hard to take?"

"I think I passed my geography test," I told her.

She looked up at DJ, who nodded. "I think she handled it just fine, ma'am."

Mom stopped crushing me to her chest, but kept one hand on my shoulder. "I made cookies."

"Great," I said, trying to muster up some enthusiasm. Cookies, to my mom, usually involved some form of natural sweetener that isn't called sugar. And while I thought that sugar was the only natural sweetener, it is not.

Two weeks ago, she'd made a batch of honey and wheat germ cookies. No refined sugar, no white flour.

"You are supposed to dip them into a nice, hot cup of tea," Mom said to me and Dad when she served them.

Dad had made a face and then dunked his "cookie" into the tea and shoved the whole thing in his mouth. "Mm!" he managed and then got up from the table.

The cookie was rock solid. I think you had to dunk it in the tea to help it soften enough for your temporomandibular joint to work.

So I wasn't too excited when Mom mentioned cookies. This meant more acting and after seven hours of acting like I was fine and focused at school, I was ready to just have some alone time.

And by alone time, I meant me in my bedroom with the door open while DJ took his post in the hallway.

"Chocolate chip." Mom nodded.

My head snapped up so fast, I nearly bit my tongue. "You made chocolate chip cookies?" I gasped.

I had to see it to believe it. I went into the kitchen and lo and behold, there on the counter were dozens of cookies dotted with dark chocolate chips.

DJ and Mom followed me. "It's not like I never make chocolate chip cookies," Mom was telling DJ.

I was pretty sure that the last time she made them, I was still learning the Pledge of Allegiance.

"With real sugar?" I asked, dubiously sniffing a cookie.

"Yes," Mom said.

Then I rethought my question. "I mean, with fake sugar?"

She sighed. "Just eat the cookie, Kate."

I took a bite. And it was definitely not a chocolate chip cookie.

But I pulled on my theater skills and managed to swallow it. Whatever was in the cookie was acting like a vacuum on my saliva. I could barely get the last of it down, my mouth was so dry. "You did use real sugar," I said after downing a glass of water.

"Yep. This one is made from the leaves of the stevia plant," Mom said proudly. "And that's whole wheat flour, carob chips, and don't tell your father, but I added some whey protein powder to give them a little nutritional boost."

DJ was staring at the cookies like they were on the same playing field as our lunch today.

So much for starving. "I won't tell Dad," I said and then grabbed my backpack and went to my room.

My room was possibly my favorite place in this house. I painted it a deep chocolate color last year, and I'd slowly been adding different colors and textures in my accessories to provide visual depth and interest. My bedspread was a rich ruby red, I'd hung a few shelves that were a creamy color, and I was trying to locate some textured pillows for my bed.

I plopped my backpack by my desk and climbed up on the bed, dragging my sketchpad, pencils, and half-finished menu over.

The menu was due on Monday, and since art was my favorite subject, I always tried to do that homework first.

I heard the TV turn on in the living room. "In South Woodhaven Falls, Missouri, yesterday, a high school junior was directly related to the arrest of famed murderer, John X ..."

"Oh my gosh!" I heard Mom say. "Kate, get in here! Katie Couric is talking about you!"

I walked into the living room, and DJ followed me. There was Katie Couric and there was my yearbook picture suspended in the air next to her.

I hated that picture. Of all the ones they had to use, they had to pick one that made me look like a squinty third grader.

Katie Couric started retelling the now-infamous story, and the phone rang. Mom answered it and then passed it to me.

"Did you know that you're on Katie Couric?"

It was Maddy.

"I'm watching it right now."

"Did you see the picture they used?"

I sighed. "Maddy, I'm watching it right now."

"I wish they'd come to me for a picture. I would have at least given them the one of us at the zoo last summer."

I knew exactly which picture she was talking about and she was right, that was a lot cuter.

"Since when do you watch the news, Maddy?"

"Since never. I was flipping through the channels, and I saw you squinting at me. Hey, if Ryan Seacrest decides to interview you, will you let me go with you? I'll give them the cute picture of you."

I just shook my head at the TV, which was now showing a picture of the jailed John X. He didn't look too happy in his mug shot, and a lone skittle of fear raced up my spinal column.

"Sure, Maddy. Sure."

Mom called me in for dinner at 5:37, yet another sign that not all was well in our house. Dad had just gotten home, and DJ was standing guard in the living room.

"How was school?" Dad asked, the first normal question I'd gotten all day.

I opened my mouth to respond.

"Oh, and I looked into getting you in some self-defense and gun handling classes. You're too young to carry a concealed weapon, but your self-defense class starts on Tuesday night at seven. You and your mother are both signed up to go."

So, it started out normal.

I nodded. "Okay." At this point, it was better not to argue.

We went into the kitchen, and Mom guilted DJ into sitting in Mike's empty chair. "I made enough for you to eat, so if you don't, I'm going to be very hurt," Mom said, putting a platter of what looked like salmon on the table.

"Okay, ma'am. If you say so."

Mom may not be able to do the sweet stuff well, but she usually made awesome dinners. The salmon smelled so good, and we all sat at the table, drooling.

Lolly was lounging on the floor, waiting for someone to drop a bite.

As was custom, Mom held out her hands and Dad made a gruffly noise in the back of his throat.

"Bless the food. Amen," he muttered, barely bothering to close his eyes.

Well. Some things hadn't changed.

Dad, DJ, and I all dug into our salmon, but Mom was more reluctant. I could tell she was trying to decide if she should say something or not.

"Guys?" she said, finally, putting her unused fork down. "We are going to church this Sunday."

Everyone just kind of stared at her in a chewing silence.

"What?" Dad said.

"Why?" I asked.

"Sounds like a plan." DJ nodded. "Great salmon, Mrs. Carter."

Mom said thank you to DJ and then looked at me and my dad. "Because it has been a long time since we were there, and I just feel like we need all the help we can get right now."

She picked up her fork and took a bite of salmon. I looked across the table at Dad, who shrugged and started on his rice.

So it looked like I wasn't going to be sleeping in on Sunday.

"What did you do in school today?" Dad asked me.

"I took a geography exam."

"Did you pass it?"

"Yes, sir."

Dad nodded, content.

A few minutes of quiet chewing took place. Lolly stirred under the table, reminding us that she was still there.

"I talked to Mike today," Mom said, and both Dad and I immediately snapped to attention.

"Is he okay?" I asked.

"Did he total his car or something?" Dad said.

Mom sent us both a glare. "He's fine."

"How's his car, though?" Dad asked.

"He's fine, his car is fine, his grades are fine, and he was just calling because he heard about Kate on the radio this morning, and he wanted to know if it was our Kate or a different one."

My brother moved out to go to college in California almost three years ago. In that time, he had only made it home for the two Christmas breaks he had and opted to stay out there for both Thanksgivings.

As for me, I hadn't talked to him on the phone the entire time he'd been gone. There's five years and personality issues between us — his personality issues, not mine.

So the fact that he called of his own free will was something of a miracle. I think that Mom tried to call him about once a week, but she only ended up getting through to him about once a month.

Mom would never admit to it, but I did see her crying a little last month when she once again got my brother's voicemail.

It made me mad at Mike. The woman went through thirty-two hours of labor and eighteen years of feeding and caring for him. You'd think he could spare a few minutes to talk to his mother on the phone.

Dad always said that an engineering degree was one of the toughest degrees out there, and we should just let Mike study.

I thought it was just another excuse for my brother.

"So, he's doing okay?" I asked. Mad or not, Mike was still my brother.

Mom nodded. "He only had a minute to talk, but he said he's doing good. Said classes are hard, but the weather is nice."

So, pretty much, he got through the perfunctory stuff and then hung up.

I shook my head slightly and kept working on my salmon and rice. DJ had already finished his plate.

At nine, DJ's night replacement rang the doorbell. Only this time it wasn't the silent Officer Colton, it was Detective Masterson at the door.

I looked up from the rerun of *Gilmore Girls* I was watching.

"You're staying tonight?" I asked, surprised when he walked in. Mom and Dad were back in their bedroom talking, and I'd heard the word *UCLA* used, so I figured it was about Mike.

DJ closed and locked the door behind Detective Masterson, and they both sat on the sofa beside me.

"What's this?" the detective asked.

"*Gilmore Girls*," DJ answered before I could.

Detective Masterson looked at DJ and then snorted.

"Excuse me," I said. "This show is a wonderful satire on life and women and small towns, and I happen to love it."

"Sure, sure," Detective Masterson said. "Whatever you say, Kate."

"I can pick a girlier show," I threatened, waving the remote. "I think that *Barefoot Contessa* is on right now."

DJ almost jumped at me. "No!"

"No more mocking my show?"

DJ shook his head violently. "No more mocking your show. Kent?" He elbowed Detective Masterson.

There was the Kent thing again. My brain could not process that Detective Masterson's name was Kent to his friends.

Kent.

He grinned. "Consider the mocking over and done with." He leaned back against the sofa cushions. "So, what does the famous Kate Carter have going on this weekend? I mean, aside from the parade with the governor and dinner with the mayor?"

"A parade?" I moaned, muting the TV right in the middle of one of Lorelai Gilmore's famous word battles with Rory.

"Just a short one." Detective Masterson grinned at me. "Just around Main Street and up to Cherry Road."

I growled under my breath. "And what am I supposed to do on this parade?"

"Oh, you know, the usual. Smile, wave, blow kisses to the eligible young bachelors in town, and toss candy to the babies."

Detective Masterson was grinning ear to ear and enjoying this entirely too much.

"Do I have to?" I asked.

"You have to." Detective Masterson picked up the remote and changed the channel to KCL, where the too-white-toothed Ted Deffle was doing the evening news.

"A six-pack of Diet Coke was found to be missing from McSweeny's earlier today," he was saying.

I looked at DJ and the detective. "Do you guys ever worry about your job security in this town?"

DJ nodded. "Every day."

"I used to," Detective Masterson said. "But then I realized that without me, the three guys who drink the weekend away at Barney's would be out there driving drunk, Mrs. Lainger would have no one to call whenever she thought her house was getting broken into, and little Lacey Cutler's kitten would have been eaten by the next-door neighbor's dog on a daily basis for the last three years."

DJ looked over Detective Masterson to me again. "Like I said, every day."

Chapter Eight

SATURDAY MORNING DAWNED BRIGHT AND BEAUTIFUL, and I woke up to the smell of pancakes.

Pancakes?

I sniffed confusedly and stumbled out of bed, grabbing my change of clothes and heading for the bathroom. Five minutes later, I had on presentable sweats and my teeth were brushed.

So long, Saturday mornings in my pajamas.

I made it to the kitchen, yawning. Mom and Dad were nowhere to be found, but DJ was blissfully eating a huge stack of pancakes, and Detective Masterson was busy flipping more.

"Morning, Kate," he hummed. "Pancake?"

Miss Yeager, should she be the one, was turning out to be a lucky girl. I nodded and sat down at the table next to DJ.

"Sleep good?" DJ asked me.

"Yes," I lied. Truthfully, I dreamt that John X's mug shot had been chasing me in the governor's parade car. He kept catching all the candy I threw and knocking over my parents and Maddy, trying to catch up to me.

"You didn't sound like you slept well," the detective said, coming over with a plate stacked three pancakes high and setting it in front of me. "You were mewling all night."

Well, this was embarrassing. I wanted my door closed at night like before this whole fiasco, so the only person who knew whether I made noise when I slept was Lolly, who usually slept on the floor by my bed.

I glared at the detective and then dug into the pancakes.

They were delicious and try as I might, I couldn't stay mad at someone who created such fluffy, tasty delights.

"Good?" he asked, sitting in one of the empty chairs, sipping from a cup of coffee.

"Kent, if I'd known you were such a good wife, I would have married you years ago." DJ grinned, shoving another forkful of pancakes in his mouth.

Detective Masterson took another sip of coffee and pulled the morning paper over. "Sadly, you're not my type. But thank you for the proposal."

"Who is your type?" I asked, squirting more syrup on my stack. "Miss Yeager?"

DJ perked up at that one. "The woman at the school?" He looked at me. "Your art teacher?"

I nodded.

"Oh, look at the headline," the detective said, not answering DJ's question.

DJ winked at me.

"'Local Hero to Be Featured in Tomorrow's May Day Parade'," Detective Masterson read.

I yanked the paper from him. There was my horrific yearbook picture slathered all over the front page.

It was like other pictures of me just didn't exist. I groaned.

"Now, now. Let me see your smile for the adoring public, Kate." Detective Masterson grinned over his coffee.

"Look at this picture," I said, pointing to the front page. "Do I really look like that in person?"

DJ studied it for a minute. "You are kind of squinting all weird there."

Mom walked in the kitchen, hair styled, makeup on, and

wearing jeans and a Western button-down shirt. "Good morning, Katie-Kin," she said, ruffling her hand through my hair.

I suddenly realized why Lolly always leaned into us whenever we petted her.

"Morning, guys," Mom said, nodding to the policemen.

"Morning," they chimed simultaneously.

Detective Masterson stood. "Pancakes, ma'am?" he asked, pouring batter onto the griddle.

Mom nodded and sat beside me. "Thanks, Detective."

I almost laughed. Here it was Saturday morning. My mother was completely dressed before ten, I had a detective in the police force serving pancakes and coffee to my family, and a police officer sleeping outside my bedroom on an air mattress.

Life could not get weirder.

Dad walked in then, 9mm strapped to his waist.

Then again, perhaps I spoke too soon.

Dad started squinting through the barely cracked kitchen blinds, and DJ elbowed me.

"That's the expression you've got right here," he whispered, pointing to the newspaper.

I sighed.

"Anything happen last night?" Dad asked the detective.

Detective Masterson shook his head, flipping the pancakes. "No, sir. It was very quiet." He looked toward the front door. "Although we did get something this morning."

Dad immediately walked out of the kitchen and came back holding the hugest bouquet of flowers I'd ever seen in my life.

"Wow," Mom and I chimed together.

"Who's it from?" I asked, clambering off my chair and over to where Dad was struggling to set it down on the counter. I ended up needing to get my chair and stand on it to see the top of the arrangement.

"See a card?" Dad asked.

"No. Oh wait," I said, pulling the tiniest white envelope from the huge monstrosity of tulips, daisies, roses, violets, and lilies.

It simply said *Kate* on the front.

I was just about to open it when Detective Masterson took it from me. "Sorry, Kate. I have to inspect everything that comes through that front door."

He opened it, read it, snorted, and then passed it to me.

I stood on the chair and started reading.

Dearest Kate—

"What's it say?" Mom asked. "Read it out loud."

I was suddenly very happy that we didn't live in the time of that *Pride and Prejudice* book. I was only imagining what it would be like to get a romantic letter from Mr. Darcy and then have to read it out loud to my mother.

I hopped off the chair. In this case, Detective Masterson had already read it. It couldn't get much worse than that.

"'Dearest Kate,'" I started again.

Dad frowned at me and Mom started getting all sappy.

DJ was snickering behind his coffee cup, I was pretty sure.

"'In gratitude for your civic service, thankfulness for your generous spirit, and hopefulness for our eventual meeting, I trust you are as overwhelmed by this bouquet as I am by your bravery. Thank you.'"

It was signed *Sincerely, Ted Deffle, KCL News.*

I felt my nose wrinkling up.

"Ted Deffle?" Dad choked on his coffee. "He's like twenty years older than you! Is that even legal?" He looked at DJ.

"To send a girl a bouquet of roses out of thankfulness?" DJ asked. He looked at Detective Masterson and shrugged. "I guess so."

"I would imagine the honorable Ted just wants to secure an interview spot with Kate," Detective Masterson said, handing Mom and Dad their pancakes. "Coffee?"

I sat back down at the table. Ted Deffle sent me flowers.

Ugh.

Maddy was not going to believe this.

"Another pancake, Kate?" Detective Masterson asked.

"Please." And keep them coming.

By the time we were heading to the mayor's house that night, I'd received another three bouquets. One from the local paper, one from the South Woodhaven Falls Rotary Club, and another one from the KCL staff.

I'd also gotten seventeen thank-you notes in the mailbox from people all over the St. Louis area. One lady claimed that she'd seen a man who matched my drawing in her grocery store last week buying processed cheese crackers.

"I wondered at the time, but it makes sense now," she'd written.

I figured that meant criminals must eat processed cheese crackers, and I asked DJ if I should add that to my Jailbird's menu.

He said that in his experience, most of them seemed to prefer the peanut butter crackers over the cheese, but he'd also known of at least three high-profile crooks who were lactose intolerant, so maybe that threw off the count.

I added both cheese and peanut butter crackers to the menu.

DJ was driving us over in an unmarked black Tahoe, but it was definitely a police vehicle on the inside. Mom and I sat in the back, and Dad sat up front with DJ.

I was wearing a light blue and brown dress that was entirely too summery for the spring weather. My shins were getting cold. I'd put a brown sweater over my arms, but now I was wishing there was a way to put sweater sleeves over my legs without looking like a complete fashion accident.

I think those are called leg warmers, but in my experience, those were better left to the girls who thought Britney Spears was a style icon and it was best for me to leave those alone. Particularly with a summer dress.

I'd never been to the mayor's house before, but as we pulled through the gate leading to the huge front lawn, I was suddenly overwhelmed by the money to be made in politics.

"I had no idea he lived in such a huge house," I said. "Tax dollars?"

"Family money," Dad answered me.

Maybe it's a life of schmoozing that pays off in the end. Mayor Arnold Walinski was a world-class butter-upper.

If that was a word.

DJ parked the car in front of the mansion and we all piled out, greeted by two guys whom I assumed were security and two dogs that I assumed were part pit bull.

"Miss Carter?" one of them said to me, putting out his hand. "Pleased to meet you. The mayor and his family have been looking forward to meeting you."

We followed the man into the house and into a huge dining room. Mayor Walinski was standing there next to a bleached-blonde woman and two dark-haired kids who were probably in elementary school.

"Greetings!" Arnold Walinski said. "Welcome to my home!"

It was all very awkward. The bleached lady looked bored to tears, the kids were too busy poking each other for me to remember their names or them to remember mine, and dinner salads were busy wilting on the gold-circled china plates.

"Please, sit," Arnold said, motioning to the table.

DJ stayed in the room, but he didn't sit down, since there wasn't a place setting for him. I started wondering if he felt like hired help.

"So, Kate, once again, I just want to say thank you for everything that you've done to keep our fair town in its safe environment," Arnold said, while his wife picked at her salad and the kids threw olives at each other.

I'm not sure when people will finally realize that this was all a big accident and all I did was draw what I was told to draw.

"You are welcome," I said, because it was starting to get old protesting.

And then we sat there in silence. Dad was done with his salad and Mom was finishing the last couple of bites. I was pretending to eat, but pushing it around instead. It was made with that bitter lettuce stuff and I was an iceberg kind of a girl.

Tasteless and crunchy. That was how I liked my lettuce.

A lady brought out the next course, which Arnold declared to be lamb.

And it looked like I was going hungry tonight, alongside DJ. There was no way I was going to eat a cute fluffy lamb, I don't care how tender it was.

"Isn't this amazing?" Arnold said, breaking the silence, chomping away. "Our cook is Grecian and she makes the most excellent lamb dishes."

"Wonderful," Mom said, lightly picking at it.

"So, tell me more about yourself, Kate," Arnold said.

I looked up at him and shrugged. "I'm a junior."

"I knew that. What do you like to do? Well, besides drawing, I mean," he said, laughing.

What did I like to do? Between homework, Maddy, and E!, I didn't have a lot of free time.

I shrugged again. "Hang out, I guess." I was realizing that aside from art and championing for non-soggy Crispix, I had zero hobbies.

No one was ever going to describe me as a well-rounded student.

"Well, that's very interesting!" Arnold burst. "Have you ever thought about a career in politics? Pretty much, you just hang out with people and try to garner their vote." Then he laughed a creepy staccato laugh.

My dad just paused right in the middle of eating his lamb steak. "What about protecting our people from total government control? What about campaigning on upholding the Constitution? What about freedom of the peoples?"

Politics were never a good dinner conversation when my dad was involved.

Arnold immediately went into apology/super schmooze mode. "Well, yes, yes, *of course* we have to work to protect the freedoms of the people. I was merely suggesting that Kate might be good at it considering her people skills and obvious good head on her shoulders, *never* that a politician's only job duty was to hang out with people."

"Uh-huh," Dad said.

We finished the meal in near silence.

"Thank you for coming tonight," Arnold said after all the plates had been cleared. "My family really enjoyed getting to meet all of you."

I wasn't sure his family agreed with that assessment, but we nodded. "Thank you for having us," I said.

Then we climbed back into the unmarked black Tahoe and headed back home.

"Kate, if you ever think of going into politics ..." Dad threatened.

"He served lamb," I said at the same time, getting sad for the poor fluffy baby.

"Those poor children are being raised in an atmosphere that is entirely inappropriate for proper growth," Mom said.

DJ listened to all of us and then grinned. "Successful evening, I take it."

"Could you please stop by Walton's? I need a burger," I said. I may not be able to eat lamb, but I can definitely eat beef. I think it has to do with calling the meat by a different name than what I call the animal.

DJ changed the direction he was driving.

"Politicians," Dad muttered under his breath, using the same tone of voice he used when he talked about the Braille print on

ATM machines. Anytime Dad wanted to point out the direction he felt humanity was headed in, he always talked about Braille on drive-thru ATM machines. "If that's not a straight shot toward stupidity, I don't know what is," he would say.

"Well, Kate, tomorrow is the May Day parade and I got word from Deputy Slalom that you can start talking to the press now. We've scheduled a press conference for tomorrow after the parade. How does that sound?" DJ asked.

It sounded like a day better off spent in the Pit of Despair, like on *The Princess Bride*, but I didn't say that. "Fine," I groaned.

DJ pulled into Walton's drive-through and I told him I wanted a cheeseburger and fries and then passed him a five dollar bill.

"I'd like a cheeseburger, fries, and double-decker chicken sandwich," he ordered.

A few minutes later, we pulled into our driveway and I settled on our sofa, unwrapping my greasy burger and turning the TV to KCL, fully anticipating a shot of our front door to be part of the news again tonight.

They had a different picture headlining, though.

"Good evening, ladies and gentlemen, and thank you for watching KCL News, the news you can trust!" Ted Deffle said, grinning that nearly blinding white smile. I ran my tongue over my teeth. I might need to go get some of those whitening strips before the press conference tomorrow.

"Tonight, we take you to the lair of a killer," he said, all dramatically. I took a bite of my cheeseburger and watched as the picture of a different front door appeared next to Ted's head.

"This is the reputed house of the killer known as John X."

I sat up a little straighter and turned the volume up a little louder. DJ came in and sat on the couch with me, eating his chicken sandwich.

"Police in the Greater St. Louis Area have been painstakingly combing through every belonging in this suburban home, looking for evidence in the four deaths of women in the surrounding area."

A map showed the four counties around St. Louis where John X had claimed lives.

"We're going live to Candace Olstrom at the scene. Candace?"

"Hi, Ted," squeaky blonde Candace said, standing outside a house marked off with bright yellow caution tape. The whole street was dark except for the news crew lights on Candace. "I'm here outside the house that police now know was the headquarters for the serial killer known as John X. Earlier today I got to talk to several of the neighbors to see what they knew."

It switched from a live feed to a tape of earlier when it was still light outside.

"Yeah, I knew 'im," one man said around a huge wad of pink bubblegum. "'E was always out in 'is yard, workin' on some old mower or sometin. 'E weren't too friendly. One of my kids 'it a baseball back there and 'e wouldn't give it back." Then the man spit the huge wad of bubblegum into his yard.

I loved how news crews out here always managed to find the pride and joy of the population to interview.

"I met him once," a lady carrying a baby said next. The baby kept trying to grab Candace's microphone. "Stop it, Lucy. I got a package that was his, so I took it over. He seemed friendly, if not a little distant. Lucy, cut it out. Who knew he was a killer? I never lock my doors, I never worry about my safety. Lucy, I swear ... I'll tell you what, though, I'm locking my doors tonight, that's for sure and certain."

"Top of the crop tonight," DJ muttered.

I smiled.

Then they switched to a picture of John X in prison, and my smile faded. He was sitting on a cot staring out of bars, and he didn't look happy at all.

Mad might be a better word.

Or livid.

He hadn't used a razor and he looked kind of dirty. He didn't really resemble the man I drew in art class as much.

"Authorities say they've uncovered several incriminating pieces that will be used in the trial against John X. Ted?"

"Thanks, Candace. In other news, the local heroine who helped aid in the capture of John X will be appearing in the May Day parade tomorrow alongside the governor, and we also will finally get a chance to talk to the notorious Kate Carter afterwards."

They were showing that awful yearbook picture of me again, but to be honest, I wasn't really paying attention.

All I could see was John X sitting behind those bars. Livid.

At me.

"Kate?" DJ asked.

I blinked and looked up at him. Suddenly, the cold, half-eaten, greasy burger in my hands didn't look so appetizing anymore. I wadded it up in the paper.

"You okay?" he asked.

I nodded. "Fine." It was better not to worry the policeman just doing his job. If I was going to tell anyone my worries, it was going to be Lolly. Mom would try to do her psychoanalyzing thing on me, Dad would start in about Miss Yeager, and Maddy would just go all drama queen.

Lolly was a dumb dog sometimes, but she was a good listener.

DJ twisted his lips like he didn't believe me, but he nodded. "Your call," he said. "Ready for the parade tomorrow? Let me see your wave."

I just rolled my eyes. "So ready. And no, you can't see my wave."

Ted was now showing clips of the families of the women John X had killed.

"We are so thankful that this man has been brought to justice for the murder of my wife," one man said, a teary teenage son and daughter beside him. He had to gather himself for a minute and then continued. "We will never heal completely, but with God all things are possible. Thank you, Kate Carter and the fine men and women of the St. Louis area police team. May God bless you and yours." Then he had to step away, wiping his eyes and holding onto his kids.

They looked like they were a nice family. Why did bad things always seem to happen to nice people?

DJ was watching me again.

"What?" I asked, looking over at him.

He squinted at me. "You did a good thing, Kate. I just want you to remember that. And I know you're freaking out right now, but remember that he's in prison and you are safe. Okay?"

I liked that DJ was young enough to use *freaking out* in its proper context. My dad tried to do that once and it didn't turn out quite so well.

I didn't like that DJ could read me like an open book. In a lot of ways, he was like the brother I always wanted and never got in Mike. Mike was always too concerned over things that concerned him.

Never things that concerned his annoying little sister.

I nodded to DJ. "I'm fine," I said again.

"Sure," he said. "I know."

I watched a couple more of the victim's families' interviews and tried to stop grinding my teeth. "Just fine," I mumbled again.

Chapter Nine

SUNDAY MORNING AND MOM, DAD, DJ, AND I WERE ALL sitting in one of the very uncomfortable pews at South Woodhaven Falls First Baptist Church.

Which I thought was an entirely-too-long-name for a building that could probably only hold about two hundred people.

Maybe.

We were handed a piece of paper with the order of the service on it when we sat down, and right as we sat an old lady slammed a chord down so hard on the organ at the front of the sanctuary that all four of us jumped.

About a third of the people in the room stood up then and gathered on the stage, wearing what looked like something flamboyant monks would wear or maybe something that a color-blind school would use for graduation. And they were all holding books in front of them and clearing their throats.

"Join us, won't you, in standing and singing Hymn 239," a man also wearing the monk outfit said into a microphone. The lady at the organ started busting out a long chord succession and then the people in front starting singing.

"Lord, who dost give to thy church," they all started, and that's where they lost me.

Who was dost? Or maybe it was a what?

Dad was standing stoically and looking at the choir in a mix of peevishness and boredom. Mom was fumbling with a book she pulled out of the back of the pew in front of her, which I realized was a book of music. And DJ was squinting at another one of the books, trying to follow along.

The organ lady finished with an ear-shattering ending and then started up again. "Hymn 197!" the same man yelled out. "And sing with joy!"

"We're marching to Zion," the people around me and on the stage sang loudly. "Beautiful, beautiful, Zion!"

I'd never heard of Zion, and other than it sounding very similar to a large cat found in our local zoo, I wasn't sure what it was.

Again, another eardrum-splitting finale, and then we all sat and listened to a man in a poor-fitting suit who said "amen" after every sentence.

Including one that made a reference to McSweeny's market. I'd never heard McSweeny's market amened before.

"And I said to a woman in the middle of McSweeny's market, 'Woman! You can have peace!' Amen?"

"Amen!" the people around us shouted, making me jump yet again.

I tried to subtly look around while the man was talking. There were primarily people in what I would guess were their late sixties, maybe early seventies around us. I didn't see anyone who was my age, and I only saw one other couple who was my parents' ages.

After the final "amen" had been shouted, the organ lady took up her post again and everyone started milling around the room, talking very loudly so they could be heard over the organ.

"Well, hello there!" a tiny old woman with hair that was whiter than anything OxiClean had ever treated said to us when we got ready to leave. She stuck her hand out to my dad. "I'm Sister Elizabeth Parker. And you are?"

It would be very hard to go through your whole life with the nickname "sister." She seemed to take it well, though.

"Dale," my dad said gruffly.

Sister Elizabeth Parker grinned brightly. "Welcome to South Woodhaven Falls First Baptist Church!" she said with more oomph than the organ lady played with.

And that was a lot of oomph.

Especially for a little woman like Sister Elizabeth.

"I'm Claire," Mom said, shaking the woman's hand. "This is my daughter, Kate, and ... our friend, DJ."

It was a nice save and DJ smiled.

"Well, it's very nice to meet you all. I must say, I haven't seen a hair untouched by the Master Grayer in this service since 1998!" She stuck her hands on her tiny hips for emphasis. "Most of you young folk tend to go for the late service. Contemporary music and that stuff that hurts my ears." Then she grinned all big at us.

Despite the fact that I'm pretty sure she was one of the loudest "amen"-ers behind us, I decided I kind of liked Sister Elizabeth. She seemed spunky.

"Well, now. You fine folks should sure come back now, you hear?"

"Yes, ma'am, we certainly will," Mom said.

Judging by Dad's expression, I didn't think that was what he was planning for next Sunday.

We walked out to the foyer before the exit, and I finally saw a group of people my age moving toward the sanctuary.

And my mouth dropped.

At the center of the group, loudly telling a joke that had the other nine kids laughing hysterically — none other than Justin Walters from art.

Aka Silent Justin.

I just stood there gaping at him. I don't know if he felt the complete shock in my gaze melting toward him or what, but suddenly he stopped talking and looked over at me.

And blinked. "Kate?" he said.

Apparently I gasped from the total surprise at the first time I'd heard him say my name, which made DJ and my father panic.

"What? What?" Dad shouted, grabbing my right arm.

"Let's get you to the car immediately," DJ said, grabbing my left arm.

I wrestled out of their reaches and Justin walked over. Smiling.

"Hi, Kate," he said easily, like we were good friends and talked all the time. "How are you? I didn't know you came to first service."

At this point, I was waiting for either Ashton Kutcher to arrive on the scene and announce that I had just been *Punk'd* or for Justin to introduce himself as Justin's previously-unheard-of identical twin, Dustin.

I glanced around, but I did not see Ashton or another Justin lookalike, and the Justin who was in front of me was now giving me a very weird look.

"You okay?" he asked.

"You speak?" I asked.

He said, "What?"

"I have never heard you talk, ever," I said.

Dad and DJ exchanged a look and then walked with Mom a few feet away. I appreciated the privacy. Should Ashton Kutcher appear, it would be nice to not embarrass my entire family.

Justin shrugged. "Sometimes I like being quiet."

He said it the same way he would say he sometimes liked Canadian bacon on his pizza. Nonchalant.

"Sometimes? We're almost halfway through the school year," I said.

He shrugged again. "So a lot of times. Especially at school."

"How come?"

Yet another shrug. I was beginning to feel the ache in my shoulders. "I don't know," he said. "Guess I don't have much to say." Then he changed the subject. "So, when did you start coming to SWF First Baptist?"

"This morning," I said.

"Oh. Well, you should come to the late service next time. It's more contemporary."

"Meaning no organ?" I asked quietly.

He shook his head. "No organ. Guitars, drums, keyboard."

"And the Amen-ers?"

He crinkled up his forehead. "What?"

"Never mind."

He just nodded at me. The group he'd been talking to came over and he smiled at them. "Okay, well, I have to go. But I'll see you tomorrow at school. Bye, Kate."

Then he and his group disappeared into the sanctuary.

Talking.

I shook my head slightly. Don't visions typically happen around churches or church people? Maybe I just had a vision.

A vision of what could be.

"Who was that?" Mom asked as I walked over to where they stood next to the door.

"A guy from art class."

Dad mumbled something about artsy boys under his breath but I chose to ignore it.

DJ looked at his watch. "It's almost ten thirty and you are supposed to be at the parade grounds in an hour," he told me.

"Oh, yay," I said, sighing.

"Try to contain your enthusiasm, Kate. We are in a public building. You don't want to cause a scene." Mom grinned, leading the way outside.

A parade. I hated even going to a parade. Being in one had to be a zillion times worse.

I had just walked out the door, squinting into the sun, when someone said, "Kate Carter?"

I turned and it was a lady in her forties I didn't recognize. "Yes?"

She gasped and clasped her hands to her chest. "Kate Carter?" she screeched again. "*The* Kate Carter?"

"And it's time to go," DJ said, quickly grabbing for my elbow.

"Oh my gosh, I am *so* thankful for you!" the woman yelled. "You are a hero, young lady, do you hear me?"

I was pretty certain that everyone in the neighborhood could hear her. I managed a short smile before I got hustled into the black Tahoe by DJ and Dad.

"You are too recognizable," DJ huffed as he climbed into the driver's seat.

"I squinted," I said, sighing.

"What?" Mom said.

"I squinted. Like in my picture in the yearbook." I squeezed my eyes halfway shut to show her.

Mom waved her hand. "Please. Your yearbook picture does not look like that."

"Does too. Check when we get home. Why else would she have recognized me only after I was staring into the sun?"

DJ cleared his throat. "She is kind of squinty in the picture."

"See? Thank you, DJ."

Dad looked out the passenger window. "Yet another reason I carry at churches."

We all looked at him. "Carry what?" I asked cautiously.

Dad turned toward me in the backseat. "My pistol. I've been carrying constantly since all this started. You can never be too careful, Kate. Did you hear those people at church? Yelling 'amen' at the preacher?"

"I think they were encouraging him," Mom said.

"Constantly being told to be quiet is not encouraging someone, Claire."

DJ opened his mouth to respond and then apparently thought better of it. "The parade," he said, changing the subject. "Kate, we're going to have continuous security on you at the parade, so there is nothing to worry about there."

I think he was speaking more toward my dad and his 9mm than he was to me.

"Okay," I said, and looked out the window. We were driving past Main right then and the town was already being littered with tons of May Day décor. Huge papier-mâché daisies, Chinese lanterns made to look like giant rosebuds, and yards and yards of pastel-colored streamers were hung everywhere along the street.

Soon, all the people in South Woodhaven Falls who owned an antique car would line up for the parade, and the school's marching band and cheerleading squad was going to perform. Mr. McSweeny closed his market and put on a clown costume most years. People even came and sold cotton candy and hot dogs.

It was a real event if you liked events.

I, however, did not like events. I spent most May Day parades catching up on homework or practicing my sketching. It was going to be a long day.

The governor owned a 1937 Packard convertible. Which if you were into cars was apparently a big deal because I guess that car was worth a lot of money. DJ told me on the way home that the governor was going to drive, his wife was going to be in the passenger seat, and me, DJ, and two other policemen were going to be in the backseat.

So it was going to be a crowded and claustrophobic long day. Great.

DJ stopped at my house, and yet again there were news vans in front. I bit back the groan. Weren't they going to get enough of the squinty-eyed heroine at the parade? Could they not wait until then?

"Hustle in," DJ said, pushing me in front of him and into my house while all the reporters yelled my name.

We got inside and Lolly came over, wagging her tail and looking at me all friendly-like.

I knelt down and gave her a hug. "Thank you for not speaking," I told her.

She licked my hand.

I had already decided that I was going to wear my favorite pair of dark-rinsed jeans and a forest green short-sleeved shirt. It was a gorgeous day outside and I really didn't think I'd need a jacket sitting in the back of a convertible.

I carried my clothes to the bathroom and changed quickly, trying not to mess up my hair from church. I'd run a straightener through it early this morning. Hopefully, it would stay straight and not get all frizzy like it was prone to do.

I touched up my makeup and stepped back to look in the mirror.

Well. It would have to do.

Mom was coming down the hall when I opened the bathroom door. "All set?" she asked, pulling a tube of lipstick from her purse.

I nodded as she smeared the bright raspberry color all over her lips. "You want some?" she asked when she finished.

"No, thanks." I wasn't a lipstick person. Lip gloss occasionally. When Maddy made me wear it. But never lipstick.

"Are you sure? Just add a little bit of color?" Mom asked, pointing the tube at my face.

I shook my head. "I don't think so."

"Girls, you need to get something to eat!" Dad yelled from the kitchen. "We have to leave in half an hour!"

My dad was nothing if not on time. My mother was one of those people who believed in fashionable lateness. Dad always said that if she were meant to be fashionable, she wouldn't have married an engineer.

Wise words, I always thought.

Dad was standing in the kitchen spreading mayo on two slices of bread. He was wearing jeans and a polo shirt. "Want a deli sandwich?" he asked when I walked in.

"Um." Now to decide how to answer this one. Yes, I did want a sandwich, but I didn't want Dad to make it for me. Dad uses way too much mayo for my tastes.

"Yeah, but I'll make it," I finally said. "Go ahead and finish yours."

Dad shrugged and stacked a healthy helping of deli-sliced turkey, tomatoes, lettuce, and pickles on his bread. By the time he finished, it was a good four inches high.

"Now that," Dad said, proudly. "That is a sandwich."

"Nicely done."

"Sure you don't want me to make yours?" he asked.

"Very sure." Especially if the outcome was going to be bigger than my head.

I slathered some mustard and mayo on two slices of bread, added a little bit of meat, one tomato, and two lettuce leaves. When I got to the table, Dad just shook his head.

"Weakling," he said.

"The camera adds ten pounds, Dad," I said, sitting across from him.

"Good. Then you'll finally look somewhat healthy."

I took a bite of my sandwich. All of the women on my mother's side of the family were tiny. I think Mom was the tallest and she was only five foot three. My grandma was four foot nine. And she maybe weighed ninety-five pounds.

Dad, though, had a coworker who discovered three years ago that his daughter was anorexic, and now Dad was completely panicked that I might be too. I kept telling him about my love of cookies and carbs in general, but I don't think he believed me.

If I had to change anything about my appearance, I'd change my height. To taller. Much taller. It got old having to tilt my head all the time.

Mom and DJ came into the kitchen then. Mom made a quick lunch of crackers, lunch meat, and cheese, and DJ made a sandwich.

"We're going to wait here for Kent to come. He's going to drive with us," DJ said, swallowing a bite of his huge sandwich.

I wondered if Miss Yeager was going to be at the parade. She was all nostalgic about the weird traditions this town had.

"Where should Claire and I be?" Dad asked.

DJ said, "You can stand wherever you like. We've got another guy coming to shadow you two, but I think everything will be fine today. The parade ends at two and the press conference starts at

City Hall thirty minutes later, so if I were you, I'd try to find a spot close to there if you can."

Mom nodded. "Wow, Katie-Kin. City Hall. That's pretty impressive!"

I sighed. "What exactly do they want me to say at this press conference?" I wasn't good in front of cameras anyway — as evidenced by my yearbook picture — so I had no idea how I was going to be in front of several and still have coherent things to say.

"Just tell them about the drawing," DJ said. "Don't mention anyone's name and don't say anything about where you live." He shrugged. "It'll be fine, Kate."

"Easy for you to say. You don't have to be in front of the cameras."

"No, but Detective Masterson will be up there with you, so at least you won't be alone in front of the cameras." Then he got very serious. "And Kate? The most important thing you need to remember?"

I waited. "Yeah?"

"Don't squint."

I threw my one tomato slice at his face.

Chapter Ten

THE GOVERNOR WAS ALREADY THERE WHEN WE GOT TO the beginning of Main. Our governor was a nice, round man. And I couldn't think of another way to describe him. He was just very ... round.

His face was round, his torso was round. He even did his hair in that comb-over style, so that even looked round once a nice breeze kicked up.

But he was nice and as far as I knew a good politician, and he couldn't remember my name to save his life.

"Sarah!" he said warmly when we walked over to his old-fashioned convertible.

I looked around, but my mom's name is Claire and the two of us were the only girls there beside the governor's wife, whose name is Patricia.

Detective Masterson, who had picked us all up a few minutes ago, leaned closer to the governor. "Kate," he said quietly.

The governor shook his head. "My apologies." Then he started over. "Kate!" Once more, the warmth just flowed. "My thankfulness and appreciation to you, my dear!"

I nodded, smiling. I liked our governor. His wife was a tiny little thing with grayish-blonde highlights cut into a Jackie O style. She smiled at me in one of those "yeah, what he said" smiles.

Our town does not have a very big Main Street, so in order for the parade to last two hours, we had to drive five miles an hour the whole way.

People were milling around everywhere. Finishing the decorations, parking their antique cars in a parking lot across the street so they could get in line a little later, already snacking on foot-long corn dogs and Dippin' Dots ice cream.

Which looked really good, and I decided that after our spot in the parade was over I was definitely getting one of the corn dogs.

There were a few speakers placed strategically down Main Street and all of a sudden they kicked on. Dean Martin started crooning *Ain't That a Kick in the Head*, and my mom started whistling to it.

"I love Dino!" Mom said.

The governor nodded appreciatively. "I certainly agree. He was one of the best musical artists of the entire last century."

"Americana would have been much different without him." Mom sighed.

"How is security going to work here?" Dad asked, apparently not caring about Dino and his effect on Americana.

Detective Masterson took over. "Governor, you and your wife will be driving. I'm going to have Kate sit on the top of the trunk — "

I blinked. "What?" I said.

Detective Masterson kept talking. " — with Officer Kirkpatrick and Officer DeWeise on either side of her."

So I was between DJ and another officer, a Mr. DeWeise, who looked like he was probably a lineman back in his college football days. He smiled nicely at me and I noticed the missing right eye tooth.

Wrong sport. Maybe hockey?

"Meanwhile, I've got another four guys coming. Two will be driving in a squad car in front of you and me and two other guys will be directly behind you in another squad car." The detective looked at Dad. "How does that sound?"

It looked like it pained Dad to admit that it did sound good. "And where should Claire and I be?"

"You can just feel free to enjoy the parade. Get a Dippin' Dots or a cotton candy or something."

Considering that Dad is about as excited about parades as I am, he handled the day's activities well. "Fine," he said quietly. "We'll wait here until Kate is leaving."

"Perfectly okay," Detective Masterson said.

At ten minutes before the parade was scheduled to start, all of us had to take our place in the car. I perched myself precariously on the trunk of the car with my feet dangling into the backseat. The metal of the car and the leather on the seats were hot and I was glad I'd opted to not wear a skirt, since the back of my bare legs would have been touching it.

DJ and Officer DeWeise were going to be roasting by the end of the parade, since they were in full uniform complete with their bulletproof vests.

"Are those heavy?" I asked as DJ adjusted his.

He thought about it and then shook his head. "They're pretty lightweight. They make custom ones now, but South Woodhaven Falls doesn't have a big enough budget to cover getting those for all of us. Especially since you've heard about our daily adrenaline rush of getting cats out of pit bull's teeth."

I grinned.

"But these ones aren't too heavy. Just bulky more than anything."

Officer DeWeise squinted at me. "We might have one that will fit you at the station. We've got a girl officer who left for maternity leave and she was about your size."

"Before or after the maternity part?" I asked, wondering if I should take a more proactive approach to my workout routine.

DJ rolled his eyes. "Before, Kate. Please don't tell me you are like other girls and all uptight and overly concerned about your appearance."

"I'm sorry, have you seen my yearbook picture?" I said.

He grinned.

"What yearbook picture?" Officer DeWeise asked.

"The one that's headlining everything they ever say about me," I groaned. "I look like this." I squinched up my eyes at him.

He tilted his head. "Actually, yeah, that does look kind of familiar."

I sighed. "Anyway, I think I have some small right to be a little bit concerned about my appearance now."

DJ conceded with a shrug. "Whatever. Did you at least bring sunglasses?"

I brought them in my purse, which I'd stuck below my feet on the passenger seat. "Got them. Think I should put them on right now?" The road ahead was pretty shaded for the first mile.

Officer DeWeise shook his head. "Just wait. Practice smiling with your eyes open for the first little bit."

DJ thought that was hilarious.

Our police force employed a regular lineup of comedians. I shook my head. The governor and his wife were climbing into the front seat and Mom waved at me.

"Smile pretty!" she said all happily. She loved the parade, so I was imagining she was just excited to get Dad out there without major arguments about how it wasn't even a real holiday.

"You listen to the cops," Dad told me. "And pay attention. Keep your eyes open."

"Yes, sir," I said.

"Don't worry, sir, I just told her the same thing," Officer DeWeise said.

The governor started up the car and we lurched once, nearly throwing all three of us into the backseat.

"Whoa!" The governor said. "Sorry about that, folks. Forgot the clutch was on. Here we go!"

We started chugging along Main Street, and I have to admit, I was amazed at how many people showed up to this kind of stuff.

People were milling around and everywhere I looked, I kept seeing foot-long corn dogs.

My stomach growled.

"You cannot be hungry," DJ said. "We just ate."

"Those corn dogs look really good," I said.

"Don't forget to wave, Kate!" Patricia, the governor's wife, told me.

I nodded and lifted my hand as we came to a section where people were actually lined up to see the parade, not just to flaunt their foot-long corn dogs.

The squad car in front of us was keeping a nice casual pace of five miles an hour, so I got to get a real good look at those corn dogs. A few people saw me and started waving.

"Kate Carter!" one lady yelled. "It's Kate Carter!"

"Thank you, Kate!" a man hollered from the other side of the street.

Soon there were probably a couple hundred or more people gathered along the sidewalk, and a chant started.

"Kate is great! Kate is great! Kate is great!"

I just waved and focused on smiling with my eyes open. Though, I have to admit, I liked that chant better than the one that Sean and Kyle Prestwick yelled at me in the second grade. They were twins, and they were both evil. They would always say, "Kate, Kate, Gator Bait!" every time I passed by them.

This was especially traumatizing because I believed then that there were really alligators in the Mississippi River, which is fairly close to South Woodhaven Falls. We took a field trip there every year from kindergarten to the fifth grade. And every year we looked at the same portion of the flood wall and heard how high the river had gotten in years past. And every year, the Prestwick boys would pretend that they were going to throw me in while I screamed and pleaded for my life.

I was not sad at all when they up and moved to Kansas City.

I blinked back to the present right as someone threw something large at the car and I ducked, squealing.

DJ caught it and laughed. It was a bouquet of roses.

"Thank you!" I yelled.

"Kate is great! Kate is great!"

I kept waving.

"I feel ignored," Officer DeWeise said a few minutes later, when everyone was still chanting "Kate is great!" and applauding.

"So do I," the governor said, smiling at me in the rearview mirror. "But goodness knows, you deserve it, Kate. Ever thought about running for office?"

I shook my head. No, most of my future plans involved me not being the center of any kind of attention. My stomach was about to implode. Public functions are not my thing. And to make matters worse, I kept thinking about how I had to talk in front of all these people after the parade.

We were starting to get to the part of Main that wasn't covered by trees, and I decided it was time to pull out the sunglasses rather than risk another squinty picture showing up in the newspaper. Which would happen because everyone had digital cameras out and flashing.

I leaned forward to get my sunglasses out of my purse, but I ended up leaning forward a bit too much and I slipped off the trunk and landed on my knees in the seat, half-crunching my purse.

Something cracked and I just knew it was my sunglasses.

I heard a guttural cry, but it wasn't me. DJ started yelling and grabbing for his gun. The governor started driving recklessly around the squad car in front, which immediately put on its siren. Patricia was screaming.

I looked up and Officer DeWeise was slumped over in the space I'd just vacated when I fell onto the seat, clutching his chest, eyes swinched tight. Blood was seeping around where his hands were on his chest.

I screamed. People all around us at the parade started screaming and running.

"Kate, get down and *stay down!*" DJ yelled at me. "Down to the floorboards, now!" He grabbed his radio while I scooted off the seat and onto the floorboard. DJ pushed Officer DeWeise onto the seat and then dove on top of him. "This is Officer Kirkpatrick! DeWeise has been shot. Repeat, DeWeise has been shot!"

The governor was still driving erratically. Patricia kept on screaming, covering her head with her hands.

I looked up at the pain-filled face of Officer DeWeise directly above me, one cheek smashed on the seat. "Are you okay?" I yelled. "Get to a hospital!"

The governor seemed stunned, scared, and started fumbling around, mashing the brake instead of the gas, and Officer DeWeise nearly fell on top of me. DJ braced himself against Patricia's headrest, so he didn't crush DeWeise.

"We need a driver!" DJ shouted into the radio.

The radio cracked something back and half a second later, someone was pushing the governor into the middle seat and was slamming the accelerator to the floor. The air whooshed around us, sirens blared, and I kept my hands knit together and my face down on the carpeted floorboards.

My heart was racing like crazy. I couldn't get a full breath in. Someone had been shot, and they'd been shot because I wasn't sitting where I was supposed to be sitting.

"No, no, no, no," I mumbled. "Oh no!"

"It's okay, Kate. It's okay," DJ said from where he was kneeling on the seat behind the prostrate Officer DeWeise. "Talk to me, DeWeise."

"Kid ..." he huffed, his eyes tightly closed in pain. "Are ... augh, are you okay?"

I was hyperventilating. "I'm okay," I managed.

"Kate, breathe. Breathe, Kate. In through the nose ..." DJ instructed. He scraped his knuckles down his cheek and just looked helplessly at me.

I squeezed my eyes shut and tried to concentrate on the breaths

I was taking. But really, all I could see when I closed my eyes was John X standing in the crowd aiming for me and shooting the funny Officer DeWeise instead.

"He's supposed to be in jail," I mumbled.

"He is," DJ said.

"Who did this then?" I looked up past DeWeise's tortured face and saw DJ's face get very hard.

He didn't answer me. We pulled to a stop and DJ hopped out over the window, and a second later they were helping Officer DeWeise out. He was gasping and moaning with every movement. Once he got out, I sat up on the floorboards.

There was bright red blood all over the shiny, velvet-white interior. It dripped down from the lid of trunk and was smeared on the backseat.

It should have been my blood.

Would have been, if I hadn't reached for my sunglasses right at that moment.

I couldn't help it.

I lurched out of the car.

And threw up.

Chapter Eleven

TWO HOURS LATER AND I WAS SITTING IN ONE OF THE hospital waiting rooms, clutching a crumpled Styrofoam cup that used to contain water in it.

Dad was pacing the floor in front of me, Mom was sitting beside me, arm around my shoulder.

I was staring at the crumpled cup.

What was Styrofoam anyway? Who made it? And was it really one of those materials that never decomposes and will be around after a nuclear explosion?

DJ and Detective Masterson were behind the big number 237 written on the door in front of us. That was Officer DeWeise's room. And last I'd heard, he was fine. The bullet had bounced off of his bulletproof vest but not before nicking him on the right side of his chest.

The doctor said he couldn't tell us any more because we weren't family or even friends. I told him that I was the person he took the bullet for, but the doctor didn't seem to care. And about thirty minutes ago, a sobbing woman ran down the hallway and burst into his room.

I was assuming a wife.

The press conference had been canceled. Now all the reporters were gathered outside the hospital. I was scared to leave.

Finally, DJ came out of the room.

"What happened? Is he okay?" I immediately asked.

DJ rubbed his face, looking ten years older this afternoon than he did this morning. "He's fine. His wife is here now. He got twenty-two stitches, but he should be back to normal within a couple of weeks. The doctor said that the force of the bullet cracked two of his ribs."

Detective Masterson came out then too. "We should let them be alone," he told DJ. Then he looked at me and my parents. "Come on, guys. We're taking you guys to the station," he said wearily.

I looked back down at the Styrofoam. Officer DeWeise had twenty-two stitches, two cracked ribs, and a sobbing wife.

Because of me.

Me and my dumb dream of being an artist.

I felt tears pooling in the corners of my eyes, but I tried my best to blink them away. Kate Carter never cried. That would be a sign of weakness, and Carters weren't weak.

Or so Dad said. Mom claimed that crying was good for the soul.

Dad nodded at the policeman. "Fine," he said crisply. I knew he was mad. He'd barely said a word after making sure I was okay when they got to the hospital. Just paced.

We stood and I gathered myself as I threw the crumpled cup away and followed DJ down the hospital corridor and to the front door.

Then I got scared. Someone had already tried to shoot at me once. What if he was out there waiting for me now? What if he was just around the other side of the huge grove of trees on the other side of the parking lot?

A throng of reporters were gathered outside the doors. Most were wearing suits, but there were a few who were dressed in jeans from the waist down and a collared shirt, tie, and sport coat from the waist up, like they'd been enjoying a nice day off before the parade happened.

DJ looked over at me. "Wait here with Detective Masterson," he

95

said. Then he made his way through the crowd of yelling reporters, jogged out to the parking lot, and pulled up right in front of the door in the familiar black Tahoe.

We got inside as quickly as we could, pushing past a few reporters who kept yelling at me, asking me what I knew.

"Did you know he'd get shot, Kate?"

"Kate, why did you duck? Did you know the shooter was out there?"

I wanted to tell them I wasn't ducking, I was trying to prevent another squinty-eyed picture of me from showing up in the newspaper. But Detective Masterson didn't give me any time to respond. He half shoved me into the backseat of the Tahoe.

Everyone else clambered inside. My heart was racing.

Detective Masterson was sitting on one side of me, Mom on the other. Dad rode in front with DJ.

The detective glanced over at me. "Kate?"

I took a deep breath and looked up at him. "Yeah?"

"Welcome to the life of a forensic sketch artist."

"Being shot at is part of the life of a forensic sketch artist?" I asked.

He shrugged. "It can be. You're a member of the police force. Police have to be prepared for anything."

"Apparently that's true even in a place like South Woodhaven Falls," I said softly.

"Even in South Woodhaven Falls," the detective nodded.

We pulled up to the police station and DJ pushed me through the doors and into the busy hum of the police station.

Deputy Slalom greeted us at the door and quickly ushered us into his office.

He turned to us after the door closed, looking tired, old, and defeated. He was wearing another business suit, but he now had the jacket on the back of his chair, his sleeves rolled to his elbows and his tie loose and hanging to one side.

"Well," he said, taking a deep breath. He looked at DJ and Detective Masterson. "What's the latest on DeWeise?"

"Doctor said two weeks recovery for the wound. Twenty-two stitches and two cracked ribs. He won't be in the field for a while, sir," Detective Masterson said.

"Especially if Mrs. DeWeise has anything to say about it," DJ said.

"Police work is hardest on the wife," Deputy Slalom said quietly, looking down at a picture frame on his desk. He shook his head slightly and looked up at Mom, Dad, and me.

"Kate, Mr. and Mrs. Carter, I'm very sorry you had to endure this today."

"Obviously, we now know what kind of danger Kate is in," Dad said darkly.

"Yes, sir. And preventative measures are going to be strictly enforced. Kate, when you go to school — "

"I'm sorry, what?" Dad interrupted loudly.

" — we will now have four officers around you at all times. Officer Kirkpatrick will continue to be your primary bodyguard."

"She is *not* going to school!" Dad burst, standing. "My daughter will not be going anywhere! She will stay home and will be constantly surrounded until we find whoever just fired a gun at her! Do you hear me?"

Deputy Slalom looked at Dad for a long moment. "Then John X just won."

"What?" Dad shouted.

"John X just won. Kate is no longer a free citizen of the United States and in a sense he put her in jail just like him. Oh, she might have a cushier couch to lounge on, but mark my words, Mr. Carter. John X will be thrilled to know that he has succeeded in stripping Kate of everything she took from him."

Dad sat down and covered his face with his hands. "She's my daughter," he said, quietly.

I'd never heard that tone in my dad's voice before. Particularly as it related to me.

More tears pooling in the corners of my eyes.

"I know that, sir. Believe me, I know that. I have a daughter too. And I don't envy the position you are in."

"So," Mom said, "you are saying that we should just continue on like today never happened."

"Absolutely not," Deputy Slalom said. "I'm saying that we should continue on as if today definitely happened. John X is mad. And because he's mad, one of his friends came out of the woodwork to the parade today. We weren't aware that John X had friends and I fear that if we don't find these people, we're looking at many more graveyard plots to be dug in the near future."

I really didn't like the term *graveyard plots* used in the same conversation that involved me.

It made me start thinking.

What did come after life? Was it really just a long nap like my dad thought? And if you never woke up again, was it technically considered a nap?

I'd asked my parents about heaven once. I was ten and the dog we had before Lolly had just died. So I'd asked if the dog had gone to heaven.

Dad told me heaven didn't exist. "It's a figment of some ancient writer's imagination," he'd told me. "And a nice idea. But honestly, I'd rather be sleeping than playing some little harp on a puffy white cloud for forever."

Mom had said that she thought heaven was more a state of mind than an eternal destiny. "I think that everyone goes to some kind of 'heaven,' if that's what you want to call it," she'd said, using her fingers for quotation marks. "But really I think you just remember your life after you die."

I'd always liked Mom's theory of heaven better than Dad's, because it was nice to think of our old dog just remembering all the fun days we'd had, but now I was wondering again.

Deputy Slalom was still talking. "It's your decision, Mr. Carter, but I would ask you to reconsider allowing Kate to attend school. Like I said, we will have four officers there at all times, plus Officer Kirkpatrick. I'm going to increase the amount of security at your house as well."

I raised my hand. "Does this mean I don't have to give a press release?" I asked.

The slightest hint of a smile crossed Deputy Slalom's mouth. "No, Kate," he said. "You don't have to give a press release."

"Good."

He looked back at Dad. "What do you think, Mr. Carter?"

Dad rubbed his face. "Your men protected her once already," he said, quietly. Which was Dad-speak for "I guess it's okay."

Deputy Slalom nodded. "Good." He looked at Detective Masterson. "I want you to be one of the ones constantly by Kate. And get Porter, Starr, and Klein. The four of you can be at the school too."

The detective nodded. "Will do, sir."

"Good." Deputy Slalom then looked at DJ. "Are you still up to this?" he asked him.

DJ nodded, chin set. "Yes, sir."

Deputy Slalom nodded. "Please rest assured that we have people working night and day on this case," he told us. "We will find out what's going on. Actually, there's a team from St. Louis coming up today to start working on this as well."

We finished talking and DJ stood. "Let's get you home," he said to me, but I think he was talking to my parents as well.

We rode home in silence. Dad was staring out the passenger window, Mom had her head leaned back against the headrest with her eyes closed, and Detective Masterson alternated looking out the window and looking at me.

A few reporters were outside my house when we pulled up, but DJ and the detective got us inside without too much trouble.

"Kate!" one lady kept yelling. "Kate!"

"No questions!" DJ snapped at her.

Lolly was wagging for us when we got inside.

"Hi, Lolly," I said, rubbing her silky black head. She wagged even harder and leaned against my leg, begging for more attention.

So I sat down on the sofa. Lolly put her drooly head in my lap and for once I didn't care. I turned on the TV and leaned back, trying to make myself relax.

The TV was tuned to the news channel, and they were showing footage of the parade that someone had caught on a personal camera. I watched it for a minute. There was me reaching for my sunglasses, there was Officer DeWeise clutching his chest and sagging sideways, and there was DJ yelling and pushing DeWeise on the backseat.

I shook my head slightly and changed the channel to something brainless. Ryan Seacrest was going on about Miley's new hairstyle and I left it on that channel, rubbing Lolly's head.

Someone had shot at me.

I closed my eyes, but all I could see was the blood dripping down the trunk of the governor's car and smearing on the pristinely white seat.

I kept my eyes open.

DJ sat down on the couch beside me. "Well," he said, looking at the TV. "This is definitely going to make me rethink getting those highlights I was thinking about."

I managed a smile at him.

He smiled back at me. "You have to stop thinking about it, Kate."

"Easier said than done, DJ."

He nodded. "Let's talk about something else then."

"Like what?"

He shrugged. "I don't know. We can talk about Miley's new hair color, but I'd kind of prefer if it was something other than that."

The detective came in from the kitchen then and sat on the rocker. "Long, long day," he said, stretching out, putting his feet on the ottoman. "What are you watching?"

"Miley's thinking of going blonde again," DJ told him.

"Oh," Detective Masterson hummed. "I think if I were her, I'd stay brunette. But then, what do I know about the fashions of dim-witted, psychologically stunted multibillionaires?"

"They brought in a renowned makeup artist to talk about it," DJ told him. "They think her skin tone isn't right for blonde. Apparently, you know more than you think you do."

The detective smiled proudly. "What can I say? I know lots about lots of things."

I knew they were bantering to get me to stop thinking about today.

It wasn't working very well.

"Does Officer DeWeise have any kids?" I asked.

DJ sighed and Detective Masterson answered me. "Yes, Kate. He's got two girls."

I nodded, picking at my cuticles, trying to swallow despite the huge gaping hole in my gut. "How old are they?" I asked quietly, trying to imagine what I would be thinking if my dad had been shot and was in the hospital.

"Nine and six." Then the detective straightened. "Kate, look at me."

I bit my lip and looked up at him.

"It's not your fault, Kate. Do you hear me?"

I nodded, but we both knew it was my fault. If I hadn't drawn John X, then those two girls wouldn't be scared for their dad tonight.

"Now," Detective Masterson said, "I want you to stop thinking about it and try to focus on something else."

"Do you believe in heaven?" I asked.

The detective didn't hesitate. "Yes, Kate, I do."

"What do you think it's like?" I remembered what Detective

Masterson told my dad about God. I was willing to bet that his view of heaven was a lot different than my parents'.

He took a deep breath. "I believe that heaven is where God resides, and it's where people who have trusted Jesus as their savior go after death."

Good solid churchy answer. "Do you think there are harps there?" I asked.

Detective Masterson grinned. "As in, are we playing them? No, I don't think we spend eternity playing harps. Or sitting on clouds. Or wearing diapers."

I wrinkled my nose at the last one. "What?"

"All those little angels sitting on a cloud playing harps and wearing a cloth diaper? Yeah, that's not a good view of heaven."

DJ had been very quiet through this whole conversation, so I turned and looked at him. "What do you think?" I asked him.

He shrugged. "I'm still trying to figure that out." Then he stopped talking and just watched the TV, where Ryan was now informing America that Usher was planning a new tour involving a few stops in Dallas, Austin, and Memphis.

"My mom thinks it's a subconscious thing and after we die, we just sort of remember and relive our previous life," I said.

Detective Masterson nodded. "I've heard that one before. So when does that end?"

"When does what end?"

"The remembering. When do you just stop having things to remember?"

I hadn't thought about that before. "I don't know."

We were all quiet for a minute. Now they were showing a music video of Usher. I decided that Usher was a fairly decent dancer.

I couldn't dance. My father was an engineer, so I had a good excuse. But still. I could never hope to have a future on *Dancing with the Stars*.

Not that I would want to wear any of the outfits they had to wear anyway. I have a thing about too many glittery sequins.

Mom and Dad had been talking in their room since we got home. I hadn't heard their door open, so I assumed they were still in there. Lolly still had her head planted squarely on my lap, and I was lazily drawing circles on the top of her head.

"So," I said.

"So," DJ parroted.

"School tomorrow." I looked at the detective. "You're coming too?"

He nodded and rocked in his chair. "Appears that way."

"I've got art first," I told him.

"Mm," he said, suddenly very interested in Usher's music video.

I looked at DJ, who just smiled at me. He leaned over a little closer. "I'll bet you ten bucks that he wears his blue polo shirt tomorrow," he whispered.

"What's with the blue polo?" I whispered back.

DJ opened his mouth to answer but got cut off. "I can hear you both, you do realize," Detective Masterson said grouchily.

"Okay. What's with the blue polo?" I asked him.

Detective Masterson glared at DJ. "I have no idea what you are talking about," he said, icily.

"He thinks he looks particularly nice in blue," DJ told me, no longer bothering to whisper.

I grinned. Especially when the detective blushed.

Bright red.

"I," he sputtered. "I do not think I look better in blue!"

"Sure you do," DJ said, easily. "It brings out your eyes, remember? Plus, if you wear navy, it's got the added bonus of being rather slimming as well, which we both know you need."

I was laughing by this point, and the detective picked up a throw pillow from the couch and chucked it at DJ, who ducked behind me. He didn't end up needing to duck — Detective Masterson had really lousy aim.

Mom and Dad walked out at that point. "What is going on here?" Mom asked, hands on her hips. "That pillow was a wedding gift. My great-aunt Charlotte crocheted that pillow. Are you pre-pared to replace it?" she lectured Detective Masterson.

He shook his head, instantly contrite. "No, ma'am. I'm sorry, ma'am."

"Good." She narrowed her eyes at DJ, who immediately stopped snickering.

"Sorry, ma'am."

"Thank you. You boys go wash up for dinner. And Kate? I could use your help."

I nodded and followed her into the kitchen while Detective Masterson and DJ went to wash their hands.

"Sheesh, all men are the same, Kate. They never grow up," Mom said, rinsing her hands in the kitchen sink. "Isn't that right, Dale?" she asked Dad.

Dad, who appeared to be in a better mood after having some time to cool off, nodded. "It's true, Kate. Marry wisely."

I wanted to remind my parents that I was sixteen and in no hurry to get married, but they continued on talking.

"Take Mike for example," Mom said, pulling a head of lettuce out of the fridge and handing it to me. "Mike is fairly mature for being a male, but he will probably never remember to call his wife when he's on his way home for dinner."

I thought that as long as Mike continued to exist as the Mike we all knew he probably would never get married. Maybe that's why my parents were already bringing up the *M*-word with me. They wanted grandkids.

Mom gave me a cutting board and a knife. "We're making taco salad. Chop the lettuce into small pieces," she said.

The police department had been giving Mom a grocery stipend for having DJ living with us. I imagine they'd increase it now that Detective Masterson was going to be here full-time as well.

I started chopping.

Dad sat at the kitchen table with the newspaper spread in front of him, since he didn't really get a chance to read it earlier today, what with church and all.

I sighed. It was still the same day that I'd seen Not-So-Silent Justin at South Woodhaven Falls First Baptist Church. It seemed like a long, long time ago.

"Look at this," Dad said, pointing to the sports section. Mom was busy browning two pounds of ground beef, and I was holding a sharp blade in my hand, so I was going to assume that he meant "listen to this."

And apparently he did mean that, because he started telling us about it. "There's some freshman kid at the high school who has started playing basketball and the guy is like six foot seven or something already." Dad shook his head and looked at me, whistling. "Can you imagine?"

"Yeah. That's Pete Somebody. He's only six foot seven?" I'd seen him in the hallways and always felt really bad for him. He looked like he'd rather be anywhere but surrounded by a school full of people who were mostly six feet and under. I tried not to stand by him. He made me feel abnormally short.

"I guess he's supposed to be really good. This says he scored thirty-one points and made seventeen free throws in the last game against one of Franklin County's high schools."

Sometimes I think Dad forgets that Mom and I were two girls who really didn't care too much for sports.

And by didn't care too much, I mean we were basically clueless. A free throw, to me, was something that you got at Peter Piper's Pizza in St. Louis at that ski ball game that I loved. Hit ten one-hundred-pointers in a row and you got a free throw. And a huge stack of tickets to redeem for cheap, made-in-China trinkets.

"Hmm," Mom said, stirring the meat. "That's neat, dear."

"What are we talking about?" DJ asked, coming into the kitchen and followed by Detective Masterson.

"Pete Walker, the six-foot-seven freshman at SWF High," Dad said, pointing out the article to them.

DJ nodded. "I heard about him. He's supposed to be really good. Especially at defense."

Dad looked so excited to have someone who cared about sports in the kitchen. The three of them started talking basketball and didn't finish until Mom and I were setting the bowls of chopped lettuce, steaming ground beef, diced tomatoes, onions, grated cheddar cheese, salsa, sour cream, and guacamole in front of them.

Mom brought over a bag of tortilla chips and we all sat down, pulling in an extra chair for Detective Masterson.

I looked around the table.

We'd gone from three people to five in a week. How much were we going to grow by next weekend?

Chapter Twelve

MONDAY MORNING AND THE CRISPIX WERE WINNING THE battle of sogginess.

I was tiredly fishing around for them in the bowl. I'd barely slept at all the night before, and when I did sleep, I kept seeing John X on the side of the street during the parade. He was holding a gun, and he kept laughing as he fired it. Then I'd see the bloodstain on the backseat of the convertible, only instead of Officer DeWeise getting hit, I would look down and see a big, round cannonball hole in my stomach. I would walk into the hospital and they would look at the huge hole in my stomach, just shake their heads, and hand me a pillow to try and shove into the gaping wound.

I'd wake up in a panic with my pillow clutched to my gut.

I chased another Crispix around in my bowl and caught it. It had no crunch left.

Yuck.

Dad looked over at me. "You understand that you are to go nowhere, I repeat *nowhere*, without the policemen. Is that understood?"

"Yes, sir," I yawned.

"And I'd prefer if you didn't even talk to anyone. Go to school, turn in your homework, do your classes, and come straight home. *Straight* home."

Suddenly, Dad had a fondness for stressed words, I guess. That and repeating things.

Mom came in, trying to put her earrings in. "Kate Carter, you listen to what your father says, and if you so much as even *think* something isn't right, you leave school right away with DJ and Detective Masterson. Agreed?" she asked sternly.

I nodded. "Agreed." Lots of italicized words in this house this morning.

"Good." She looked at the clock. "I have to run. You be safe at school." She kissed Dad good-bye and ran out the door, grabbing her briefcase as she went.

Dad and I left a few minutes later. DJ drove me to school in the black Tahoe. I rode in the backseat. I was going to forget how to drive if this kept up too much longer. I hadn't been behind the wheel since my drawing of John X had been flashed all over the news.

Detective Masterson was in the passenger seat and, yes, he was wearing the blue polo.

"Nice shirt," I told him as we pulled into the school parking lot. "Brings out your eyes."

Detective Masterson just glared darkly at DJ. "Thank you, Kate," he bit out.

DJ parked the Tahoe in the parking lot and then they walked with me into the school, one on each side of me. I was starting to feel like a prisoner. All I needed was one of those fashionable orange jumpsuits and an ankle-bracelet tracking device.

Art was up first and Miss Yeager was busy writing the assignment on the whiteboard when we walked in. She looked over and blushed a pretty shade of pink when she saw Detective Masterson.

"Oh, uh, hi!" she stumbled around.

The detective just smiled back at her, but there was a telltale flush to his face as well. I grinned over at DJ and then sat at my empty table.

DJ was much too punctual for Miss Yeager's class. No one

showed up in here until the bell was on its last chime over the intercom.

Not-So-Silent Justin came walking in right then and sat next to me at the table. He smiled at me but said nothing. Just pulled his sketchpad from his bag and found the pencils he'd rubber-banded together and sat there quietly at the table.

Okay, what was this?

I just looked at him. "Justin?" I said finally.

He looked back at me.

"You're doing it again."

He frowned.

"Not talking? Remember? I thought you were, like, stricken mute until we saw each other yesterday morning at church."

He made a noise deep in the back of his throat. "I'm not mute," he said, so quietly I had to lean forward to hear what he was saying.

"Then why don't you talk at school?" I asked.

He shrugged. "I don't have much to say here."

I just looked at him.

"But that does remind me, are you okay? I heard you had a rough afternoon," he said. He leaned forward. "Is the other cop okay?"

I nodded. DJ had talked to Officer DeWeise that morning and everything seemed to be healing as it was supposed to be. The hospital had even told him that if he continued feeling okay, he might be able to check out of the hospital tomorrow and finish recuperating at home.

"And you're okay?" Justin said.

"I'm fine," I said robotically, sort of like when I went to the doctor's office for my yearly checkup. Mom always said that I could have rubella and whooping cough, and I'd still croak out that I was fine.

Sometimes, it was better not to think about what was wrong. If you could forget, then everything would be okay again. So I was trying to forget yesterday.

DJ found an extra chair and sat down a couple of feet behind me while the detective stood in the back.

I felt like I was on display.

The bell rang and kids flooded into the art room. Allison Northing sat down next to me.

"Oh my *gosh*, Kate! You were *totally* shot at!" she screeched.

I winced from the decibel level she reached. That and the fact that I'd been trying to forget about it.

"It was *just* like one of those action movies my brother likes to watch!" Allison continued, oblivious to my pained expression, I guess.

"I'd rather not talk—" I started, but it was for no good. She kept on.

"There was a gun, someone got shot for you, you just *happened* to be reaching into the backseat. I mean … *oh my gosh!*"

"Yeah, Allison, we could stop talking about—"

"I mean, someone was *shot* yesterday. Right next to you! I mean, the guy was probably aiming for *you*." She gasped. "Doesn't that, like, completely freak you out?"

I just looked at her, my gut twisting.

"Hey, I think we're starting, Allison," Justin said suddenly.

That shut her up completely. She stared at Justin, mouth open, eyes wide. He calmly turned and faced the front.

"All right, class!" Miss Yeager said loudly as everyone pulled out their sketchpads and pencils.

Allison elbowed me in the ribs. "Dude, did you *hear* that? Justin just spoke to me!"

"Allison?" Miss Yeager said, the warning in her voice.

Allison nodded.

"All right, I need everyone's menus from Friday and then we'll get started on today's lesson."

There was a loud rustling of papers as everyone dug their menus from their backpack. I'd finished mine on Saturday and I was very glad I had. There was no way I would have been able to concentrate on it last night.

Jailbird's Café looked like a rather charming place. There were pictures of men in striped black-and-white pajamas, carrying balls-and-chains, and lots of little touches like handcuffs around all the menu titles.

Miss Yeager gathered our menus and then turned to the whiteboard. She'd drawn a picture of the Froot Loops toucan on there.

"Anyone recognize this guy?" she asked.

"Toucan Sam," we all said dutifully.

"Very good. And welcome to another fascinating career in the art field, commercial art."

She continued to talk about how artists were paid to create characters such as Toucan Sam for different brands.

Again, I had trouble concentrating. I kept thinking about what Allison had said.

"The guy was probably aiming for you."

Miss Yeager was talking and drawing the Trix rabbit on the board, but I didn't hear a word of what she was saying.

Aiming for you.

The day passed by very slowly. Everyone I passed in the hallway was taking care to walk at least thirty feet away from me. I felt like I'd been diagnosed with scurvy or something. No longer were people yelling out my name in adoration.

Now they whispered it as I passed.

"There's Kate Carter," I heard one guy hiss to another. "She got shot at yesterday. Put a cop in the hospital."

I tried to just stare straight ahead and I tried even harder to not listen, but it was hard when the halls became so quiet I heard the rattling of people's teeth against their orthodontia whenever I stepped outside the classroom.

DJ and the detective were never more than a few inches away, but it didn't make me feel any less alone. Even Maddy wasn't at school today. She'd texted me this morning saying she'd woken up with white patches on her tonsils, and her mother was making her go to the doctor before she had to get her throat amputated.

I texted back that she probably just had tonsillitis, and people lived from that every day without the threat of amputation. But Maddy's mom is something of a hypochondriac, and any time Maddy got even a case of the sniffles, she was immediately marched to the doctor in case it was something serious like the German measles instead of the common cold.

Sometimes I wondered if being a hypochondriac made you more susceptible to diseases. Everyone I knew who was constantly freaking out about getting sick and rubbing their hands with that sticky goopy stuff was always getting sick. So either the goopy stuff wasn't working or their immune systems were so overprotected that they weren't even sure what to do with a germ anymore.

We drove home from school in silence. Detective Masterson kept looking in the rearview mirror at me with a worried look on his face. DJ kept clearing his throat like he was going to say something, and then he'd stop before he did.

Detective Masterson finally spoke as we turned the corner onto my street.

"You okay, Kate?"

"I'm fine." There it was again.

"You seem kind of…" He let his voice trail off and shrugged as he parked in my driveway. For once, there weren't any reporters around.

I felt a huge wave of relief crash over my shoulders at that fact.

"I'm fine," I said again. "I'm just tired."

"You definitely didn't sleep very well," Detective Masterson said. He turned in his seat and looked at me. "Nightmares?"

I hated having to leave my door open at night. This was getting embarrassing.

I shrugged, which was my way of saying, "Yes, but I don't want to talk about it." I guess he picked up on the clue, because he unbuckled and hopped out of the car, opening the back door for me.

"You've got lots of homework," DJ said. "I'd forgotten how much homework high school teachers give."

"Keeps kids off the streets," Detective Masterson said as we walked inside.

The detective was going to be one of those fathers who tried to give his kids more homework than was needed just so they were doing something productive. I know this because my dad has said many times that if teachers were stricter with homework, we'd have far fewer juvenile delinquents in prison these days.

I'd felt the need to point out that the definition of juvenile delinquent was someone who just didn't care regardless, and if they didn't care when there was less homework, what made Dad think that they would care if there was more?

Which is when Dad had pulled out a stack of his college math textbooks for me in case I ever got bored.

I tried very hard to look busy around Dad most of the time.

I took my books to the kitchen table and tried to focus on my algebra homework. We were learning about how x and imaginary numbers worked together.

I hated math. Was I ever going to use imaginary numbers in any career I picked? No. There was zero point to me learning this.

"How's it going?" DJ asked, walking into the kitchen a minute later.

I shrugged. I was in the middle of finding x and it was just better if I did it robotically instead of thinking too much about that sentence.

"Finding X" had too many other meanings for me right now.

"I just got off the phone with Officer DeWeise," DJ said.

I looked up at him. "Is he okay?"

DJ nodded. "He'll be fine. The doctors told him that everything is looking really good."

I breathed a sigh of relief. "Good."

"Yep." He pulled a pear from the fridge and started cutting it into slices.

I looked back down at the page in my math book that I was working on.

Find X *in the following problems.*

I slammed the book shut.

Tuesday and Wednesday passed by like they were on repeat from Monday. I went to school, everyone pointed and whispered about me in the hallway, I turned in homework, Miss Yeager and Detective Masterson blushed at each other but didn't talk, and Justin said "hi" twice and that was it.

Every night, I'd watched the news and every night, Ted Deffle at KCL would tell some new shocking story about John X's life before prison. New people who knew him were coming forward and all of them couldn't believe he was a serial killer.

"Why, I would have left my kids with him while I ran to the grocery store for milk," one lady from Franklin county said on Wednesday night's news.

Detective Masterson had said that the police there should just go ahead and write her info down because she was likely going to be calling in a missing child's report sometime in the near future.

Thursday didn't start that much differently.

The school again went painfully quiet when I walked in the doors. I hadn't decided if it was because they were worried about being shot if they got into near proximity of me or if it was the two very obvious, despite their attempts at plain clothes, cops next to me.

Maddy, though, was back on Thursday.

She came hustling over, shoving her backpack onto one shoulder. "Kate, I'm so glad you're here," she whispered.

"What's with all the whispering?" I asked. "How come no one is talking in a normal-toned voice anymore?"

She gave me a *duh* look. "Because. No one wants to get shot."

I sighed.

"Anyway, I'm glad you're here. I was talking to Tyler and he said that he heard that John X had a cousin named Bridget who goes to this school."

Detective Masterson and DJ exchanged a look, and I saw the detective pull his phone from his pocket and start texting someone.

"Wait — Tyler?" I asked.

She nodded.

"As in the same Tyler who broke your heart all of a week ago?"

"We're back together," she announced, flashing a big smile. "He apologized. He said that he was totally in the wrong, and he never meant to hurt me."

Fabulous. I managed a smile. "Great, Maddy. That's great." I wished I could have been more excited, but now I simply got to watch the dramatic breakup again sometime in the future. Tyler really was a big jerk. I never could see what made Maddy so in love with him. He treated her like garbage.

"Thanks!" she said all perkily. We passed by a group of football players who were gathered in the hall, and Tyler immediately came over.

"Oh, hi, Kate," he said, slinging his arm around Maddy. "And you guys must be the undercover cops." His voice dropped a couple of decibel levels. "Do you really think someone will try to shoot Kate here?"

A real winner, that Tyler. Always had the nicest thing to say and the most perfect time to say it.

Detective Masterson frowned at Tyler — he didn't even bother answering him. We stopped outside the art classroom.

"Well. Anyway. See you later, Kate."

Tyler left and Maddy rolled her eyes. "I don't know why he asked that." She looked at the policemen. "He's really not that callous most of the time."

Oh, he really was. But I didn't say anything.

"So, Kate, can I come study with you afterwards today?"

I nodded. "Sure." Honestly, I'd missed Maddy's incessant chatting over the noise of Ryan Seacrest while I was trying to do my homework. "How are the tonsils?"

She waved her hand. "Oh, they're fine. The doctor said that I'd probably have to get them out sometime this year, but I'm going to wait until summer to do it so I don't have to miss a bunch of school. He said that I probably should have had them out when I was a kid. Want to see them?"

I winced. "No, thanks." Looking in people's mouths was not a favorite pastime of mine. Dentistry was out as far as a future career choice.

She nodded. "All right then. I'll see you after school. Bye!" She waved and left, running down the hall to make her first class on time.

"Charming friend," Detective Masterson said under his breath.

"Equally charming boyfriend." DJ nodded.

"Hey," I said. "Maddy is my best friend, so please be nice to her."

Detective Masterson shrugged. "I'll be nice."

We pushed through the door to art class, and there were only six other people in there as the bell rang. I frowned and looked back into the hallway. Usually, there are around fifteen more kids in my class.

Miss Yeager turned from the board and looked at all of us. "Good morning, everyone," she said.

I sat down next to Justin and Allison and looked around. I raised my hand.

"Yes, Kate?"

"Where is everyone today?"

Miss Yeager tried to hide a wince in my direction, but then I understood.

"Oh," I said, shaking my head slightly. "I get it. Never mind."

Allison elbowed me in the ribcage. "I heard that all these moms had this meeting last night because they think that it puts all their kids in danger for you to be here, and so they pulled all their kids out of school," she whispered.

"Allison!" Miss Yeager said sharply. "Now is not the time."

She shrugged at Miss Yeager and then pulled her pencils out of her backpack, looking at me. "I'm just saying what I heard."

I sat there quietly in my chair, facing the whiteboard and trying not to look around at all the empty seats. The moms panicked? They had a meeting? I was preventing fourteen kids from coming to school today?

This was getting to be too much. Didn't they realize that's why Detective Masterson and DJ were here?

Miss Yeager sent an apologetic look my direction and started the lesson. It was just a review, so I started to drift off in the midst of it.

My stomach was cramping. I'd always been the girl that no one even noticed, and now, everyone noticed me. Everyone was scared to stand close to me.

I felt like a walking time bomb.

Miss Yeager finished class right as the bell rang. "Kate, hold on a minute please," she said over the clanging. The rest of the class gathered their stuff and left.

Justin sent me a half-smile as he packed his backpack. "Chin up," he whispered, and then left.

Miss Yeager came over and sat down in Allison's vacated chair. "You are not the cause of this," she said.

"Come on, Miss Yeager," I said. I was so tired of people telling me this was not my fault. It was my fault. If I hadn't drawn John X, then I never would have caused Officer DeWeise to get shot or have part of the school staying home out of fear.

"Kate, people get scared over situations that they don't need to be scared about," Miss Yeager said.

I just sighed at her and the two policemen standing next to us. "They don't need to be scared about this? I've got two cops following me around like I'm the President's daughter, I've gotten a cop with a wife and two kids shot and put in the hospital, I can't sleep at night because of the nightmares, and my mother has stopped buying me Crispix because she saw me tracing the x in the title yesterday." I let my breath out.

Miss Yeager reached over and rubbed my shoulder. "I'm so sorry, Kate. This is all because of me and a stupid idea I had. I'm so sorry."

"If it's any consolation," Detective Masterson said, "people still think you're a hero, Kate. Those people who were waiting for vindication for the women who died have gotten it. And John X will never be released from prison."

"Apparently, he doesn't need to be, and people still get shot," I said bitterly. I slammed my hands down on the table. "You know what? I think I'm going to go home for the rest of today."

I stood, grabbed my backpack, and left. Detective Masterson and DJ hurried to keep up with me as I marched out of the school and to the black Tahoe.

"Kate. Kate, slow down," DJ said, grabbing my forearm. "Are you sure you don't want to stay for the rest of the day?"

"What's the point? So I can see all the rest of the empty tables at school? No thanks. Everyone wishes I would just stay home anyway."

Detective Masterson unlocked the Tahoe, and I climbed in. It was a quiet drive home.

DJ parked in the driveway, and we walked to the front porch. There sat three more bouquets on the front porch. I was willing to bet that at least one was from the news crew at KCL who was still begging for an interview. We each grabbed one and went inside.

I set my bouquet on the kitchen counter next to the other two. They were pretty. Daisies, roses, tulips ... it looked like a funeral had happened in our house, because these were everywhere.

I was beginning to hate the smell of flowers.

I yanked the notes from the bouquets.

Dear Kate, thank you for your selfless contribution to society ...

Kate, we are so grateful for such patriots in America ...

Dear Kate, if you could please call our newsroom at 555 – 3422, we'd love to have you on our show ...

The last one was from KCL. The first two were signed from Phyllis in St. Louis and the Kleins in Springfield, Missouri.

I put all the notes in the teetering stack of notecards on the kitchen counter and left the flowers where they were. One thing was sure — South Woodhaven Falls florists had been reaping the benefit from my actions.

They were about the only ones who were.

It was only ten o'clock in the morning, and I had no idea what to do with the rest of the day. I didn't have any homework, since I'd skipped out on classes. Mom and Dad were both at work for the remainder of the day.

It was just me and the cops.

Two men and a high school dropout.

Wasn't that the name of a movie?

I wondered if skipping school today classified me as a juvenile delinquent. I'd have to ask Dad later tonight.

"So," DJ said, joining me in the kitchen. "What do you want to do for the rest of today?"

I shrugged. "I don't know." Usually, when I was completely bored, I would go to my room and draw for hours.

I was starting to hate drawing. Anytime I sat down to sketch, the only face I saw was John X's.

Detective Masterson came into the kitchen, holding his cell phone. "Guess what?" he said, though I wasn't sure if it was directed to me or DJ.

Judging by DJ's lack of a response, he didn't know whom the question was for either.

Detective Masterson didn't bother to wait for one of us to answer. "There was a witness at the parade."

DJ immediately straightened. "Witness? Someone saw the shooter?"

"Apparently, they saw them clear as day. They've just been too scared to come forward with that information."

They both exchanged a look for a minute and then both turned to me. I was fishing in the pantry for the stash of M&M's Dad and I had hid weeks ago. I could feel their stares on my back.

I winced. "No," I said, knowing what was coming.

"Kate," Detective Masterson started.

I found the bag of M&M's and tore into it. "I don't want to. Have the real artist guy do it."

Detective Masterson let out a single, staccato laugh. "Ha! Like that would help us at all. Larry's sketches have only gotten us leads for nice old ladies buying their grandbabies teething rings. We've never caught the person we were looking for off of Larry's sketches."

"Seems like it's time to hire a new sketch artist then," I said, popping a handful of M&M's into my mouth. "And one who's legal to vote," I said around the colored globs of chocolate, since both of them opened their mouths at the same time.

"Kate," DJ said again. "If we find this guy, maybe we can get him to talk. We can find out if there are more people after you. We can find out how many more friends John X has."

I chewed in silence, looking at them and then at the floral shop in my house. Then I thought about Officer DeWeise and his two kids waiting at home for their daddy. And how my dad's voice cracked when he was talking about me staying protected.

It made sense. If we caught the guy who shot at me during the parade, maybe he was the last of my worries. Maybe he was John X's only friend, and maybe if they were stuck in prison together they'd only get to reminisce about the good old days of killing innocent women instead of continuing to do it.

Maybe.

I looked again at the flowers decorating our entire house. From the kitchen, I could count at least twenty-two bouquets scattered around our house. That didn't count the handful that were upstairs. Mom said we were going to need to start giving them out to the neighbors.

About half of them were from KCL, but the other half were all families and couples and women who had written some really sweet thank-you cards.

I was scared to leave my house for fear of John X, one woman had written. *Thank you for giving me my freedom back.*

Now if only I could find a bit of that freedom as well.

I sighed and swallowed and looked at the two policemen in front of me.

"Fine." I said it quietly, but both of them reacted like a firework had exploded.

"Great!" Detective Masterson said, doing a fabulous impression of Tony the Tiger. "I'll call Deputy Slalom right now." He immediately left, dialing as he went.

"Awesome," DJ said, patting my shoulder. "I knew we could count on you, Kate."

Detective Masterson appeared back in the kitchen seconds later. "We're going to the station right now," he said. "Think you should call your parents? Don't forget the code we talked about."

I nodded. I picked up our house phone and dialed my mom's work first.

"Hello, Claire Carter's office." Madge, Mom's ancient secretary, answered the phone.

"Hi, it's Kate."

"One moment."

A second later, my mom answered. "Kate? Honey, is everything okay?"

"Just wanted to be sure you remembered my dentist appointment was today," I told her, nodding at the policemen. We weren't supposed to say exactly where we were going, just in case.

I felt like I was in one of those spy movies.

Only I felt like I should be cooler. I felt a little like Steve Carell's character in *Get Smart*. Kind of goofy.

Mom cleared her throat. "Okay, honey. Thanks for reminding me."

So now Mom knew that I was not at school, I was going to the police station, and everything was fine.

"Okay. Bye, Mom."

"Love you, Katie-Kin."

I paused, holding the phone with both hands. "I love you too, Mom."

Dad didn't take it quite as easily. "The dentist?" he repeated. "Why in the world are you going to the dentist right now? Shouldn't you be in school?"

He either didn't remember the code or was trying to find out why I was going to the police station, but we hadn't discussed the code past the dentist part.

"Well, I, uh, have a cavity, I think," I said, around a mouthful of M&M's. "It's kind of painful, so I called the dentist. They said to come on over, and they'd take a look at it. It's pretty urgent, Dad."

Then it clicked.

"Oh," Dad said, suddenly. "Right. Well, then you should probably go in."

"Yep. I'm on my way there."

"Okay. Well. Buckle your seatbelt." *Bring the cops.*

"Always, Dad. Love you."

"Love you back."

I nodded to DJ and Detective Masterson. "Okay. Let's go."

Chapter Thirteen

I FOUND IT KIND OF SAD THAT THE POLICE STATION LOOKED so familiar. Same desks, same cubicles. Same feeling of being in an office hawking paper supplies instead of a place dedicated to upholding the law.

Deputy Slalom was waiting for us when we got there. He was wearing his typical outfit of a button-down, long-sleeve shirt and a tie. This time, he was still wearing his jacket.

Must have been a slow day.

"Hi, Kate," Deputy Slalom said, holding open the door to one of the conference rooms. "Glad you were able to come."

I'd never heard a policeman excited about a high school student skipping classes, but things have been a little weird lately.

I nodded. "I brought my pencils," I said, holding up a handful of pencils rubber-banded together. I didn't bring my sketchpad. I figured surely the police station had paper.

Then again, with all the city and county budget cuts that have been happening constantly, maybe that wasn't a good assumption.

Deputy Slalom showed me into the conference room and DJ followed me. Detective Masterson went to go check his office.

There was a huge sketchpad set up on an easel in the room, as well as a couple of chairs, two tables, a box of facial tissues, a huge binder, and a water dispenser.

I'd never drawn on an easel before. Miss Yeager didn't have the money to buy easels for everyone in art class, so we got to draw on the table. And at home, I always drew on my desk.

I've heard it's better for your wrist if you use an easel, but since I've never practiced on one, I'm not sure if I could draw as well.

"Make yourself comfortable," Deputy Slalom said to me. He patted DJ on the shoulder. "And feel free to take a break, if you want. I'm going to hang out in here for a few minutes."

DJ nodded and looked at me. "You okay?" he asked.

"Go take a break," I said, filling a paper cup with water. "I'm fine."

DJ left.

Deputy Slalom nodded to the chair next to the easel. "The witness is on her way in. Let me explain a little about how this works."

I sat down and took the rubber band off my pencils. Deputy Slalom sat in the chair opposite me.

"We don't give out the witness's last name," he started. "But this woman's first name is Carol. She was at the parade with her three kids when she saw the shooting."

"How old is she?" I asked.

"Probably forty. Maybe forty-five. With all these new creams women are putting on their faces, it's getting harder to tell." Deputy Slalom nodded to the huge binder. "In that book are nearly a thousand different facial components. Everything from noses, ears, and moles. Our former sketch artist liked to use it to try and draw out the memory from the witness."

Former sketch artist. I sighed. Poor Larry.

I picked up the heavy binder and flipped through about ten pages of eyebrows before even I was confused at what I was looking at. They started looking more and more like dead centipedes.

If I were asked to describe someone after looking at one thousand different facial features, I don't think I'd even be able to accurately describe my mother, much less someone I'd seen for barely a minute.

No wonder Larry's sketches always came out wrong.

"Do I have to use this?" I asked, closing the binder.

Deputy Slalom shook his head. "You can do whatever you want to. Normally, I wouldn't give that much freedom to an artist, but considering how much that sketch of John X was picture quality, who am I to judge your methods?"

There was a rap on the door and a policeman I hadn't met stuck his head in. "She's here, boss."

"Send her in," Deputy Slalom said, standing.

A short woman with cropped brown hair walked in, clutching her purse nervously. She didn't wear a lot of makeup, just some eyeliner and mascara as far as I could tell. Her cheeks were flushed though.

I was hoping it was from the nerves and not the flu. Getting sick right now wasn't a high priority for me.

"Hi, Carol. Thank you for coming in," Deputy Slalom said in a nice, soothing voice. He ushered her in and had her sit in the chair opposite me.

She just stared at me. "You're okay?" she said quietly, in a sweet Southern accent.

I nodded. "I'm okay."

"And the policeman who was shot?"

I looked at Deputy Slalom, imagining he had the more up-to-date information.

"He was discharged today," he said. "A couple of cracked ribs and a few stitches. You have to love bulletproof vests," he said, lightly. I knew he was trying to lessen Carol's anxiety, but I think just the sight of me was enough to send her back into a fit.

She only nodded.

"Carol, Kate here is going to draw what you remember. Okay? You two take as much time as you need, and let us know if we can get you anything."

Deputy Slalom's secretary brought in a plate full of cookies, brownies, and fruit then. "Here you go, ladies," she said, setting it on the table in between us.

Deputy Slalom looked at me. "You good?"

I nodded.

"Okay. Let me know if you need anything. I'll send Kent in here in a minute."

He left.

The room was very quiet. Carol was alternating between staring at me, the easel, and the plate of food.

I was trying to figure out what to do next.

"So, uh," I started strongly, just like my speech teacher loved. "Um, what do you do?"

Carol blinked and looked away from the cookies and up to my face. "I'm sorry, what?"

"What do you do for a job?"

"I'm a stay-at-home mom."

I nodded. "That's neat." Evidently, her daughters don't have to worry about going on imaginary adventures like that story about the little kid who was home too much by herself. "How old are your kids?"

She took a deep breath, relaxing her iron grip on her purse slightly. "Nine, seven, and four. The older two are at school right now. The baby is with my husband." She dug into her purse and pulled out a wallet-sized photo. There was a huge Christmas tree in the background and a bunch of little blonde girls, a blond man, and Carol in the picture.

"Aw, they are cute," I said, taking the picture and staring at it for the appropriate amount of time before handing it back.

"Thanks." She managed a small smile at me. "If you don't mind me asking, how old are you?"

"Sixteen," I said.

"Wow," she breathed. "You are young."

There are only a few statements that put a complete end to a conversation, but that is one of them. What was I supposed to say to that? Yes, I am? No, not really?

I cleared my throat. "So, um, I'm actually not sure why they wanted me to come draw for you, but I'm trying to do anything I can to help this investigation," I said.

She nodded. "I'm sorry it took me so long to come forward. My girls …" She looked away and shook her head. "Well. You understand."

I didn't, but I nodded like I did. "Did your girls …" I winced. "Did they see …?"

She shook her head immediately. "No, they were with their father. I was trying to find the stand with those corn dogs."

Oh, the corn dogs. Which I hadn't tasted.

"Anyway, I couldn't find the stand and I was over on the side of the street, and there were a bunch of people cheering for you, so I walked over to get a better look at you."

"Did you ever get one?" I asked.

She shrugged. "There was a tall man in front of me, so I kind of caught a side profile of you."

I shook my head. "No, I meant, did you ever get a corn dog?"

A tiny smile crossed her face. "No. The parade was canceled."

"Sorry about that."

"Me too."

She looked more at ease. She even set her purse on the floor instead of clutching it tightly in her lap.

I arched my back in the uncomfortable, hard plastic chair. I wasn't sure what to do at this point. When I sketched John X, Miss Yeager just read me a long description of what he looked like. I didn't have to do the probing thing.

It felt weird asking a woman I barely knew a million questions, though. Sort of rude, even.

"What are your daughter's names?" I asked, just trying to get to know her better.

"Meghan, Rachel, and Elise," she said.

"Pretty." I smiled.

"Do you have any siblings, Kate?"

I nodded. "I have a brother. He's not around very much. He's in college in California. He's going to be an engineer, so he can't take very much time off school." I shrug. "We don't talk much."

She nodded, knowingly. "I have a brother like that. He lives in Maine and we never talk unless I'm in labor."

"You had a long stretch of not talking then, between your second and third girl," I said. "Is he an engineer too?"

She laughed. "No, he's working as a technical support something or another. He's in charge of a bunch of wires, basically."

"Do you want a cookie?" I asked, pointing to the tray. I wasn't starving, but breakfast had been early morning and it was nearing eleven thirty. Almost lunchtime. I pulled a chocolate chip cookie off the plate and Carol picked a brownie.

"I really don't need this," she fretted, rubbing a hand on her hip.

I tried very hard not to roll my eyes. All adult women are the exact same. I was just thrilled that there was real — or fake, according to my mother — sugar in the cookies. I hadn't had a real chocolate chip cookie for far too long.

"Careful," Carol said, smiling at me. "You'll worry about it too."

Apparently I wasn't as good at hiding the eye roll as I thought I was.

We talked about nothing and everything for the next thirty minutes. She grew up in Arkansas, which explained the accent, married her husband in Georgia, and then moved to South Woodhaven Falls when her husband got a job in the St. Louis outskirts.

"I hate that he commutes so far to work every day, but I love living in a small town," she said. "It's so good for the girls."

We finally got back around to the parade after noon.

"I guess I first noticed him because he was wearing a hooded sweatshirt and had the hood on," she said, pulling a pineapple chunk from the tray. "And it was very sunny, you remember. And warm. You definitely did not need a hood on."

I looked away from Carol nibbling on the pineapple so I could start imagining the man.

"He wasn't very tall," she continued. "He was probably close to Steve's height." Steve was Carol's husband. She'd already told me he was five-eight and therefore had solidified their daughters' shortness forever.

"And he was wearing sunglasses," she said. "Those kind that look like something Tom Cruise would wear in *Top Gun*. Wait, is that too old of a reference for you?"

I grinned. "My mom loves *Top Gun*."

"Meg Ryan was adorable in that movie."

I nodded.

She talked for the next hour and I listened carefully. The man she'd seen had what looked like short brown hair under the hood, the aviator sunglasses, a five o'clock shadow, and a sharp chin. She hadn't seen his ears, but he had nice cheekbones.

"He was probably around thirty, I'd guess," she said.

I still hadn't drawn anything. There was no point to drawing something I'd only have to erase later.

"How about his nose? His lips? Is Elise excited to start kindergarten?" I prodded her with questions about the man and about her family whenever she stopped talking.

Detective Masterson came in and out during the meeting, and when he came in at one, he brought hamburgers.

At two, I picked up my pencil and pulled the sketchpad off the easel. Carol was still talking about how she'd kind of thought something shifty was going on with the man.

"He kept looking back and forth and back and forth," she said. "And he kept both of his hands in the front pockets of his sweatshirt. Like I said, it was much too warm to be wearing something like that."

I started drawing. I closed my eyes and saw the face of the man she had described. But it's not just physical description that mattered. There were indefinable qualities that played into how someone looked. How they acted, what they lived through.

I worked on the sketch for almost an hour. Carol would lean over and look at it and make a few comments.

"His nose was a little more straight," she said.

I fixed the nose and kept working.

"Kate?" she asked about thirty minutes later when I took a break to stretch.

"Yeah?"

She fidgeted and I braced for a hard question. "Why did you lean forward?" she asked quietly.

The question of the week.

I put my pencil down. "I don't know," I said, truthfully. "I needed my sunglasses, so I leaned forward to get them because my purse was in the backseat. But I have no idea why it was exactly at that time."

She looked at me and nodded. "Okay."

I picked up my pencil and looked at my half-finished sketch. The man's forehead and eyes were done, his nose was coming along.

"Carol?" I asked.

"Yes, Kate?"

I set the pencil back down. "Do you believe in God?"

She pursed her lips, eyes going a little bit dark. She didn't answer me for a long minute, and then she let out her breath. "I don't know, honestly."

I nodded. "Okay."

"You think that's the reason you leaned forward right then?"

I shrugged. "Well. I don't know. I mean, if I hadn't, I would have been shot. And I wasn't wearing a bulletproof vest, so the odds are good that I could have died. So, for me to bend over at exactly that time ..."

I let my voice trail off, and I picked up my pencil again.

Carol didn't say anything.

It took me another forty-five minutes before I finished the drawing. We didn't talk as much during the last part of it.

I held it up when I finished. "What do you think?" I asked quietly.

She looked at the drawing and then closed her eyes. "That's him."

Detective Masterson walked in.

"How are we doing, girls?" he asked.

Carol picked up her purse. "That's him," she said, pointing. "That's him and it's time for me to go." She looked over at me as she stood. "Thank you, Kate. Stay safe."

She left.

I looked at the drawing. A man in his early thirties wearing a hood and aviator glasses looked back at me.

"Think it will help?" I asked Detective Masterson.

He picked up the pad. "I think you are a very talented artist. And beyond that, you have a natural affinity toward forensic sketching, Kate."

I shook my head. "I doubt it. I didn't have a clue what I was doing."

"You put the witness at ease, you asked questions that went beyond the description, and you really made her feel comfortable enough to tell you what she saw." Detective Masterson was smiling proudly at me. "I think you did great."

I smiled.

I stretched my hands out in front of me, popping my knuckles. My fingers were sore, but my headache was worse. I chugged another cup of water and stood, stretching.

"Well, how did it go?" Deputy Slalom asked, walking in.

"She did great, sir. Here's the sketch." Detective Masterson handed the pad to the deputy.

Deputy Slalom took it and studied it for a minute, eyes narrowed. "Hmm," he said. "Send this to all the news networks and let's get some flyers made. I want the hermit who lives four counties over to know what this guy looks like. Got it?"

Detective Masterson grinned at me. "Yes, sir."

Chapter Fourteen

THE SKETCH WAS ON THE FIVE O'CLOCK NEWS WHEN WE got back to my house. Mom had apparently just gotten home; her car was making those weird popping and hissing sounds like when you first turn the engine off. Dad still wasn't there yet.

She was sitting in the living room watching Ted Deffle on KCL when DJ, Detective Masterson, and I walked in.

The picture I drew was plastered on the TV. Mom looked over at me from the sofa.

"Your work?" she asked.

I nodded and sat next to her. She put her arm around me.

Ted was talking. "This is the description of a man thought to be the shooter at last Sunday's parade, which left a member of our fine police force in the hospital. If you recognize this man, please call the hotline number listed on the screen. All calls are considered anonymous."

The picture changed back to Ted's fake-sun-tanned face. "In other news, people are still talking about the devastating events that occurred at the May Day parade ..."

"So," Mom said, turning Ted to mute. "You skipped school and went to 'the dentist.'" She looked at DJ and Detective Masterson, then back to me. "Your idea or theirs?"

"Mine," I said. "The skipping school part, at least."

"Uh-huh. Remember last year when you caught mono? You

refused to stay home and sleep? I basically had to tie you down in bed because you were so worried about missing school." She looked at me in the eyes. "Today doesn't sound like you."

"Does anything that's happened in the last week sound normal?" I asked. "Other kids' parents are flipping out about their kids' safety now. There was like a third of school who wasn't there today, thanks to me."

Mom sighed. "So, you left."

"Maybe it's better if I just stay here for a while. Maddy can bring me my homework and I'll keep up with everything here." I gasped. "Maddy!" She was supposed to come over today after school and I totally forgot about it.

I don't have a cell phone. What if she waited on my front porch for an hour before finally giving up? Or worse, what if a news crew was here and they made her give an interview?

Or much worse . . .

I shut my eyes, not wanting to think about *that* scenario.

"She left a message saying she wasn't going to be able to come over today after all," Mom said, patting my arm. Then she looked at me wryly. "She had a dentist appointment."

Detective Masterson started laughing. DJ smiled.

Mom just smiled and sighed. "Your father is on his way home, so I'm going to go start making dinner. We can talk about the you-staying-home-from-school idea when he gets home." She ran her hand through the back of my hair, like she used to when I was a little kid, before she stood and left the room.

Detective Masterson sat down in the recliner. "So, no more school for you?" he asked.

I sighed. "What if the other kids' parents are right and I'm just a big bull's-eye to all of them?"

The muted TV was flashing the picture I'd just drawn again, along with the hotline number.

"How many calls do you guys usually get on stuff like this?" I asked.

DJ sat on the opposite end of the couch from me and sighed, looking over at Detective Masterson. "Um ... maybe a good two hundred? Three hundred depending on how publicized the case is." He shrugged. "Most of them are from people who swear they saw that man in front of them in the grocery store."

"Do you go check all of them out?"

Detective Masterson nodded. "Unless they are completely ridiculous, then yes, we do."

It seemed like a lot of busywork to me, but I didn't say anything. Instead, I reached for the phone, because I needed to tell Maddy to get my homework for me.

She answered her cell phone on the second ring. "Well, if it isn't Kate Escape," she said, and I could hear the grin in her voice.

"What?" I asked.

"Kate Escape. It's what everyone at school is calling you since you left this morning. Personally, I think it's kind of catchy." She sighed. "Wish I'd come up with it."

Fabulous. Now I'm a juvenile delinquent and I have a trendy new nickname. Dad was going to make me memorize his calculus books for fear that I'm morphing into the next resident at the juvy hall near here.

"Clever," I said.

"So, why'd you leave, Kate?"

"Everyone is scared when I get there. All the parents are rioting. It's better for me to just stay home."

"Oh, yeah, I heard about the parent thing. They asked my dad if he was going to go."

"Did he?"

"Kate, considering he didn't even make it to my junior high graduation, what do you think?"

True. Bad question to ask. Maddy's parents tend to use stuff to make up for their lack of affection. They missed junior high graduation and gave her the complete set of *Friends* DVDs. Her shiny brand-new Tahoe? She had been asking them for weeks to try and make it to the huge school debate that she was in, and both her mom and dad had promised to be there. Then they didn't show.

So, they gave her a car.

Maddy rarely talked about it.

Part of me figured that's why she had such bad taste in boys.

"Anyway, I had a dentist appointment this afternoon, so I'm sorry I didn't come by. But I'm cavity free and the dentist said that for as straight as my teeth are, I should never need braces."

"Nice," I said, looking at the TV. DJ had switched it from the news to a baseball game.

"Yeah. And I didn't finish there until almost four, so I just decided to come home instead."

"That's fine," I said. The pitcher had now thrown six pitches to the same batter.

This is why I dislike baseball.

Actually, sports in general. What's the point?

Answer — there is no point. It's a bunch of grown men in weird costumes accomplishing nothing.

I was never a big fan of those little-kid sports movies.

"Maddy," I said, before I forgot. "I think I'm going to stay home tomorrow, so could you bring my homework by after school?" Tomorrow was Friday. Maybe something drastic would happen over the weekend, and I could go back to school as just boring old Kate Carter. None of this Kate Escape business.

"You're staying home? This isn't because of what those mean old parents were talking about, is it? Because, gosh, Kate, they are just being ridiculous."

I thought about Officer DeWeise getting out of the hospital today and shook my head. "Maybe not so ridiculous, Maddy."

"Whatever. *I* think it's ridiculous."

"Anyway. Could you just gather up my homework for me?"

"I guess. I still think you should just come to school. But yeah, I'll get your homework. Need anything dropped off?"

I knew I had a big math test on Monday, but maybe the policemen could get my teacher to let me do a makeup. He hated giving makeups.

"I don't think so. Not right now, anyway."

"All right. I'll see you tomorrow afternoon then."

We hung up.

Friday morning dawned bright and sunny, and my eyes popped open at six forty-five out of sheer habit.

I was going to live to be one of those old people who couldn't sleep in if someone paid them.

I tried to roll over and go back to sleep, but my brain was already buzzing.

What if someone had identified the sketch I drew? What if that man was in prison right this very minute? What if Detective Masterson was making pancakes again for breakfast?

My stomach growled.

I sighed and gave up on going back to sleep. There was a stack of calculus textbooks from Dad next to the bed.

"I'm just worried that you'll be bored at home," he'd said last night at dinner.

Because calculus is usually the first thing I turn to when I get bored.

Mom had another option. "Why don't you get out that journal I gave you a long time ago and start writing down some of your thoughts?" she'd suggested.

That sounded about as fun as the calculus, considering my thought processes these days.

She'd given me the journal back in the eighth grade, and I'd written in it once.

Mom gave me this journal so I will grow up to be a healthy, active adult who cares about her psyche and her community.

Yay.

And that was all I'd written. I was pretty certain that journaling was not going to be my stress-relief method of choice.

I finally got out of bed at seven and went to take a shower. DJ was already up — his air mattress was already stowed out of the way. He and Detective Masterson were alternating sleeping on the mattress in the hallway during the night.

I had no idea how they still managed to carry on an intelligent conversation when they each only got about four hours of sleep every night. But I'd yet to hear them complain about being tired or even seen them yawn.

Policemen are a different breed of males.

I pulled on a pair of black track pants, white socks, and a white short-sleeve T-shirt after my shower. I ran the blow-dryer over my hair and decided to skip the straightening iron today.

After all, it was just me and the cops stuck at home today. And when someone has seen you talking in your sleep, you just don't have the same motivation to fix your hair as you did before that.

I did put on a little bit of makeup, though, to cover the dark circles under my eyes. Apparently, I still wasn't sleeping very well. I added some mascara and went to go see where everyone was.

Mom and Dad were sitting at the kitchen table, eating breakfast. DJ was leaning against the island counter reading the paper, and Detective Masterson wasn't around, which meant no pancakes.

Lolly was sleeping on the kitchen floor.

"Morning, Katie-Kin," Mom said, smiling at me. "How did you sleep?"

I shrugged, because that seemed like the safest answer.

"See, Claire? Even when she doesn't have school, Kate is up and ready to get to studying and increasing her knowledge. Isn't that right, Kate?" Dad said.

"Sure, Dad," I said, because again that seemed like the safest answer.

Since Mom had stopped buying me Crispix, my only choices for breakfast were Mini-Wheats or some weird granola stuff Mom liked.

I sighed. Mini-Wheats had a weird texture to me.

"There's toast too, honey," Mom said.

It sounded better than my other choices. I put two slices of bread in the toaster.

Detective Masterson walked in then, putting his cell phone in the pocket of his jeans. "Good morning, Kate," he said.

I nodded to his pocket. "Any leads on the sketch?"

He just gave me a short laugh. "Any? How about four hundred and thirty-nine? Apparently, everyone and their grandmother has seen this guy around town."

Mom looked up from her section of the paper. "Well, that's good then, isn't it?"

Detective Masterson shook his head. "Not really, ma'am. Whenever a well-publicized case like this is using a hotline, *everyone* wants in on the action. We can legitimately throw at least half of those tips into the garbage."

"Plus, since he was wearing sunglasses and a hooded sweatshirt, it makes it even more likely that we'll have a lot of tips that are just no good," DJ added.

My toast popped, and I spread a healthy layer of peanut butter all over it. I carried it over and sat down at the table with Mom and Dad.

"So the other half of the tips?" Dad asked.

Detective Masterson said, "We've got men checking those out today. A team from St. Louis came up and has been assisting Deputy Slalom in this investigation. Missourians are ready to relax again when they leave their houses."

Mom and Dad finished breakfast and then left about thirty minutes later. I was sitting on the floor in the living room petting Lolly when they headed out the door for work.

"Be careful," Dad said in his new way of saying good-bye.

"Journal," Mom said. "Try to write in your journal. And I'll call you later today."

They left.

I rubbed Lolly's silky ears, and she moaned like a cat. I reached over and pulled the remote off the coffee table. Surely something interesting was on TV at eight o'clock on a Friday morning.

I flipped through the channels for ten minutes. Or surely not. There were old sitcoms I'd never heard of playing reruns, Regis and Kelly were cracking not-so-funny jokes to an audience who was probably paid to laugh at them, a show where women found out they were pregnant in the delivery room, which just sounded ridiculous to me, and then a few true-crime shows.

I stopped on one of those, even though I knew I probably shouldn't be watching this stuff right now.

Detective Masterson came in before I really caught what was going on in the plot. So far, it was about an attorney who had a history of representing criminals who were most likely guilty and getting them off scot-free.

"What are you watching?" he asked, frowning at the TV.

I clicked the guide to see what the name of the episode was. He read it and immediately started shaking his head.

"Nope, nope. Sorry, Kate. You have enough nightmares as it is," he said, yanking the remote from my hand and turning the TV to Regis and Kelly.

Fabulous.

The day passed by very slowly. I watched mindless TV, painted my toenails, played tug-of-war with Lolly, and organized my bookshelf.

When I finished with my bookshelf, I looked at the clock, expecting it to be at least almost three and Maddy on her way here.

It was eleven. In the morning.

I sighed. I would never make it under house arrest. There was probably a good reason my parents never had to ground me. This was awful.

I went back out to the living room. Detective Masterson was reading something from a three-ring binder, and DJ was on the phone in the kitchen. Lolly sat with her head resting on the detective's feet. She would probably miss them when they didn't have to live here anymore.

"Bored out of your mind yet?" Detective Masterson grinned at me when I walked in and slumped on the couch.

"I don't understand why people skip school on purpose," I said. "There is absolutely nothing to do here."

"You could start on those calculus books," he said, grin widening.

"I haven't reached the suicidal stage of boredom yet." I looked around, thinking. I had no homework, there was nothing on TV, and I couldn't concentrate long enough to read anything.

"Any new leads?" I asked, hopefully.

Detective Masterson smiled at me. "Give them time, Kate. They'll find him."

I sighed.

He looked at me for a long minute and then closed his three-ring binder. "All right. What do you want to talk about?"

"What?" I asked.

"You're just going to sit there until Maddy shows up with your homework, aren't you?"

I shrugged. "I'll probably eat something in there too." I looked over at him. "This is what causes childhood obesity, huh?"

He grinned. "Witness protection?"

"House arrest."

"Considering the rise of childhood obesity and the few people every year who are put under protection, I'm thinking it's probably not the sole cause of it. Personally, I blame Xbox."

I'd never been a fan of video games. There were the kids at school who played them nonstop, and I'd always thought they were very strange people. They came in wearing their *Darth Vader could totally take Frodo* shirts, with their hair all straggly and their eyes all bloodshot.

Dad said that the effects of playing video games had to be similar to having a drinking binge the night before. He called it the "brain cell murderer."

"We aren't allowed to have an Xbox," I told the detective. "Dad thinks it ruins your brain cells, and Mom said it prohibits healthy family communication."

"You have smart parents," Detective Masterson said.

At noon, I turned the TV back on. *Miss Congeniality* was on and I watched the rest of it, snacking on deli meat and cheeses in the meantime.

Finally, the phone rang at two thirty. It was Maddy.

"So, Kate, about this whole bringing you your homework thing," she started.

I tried not to sigh too loudly, because that was Maddy's way of saying that she wasn't going to do it after all.

"Tyler asked if I wanted to go watch his football practice, and things are kind of on a slippery slope for us right now, so I really feel like I need to go do that if I'm going to make this work," she said.

"Didn't you guys just get back together yesterday?" I asked.

"No. Wednesday night."

"And things are already on a slippery slope?" I asked.

"We just have communication problems," she said.

Sometimes, Maddy and Tyler's problems seemed like they belonged more to a couple who had been married for ten years. I could just see them going to counseling for this.

"Well," I said. "Okay."

"Yeah, but don't you worry about getting your homework. I've already given it to someone else, and they're coming by."

It was probably Allison Northing, and I'd have to listen to her chatter mindlessly for an hour before she'd leave and let me get to studying.

Even though mindless chatter was totally welcome at this point in my house. Detective Masterson was back to reading from his three-ring binder, and DJ was again on the phone.

"Okay," I said. "Have fun at the practice."

"Thanks, Kate! Have a fun day at home! You are so lucky you got to stay home all day, by the way."

"Not really," I said. "Bye."

Detective Masterson looked over at me when I hung up. "No homework?"

"She sent it with Allison Northing. Remember the girl who sat next to me in art class?"

He didn't do a very good job at hiding his wince.

"Yeah. Just be prepared," I said, sounding an awfully lot like Scar in *The Lion King.*

Fifteen minutes later, my doorbell rang. DJ answered it, since I was not allowed to answer the door alone.

I steeled myself, waiting for Allison's loud voice.

I didn't hear anything. A second later, DJ walked into the living room followed by Justin Walters.

I was a little bit shocked. Or a lot bit.

"Hi, Allison," Detective Masterson greeted him, grinning. "You look different outside of school."

Justin smiled confusedly at the detective. "I'm Justin Walters. I have Kate's homework," he said, like he was being interrogated.

"Sure you do," Detective Masterson said, still grinning. "I'll just go get something to drink. DJ, you want something?"

DJ was standing behind Justin and looking at me. "What? Oh yeah. That sounds great."

They both left, leaving me and Silent Justin standing in the living room.

Lolly wagged over to Justin, and he petted her ears. "Pretty dog," he said, though I wasn't sure if it was directed to me or Lolly.

"Thanks for bringing my homework," I said after a minute. First, Justin doesn't talk to me for three straight years — well, almost — and now he's bringing me my homework.

It was a little awkward, to say the least.

"Sure, no problem," he said, handing me a stack of papers.

"Miss Yeager's homework is to pick one of the careers we talked about and draw something for that career. She said you didn't have to do it, though."

I frowned. "How come?" Suddenly I'm not only not welcome at school but I can't even do the homework?

I felt like a homebound invalid. Next thing we knew, someone was going to be calling that traveling meal service to come feed me.

Justin must have seen the anger, because he immediately stopped petting Lolly and put both hands up. "Just because she said that you had already done it," he said quickly, in a soothing voice. "She said you'd already done it at least twice, which was all the rest of us were required to do."

So Miss Yeager had recognized my work on TV again.

I sighed. "If it's an assignment, then I'm going to do it too."

"Fine by me," Justin said.

"What are you going to do?"

He shrugged. "I don't know. I kind of like restaurant and commercial art. Honestly, it's just a hobby."

This was the most he'd ever talked to me, so I tried to keep the conversation going. "What do you want to do then?"

Another shrug. "I'm good at math. I've thought about engineering."

I just looked at him.

What is with me and this apparent magnetic force I have toward engineers? My dad. My brother. Now Justin.

Justin is the only one of those three, though, who appreciates art. My dad and Mike think art is a waste of time and a ridiculous use of pencil lead.

"Oh?" I said, because I couldn't think of anything else to say.

"Yeah. And with the art background, I'm kind of interested in something along the lines of architectural engineering."

"So you want to design buildings?"

He shrugged. Yet again. "I don't know. Maybe. It's a thought, anyway. I still have two years to decide."

"Well. A year and a half."

"Yeah." He finished scratching behind Lolly's ear and looked at me. "So, what do you want to do?" Then he grinned. "That might be kind of an obvious answer, huh?"

My turn to shrug. "I don't know." I sat down on the couch. "Do you think that if you are good at something that's a sign you should do it?"

He thought about it for a minute and sat on the recliner. Lolly scrambled over to lay her head in his lap.

"Not necessarily," he said. "Like, my sister is good at cooking but she's a finance major at Missouri State."

"You have a sister?"

He nodded. "And a younger brother. He's nine."

So much I didn't know about this guy. It was amazing that we'd been sitting next to each other in classes for the entire last year.

I looked over at him. "How come you don't talk like this at school?"

"I don't know. Allison talks enough for the entire class. And I like to just concentrate at school." He leaned back in the recliner. "So does that mean you don't really want to be a forensic sketch artist?" he asked, going back to my earlier question.

I sighed as I thought about it. On the one hand, I loved the art aspect of it. Faces had always intrigued me and I'd always loved to draw them. And the idea that I was helping people by doing it. That was cool.

On the other hand, I didn't like this part of the job. The staying in hiding, getting shot at, worrying about my friends and family and the people protecting me part of it.

Surely not *all* sketching jobs for the police department were this dangerous though. I mean, look at Larry, whoever he was. He was apparently safe. Unemployed, but safe.

Poor Larry.

I realized Justin was watching me then and I shook my head. "I like parts of it. I don't like other parts of it."

"Sounds like any job then," Justin said. "My dad is an attorney. He said that he really likes the helping people and the money parts of it, but he hates the actual legal process."

"Why did he become an attorney then?"

Justin grinned suddenly. "Because my mom was in school to be a legal assistant, and Dad thought she was cute."

"That's funny," I said, smiling.

"Yeah. So did you draw the picture of the guy they think shot at you at the parade?" he asked.

I nodded.

"It was a good picture."

"Thanks."

"Think you'll come back to church on Sunday?"

I hadn't even thought about it. It was more Mom's thing than mine anyway. "I don't know," I said. "Maybe. We'll see what happens by the time Sunday gets here."

He smiled. "It's only two days away."

"A lot can happen in two days."

"If you come, you should come to the second service. It's more laid back."

I thought about Sister Elizabeth Parker and her boisterously loud amens. For being such a tiny woman, she could sure get loud.

"Do people say amen as much?" I asked.

He shook his head. "Hardly ever. Why? Do people say it a lot in the first service? I haven't been to first service in years."

"Oh yeah," I said, nodding. "A ton. Like Sister Elizabeth Parker? She gets nice and loud. I jumped every time Sister said it."

He grinned widely. "You know, Kate, you don't have to call them 'sister' and 'brother' unless you just want to," he said.

"What?" I asked.

"Sister Elizabeth Parker? Her name isn't sister."

I just looked at him. "Then why did she introduce herself as Sister?"

"Because sometimes people in the church say that as a way of saying that we're all part of the body of Christ." He was still grinning. "Her name is just Elizabeth Parker."

Christians were very weird.

And I felt pretty dumb. "Well," I said, fumbling around for some shred of pride left. "Since you know everything, where is Zion and why are we marching there?"

He just laughed.

Chapter Fifteen

SATURDAY AT NOON, DEPUTY SLALOM CALLED DETECTIVE Masterson. I could hear the deputy's deep voice over the phone even though Detective Masterson was sitting on the other end of the couch from me. We'd been playing a game of Phase 10.

Dad was killing us all.

I think it was starting to bug DJ. I never noticed he was competitive until right then.

"One second," Detective Masterson whispered to all of us and stood and walked into the kitchen.

It was Mom's turn, and she was busy staring at the top card on the discard pile.

"Pause," DJ said, rolling his shoulders and laying on his back on the floor. We were all gathered around the coffee table. Mom and DJ were sitting on the floor, Dad had the recliner, and the detective and I had the sofa.

Mom laid her cards face down and then started doing a couple of back stretches.

"Do you want to sit here?" I asked her for the thirtieth time that day.

She shook her head. "I sit on a couch all week long, Kate. I like the floor."

Mom's office had two couches in it. One for her and one for her patient. Sometimes I think she sat at her desk, but the majority of the time she was on the couch.

I nodded and everyone got quiet. I think we were all trying to overhear Detective Masterson's conversation in the kitchen, but he was talking too quietly for us to hear.

Dad was looking at the score sheet. He had his glasses on, which I thought made him look at least fifteen years older.

"So, I'm on phase six, Kent is on phase five, and you three are all still on phase four," he said.

I could see DJ stiffening on the floor. "I hate this game," he mumbled.

"What was that, DJ?" I asked.

He sat up. "Nothing." Then she shot a look of challenge at my dad. "It can all change in one hand, Dale. Just one hand."

"Heh. We'll see," Dad said.

My dad can be quite the competitive person as well.

Detective Masterson came back in the room then, sliding his cell phone back into the pocket of his jeans. All of us immediately quit talking and looked up at him.

"Kate, you've got a press conference at three," he said, squinting at the clock over the fireplace.

"Press conference?" I asked.

"What?" Mom said.

"I thought you guys said that wasn't a good idea." Dad frowned.

"Also, we've had three separate leads all tell us that they saw a man who fit the description of the one you drew at a grocery store in Ballwin. We've got a team headed over there right now." He sat on the couch and picked up his cards.

Ballwin is closer to St. Louis than South Woodhaven Falls. It's almost straight to the west of the city, and we're more to the northwest.

"Is that what I'm supposed to talk about then?" I asked.

"What?" he said.

"The lead. The grocery store?"

"Oh," Detective Masterson said, shaking his head. "No, no. You just need to talk about drawing. Don't mention anything about the lead. We don't want this guy to leave Ballwin if he hasn't already."

A press conference.

I tried to hide the groan. I thought I'd gotten out of giving a press conference.

"So, we'll leave here around two or two fifteen to give you time to get ready, okay?" Detective Masterson said. "You'll be giving it at the station, so don't worry about safety." He said that mostly to my dad.

"Great! Let's play," DJ said, picking up his cards.

"So I'm just supposed to talk about drawing?" I asked.

Detective Masterson nodded, and DJ laid his cards face down again. "Just talk about your techniques, your excitement over John X being caught, and how you're hoping this new drawing will bring enough notice to find his accomplice," he said.

He made it sound very easy.

"Ready?" DJ asked as soon as the detective stopped talking, grabbing his cards again. "Ready to play?"

"What are you, six?" I asked him, rolling my eyes.

He shrugged. "I have to beat your dad, Kate."

"Just so you know, Dad has not lost at Phase 10 since he had the Great Stomach Flu of 2003, and even then, he didn't actually *lose*, he quit early because he couldn't stop throwing up."

DJ made a face. "Is that true, sir?"

Dad nodded. "Man, that was a miserable night. I rarely get sick, but that night I thought it was the end of the line for me." He looked at Mom. "Remember that night, Claire?"

She sighed. "How could I forget? You made me pull out the will and go over it before you went to sleep." She was rolling her eyes now too. "All men are hypochondriacs."

DJ said, "I meant about the Phase 10 record, not the stomach flu."

"Oh," Dad said. "Yes, it's true."

He straightened. "Well, it ends today."

Dad just shook his head. "Words I've heard before. Never seen the fruit of it, though."

Detective Masterson looked over at me. "So, you're good for today?"

"Do I have a choice?" I asked.

"Not really."

I shrugged. "Then does it matter?"

He looked at his cards. "I guess not. Just ask me if you need help preparing something. Mostly it will just be a chance for people like Ted Deffle to finally ask you some questions."

"Maybe he'll stop sending flowers then," Mom said. "I love flowers, I really do. But when it takes me thirty minutes just to water all of them and when the air in my house is starting to get a yellowish pollen hue to it, I start to think otherwise."

It would be nice. We had three more bouquets today. One was from KCL and the other two were from people in Springfield, Missouri.

We finished playing the game — Dad won again much to DJ's distress — and I went to go find something to wear to the press conference.

What in the world are you supposed to wear to press conferences? The only ones I've ever seen involved people confessing that yes, they did cheat on their wives just like the whole country knew they had. They always wore a collared polo shirt and sunglasses.

I would assume the attire would be different for today's occasion.

Mom knocked on the open door, while I stood and stared at my closet.

"Need some help?" she asked, coming in.

"Skirt or pants? Short sleeve or long sleeve?" I tugged on a couple of clothes but didn't pull them out of the closet.

Mom let out a long sigh. "Well," she said, coming next to me to join in staring at my closet. "I'm always a fan of longer sleeves on

TV. I think it makes your face more of the focus instead of people staring at your arms."

I found a couple of three-quarter-length shirts and pulled them out. It was too warm to wear long sleeves.

"And I would just wear jeans. You're sixteen, and you'll probably be sitting down," Mom said, shrugging. "You might as well be comfortable."

She had a point. So I picked out a cranberry-colored, three-quarter-length shirt and my favorite pair of jeans. Mom told me to pick the cranberry top because, apparently, I was a person who looked better in winter colors.

Until then, I had no idea that cranberry was in any way associated with winter other than being a traditional side dish for Christmas dinner.

For once, my hair actually straightened correctly, and I practiced smiling without squinting as I put on my makeup.

"Time to go, Kate," Detective Masterson said as I came out of my room.

I nodded. We all piled into the Tahoe, and DJ drove us to the police station.

The good old familiar police station.

Tons of news vans were there. South Woodhaven Falls only has one news crew, KCL, so I asked DJ as we pulled to a stop in front of the building where all the other vans had driven from for this conference.

"All over," he said, shrugging. "Like that one? WGDB? I think they are one of the main ones in Saint Louis."

A few news people and their cameras were gathered out front of the building, but DJ and Detective Masterson hustled me in so I didn't even hear their barrage of questions.

Plenty of time for that soon.

The station had two conference rooms. One was the conference room that I'd sketched the parade shooter in and where I'd met with Deputy Slalom. The other I'd never been in. It was much larger and had enough room for about fifty people to sit comfortably. There was a long table at the front of the room on some risers.

"I have to sit there by myself?" I whispered to DJ.

He shook his head. "Kent's going up there with you. And so is the boss."

That made me feel a little better. I was also glad I hadn't worn a skirt. That would have put the edge of my hem on eye level with the cameras.

A lady stepped up on the risers and attached a couple of microphones onto the table.

People were milling around everywhere. Mostly well-made-up people wearing suits with big, coiffed hair and earpieces. Cameras blocked every possible walkway.

Deputy Slalom walked in then and clapped his hands. "All right, let's do this," he said, climbing up on the riser. He was dressed nicely today. Slacks, a button-down collared shirt, and a sport coat.

I looked like a little kid they'd dragged out of school next to him.

Which was sort of the truth.

Detective Masterson was wearing his uniform, which had become kind of a rare sight for me. He helped me climb onto the tall riser, and I sat down in the middle chair.

I felt like a little person. Deputy Slalom is probably an inch or two over six feet tall, and he's shaped like a big barrel. Detective Masterson isn't a big man, but he is tall. He really does look a lot like a tougher Orlando Bloom.

And then there was all five feet one of me. In front of a table that sat a few inches higher than a normal table, and I had to reach a microphone on top of that.

The people with the news crews were slowly arranging themselves on the chairs below. The cameras were mostly in the back and along the sides of the room.

I felt like I needed to make an apology to my significant other.

Thanks to my No Dating High School Boys rule, though, I wouldn't have to deal with that.

"All right, all right," Deputy Slalom said gruffly, pulling his microphone closer. "Everyone take a seat, we're going to make this short and sweet."

I wondered if he realized he rhymed.

I pulled the microphone closer to me as well, and it squealed super loud in protest. Everyone in the room groaned and covered their ears.

"Sorry," I muttered.

Detective Masterson grinned at me. "Ladies and gentlemen, thank you for coming today on such short notice, but you can understand why, considering the security breach at the parade last week. You'll have fifteen minutes to talk to Kate Carter, so please make your questions brief. Kate, go ahead."

Go ahead and what? I just smiled — being careful to avoid squinting — and looked around. "Um. Any questions?" I asked.

All of the reporters started shouting right then, so loud that I couldn't make out one question from another.

Deputy Slalom rolled his eyes. "One at a time!" he yelled darkly into the microphone. Then he pointed. "You. Talk."

It was Ted Deffle from KCL. I half wondered then if he'd been sending flowers to the police station as well, and that's why he got picked first.

"Kate, Ted Deffle from KCL," he said, standing and flashing his teeth that were so white they probably caused traffic accidents.

"Hi, Ted," I said.

"Let's start with John X. How did you manage to draw such a picture-perfect image? And were you the artist who created the portrait of the proposed shooter at the parade?"

I looked briefly at Detective Masterson, who just smiled encouragingly at me. "Well," I said, "I heard a description of what John X looked like, and I just drew what I saw." Simple enough answer. "And yeah, I drew the shooter at the parade."

"Kate! KATE!"

"Enough!" Deputy Slalom yelled again. He pointed. "You. Go."

Another man, this one with hair that looked like he'd emptied a can of shine serum into it.

Ew.

"Hi, Kate, Ralph Robins from Springfield. I think we're all wondering the same thing," he said. "You're sixteen, you're a junior in high school, and you're not even old enough to vote. How is it that you are the one who is now drawing all these criminals? Might I say, very *dangerous* criminals?"

He was looking more at Deputy Slalom and Detective Masterson than he was at me, but the question was still addressed to me, so I cleared my throat.

"Well, um, I don't think you can ever be too young to assist your country when it's in need," I said, trying not to flinch. Now I sounded like a miniature politician. Cue the national anthem and the big flag dropping behind me.

Detective Masterson leaned forward then. "Every measure has been taken to ensure Kate and her family's safety and health during this time. We have also been very aware of child labor laws and are actively guarding Kate's delicate psyche."

I glanced over at my mom, who was nodding like Sister Elizabeth Parker during the preacher's sermon last Sunday. I was almost waiting for a loud "amen!"

Deputy Slalom pointed out a brunette lady this time whose hair was teased so high, I had trouble seeing any cameras behind her.

"Cindy Treller from St. Louis. Kate, why did you lean forward at the parade?"

Oh, the question of the week.

I still got a tight, tingly feeling in my gut when I thought about it. Sort of like when you find out that you're going to have to get shots at your doctor's visit and it was never just a checkup.

I looked around for a minute, trying to figure out what I was going to say. "I don't know," I said, honestly. "I had put my sunglasses in my purse on the backseat, and we were starting to get to the part of the parade that was in the sun. So, I was trying to pull my sunglasses out." I took a deep breath. "Why it was at that particular moment, I don't know."

Detective Masterson and Justin would say that God was watching out for me.

I thought that God, if there really was a God, had better things to do than worry about what a five-foot-nothing average student was doing.

On and on the questions came.

"Have you always liked art?" one man with something of an afro asked.

"I assume that a career as a criminal sketch artist is in your future?" a lady wearing a suit that looked like it was from the eighties said.

"Anything you'd care to say to John X?"

The last question was from a man in the back. He was tall, blond, and had the prettiest chocolate-brown eyes I'd ever seen. He'd introduced himself as Rick Litchfield from a southern St. Louis station.

If I lived in St. Louis, I would definitely be watching his news station.

I wasn't a huge fan of his questioning skills though.

I thought about it, looking at the big green x in the EXIT sign hanging over the conference room's closed doors.

If I had anything to say to John X . . .

I would want to know why. Why did he kill those four innocent women? They hadn't done anything to him, he didn't know them from anywhere. They were just moms, wives, girlfriends minding their own business, going about their own day. Not causing any harm to anyone.

I would want to know if he was sorry. Judging from the one picture I'd seen of him in prison, I would guess no, but it never hurt to ask.

I would want to know how many people he had working for him. He had at least one friend who liked to wear a hooded sweatshirt. How many more?

I leaned forward to the microphone. "I'd say enjoy that prison pot roast."

The reporters all started laughing. Rick Litchfield in the back smiled.

"Good answer," he said.

"That does it for today," Deputy Slalom said gruffly. "Thank you for coming to the press conference, enjoy your day."

Both he and Detective Masterson stood, and I followed suit. We stepped off the risers and they escorted me, Mom, and Dad into Deputy Slalom's office.

"Great job, honey," Mom said, giving me a hug. "You looked beautiful up there."

"Did you really have to end with a threat to John X?" Dad asked, face tight. "Come on, Kate."

I shrugged. "It wasn't a threat." I looked at Detective Masterson. "Did it sound like a threat?"

He looked at me and my dad and chose his words carefully. "It was a, uh, tease," he said. "But you managed to end on a light note and for that, I'm grateful. Coffee, anyone? Tea? Coke?"

"Coke," I said. Deputy Slalom was nodding to the chairs in front of his desk, so I sat.

"Nothing, thanks," Dad said, sitting down next to me. Mom asked for a bottle of water and then sat on the other side of me.

Detective Masterson went to go get the drinks, and Deputy Slalom sat behind his desk, knitted his fingers together, and laid his fists on the desk.

"So, we'll just hang out in here for a bit, just so they all leave." He looked out his window where several of the news people were now giving reports in the parking lot. He sighed. "Might be awhile."

Detective Masterson came back with my Coke, a bottle of water for Mom, and two Snapple Peach Teas. He handed one to the deputy and kept the other for himself.

"Anyway, good job, Kate. I thought you did very well handling yourself," Deputy Slalom said in his gruff voice after a long swig of peach tea.

"Thanks."

"Professional and short answers. I like that."

I nodded. "Did anything turn up at that grocery store in Ballwin?" I asked.

He took another long sip of his tea. "Not yet, Kate. Give it time. We've got a team down there, but phone tips can take weeks, if not months, to turn up anything."

"You guys got John X awfully quick," I said.

"That was completely a matter of being at the right place and at the right time with the right photograph," he said. "I heard you aren't going to school anymore." He looked at Dad as he said it.

"Yes, sir. And it's completely my decision," I said, taking the blame away from my dad. "The parents of the other kids at school were starting to keep their kids home so they wouldn't have to worry about them standing in the same hallway as me and getting shot."

Deputy Slalom rolled his eyes. "It's those panicky people that make my job so much harder than it really is," he said. "The last thing this guy or John X wants is another murder other than yours to chalk up to his name. He's already facing the death penalty. Committing a crime against a minor isn't going to help his case."

I popped the top on my Coke. "Still, that's the way it is at South Woodhaven Falls High."

"Okay. Well, hopefully, something will turn up on this shooter in Ballwin. In the meantime, keep up with your studies. And, Kate," he said, his voice getting softer, "did you get a chance to consider my offer from last time?"

I shook my head in mid-swallow. "No, sir. Not yet."

"No worries," he said. "Take your time."

Mom and Dad were looking at me curiously, but I did my best to ignore them and finish my Coke.

There would be plenty of time for questions later.

Chapter Sixteen

SUNDAY MORNING AND MOM DECIDED WE WERE ALL GOING to church again. "I don't know what's going on here right now, but I know that we can't handle this by ourselves," she said last night at dinner. "Now, DJ and Kent will be along with us to watch out for Kate's safety, so we have no excuses," she said, cutting off my dad before he even got a word out of his open mouth.

I was pretty sure that Dad wasn't too excited about it.

But we all piled into the Tahoe at ten o'clock on Sunday morning. I was wearing a pair of jeans and a nicer top. Detective Masterson had dressed up in khakis and a button-down. Mom was wearing one of her business suits minus the jacket.

The first service was just leaving at South Woodhaven Falls First Baptist Church when we got there. I saw Sister Elizabeth Parker talking animatedly with the man who stood on the stage asking for amens last week.

"Kate!" someone yelled.

I looked around and Justin Walters was waving at me, leaving his group of friends to come say hi.

"I'm glad you came," he said, smiling. "You're just getting here, right?"

I nodded, noticing Detective Masterson not-so-subtly grin at DJ. "Yes, we just got here," I said loudly, moving so the two cops weren't behind me. Hopefully, Justin didn't notice them.

He grinned wider. "Great! You guys can sit with my family. Come on in." He waved to his group of friends and led us into the big meeting room.

It looked a lot different from last week. The organ was still on the stage, but it was buried behind a set of drums. Three guitars, a bass, lots of microphones, and a few skinny, punked-out guys were up there. The guys were milling around, adjusting their girl pants and swiping their longish hair out of their eyes.

I glanced over at Dad, who was already shaking his head. I don't think Dad liked the hymns last week, but he really hates men in women's clothing or hairstyles. Dad believes that all guys should have buzz cuts and wear pants that fit relaxed in the rear and legs.

Justin had a buzz cut. And was wearing simple, straight-cut jeans.

"Guys, this is my mom and dad," he said, pointing to one pew where a blonde woman and a gray-haired man sat. "Lucinda and Jason," he said.

My parents introduced themselves, and I shook their hands as well. We introduced DJ and the detective as old family friends.

Lucinda clasped my hand tightly. "How are you, dear? We've been praying so hard for you!"

"Uh, good. Thanks." Her hand was squeezing my first and fourth knuckles together. It kind of hurt.

"Yes, we have!" Justin's dad boomed. "And Dale, if you need anything, you just holler, okay?" He clapped my dad's shoulder.

Dad just nodded.

Someone plucked a couple of strings on a guitar, and the lights immediately dimmed everywhere except for the stage. We all filed into the pew, except for DJ, who was going to stand in the back. He whispered some lame excuse about having a bad back to Lucinda when she protested that there was plenty of room in the pew.

I knew he was back there to keep an eye on things. I sat between Dad and Detective Masterson and looked up at the stage.

"Hi," one of the girly looking guys said. "My name is Shaun, and welcome to SWF First Baptist. Let's worship, shall we?"

He strummed down his electric guitar, and the drummer and other two guitarists and bass player picked up the beat.

Shaun started to sing and the words suddenly appeared behind him on a big screen that I hadn't noticed last week.

The weird, flamboyant monk outfits were nowhere to be seen. Everyone around us immediately stood and started singing, raising their hands and moving to the beat of the music.

I felt like I was at a concert. Only, a weird, sing-along concert.

It sounded like the detective knew all the words. I could hear Mom trying to sing along as well. Dad just stood and stared at the stage.

I tried to sing. There was no mention of Zion or dost or thou or any of those weird words that I wasn't sure what they meant.

"We are hungry, we are hungry," the lead guy sang. He really had a great voice. And while the song was actually making me hungry, I did enjoy listening to it.

I peeked around Dad and Mom and saw Justin singing with his eyes closed and his right hand lifted about waist high.

I didn't get the raising hands thing. It was like half the people here were calling that it was their turn to sing next or saying they had a question.

I had a question. If we were so hungry, why were they only serving the tiniest fragments of crackers and the smallest glasses of grape juice I'd ever seen to wash it down with? It was like what I imagined you gave an infant for their first meal.

The same man who talked last Sunday got back on the stage. Only now he wasn't wearing a suit coat or a tie or even nice pants. He'd pulled the tail of his button-down shirt out and had changed into straight-cut jeans.

"Thanks, Shaun," he said into his wireless lapel microphone. No more standing behind a lectern, he just carried a worn Bible and carried a stool over to the middle of the stage.

"Good morning," he said warmly, sitting on the stool and opening his Bible. He taught for about thirty minutes, and he didn't once say the word "amen" except at the end of a prayer.

No one said it in the audience either. And after he finished teaching, the band came back up and did one more chorus from one of the songs they'd sung earlier.

Afterward, the people around me exploded out of their seats.

"Hi!" one very exuberant boy about the age of ten or so said, popping up behind me. "You're Kate Carter!"

I nodded. "What's your name?"

"James," he said, grinning, two dimples appearing on both of his cheeks.

Justin stood and leaned around Mom and Dad. "This is my little brother."

"Oh," I said. "Well, nice to meet you, James."

A bunch of people came over then to talk to the new family, I guess, but I noticed that Detective Masterson was looking more and more anxious about the growing crowd.

"Wow, Kate Carter!" one high school–aged boy said, coming over. "I'm Sam Lawry, and can I say that you are one of the bravest girls I've ever heard of?" He stuck out his hand to me. "I've always hoped we'd meet at school, but the grade difference probably prevents it."

I squinted at him. *Sam Lawry* was ringing bells and I wasn't sure why. "Have we met already?" I asked, and even though it sounded like a horrendous pickup line, I really thought we'd already met.

"I play on the football team," he said, grinning one of those "I'm important" smiles at me. "Defensive end."

He could have told me the name of the part of the car that makes it go forward for all I understood about his last sentence. "Cool," I said like I knew what he meant.

"We should get together and talk or something," he said.

Right then, three squealing girls ran over.

"WE SAW YOU ON TV!" they screamed.

"Oh my gosh, that was *so* cool," another guy chimed in.

Soon, it was a loud madhouse. I couldn't see my parents anymore. Somehow, I'd gotten sucked into this circle of kids who were all going crazy.

Detective Masterson reached into the mob, grabbed my forearm, and hustled me toward the door. "No more teenage hormones," he mumbled as he yanked me outside.

DJ was also looking concerned as he hurried over to help get Mom and Dad, and the two cops rushed us to the Tahoe.

"Okay," Detective Masterson sighed when we were all in the car. "Kate, no offense to your social life, but I liked it better when no one wanted to talk to you."

Mom frowned her disapproval of his comment but refrained from making one herself.

Dad was shaking his head. "Did you see the pants on that singer guy?"

I had to smile.

We got home and piled out of the Tahoe. The day was beautiful. I sniffed. Something smelled really good. One of our neighbors must be barbecuing.

I walked to the front door and stopped.

Instead of the usual assortment of flowers, there was a pan covered in aluminum foil sitting right in front of the door.

Detective Masterson joined me, saw the pan, and immediately moved into police mode. He called for DJ to come help him and together they slowly approached the pan. One of them reached down and pulled a white card off the top of it.

In the process, they nudged the foil, and the savory scent of roasting beef was even stronger.

I froze.

"What is it?" Mom asked, slinging her purse over her shoulder. She squinted at the foil-covered meat and nodded. "See? People should always send food instead of flowers. I wish this idea had caught on a long time ago."

I stayed rooted where I was on the porch. Detective Masterson's chin was set so hard, I worried about his back molars.

DJ exchanged a look first with the detective and then with me.

"What is it?" Dad asked, echoing Mom behind me.

It was a pot roast.

Barely ten minutes passed by before our yard was swimming with cops. Uniforms were everywhere—in the house, in the bushes, combing the neighbors' yard.

The fabulous-smelling pot roast had gotten shipped off to the police station for testing, but not before I'd seen the note.

I'm nothing if not generous, Kate.

It wasn't signed, but we all knew who it was from. He had nice handwriting, that friend of John X's.

I was watching out the front window. A forensics team was scouring the front yard for footprints, hair, anything that might lead them to the shooter from the parade.

DJ came back inside then, pulling a pair of aviator sunglasses off his face. He looked over at me. "You doing okay, Kate?"

I nodded. I was kneeling on the couch, holding the curtain back with one hand, my chin balanced on the back of my other hand, which was on the back of the couch.

I watched as two policemen bagged just about everything in our front yard except for Mom's frog garden decoration that sat in the front flower pot. But sod, dirt, leaves—you name it, and it got stuck in a bag with a label on it.

"Look at it this way, Kate. It was a pot roast. It wasn't a gun, it wasn't someone waiting for us when we got home. It was just a harmless pot roast."

Harmless to everyone except the cow, I guess.

I nodded again, though, because I knew that was what DJ wanted me to do. "Okay," I said.

He gave me a sad smile and went into the kitchen, where Detective Masterson and a few other cops were having a powwow around our kitchen table.

Mom and Dad were sitting on the other couch. Dad hadn't said anything else about the pot roast comment I'd made, but I knew he was thinking it.

I felt bad. If I'd just brushed off the reporter's question, our house wouldn't have become the newest branch of the South Woodhaven Falls police department.

I should've just said that I didn't have anything to say to John X.

I let the drape fall back down and turned to look at Mom and Dad. They were watching the news. All media vans had been blocked at the top of the street, so they were reporting from the corner.

"And I'm getting another report, hang on a second," Candace Olstrom, the peppy, blonde reporter, squealed to the camera. She turned to a guy I didn't recognize who wasn't from the police department, because he wasn't in uniform, and talked to him quietly for a minute. Then she turned back to the camera.

"Well, it seems that authorities are still busy trying to find out who left a mysterious package on heroine Kate Carter's doorstep earlier this afternoon."

Shocking report. I stood and went to my room.

I sat down at my desk and tried to think about my homework. It was Sunday, after all. Justin was going to drop by tomorrow morning on his way to school to pick up my completed assignments.

Or at least he was before this fiasco.

I'd finished my math and science homework. I had a take-home quiz in English, but that wouldn't take me more than about half an hour to do.

I pulled over my sketchpad. Miss Yeager had wanted us to draw something that was an example of what we wanted to do in an art-centered career.

I closed my eyes for a minute.

John X's face had been replaced in my brain by the parade shooter. I'd already drawn him though.

I started just sketching whatever came to mind.

I could still smell the remnants of pot roast in the house. My stomach began growling, and I remembered that I'd never eaten lunch.

The sketch started to have a face.

Medium-spaced brown eyes framed by thick, whiteish-blond eyelashes. Freckles stood out along the cheekbones. A straight, red-haired buzz cut with a nice hairline.

I worked on it for about an hour and then went into the kitchen, hoping the police had found a new meeting spot.

But they were all still there. Maps were spread on the table and people were talking softly, using words like "perpetrator."

I tried my best to sneak in so I could just quickly make a sand-wich and leave. I had the bread out of the pantry when Detective Masterson looked over and saw me.

"Kate," he said, and everyone stopped talking and looked over at me.

Now I felt like I was stealing bread from my own house. "I was just making a sandwich," I said quickly.

He smiled then. "You aren't in trouble. Are you okay?" He stood from the table and came over, leaning against the counter while I grabbed a package of deli turkey meat, mustard, swiss cheese, and lettuce from the fridge.

The other people around the table started talking again.

I shrugged. "I'm fine," I said, pulling my standard facing-the-doctor answer out for him. "Sorry to interrupt. I'm just getting lunch."

He looked at the clock on the oven and sighed. "It's late for lunch. I'm so sorry about all this, Kate."

Another shrug. "I'm the one who had to make the pot roast reference at the press conference."

"If it's any consolation, it was a really funny reference," he said, trying to lighten the mood.

I spread a thin layer of mustard on the bread and stacked on the turkey, lettuce, and cheese. "I thought so too."

"We will find him, you know," he said in a quiet voice. "And everything will go back to normal for you."

Funny how it had only been two weeks and I could barely remember what normal looked like for me.

Justin rang my doorbell at seven o'clock the next morning. I hadn't slept more than about two hours Sunday night thanks to more nightmares, so I was up, showered, and reading *The Grapes of Wrath*, since we had to have it finished by the end of the school year.

Which was in almost six months. Better to get a head start on it now.

I was so bored I was scaring myself.

DJ opened the door and escorted Justin into the family room. "Morning, Kate," Justin said, looking all awake and refreshed after what could only have been a great night's sleep.

He looked around my living room. I was slumped on the sofa, eyes bleary. DJ had black circles so thick under his eyes that he looked like he could have been playing on a football team. Detective Masterson was rubbing a three-day-old beard, and Mom and Dad were silently eating breakfast, staring at the table.

"Lively bunch today," Justin said to me.

I rubbed my eyes. "It was a long day yesterday."

He nodded. "I heard about that. Someone left a package on your doorstep? What was it? Was it a bomb or something?"

"No. It was a pot roast."

He was quiet for a minute, staring at me. Finally he cleared his throat. "Maybe I'm missing something, but I actually like pot roast, and I'm not sure why someone leaving one of those would cause so much sleepiness today." His eyes widened. "Unless the pot roast was drugged or something."

I think that Justin has watched too many crime shows on TV.

Either that or read too many Hardy Boys books as a kid.

"We didn't eat it," I said. "I made a comment about how I hope John X is enjoying his prison pot roast at the press conference, and then one showed up on my doorstep."

DJ started clearing his throat, and I guessed I'd talked too much. "But anyway," I said offhandedly, like it was no big deal and we were just all completely zombied-out for no reason at all. I grabbed my stack of papers for him. "Here's my homework. Thanks again for doing this, Justin."

He tucked the papers into his backpack. "Sure, no problem. You positive you don't want to come to school today? I came here a few minutes early to try and talk you into it."

I shook my head. "Nope. I'm putting myself under house arrest until this guy is caught and happily eating his share of the prison pot roast."

Justin quirked his head. "Do they even serve pot roast in prison? I mean, I'm no expert, but I've seen a few of those documentary things they show on TV about life in the slammer, and I've never seen anyone eating a pot roast." He shrugged. "But then again, I don't think I've ever really seen anyone eating. I think that show likes to only show the fight scenes."

Must have been the same documentary I'd watched before. We both just looked over at Detective Masterson, who was skimming the paper through red-rimmed, sleep-deprived eyes.

He looked up at us after a few seconds. "What?" he asked.

"Do they serve pot roast in prison?" I asked. I'd asked DJ before and he hadn't been sure.

Detective Masterson shrugged. "You'd need to contact a warden with that question. But I can tell you that one of the times I was there they were serving meat loaf." He rolled a shoulder. "I guess that's almost like pot roast."

Except it's much grosser.

My mother hated meat loaf with a passion. I could only think of one time that we'd had meat loaf in this house, and it was when my grandfather died and some people from my dad's work brought dinner for us.

Mom said it was like the bologna of dinner meats. She said that someone out there must have not wanted to go grocery shopping that day so she just threw everything she had into a bowl, mixed it all together, and baked it, and unfortunately invented meat loaf.

Mom could barely even stand to say the words. She called it "that horrendous meat product."

My dad, on the other hand, loved meat loaf. He said that my grandmother used to make it all the time for them for dinner when he was growing up. "It's an amazing meal," he told me one time after one of Mom's tirades on it. "Cheesy, melty, juicy ..." Then he'd just sighed and poked at the plain chicken breast on his plate.

Justin shrugged. "Well, anyway. I know there aren't kitchens in the jail cells, though, so how did John X get the pot roast over to you?"

At the conclusion of yesterday's cop invasion, they'd decided that there were two possible candidates for the cook who created the pot roast. One was the mysterious, hooded parade shooter, and the other was someone who had watched the press conference and thought it would be a way to end up on the news.

I thought the second choice was just horrible. "Someone would do that?" I had asked.

All of the police people just looked at each other and then shook their heads. "Every day," someone said. "Fame is a powerful motivator, Kate."

Which was partially why they had concealed what the package

was from the media. No use in giving the cook — if that really was his motive — a sense of satisfaction.

"They aren't sure yet," I answered him. "And by the way, you can't mention that it was a pot roast to anyone else, okay?" Not like I had to worry too much about that. He didn't talk to anyone at school.

He nodded. "I won't. That's pretty weird though." He zipped his backpack shut and squinted at the clock over our mantel. "Guess I need to get going. Have a good day, Kate."

"Thanks again, Justin."

"I'll be back around two thirty or so."

He left.

Sometimes it still weirded me out how much we talked now.

Mom came into the living room as Justin left. She looked exhausted, and she was massaging the sides of her forehead. "Got your homework taken care of?"

I nodded. "Sure you can't stay home today, Mom?" Surely she needed a break.

She shook her head. "I wish I could, Kate. I know I'm completely booked back-to-back this morning. I'm going to check my schedule though. If I don't have very many appointments this afternoon I might have Madge move them all to next week instead and just come home early." She disappeared into her room to finish getting ready.

She and Dad both left at the same time. "Be careful," Dad said.

"Pay attention," Mom said.

"Don't answer the door," Dad said.

"But please answer the phone," Mom said.

"Stay inside and lock the doors," Dad said.

"Bye guys," I said.

They both left. I sat back down on the couch and pulled over *The Grapes of Wrath* again, but I didn't feel like reading anymore. All the words were starting to blur in front of me.

So I leaned my head back against the cushion, pulled my feet up next to me, and turned on the TV.

Almost eight o'clock on a weekday morning. I flipped through the channels and settled on an old *I Love Lucy* rerun. Lucy was yet again trying to get Ricky to let her into show business, and I half wondered what my life would be like if I married a Cuban bongo player.

Probably louder. Definitely louder than my life was right now. Detective Masterson was still quietly flipping through the paper, and I think DJ had decided he was going to try and get in a power nap because he just wasn't feeling very alert. Lolly was lounging on the floor, licking a rawhide bone. She never chewed them, she just licked them.

The show ended and another episode started. I curled up tighter and moved my head to the armrest.

My eyelids felt heavy. And my eyes felt completely dry, like I might need to invest in a humidifier soon.

I blinked to moisten them, but then just kept my eyes closed because it felt good.

The doorbell was ringing. The doorbell was ringing, and no one was going to answer it. So I walked over and opened the door.

John X stood there holding a fork in one hand and a spoon in the other. "I thought I'd join you for some meat loaf," he said in a deep, bass voice. A man in a hooded sweatshirt came up behind him, also holding utensils.

"I don't have any meat loaf," I told him.

"It's okay. We'll make some. I have a great recipe from my great-grandmother," John X said, walking into my house and into the kitchen, where a few bowls were already laid out on the counter.

"Let's see," he said, setting his fork and spoon down and rubbing his chin. "We need meat and a loaf of bread."

The man in the hooded sweatshirt got the bread for John X from the pantry. He didn't say anything. I looked at him and he smiled politely, but he still didn't say anything.

John X was looking at me. "Where's the meat?"

I opened the freezer and there was only frozen rawhide bones in there. "We don't have any," I said. "My mom hasn't been grocery shopping in a while."

John X looked around the kitchen for a few minutes. "Well, then. Do you have a dog?"

I nodded.

"I guess we found our meat then. Go ahead and call the dog in here." John X rolled up his sleeves and motioned to the hooded man. "We'll need your help too. Sometimes dogs can get a bit hard to skin."

I shook my head. "I don't want to use Lolly."

"You just said you don't have any other meat," John X in a *duh* tone of voice. "We have to use the dog."

"No, we don't. We can go to the store."

The hooded man started to look impatient.

"Look, just call the dog in here," John X snapped. "Call the dog or we'll use you instead."

I started crying. "Why can't we just go out to eat?" I asked. "Why do we have to eat Lolly or me?"

"That's it," John X said, grabbing my arm. "Get a knife," he instructed the hooded man. "We'll use her leg. She's got more meat there than anywhere else."

I started screaming and tried to run, but John X had a firm grip on my arms.

"Kate," he said sharply over my screams. "Kate!"

I screamed all the louder.

"*Kate!*"

Suddenly, I was being jerked up and shaken. I blinked awake. Detective Masterson was gripping me by both arms, shaking me and yelling, "Kate! Kate!"

The room started to settle into place. *The Price Is Right* was on the TV. Lolly was licking my toes.

Detective Masterson looked scared. He set me down on the couch and exhaled, rubbing his hands together.

I was shaking uncontrollably and tears were pouring down my face.

"Are you okay?" he asked, sitting down beside me and rubbing my shoulders.

"What happened?" I asked.

"You started screaming. You were sleeping, and you just started screaming." He shook his head. "Then you wouldn't snap out of it." He looked over at me. "Are you okay?"

I sniffed and tried to stop the torrent of tears. "He wanted to make meat loaf using me," I hiccupped.

"John X?" Detective Masterson asked quietly.

I nodded, lifting a shaking hand to wipe my cheeks. Lolly was now laying on my feet.

Detective Masterson sighed and rubbed his eyes. "Well, that wouldn't have been too tasty," he said, smiling shortly. "You're kind of skin and bones, Kate."

"He was going to use my leg."

"That makes more sense." He smiled again at me and took a deep breath. "Sheesh, kid. You scared the daylights out of me."

I looked around. "Where's DJ?"

The detective brushed a hand nonchalantly. "That guy could sleep through a root canal. I'm worried about you. Kate, I don't think you should take the sketch artist job."

I got the tears to stop and rubbed my cheeks. "Why?"

"Look at you. You can't sleep, you hardly eat anything anymore. You won't go to school." He shrugged. "You are extremely talented, and we'll be losing a huge asset to the team, but you can't handle this."

Now I just sounded weak. There were hundreds of people out there who made their living doing far more dangerous things than criminal sketches. You never heard of any of them having nervous breakdowns.

I'd never had a nervous breakdown, but I wondered if the not sleeping and hardly being able to eat was part of one.

Mom would probably know the answer to that.

Not that I would ask her.

That would be about as bright as giving Allison Northing a megaphone for Christmas. No good could come from it. Sort of like when Grandma Carter got my dad the *Complete Guide to Engineer Jokes, Riddles, and Slap-Knees* for his birthday about five years ago. He still drags that thing out every so often.

Mom and I still don't find any of the jokes very slap-kneeish. And what's with that word anyway? I wasn't aware that you could just randomly turn verbs into nouns.

"I'll keep thinking on it," I said to Detective Masterson. "Maybe I won't take the job, maybe I will. We'll just have to see."

He gave me a long look before nodding. "Okay."

Chapter Seventeen

THE WEEK WENT BY VERY SLOWLY. JUSTIN CAME EVERY morning at seven to pick up my homework and every afternoon before three to deliver it. Most of the days he didn't stay and chat.

There had been no new leads on the parade shooter. The cops still had a couple of guys watching the grocery store in Ballwin, but no one resembling the man at the parade had been there in the last two weeks.

Detective Masterson and DJ tried to be encouraging, but I could tell that they were starting to get sick of this.

Mom and Dad went to work exhausted and came home even more exhausted.

And I tried every method possible to get myself to go to sleep at night. I had Detective Masterson pick up some lavender-scented lotion at the store and tried using it before I went to bed to get me to be more tired. I tried taking that cough medicine that knocks you out, even though I wasn't coughing.

None of those seemed to work. I tossed and turned from the moment I got into bed Thursday night. I looked at the clock at one point and it was three fifteen in the morning.

I'd probably slept a whole two hours.

Finally, I gave up. I turned on my bedside lamp and dragged my sketchpad over. I'd been working on one sketch all week, and I was nearly done.

The red-haired man with a buzz cut smiled back at me from the pad, and I started working on his chin.

It was DJ.

I don't think he knew that I was sketching him. Next up was Detective Masterson and then probably my parents.

I had nothing better to do.

At three forty-five, I finished DJ's chin and pushed the pad back a few inches to get a better look at it. It looked just like him, and I was rather proud of my efforts.

I yawned and tried to decide if I could fall asleep now. Sometimes just getting a little bit of energy out seemed to help.

I tried shutting my eyes, but sleep didn't come. My brain was still working overtime. I wondered if John X's friend had somehow gotten the tip that so many people had seen him at the grocery store in Ballwin, and he'd moved on to a super Walmart or something.

Some of those had self-checkouts. You could go in, get your groceries, pay for them, and leave without anyone so much as even noticing you.

We had gotten some reports back on the pot roast. There was absolutely nothing wrong with it. It apparently had been cooked to perfection, according to some of the people down at the lab. And the note that came with it?

Zero fingerprints, zero DNA.

Not that it was a shock, but it was a little sad. I was hoping that whoever had cooked the pot roast had lost a hair in there or something.

Maybe our hooded sweatshirt friend also wore hairnets occasionally.

I wasn't going to be able to go back to sleep. I started drawing another head and shoulders shot.

Detective Masterson really did look an awful lot like Orlando Bloom. Same nose, same jawline. The only thing that was different was his hair and the slightly tougher quality in his bone structure.

I worked on the sketch until six thirty and then took a quick shower. I blow-dried my hair, added some cover-up over the increasingly dark circles under my eyes, and pulled on a pair of worn jeans and a blue T-shirt.

Justin was almost annoyingly punctual. I was just walking into the living room when he rang the doorbell. DJ answered it, yawning. "Hey," he said, letting Justin in.

"Morning, guys," Justin said. He joined DJ in yawning. "Thankfully it's Friday, right?"

I nodded, but really, my weekends weren't that much different than my weekdays now. Everything just kind of blended together. I handed him my stack of homework. "Thanks again, Justin." We were starting to sound like a broken record. He came in, said good morning, I said thank you, he said no problem, and then he left.

"No problem," he said, shoving my homework into his backpack.

Then it was his cue to leave. Instead, he sat down on the sofa.

DJ and I exchanged looks, because this was not according to schedule. Then DJ cleared his throat and left the room.

Justin looked at me. "So, have they found that guy from the parade yet?"

No offense to Justin, but you'd think this would have been fairly obvious.

"Um. No. Not yet," I said. I was still standing by the recliner, just looking at him, waiting for him to leave before I started my new morning routine. *Happy Days*, a show I'd never seen before but was apparently about life in the 50s but was made in the 70s, came on at seven. Then I watched *Friends*, watched a guy named Bobby Flay do cooking competitions, and napped during *I Love Lucy*.

So far, Detective Masterson had only had to wake me up once since Monday because I was screaming in my sleep again. But other than that, I was getting fairly decent three-hour naps in every day.

"Are you going to wait until after he's caught before you come back to school?" Justin asked, apparently staying to chat today.

I sat down in the recliner, rubbing my cheek. "I don't know," I said. I had thought about it, but not very much. What if he never was found? Did that mean I never went to school again? Would Detective Masterson and DJ have to live with us forever?

"Well, I think you should just come on back to school. What's the worst that could happen?" he asked.

I blinked as a hundred different scenarios that would fit the "worst thing that could ever happen" adjective raced through my head. Classmates could get shot, teachers could get hurt, I could put another cop in the hospital.

Justin apparently noticed the look on my face and winced, rubbing his cheek. "I, uh, I didn't mean that question, Kate."

Maybe it would be better if I didn't take the police department job. Maybe after all this was over and done with, I could get a full night's sleep, go to school like a normal sixteen-year-old, and have a nice life of homework and Crispix. I was even starting to miss my beat-up, barely working car.

I shrugged. "No big deal," I said. "But that's why I won't go back until he's caught." I hadn't elaborated on the *why* but I had a feeling that Justin got my drift.

He just nodded. "Okay, then." He stood, pulling his backpack up off the floor. "All right, I'd better get to school. Have a good day, Kate. I'll see you this afternoon."

"Thanks again, Justin." I walked him to the door.

"No problem."

I locked the door behind him, but not before poking my head outside first. It was a gorgeous day outside. And despite the trampling our front yard had gotten on the day of the pot roast fiasco, it looked like the grass would probably grow back just fine.

Thank goodness. Dad about died when he saw the yard after the barrage of uniforms left.

"What in the ..." His voice had trailed off and I knew better than asking him to finish his sentence as he stood in the front door, staring at what used to be his lawn of perfection. He'd had complete strangers coming to the door in years past, asking him what kind of fertilizer he used and how he kept his yard so green.

I closed the door and turned on *Happy Days*, though by this point I'd already missed the first few minutes of it.

Detective Masterson came in and settled in the recliner with the newspaper, like he did every morning. DJ was on the phone in the kitchen like he was every morning.

And Mom and Dad finished breakfast and left with their usual warnings like they did every morning.

I had just woken up from my nap during *I Love Lucy* when I saw Detective Masterson close his cell phone and look over at me. "Kate," he said, "time to pay another visit to the dentist."

I nodded, rubbing the lines on my cheek from the corduroy pillows. "Okay." Suddenly, I was wide awake. Maybe they caught the grocery store parade shooter! Maybe they'd run him down and I could go to school on Monday!

"And bring something to do," Detective Masterson said as I jumped off the couch and ran to my room for my shoes. "We'll probably be there a while."

"Okay!" I said.

I grabbed my shoes, changed into jeans quickly, and slapped a quick coating of mascara on. I closed my sketchpad and picked up my favorite pencil set, tucking both under my arm.

I could work on my drawings while we were at the station, since apparently we would be waiting there for a little while.

We left a few minutes later. DJ was driving over the speed limit and Detective Masterson kept looking at his cell phone.

"Did they catch him?" I asked excitedly.

"I don't know," Detective Masterson said.

"Did they see him?"

"I don't know."

"Did they at least identify him?"

He turned and looked at me. "I don't know, Kate. All they said was come down to the station right away."

"You didn't ask why?"

He shrugged. "We'll find out when we get there."

I just shook my head and looked out the window. All men were the same, my mother would have said. Any time Dad got off the phone with his side of the family, Mom would ask him what they said, what was going on with everyone, whether or not the dates for the family reunion would work for everyone this summer. And Dad would have absolutely no answers for her.

"I guess they were all fine," Dad would say.

"You didn't ask?" Mom would rant.

"I didn't think to."

We pulled up at the station and hurried inside. Deputy Slalom was sitting at his desk, and we were told to go on into his office.

I decided that you could always tell what kind of day it had been for the police station by the condition of Deputy Slalom's wardrobe.

So it kind of scared me when we walked in and his button-down shirt was completely unbuttoned, showing his white under-shirt. His sleeves were rolled up past his elbows, and his tie was in a wad on the desk.

"Sit," he barked as soon as we walked in.

Definitely not good news. I sat immediately, setting my sketch-pad and pencils on the floor under my chair. Detective Masterson sat in the chair beside me, and DJ stood behind us, since there wasn't another chair.

Deputy Slalom was pacing now, his shirttail flapping behind him. He was seething.

I watched him, my stomach knotting tighter each time he passed in front of me. I'd already resigned myself that this was not going to be the good news I was hoping for. Now, I was just hoping that there was a light at the end of the house arrest tunnel.

"Well," Deputy Slalom growled finally after five minutes

of pacing in front of us. He stopped behind his desk chair and gripped the sides of it. "Good news, Kate. They found the parade shooter."

He was still seething though, so I didn't bust into a happy dance just yet.

He squeezed the chair sides tighter. "And I just got off the phone with the Clayton county office."

Clayton is another suburb of St. Louis.

"It seems that our friendly and entirely *ridiculous* prison system has somehow *misplaced* a certain inmate!" Deputy Slalom shoved his chair against his desk so hard, the three framed pictures he had sitting on it fell over.

I jumped. I'd never heard so many stressed words from Deputy Slalom. At first, it didn't really register what he'd said because I was so shocked by the chair slamming and the yelling.

He'd seemed like such a docile man.

Guess not.

Detective Masterson went pale. "I'm sorry?" he said.

"Yeah! Yeah, that's all the guy from Clayton had to say!" Deputy Slalom was back to pacing. "'I'm sorry.' I'm sorry?! Does that suddenly help things? Are we finally living in a society where all people have to do is halfway apologize, and suddenly everything is all rainbows and butterflies and Hostess snack cakes?!" He banged his fists down on the desk and this time a paperweight fell over.

I kept scooting farther and farther back in my chair. I'd spent many a time in the principal's office hearing about how being tardy to class is setting myself up on a road of failure and disappointment, but Principal Murray had never yelled like this at me.

Somehow I got the feeling that Deputy Slalom wasn't yelling at us as much as just venting to us.

He flung himself into his chair with a huff. "John X is missing," he said in a sullen, deathly quiet voice.

The room immediately felt like it shrunk six feet in every

direction. My chest got tight, my lungs had trouble expanding. I couldn't feel anything past my waist. Any joy about the parade shooter being captured vanished like the rare package of Nutter Butters in front of my dad.

"Missing," Detective Masterson repeated after a few minutes of complete silence in the room.

"Missing. Gone. Kaput. MIA." Deputy Slalom waved a wrist around while he spoke, his eyes glassy, his gaze fixed on the window. "He was in his cell for breakfast, and there was no one there by lunch."

My hands were shaking violently, and I tried to control them by weaving my fingers together so tight, my knuckles turned white.

"The clever man from Clayton said he thought it was his 'responsibility' to let me know that they'd somehow 'misplaced' John X, and if he happened to show up here in South Woodhaven Falls, could we 'please arrange a transport' back to the prison." Deputy Slalom started shaking his head.

"What did you say?" Detective Masterson said.

"I said a bunch of words that I'm not going to repeat in front of a minor." He looked over at me. "And a girl minor at that." He let his breath out for a long minute and kept looking at me. "Kate. This changes a lot."

I managed a nod, but I'm not sure how I did. My muscles felt frozen and stiff, like when it would snow a lot on the hill behind my house and Dad and I would go sledding on Mom's cookie sheets when she wasn't home, much to her dismay when she'd return.

Detective Masterson looked at me as well and reached over, patting my shoulder. "Don't panic, Kate."

He said it in the same tone he'd use if I'd burned myself cooking. If any situation was worthy of a good panicking, I would think that this one would be it.

DJ had been awfully quiet behind us. I looked over, and he was standing there with his arms crossed over his chest, jaw muscles set, eyes glaring.

Maybe it was better that he wasn't talking.

Deputy Slalom took another deep breath and simply shook his head.

Right then, his secretary came in and gave him a manila folder. She looked at me and gave me a sad smile before she left.

He opened the folder and nodded at the contents. "Kate, you're going into official witness protection."

I thought I was in official witness protection. I opened my mouth to ask.

"And not just at your house with a couple of cops there." He peered over at Detective Masterson. "You're going with her."

The detective nodded. "Yes, sir."

"And Kirkpatrick?"

DJ finally spoke. "Yes, sir?" His voice was hard.

"You're staying here. I'll need all the manpower I can get. Kate, you and your parents are being shipped to an undisclosed location in the next four hours." He waved at his secretary through the window facing the room filled with cubicles, and she stood from her desk, walked over, and poked her head into the office.

"Yes, sir?"

"Have a car go pick up Kate's parents." He looked at me. "I assume they are both working?"

I nodded.

He looked back at his secretary. "The info is all in their folders. I want them back here in thirty minutes."

She nodded. "Yes, sir." She closed the door and walked back to her desk.

Deputy Slalom looked back at me. "Kate, when your parents get here, you'll have one hour to pack. Pack lightly and pack the essentials."

"Where are we going?" I asked.

He started shaking his head. "I can't tell you that." He squinted at the clock. It was almost one in the afternoon. "You will be headed to your location by three. Is that understood?" Then he looked at Detective Masterson. "I want confirmation that you are there by five tonight."

I could see a muscle jumping in Detective Masterson's cheek. He nodded stiffly. "Yes, sir."

"Kate, you are not to take any cell phones, computers, or whatever the latest gadget that starts with *i* is. No communication devices at all. Anything that could be traced to you, I want left here. Is that understood?"

I nodded.

He picked up the phone on his desk and started dialing. I sat there, numb, my fingers still woven together.

"Daniels? It's Slalom. I need you to get a forensics team over to Clayton and see if they can't find how in the blazes a level-four criminal escaped from there without anyone seeing him." Deputy Slalom listened for a minute. "Thanks." Then he slammed the phone down.

"I'm going to get any and every picture of John X that we have out there circulating. If he so much as even peeks out of his little gopher hole, I want someone there to slam him over the head with a mallet and some handcuffs. And no way in ..." He looked at me briefly. "No way in *heck* am I letting him go back to Clayton. Fool me once, shame on you. They aren't fooling me twice."

I was assuming that Deputy Slalom had been referring to the old arcade game where you had to whack the little groundhogs on their heads when they popped out of the holes before they went back in.

I was never very good at that game.

Thirty minutes later, almost to the second, both of my parents ran in, looking panicked.

"Kate!" my dad shouted when he saw me. "What happened? Are you okay? Did they catch the parade shooter?"

Apparently, no one had informed my parents why a policeman had demanded that they go with him in a squad car in the middle of the day.

Detective Masterson stood and offered my mom his chair. Deputy Slalom had spent the last few minutes before they got here trying to get the media relations guy to send out bulletins about John X to all the news stations in and around Missouri.

"I want his picture as far as he can drive in one day, you got that? And at every airport, bus station, and train depot around." Then he'd slammed down his phone so hard it probably left a resounding ring in the media guy's ear.

I was starting to worry about the structural integrity of his desk with the beating it was taking today.

Mom sat down in Detective Masterson's vacated chair and reached over for me. "Are you okay?" she asked, smoothing my hair away from my face.

"What is going on here?" Dad demanded.

Deputy Slalom was back to shaking his head. "They caught the parade shooter."

"Oh yay!" Mom said.

"Yeah. Yay. And then the idiots down at the Clayton prison seemed to have somehow 'misplaced' our friend John X."

I immediately jumped up out of my chair so Dad could drop into it, since he didn't look like he'd be able to stand for much longer.

Both he and my mom just stared at the deputy.

"They what?" Dad finally said.

Another slam on the desk, which made both Mom and Dad jump. "Look, I don't have the strength to tell it again," Deputy Slalom said, almost growling as he looked around the room. "Kent, tell them what's going on."

In short, precise sentences, Detective Masterson quietly informed Mom and Dad of the situation. "So, the four of us are going to be leaving in the next two hours for an undisclosed location," he finished.

Mom sat there, mouth open.

Dad jumped up from the chair and started pacing back and forth behind it, in front of DJ.

I stood quietly against the window.

"Obviously, our primary concern is for Kate's safety," Detective Masterson said to Dad. "So, we need you guys to go home and pack only the essentials. No cell phones, computers, or any other communication device that could trace someone back to Kate."

"What about our family?" Mom started fretting. "Our son, Mike. He's in school. What am I supposed to tell him? What about my work?"

"What about our dog?" I asked.

"How often do you talk to your son?" Deputy Slalom asked Mom.

We all just looked at Mom, wondering if she'd actually admit how little she talked to him. She sighed and shrugged. "It varies."

It did vary. It varied on how often Mike needed something.

"Don't tell him anything then," Deputy Slalom said. "Here's the thing, Mrs. Carter. I don't want another person outside of these four walls to know where Kate is, whether that means lying your tail off to your work or your son."

Mom nodded and I saw the tears building.

Dad must've seen them too, because he reached down and put both hands on her shoulders. "We'll tell work that we got offered the use of a vacation house and we decided to take it. Considering everything that has happened, I don't think anyone's going to doubt our need of a good vacation."

Mom nodded again and sniffed. "And Mike?" she asked quietly.

Dad sighed. "We'll tell him we won't be able to answer our phones for a while and if he needs to get ahold of us to have him call ..." Dad's voice trailed off and he looked at Deputy Slalom. "I guess giving him Kent's number wouldn't be the wisest, would it?"

"Tell him to call your friend Gene," Deputy Slalom said. He tapped a nameplate I hadn't noticed before on his desk. It was gold and engraved.

Deputy Gene Slalom.

Dad nodded. Mom nodded. Detective Masterson nodded.

I was too busy feeling sorry that the deputy had to go through life with a name like Gene Slalom to nod. No wonder he went into law enforcement.

"Make your calls," Deputy Slalom said. "And then you've got an hour to pack. I want every one of you gone by three."

"And Lolly?" I asked.

Deputy Slalom sighed. "What kind of dog is she?"

"Lab, sir."

He sighed harder. "My wife and I will take her for a few days."

Mom immediately pulled out her cell phone and pushed the speed dial. She waited for a while, her expression growing bleaker and bleaker with each passing second. "Hi, honey," she said, finally, and I could hear her holding back the tears as she talked. "It's Mom. We're going on something of a last-minute vacation and our cell phones won't work there, so if you need something, call our friend Gene at 555 – 8711." She paused. "Love you, Mike."

Dad was on the phone with his work. "We got offered a fabulous vacation rental for a little while, and we think that we of all people deserve a vacation," he said. "My cell won't work, so just hold all my calls and I'll return them when I get back."

I opened my cell phone and looked at it. Who did I need to call? Who did I want to call?

I sent Maddy a text message. *We are going out of town for a few days. No cell reception. Talk later.*

Then I called Justin. It was almost two, which meant last period had started a little over thirty minutes ago. I was expecting his voicemail.

Just so I could tell him not to bother with the homework.

"Hi, Kate," he answered.

I frowned at the phone. "Justin?"

"Yeah?"

"Why are you answering your phone?"

He paused. "Um. You called me on it."

"No, I know, but aren't you in school?"

"I've got study hall the last period. I went out to the hallway."

I shrugged. "Oh."

"So, uh, did you need something?"

Mom was calling her secretary, Madge, to tell her to hold all of her appointments.

"Yeah, Justin," I said, quietly. "I need you to not pick up my homework anymore. You see, there was this great vacation house that opened up, and Mom and Dad decided we needed a little bit of family time away from everything. And since I wasn't going to school anyway ..." I let my voice trail off. "But thanks for helping me out these last few weeks."

I got ready to hang up.

"Wait, wait," he said. "You're just leaving?"

"Yeah."

"Just like that?"

"Just like that," I said. It didn't seem like the people on the other end of Mom and Dad's calls were having this much trouble believing them. I must not have been a very good liar.

Justin paused like he didn't believe me and he had more questions, but I jumped in before he could start. "Anyway, good to talk to you, thanks for everything, bye!"

I closed my phone quickly, feeling bad for hanging up on him, but I would have felt worse if I'd let something slip.

Twenty minutes later, I was throwing as many belongings as I could into my suitcase that I hadn't used in two years.

I didn't even remember what my suitcase looked like. Dad had to get it out of the garage for me because I couldn't find it.

"Maybe we need to go on 'vacations' more often," Dad said, rolling his eyes.

We both knew why we hadn't gone anywhere for so long. Mom couldn't stand the thought of us going on a family vacation without Mike.

And Mike was never here.

So we never went.

I put in socks, T-shirts, long sleeves, jeans, and shorts, just so I was prepared for any type of weather, though if we were driving and Deputy Slalom was planning on us getting there — wherever there was — by five, then we weren't going very far away.

I grabbed a few books, found a couple of DVDs that I hadn't seen in a while to throw in there, and reached over for my sketchpad.

It wasn't on my desk.

Actually, it wasn't anywhere in my room.

"Mom, have you seen my sketchpad?" I asked her as she ran down the hall, hauling an armload of whites that were fresh from the dryer.

She shook her head. "Sorry, Katie-Kin. Did you check the family room?" She disappeared into her bedroom. I could see Dad in there packing ammunition beside his clothing.

I looked in the living room, the kitchen, and had DJ go look in the black Tahoe. Detective Masterson was home packing, and he would bring back the car we were going to take.

"You can't be too careful," he'd said.

DJ came back inside shaking his head. "Sorry, Kate. It's not there." He had a helpless look on his face, and he'd had it on there since we'd gotten back to my house.

I figured he was probably wishing he was coming with us. He'd spent the past three weeks living with us, after all.

"I'm sorry you aren't coming with us," I said.

He just nodded at me. "Me too."

I went back to my room to finish packing. Suddenly I remembered where my sketchbook was. I'd left it underneath my chair in Deputy Slalom's office.

I heard Detective Masterson come into our house then. He stuck his head in my room. "Time to go, Kate."

"I left my sketchpad and pencils at the station," I told him.

He shrugged. "We don't have time to stop for it. I'm sorry, Kate. Do you have another one you can bring?"

I had one from last summer that still had a few empty pages in it. I sighed and packed that one instead alongside a bunch of pencils that weren't my favorite brand, but weren't awful.

Detective Masterson had brought a white GMC Yukon and parked it in the garage. We quietly piled into it while the garage door was still closed. DJ was still at our house when we left.

"Hope we see you again soon," I said as we climbed into the Yukon.

He nodded. "Drive safely." He closed my door and walked quickly back inside, shutting the door behind him. The goal was to leave as unnoticed as possible. There was no telling whether there were still camera crews watching my house.

Detective Masterson instructed all of us to duck down in our seats for the time being. He wanted whoever was watching — if anyone was watching — to think that he'd driven up alone and left alone. I think Dad had the hardest seat to do that since he was sitting in the passenger seat.

Mom and I laid down on the backseat. All of our bags were behind us and I started thinking about where we were going. Was it a hotel? A cabin? I'd seen movies where the people had to be put in protective custody, but I'd never ever thought it would happen to me.

Finally, Detective Masterson said we could sit up again. We were on the highway, headed west.

"Can you tell us where we're going now?" I asked.

He shook his head. "You'll be able to tell the basic area soon, but it's best if you don't know details, Kate."

"Is it a hotel?"

"I can't tell you."

I looked out the window. "Is it a camping site?"

"Kate," he said, looking at me in the rearview mirror. "No details, kid. Sorry. You'll find out soon enough."

"Detective Masterson?"

He sighed. "Yes, Kate?"

"Can you turn on the radio?"

He flipped it on and it was tuned to the local country station, and I had to wonder about the detective's musical tastes. This wasn't cool country like Rascal Flatts.

This was old-school country, like whatever the guy's name was who had the long, gray hair and wore old blankets around.

Dad started humming along and settled back in his chair contentedly. "See? This was the era of good music."

"Agreed," Detective Masterson said.

I looked at my mom, who was rolling her eyes. Mom tends to be very modern-day with her musical choices. She worked out to the Black Eyed Peas and Justin Timberlake.

I told Maddy that and she's thought my mom was the coolest mom ever since then. Apparently, her mom doesn't work out and the only music she ever listens to is the commercial medleys between talk show hosts.

Mom always said that the eighties were a period of horrific hairstyles and much-too-short shorts for men, so why in the world did anyone assume that those same people who created those styles could create quality music? Her case in point was Madonna, but I would have used someone like Boy George.

He was just plain weird.

Two hours later, we were passing the signs for Columbia, Missouri, when Detective Masterson put his blinker on and exited the freeway.

I perked up. I'd been staring out the window without really watching the scenery, trying to block out the old-timer country music.

We were going to Columbia?

He kept driving through the town and turned right on a tiny two-lane road that went on and on for miles. All around us were trees, hills, and more trees. And the trees got thicker the farther we drove.

Detective Masterson made several more turns and finally

stopped in front of a tiny house in the middle of a clearing that was pretty much in the middle of a forest.

"Welcome to your hopefully temporary home," Detective Masterson said, putting the Yukon in park and turning off the engine.

The house looked creepy. I stared at it through the windshield. It was small and square and looked like it could have been the hideout for the Unabomber at one point.

Everyone climbed out, and I stepped out of the car onto a carpet of pine needles. The trees were ginormous and I wondered at what point the little house had last seen daylight. Between the thick trees, hardly any sun made it through to the ground.

Birds were chirping, but other than that, it was totally silent.

I shivered, creeped out again.

Dad picked up his and Mom's suitcases, and Detective Masterson grabbed his and mine before heading up to the front porch of the house. He unlocked the front door, and it squealed in protest as it opened.

"Come on in," he said, leading the way and flicking on lights as he went.

The house was tiny. There was a living room and kitchen directly off the front door. Then a short hallway and three miniature bedrooms. Orange shag carpeting covered everything but the kitchen. Detective Masterson set my suitcase on the creaky twin bed in the last bedroom. "Might as well get comfortable, Kate."

I looked around the room. Everything had dark wood paneling covering it, even the closet doors. The bedspread on the bed was an ivory-colored quilt. There was a short dresser in the room and no other furniture.

I walked back into the family room, where Detective Masterson was talking quietly on his cell phone.

"Yes, sir. Yes, sir." He saw me come in and waved to me. "I'll tell her, sir. All right. Bye." He closed the phone, pocketed it, and looked at me. "I need to show you something that this house has." He pointed to the kitchen, and I followed him in there.

The kitchen was old. Old orange linoleum, old appliances, old dark wood paneling everywhere.

Detective Masterson knelt down in front of the sink. "See this?" he pointed up under the countertop. I bent over.

A small white button was there.

"Yeah," I said.

"That's a silent alarm. There's one in every bedroom, two in here and two in the living room. If you push that button, a team from the FBI will be here in the next four and a half minutes."

I nodded. "Okay."

"If anything feels even off to you, you come find me. If you can't find me for whatever reason, you push that button. Got it?" He was looking at me very seriously.

I nodded again. "Got it."

"I'll show you where all the buttons are."

He took me on a tour around the house and pointed out every hidden button. I never would have seen them if they hadn't been pointed out to me.

"How often do you guys use this house?" I asked.

"This is the first time our department's ever had to use it," Detective Masterson said when we got back into the living room. "But it's open to all police and FBI in the Missouri area."

"And when was the last time someone thought about updating it?" I asked, poking at one of the yellowing lace curtains over the front window.

He grinned. "You don't like it?" He looked around, smiling. "I guess it could use a little sprucing. Hopefully we won't be here long enough to pull out the home décor books though. And really, it is pretty up to date." He pointed to the window. "All the glass in here? Bulletproof. And the alarm system, of course. And there's a sensor that tracks body heat that is within the five miles surrounding this place. All those gadgets are in my room."

"What about bears?" I asked.

"What about them?"

"Do they come close to the house?"

He shrugged. "They've never hurt anyone if they do."

Not quite the answer I was looking for. I'd seen a documentary on TV one time about a man who tamed bears and fed them on his land, and he was trying to tell the world that they really were just nice, cuddly creatures, but I had a hard time believing him.

Sort of like when people have told me that rats make good pets. I just don't believe them. Rats are disgusting.

I sat down on the olive green and orange-striped couch and looked at the TV. It had a dial on it.

Dad and Mom came out into the living room then.

"Wow, I haven't seen a TV like that since college," Dad said, excitedly. He reached over and twisted a knob, and the TV blinked a few times and then came on to pure static.

"Yeah, about the TV," Detective Masterson said. "I think since we are so thick into these trees, only a few channels make it through."

Dad twisted the knob around, and Mom joined me on the couch.

A couple of minutes later, a baseball game flickered through the static. Dad was overjoyed.

"Look at this, Claire!" he said, sitting down next to Mom. "Kate, this was what TV was for us when we were little kids. None of this flatscreen HD madness. Just good old-fashioned rabbit ears."

"Mm-hmm," I said. I was a little distracted by the pitcher's head moving from right to left across the screen without bringing his body with it.

I got up from the couch and went to get my sketchbook. The only place to draw was on the kitchen table, so I sat down and pulled out my rubber-banded pencils.

Detective Masterson was standing in the kitchen, checking out the contents in the fridge.

"No food?" I asked.

"Oh, there's food. The guys in Columbia stocked it for us before we got here." He pulled out a big jug of chocolate milk. "Want a glass?"

I couldn't even remember the last time I had chocolate milk. Probably since before Mom's big health kick. I started nodding.

He poured two glasses and then sat down at the table with me, passing my cup over.

"What are you working on?" he asked.

I shrugged. I had been working on his face, but I'd left that sketchbook in Deputy Slalom's office. "I don't know," I said. Maybe I'd draw my parents now. Or the pitcher with the wavy head.

"So, I got you something," he said. "Before I knew we were coming here, but I did pack it in my suitcase, so hang on a second."

He disappeared down the hallway and came back with a thin box. Sitting back down at the table, he passed it over to me. *NIV Bible*.

I frowned. It seemed like the box holding the Bible might be spell-checked more carefully. What in the world was a "Niv"?

"You don't have to read it," he said, watching my face. "I just thought with some of the questions you've been asking me, and your mom trying to get you guys to go to church more, that you might need a Bible."

"Thanks," I said. "What's a 'niv'?"

"A niv?" he parroted confusedly and then looked at the box. "Oh! NIV? That means New International Version."

"Oh," I said. I opened the box and the Bible was thin and on the smaller side, covered in soft, buttery-smooth brown leather.

It was nothing like the incredibly bulky and heavy Bibles I'd seen at South Woodhaven Falls First Baptist.

"Thanks, Detective Masterson," I said, smiling at him.

"You're welcome. And I would start in Luke, by the way," he said. "This isn't like a normal book where you start at the beginning and work your way through."

I nodded.

Dad stood up. "Okay, his head is making me crazy," he said, fiddling with the rabbit ears on the back of the TV.

Now the pitcher's head was standing still, but his body was moving back and forth.

"HD TV is looking pretty good right now, huh, sweetie?" Mom said, and I could hear the mocking grin in her voice.

It could be a long time in this tiny house.

Chapter Eighteen

FIVE DAYS PASSED VERY SLOWLY. BY THE END OF THE SECOND day, Dad had rigged an entire coat hanger system over the TV, and we then had about fifteen more channels than we originally had and no more fuzzy heads.

Mom had paced the short length from the front living room window to the back kitchen window two hundred and seventeen times. Then she started doing lunges from the back window to the front window.

Detective Masterson spent most of the time reading. I'd discovered he was a Clive Cussler fan. The only thing I knew about Clive Cussler was that the movie *Sahara* with Matthew McConaughey was based on one of his books.

I wasn't really a Matthew McConaughey fan. He was shirtless too much of the time.

I alternated between working on pictures of Mom and Dad while munching on Chips Ahoy and taking naps, since I still wasn't sleeping at night.

The house was starting to feel smaller and smaller.

Wednesday morning at two fifteen, I was still staring up at the ceiling with bleary eyes. When we'd first gotten there, the room had been pitch black at night, because there weren't any street-lights like at home to give a comforting glow to the room.

After the first night of no sleeping, Detective Masterson handed me a night-light to plug in.

I felt like a wimp for needing a night-light to sleep. I was, after all, sixteen years old, and night-lights were typically used with what? Two-year-olds?

Next thing I knew, I'd be asking for a blanket and a binky.

The night-light helped though. Obviously I still wasn't sleeping, but at least I wasn't laying in bed with my heart pounding wondering if there was someone in my closet or not.

I slept with my closet doors open too.

I looked at the clock again. Two seventeen.

Yay. Two whole minutes had passed.

Sighing, I reached over for the ancient Tiffany-style bedside lamp and turned it on, blinking into the sudden burst of light. My eyes felt raw and dried out, sort of like week-old grapes that probably just needed to be tossed.

The Bible that Detective Masterson had given me was laying on the bedside table. I hadn't read anything in it so far.

Start in Luke, he'd said.

I picked it up and opened it. The pages were super thin, like tissue paper. Maybe owning a Bible wasn't a good idea for someone like me who tended to accidentally rip things.

I turned the first pages until I got to the table of contents and found the listing for Luke. Page 847.

The Bible was a lot bigger than I'd figured it was.

I flipped over carefully and ended up in a section called Psalms on my way over to Luke.

There were a lot of chapters in Psalms. I was looking at Psalm 112 and there were still a bunch after it.

One line caught my eye. "They will have no fear of bad news; their hearts are steadfast, trusting in the LORD."

I wasn't sure who "they" were, but I found myself wishing that I could be like them. You know, the whole not fearing bad news.

At this point, my life was all about fear.

I read a little further in the Psalm and some of it sounded like the songs we'd sung at church last Sunday.

I wondered what it would be like to be like Justin or Detective Masterson. Both of them seemed so set that everything that was happening was God's plan. And for some reason, that made everything okay.

Everything was not okay, though. I'd already been shot at once, and now the guy who I put in prison was likely out there looking for me.

I shivered and looked at the closed blinds covering the bullet-proof window. My life had been reduced to a tiny house in the middle of the woods of Missouri.

I spent the next three hours reading in the Psalms. By the time I reached over to turn off the bedside lamp to try and get a few more hours of sleep, I could hear the birds starting their morning chirping.

I slept until almost eight, which was really good for me. I walked out into the living room after I brushed my teeth and found Mom and Dad pulling on their sneakers.

"Morning, Katie-Kin. We're going for a quick walk," Mom said, doing a couple of stretches. "Want to come with us?"

I watched Mom do a few lunges and shook my head, yawning. I might be going stir-crazy, but I wasn't about to go power walking with Mom. Mom took her walks far too seriously.

I was actually amazed that Dad was going to go with her. He mocked her mercilessly about how she walked.

He must be really bored.

"No, thanks," I said. "Have fun." I sat down on the couch.

"We'll be back soon," Mom said, kissing the top of my head.

"I'll tell Kent we're leaving," Dad said.

I looked around. "Where is he?"

He shrugged. "Something about the motion sensor. I think he's working on it in the shed out back."

They left and I went to pour a bowl of Cocoa Puffs, one of the many contraband items in our house that was luckily in plenty of supply here. Detective Masterson walked in as I was pouring the milk over them, listening to the happy sounds of chocolate snapping.

"Good morning, Kate," he said, backhanding his forehead and reaching for a bottle of water from the fridge.

"Hot outside?"

"Stuffy in the shed," he said after gulping half the bottle. "Anyway, I've got to finish working on this thing." He unclipped his cell phone and set it beside me on the table. "If you need anything or anything even seems off, push 4 – 6 – 3. That will buzz my pager."

I nodded. "Okay."

"It shouldn't take me too long. And I'm just behind the house."

I nodded again. "Okay."

"Have a good breakfast."

He left and the house suddenly felt very quiet.

Quiet, dark, and small.

I ate my Cocoa Puffs in crunching silence, reading the back of the box as I ate. Apparently, Toucan Sam had a friend who was crazy for this cereal.

I put my bowl in the sink when I finished and found my sketchbook. My parents' heads were coming along, but I wasn't quite done yet.

I sat down on the couch.

Nothing like an orange and olive green–striped couch sitting on orange carpeting and surrounded by dark wood paneling to get the inspiration rolling.

I stared at my parents' half-finished heads for about fifteen minutes before I finally just flipped the page over and started drawing something else.

Last night, one of the Psalm chapters, the first one I think, had mentioned something about someone sitting under a tree or being like a tree or something like that. That was one of the last ones I read, so it was a little fuzzy to me. But looking out the front window and seeing just a mesh of trees made me think of it.

I usually liked to stick to people but I started sketching the forest. I drew the window frame I was looking through, complete with the wood paneling on the sides of it. Then, through the window, I drew the trees.

The sound of Detective Masterson's phone ringing startled me and I jumped, my pencil making the limbs on one tree look more abstract than real.

I walked over to the table and looked at the cell. He had one of those phones that rang and vibrated at the same time, so it was jangling and turning in a circle on the table.

He hadn't told me what to do if his phone rang.

I picked it up and looked at the screen.

Slalom.

I should probably answer it if it was the deputy calling.

"Hello?" I said, my voice all mousy. I hated how I seemed to always talk an octave higher on the phone.

"Who is this?" Deputy Slalom demanded.

"Um. Kate, sir. Kate Carter."

"Kate, why are you answering Kent's phone?"

"Um. Because he's out working in the shed." Now, not only was I talking an octave higher, I was stuttering and a tattletale.

Today was going to be a great day.

"Get him. NOW!"

I nearly dropped the phone when he yelled. "Uh, yes, sir," I managed, fumbling with the phone and running for the front door. My stomach was flip-flopping like I had a dozen or so wide-mouthed bass swimming around in there.

Maybe they'd caught John X!

I shoved my feet in some flip-flops and ran out the front door, leaving it slightly ajar, and onto the porch. The birds were singing, there was a slight breeze, and the sun was shining through the trees in small patches all over the pine-needle-blanketed clearing.

The shed was in the back. I hadn't been to the back yet since I was pretty content to stay inside, all things considered.

"Did you find him?" Deputy Slalom barked at me.

"Uh, not yet, sir."

"Good grief, Kate, the house is tinier than my aunt Gladys' kitchen! Find him now!"

"Yes, sir. Right away, sir."

I tripped over the natural landscape and found myself thankful for the manicured lawn Dad cared so much about. I didn't even have to worry about stubbing my toe in his grass.

Not like I was ever allowed to walk on it.

I finally saw the shed a few feet back from the house and I hurried as quickly as I could toward it, phone smashed to my ear, trying to avoid all the fallen branches, rocks, and probably snake holes around.

I had one thing in common with Indiana Jones, and that was that we both hated snakes. Other than that, we were total opposites.

It was my goal to lead my life in relative obscurity.

Which obviously was not happening right now.

I looked up at the shed and saw someone coming out of it, closing both the doors behind him.

It was DJ.

"DJ!" I shouted, waving and smiling.

"DJ?" Deputy Slalom yelled in my ear.

"Hi!" I said.

He waved back and started walking in my direction.

"Kate! Listen to me — run! Get as far away from DJ as you can!" Deputy Slalom yelled.

I stopped about halfway between the house and the shed, frowning. "What?" I said. "It's DJ. The guy from your police force?"

"Kate, get in the house! Get back in the house *now*!"

I didn't try to argue with him, but I couldn't help thinking how ridiculous it was for me to be running back to the house when I'd just waved at DJ.

DJ had lived with us for the last month. What did Deputy Slalom think he'd do? Hug me in greeting?

"Kate!" DJ yelled behind me, and I could hear him crashing through the brush. "Kate, hold on!"

I tripped up the front steps and into the front door, closing it and locking it behind me right as DJ rammed into it, grabbing the knob. "Kate!" he shouted again.

What if DJ had news about John X? What if he knew something and had driven all the way out here to tell us?

"Are you in the house?" Deputy Slalom was still yelling at me.

My heart was pounding. I just stared at DJ through the window on the front door. "Yes, sir."

"Do not open that door, Kate. Do you hear me? Do *not* open that door!"

DJ pounded on the door. "Open the door, Kate! Don't listen to him!"

"Deputy, what — ?"

"You left your sketchbook here," Deputy Slalom shouted.

I went into the kitchen to get away from DJ's pounding on the door. "Okay."

"You left your sketchbook here and one of the guys we brought up from St. Louis started looking through it."

A sketchbook isn't the same thing as a journal, but for me, it can be. I felt myself getting a little offended. "He what?"

"He looked through it and saw the picture you did of DJ."

My heart started beating a little faster. I watched as DJ paced the front porch, staring into the house, shouting at me.

"Open the door, Kate!"

"Kate. He recognized him. From a case about four years ago."

Surely Deputy Slalom meant that DJ had worked on the case. He must have worked in St. Louis.

I couldn't get a full breath into my lungs. They felt cramped, like there suddenly wasn't enough room in my rib cage.

"Kate, a man matching DJ's exact description was an accomplice in John X's first murder."

And just like that, my heart stopped pounding. I sank to the kitchen chair, shock making it impossible for my kneecaps to hold the standing position.

"But he ... how ...?"

"We hired him exactly three and a half years ago. He had no police record, we didn't know anything about any of this. But the cop from St. Louis brought up the case records from the first murder." Deputy Slalom sighed and I could picture him rubbing his forehead. "Kate, it's him. I don't know the whys and I really don't understand the hows, but it's him."

"Kate! Open the door!" DJ yelled, pounding on the front window.

I looked at him, and the fear took over. I shook from head to toe. DJ? The same guy who slept outside my room on an air mattress for the last four weeks? The guy who panicked when Officer DeWeise was shot, the guy who tried to make me laugh when he could tell I was getting freaked out?

He, of all people, was working with the man who was trying to kill me?

DJ looked and sounded angry. His eyes were bloodshot, his face was bright red, and he was yelling constantly.

I started worrying about my mom and dad. And Detective Masterson. I'd seen DJ coming out of the shed. What if he'd killed Detective Masterson and my parents?

I started shaking harder. Tears were gathering in the corners of my eyes, and I felt like all of my muscles had turned to overcooked noodles.

"Stay on the phone with me, Kate," Deputy Slalom said. "I've got the FBI headed your direction."

"Kate! Kate!" DJ started banging both fists on the window, screaming at the top of his lungs. "Kate!"

I don't think I even realized what happened at first.

One minute I was holding the phone, Deputy Slalom talking in my ear about how the FBI was on the way, the next minute the phone was gone and I was face-to-face with a man whose face I knew better than my own.

"Hello, Kate Carter from South Woodhaven Falls."

It was John X.

Chapter Nineteen

I COULD ONLY ASSUME THAT MY CENTRAL NERVOUS SYSTEM had shut down, because for some reason I was very calm right then. The man I'd been having nightmares about for weeks was standing right in front of me closing Detective Masterson's phone and smiling smugly.

And I just sat there. I didn't scream. I didn't faint.

I didn't even twitch.

DJ, meanwhile, was continuing to pound on the door, the window, the siding on the house, yelling at the top of his lungs. "Kate! Kate!"

John X ignored him. Instead, he pulled out the chair to my right and sat down at the table with me, pushing the detective's cell phone to the other side of it.

"So, Kate Carter," he said.

His voice was different than I'd imagined it. It wasn't scarily deep. It was cultured, almost. Precise.

I just looked at him. He was, all things considered, a very nice-looking man. A strong jawline, high cheekbones. And unlike the thin-lipped, beady-eyed crooks like I'd always imagined, John X actually had a nice smile and really pretty brown eyes. He wasn't too tall and he wasn't too short. And he was dressed fairly stylishly — straight-cut jeans, a collared Polo shirt.

No wonder he'd targeted women. It was difficult to think of the man in front of me committing a moving traffic violation, much less murder.

I didn't say anything.

He knit his fingers together on the table and looked over at me. "So, you've made things a little difficult for me lately," he said.

I kept thinking about the panic buttons Detective Masterson had told me about. If only I could get up nonchalantly and push one of the buttons.

"KATE!" DJ yelled.

John X sighed and looked out the window. "Your friend is a slow learner."

"Apparently, he's your friend too," I said quietly, surprising myself with the sound of my voice.

John X's mouth curled in a small smile. "Is that what your friendly deputy just told you?"

I shrugged but inside I was worried. If he knew I was talking to Deputy Slalom, then he knew that it was only a matter of time before the FBI got here.

So why was he just sitting at the dining room table with me? Why hadn't he killed me and moved on before he got caught again?

Four and a half minutes, that's what Detective Masterson had told me. It would take the FBI four and a half minutes to get here.

It had been two since I'd talked to the deputy and he'd said they were on their way.

"You're quite young," John X said, looking at me, sounding almost surprised. "How old are you?"

"Sixteen."

"I knew you were still in high school, but I wasn't expecting ... well, when does life really go by your expectations, though, right?" He sat up straighter. "Such a shame. I bet you were going to be the shining star of the South Woodhaven Falls police force, hmm?"

My nerves were back at his use of the past tense in referring to me. I clasped my hands together to keep from shaking. I kept thinking about the Psalm I read last night. The "they" who had no reason to fear.

I had reason to fear.

It had been three minutes. I only needed another minute and a half.

I sat quietly and he watched me, leaning back in his chair. The only sound was DJ's occasional yell.

"How come you aren't letting him in?" I asked finally.

"How come you aren't?" he asked me.

"Because I heard he was with you."

"Interesting," John X said, rubbing his chin. "Because I've been hearing different reports about little Darren there." He looked over at DJ, who was staring through the window, visibly seething. "Consciences can be deadly things."

I frowned. "So DJ didn't help you kill the first lady?"

John X snapped his gaze back to me. "Oh, no. He did. He just didn't adapt as well to life after the murder. Some people just can't face who they really are, you know?"

Dad had told me that exact phrase once during one of his infamous Kate-should-become-an-engineer talks. I'd made a comment that I wasn't sure I wanted to be an engineer and Dad had only said, "Well. Some people can't face who they really are until college. You'll get there, Kate. You'll get there."

Detective Masterson believed in a whole "plan" type of life where everything was God's plan.

Was this God's plan? Me accidentally drawing a murderer and soon becoming his next victim? And who knew what had happened to the detective or my parents, for that matter.

I looked down at the orange linoleum and squeezed my eyes shut.

God. If You're there, please help me.

It was probably the shortest prayer ever prayed, but I didn't have a lot of time.

John X was looking at me again, head slightly tipped, eyes thoughtful. "So, Kate Carter, what should we do now?"

I shrugged. "You could let me go." It was worth a shot.

"Ah. See, I could. And I probably should. But you know I can't do that," he said, smoothly.

I nodded, my heart pounding. It had been five and a half minutes.

Where was the FBI?

DJ had stopped pounding on the door. He just stared at us through the window.

John X sighed. "Well, now, Kate Carter, I probably should do what I came here to do," he said.

Apparently, John X liked both my first and last name.

I looked at him and then back at the window. DJ was gone and I felt a mix of relief and panic. On the one hand, if he was working with John X, then I was glad he'd left.

On the other hand, now it was just the two of us.

And John X was pulling a small black gun from his pocket. He set it on the table between us and sighed again. "Such a waste of talent," he muttered. He looked over at me. "I hope you realize that I hate to do this."

I swallowed hard. I wasn't ready to die. I didn't know what came next. Heaven? A weird mix of memories? Eternal napping?

I heard tires crunch on the driveway right then. John X looked out the front window and frowned. "Hmm," he said.

I don't know what came over me. I grabbed the gun from the table and bolted for the front door. I had just gotten the top lock open when John X tackled me from behind. I fell forward, clutching the gun to my chest and hitting my head hard on the front door.

People were yelling outside, "FBI! FBI!"

My head was ringing. I'd fallen on my knees right in front of the door. I reached up to unlock the second lock.

I heard the snap almost before I felt it. John X had hit my left wrist so hard, he'd broken it. I started crying in pain.

The door in front of me blistered right as the windows shattered, but didn't break. They were bulletproof, after all. I screamed.

I scooted to the wall by the door, still holding the gun in an iron grip with my right hand. John X was kneeling right in front of me, pulling his fist back, shaking his head, aiming for my face.

"Stop right there."

John X froze.

My dad stood there behind him, 9mm trained directly on John X's head, his legs spread in a shooting stance. He didn't even look at me, he just kept both hands on the gun and both eyes on John X.

"Hands on your head. Now."

Slowly, ever so slowly, John X lifted both hands and put them on his head, falling cross-legged to the floor.

The front door busted open and suddenly the place was swarming with men with guns. Dad didn't move. John X didn't move.

And I sure didn't move because the two of them were trapping me against the wall.

One of the men pulled a set of handcuffs from his back pocket and wrapped them around John X's wrists, yanking him up and pushing him outside. "You know what?" he was saying as he escorted John X out. "I'm not even going to read you the Miranda warning. I'm going to let you tell it since you know it so well."

"Kate," Dad said, dropping to his knees in front of me. "Oh, Katie." He gripped me in a short hug and then stood. "I need a doctor!" he yelled, looking at my quickly swelling and bruising wrist.

I still had John X's gun in an iron grip against my chest. "DJ," I muttered, tears still streaming down my face.

Dad nodded. "They arrested him before they broke in," he said.

I blinked and looked up at him. "How did you — ?" As far as I knew, there was only one way into the house and one way out. And the front door was it.

Dad shrugged. "I shattered the back window when they were making all the commotion in here."

"It was bulletproof," I said.

"You can only make glass bulletproof to a certain extent, Kate." The engineer in my dad was taking over. "I shot three holes in it and then used the tire iron from Kent's car to break it the rest of the way. See, bulletproof glass works because it has several layers and the layers absorb the bullet so it doesn't pierce all the way through. But it does damage the rest of the glass, because — "

I shook my head and interrupted, because quite frankly, at that moment, I didn't care. "Mom? Detective Masterson?"

"Both fine. DJ knocked Kent out and locked him in the shed before he tried to come get you. I guess he was planning on taking you away from here to keep John X from finding you." Dad was shaking his head.

Mom ran into the house then, panicking. "Kate! Kate!" she screamed, dropping to the floor beside me. "Are you okay? You're alive! Where's the doctor? Where's an ambulance?" She grabbed my face in both hands. "Don't worry, Kate, we're getting you into intense psychotherapy when we leave here!"

I was worried about that. Actually, no I wasn't.

I just smiled at my parents and sniffled back the tears. "Let's go home."

Chapter Twenty

TWO WEEKS LATER

THE BELL WAS RINGING AND I LAID MY MATH HOMEWORK on my teacher's desk. "Don't forget about the pop quiz Monday!" he yelled over the bell as we left.

Yay.

It was the last class of the day and I was officially done with school for the week. In three weeks, I was going to be officially done with school for the entire summer. I stopped by my locker to grab my other books.

"Hey."

I looked over. Justin.

"Hey," I said, closing my locker and stuffing the extra books into my backpack.

"Are you coming to church on Sunday?" he asked.

I nodded. "Pretty sure." We'd been last Sunday. We again went to the late service and missed out on hearing the multicolored choir and the amen-ers, but I did meet a few more people from school, and now they waved and stopped to talk to me in between classes.

I had more friends than just Maddy. My mom was thrilled.

She hadn't made me go to psychotherapy, but she did ask me to let her know anytime I started thinking about what happened at the little house in the woods.

And she started reading through Luke with me.

So far, this guy named Jesus had made some pretty huge claims about himself. I was curious if they were going to hold true. I couldn't really understand why God had answered my prayer at the house, but he had and I was willing to learn more about him.

Justin nodded. "Want to come study with me?"

I shrugged on my ridiculously heavy backpack, sighing. "I can't. I've got work."

"Oh. Okay."

He actually looked kind of sad.

"I can come tomorrow though," I said.

He grinned at me. "Sounds good. See you tomorrow, Kate."

And then he winked at me before he left.

My stomach twisted slightly, and I cleared my throat. There was no time to think about Justin right now. I was already late.

I ran for my car and tossed my backpack into the passenger seat. We'd gotten a huge check as reward money for finding John X, and Dad had used it to upgrade my car. "I guess it's fine for you to drive something a little newer," he'd said grudgingly one day when I got home from school. A two-year-old Jeep Wrangler sat in the garage.

Now I couldn't help grinning as I drove to work. The sun was shining, the birds were singing. I had the windows down and the breeze was rifling through my hair.

I pulled into a parking place and walked inside, waving at the front-door secretary.

"They're waiting for you in the conference room," she said, smiling at me.

I opened the door and Detective Masterson and Deputy Slalom

were both sitting in the conference room. Detective Masterson stood and smiled shortly at me.

"Hi, Kate. How was school?"

"Fine. I actually—"

Deputy Slalom cut in then, stripping off his sports coat and rolling up his sleeves. "That's great, Kate, but we don't have time for pleasantries today. We've got a new witness for you, and this case is a doozy. Started in Arkansas and now this creep is moving north."

I sat down at the table, took a deep breath, smiled at Detective Masterson, and nodded at Deputy Slalom.

It was going to be a great summer.

Normal.

Acknowledgments

To my parents — Doug and Susan Mangum, thank you for loving me, raising me, and giving me the gift of a crazy imagination. I've always loved you, but I never appreciated you fully until we had Nathan! Thank you for everything you've done for me!

To my family — Bryant, Caleb, and Cayce Mangum; Greg, Connie, Allen, Vicky, Tommy, and Ashlee O'Brien: thank you for the laughs, the prayers, and for encouraging me. I am so blessed to have you as my family. I love you all!

To my friends — Clint and Leigh Ann Trebesh, Eitan and Kaitlin Bar, Mario and Elisa Martinez, Greg and Jen Fulkerson, Barb Walker, Shannon Kay, and my wonderful friends at Mars Hill ABQ — thank you for being such an incredible blessing in my life!

To the friends I've made at Zondervan, particularly Jacque Alberta — thank you! My agent, Steve Laube — thanks for helping me find a home for this novel.

Finally, to my Lord and Savior Jesus Christ — may everything I write be a way to draw closer and closer to You.

Discussion Questions for Sketchy Behavior

1. From the beginning, Maddy and Tyler have a dramatic relationship. And according to Kate, Tyler is a jerk. Why do you think Maddy and Tyler keep getting back together?

2. Kate's entry into forensic sketching is a little … sketchy. If you were Kate, how would you have reacted to the news that your art teacher had you draw a wanted criminal and the police knew about it? Do you think Miss Yeager and Detective Masterson's idea was worth the risk? Why?

3. Kate's brother, Mike, is never around. In fact, except for the time Kate's "big arrest" was on the radio, he never calls to find out how his sister is doing. How did this affect your opinion of Mike? Do you think he was aware of everything that was happening in South Woodhaven Falls?

4. Kate has a dating incident that will not be spoken about, ever. What do you think that event could be?

5. Even though she's in a lot of danger, Kate handles her sudden fame and her fear of John X with humor. If you were her, how would you have reacted? Do you think her humor in this situation is a coping mechanism, or is it just who she is? Why?

6. When Kate decides to grab her sunglasses during the parade, it ends up saving her life. Do you think that was more than a coincidence? What moments throughout the book seemed like coincidences at the time, but wound up becoming very important later?

7. Throughout the book DJ is a major person in Kate's life, living at her house as a bodyguard and interacting with her and her family in an almost brotherly way. Based on his characterization, did his past come as a shock to you? Why do you

think DJ was involved with the case and showed up at the FBI hideout? What do you think will happen to DJ?

8. Kate's mom decides that the family needs to attend church because "we need all the help we can get right now" (p. 60). What do you think of her mom's thought process? Do you know anyone who thinks the same way? What would you say to them?

9. In your opinion, why does Kate take the summer forensic sketching job after everything that happened with John X? Would you want Kate's job? Why or why not?

10. What do you think will happen between No-Longer-Silent Justin and Kate? What would you *like* to happen?

Check Out These Books
by Nancy Rue in the Real Life Series

Four girls are brought together through the power of a mysterious book that helps them sort through the issues of their very real lives.

Motorcycles, Sushi & One Strange Book

Boyfriends, Burritos & an Ocean of Trouble

Tournaments, Cocoa & One Wrong Move

Limos, Lattes & My Life on the Fringe

Also available in ebook and enhanced ebook versions.
Available in stores and online!